Whether unimaginable horrors conjured from the dark

unconscious, or magnificence challenging the feral depths of

imagination, we stand in awe, and become a changed people.

— Excerpt from Shafan

To BRYAN,

EVERY GREAT JOURNEY

BEGINS WITH A DREAM.

Ran Park

BtH
11-29-08

CIRCLE OF DOORS

A Few Words from Readers

"The story in *Circle of Doors* is about us all, collectively and individually, and about life choices. It describes who we are, why we are here, and where we are going in relation to those choices with the resulting experiences we might have. It is a book of opposites; despair vs. hope, hatred vs. love, darkness vs. light, doubt vs. faith, fear vs. empowerment. We become intimately acquainted with the characters, their strengths, weaknesses, and the challenges they must confront that cause them to progress or regress.

"Emotions are perfectly described. The story is full of miracles, symbolisms, science, time travel, mysteriously appearing people and strange organizations, visions, and other topics many authors shy away from, but which Mr. Parker assembles together in a magical way.

"Parker is a gifted writer whose knowledge of a vast variety of topics greatly enhances the work. His concepts are vividly portrayed. The story draws you in as an observer while it progresses with people who quickly become your friends or enemies. When he offers his philosophy, it is strong and directed with uncompromising values. His writing style enables the reader to see and hear things as they are, without imperfections to block the senses.

"I believe that many readers are looking for a book of this caliber and quality, and I think most will enjoy reading *Circle of Doors*. But pay attention! Much of the deliciousness is in the details."

—David Larsen
Independent Review

"*Circle of Doors* is an extremely clever, exhilarating read with compelling characters you grow to love. Parker has the ability to weave layers of meaning into a fascinating and absorbing tale. This beautifully written story will draw you back again and again. An outstanding debut!"

—*Kelly Welker*

"I just finished Ranse Parker's *Circle of Doors* and am now enshrouded with lingering mists of Ethan Grey. Parker has created a bittersweet mystery that begins in intense loss and with expert dexterity quickly moves into international intrigue. He provides an insider's scientific knowledge exposing frightening possibilities and creating within the reader's subconscious the constant nagging question, "What if?"

"It is fast paced with clear, flowing prose. A first-rate suspense novel with a great plot and characters that stay friends long after the last page is read. I'm looking forward to his next novel."

—*Sallee Drake*

"It takes an extremely talented writer to engage readers from the very first words of a novel and keep them entirely engrossed in the story until the end. Ranse Parker is that writer. He has created a masterpiece of a story that lives on in one's mind long after the last page has been turned. His ability to permeate all of the senses with such vivid descriptions of characters and places is mesmerizing. The journey does indeed open the mind to possibilities that would otherwise seem implausible."

—*Angie Larrabee*

"Once I began I found it hard to put the book down. It ended up being one of the best books I have ever read. The (story) made me feel like I, as an individual, am a person of real worth. Thanks for a great literary experience."

—*Larry Porter*

"I am so glad that I bought your book. It was hard to put down. I enjoyed it immensely and have passed it on to friends and will recommend it to everyone that I know. You are a great writer and I cannot wait for your next book."

—*Cathryn Pratt*

"An ancient voyage, fables, scrolls, scientific discoveries, all intertwined within the present, past and future. It's a fascinating story of intrigue, mystery and romance that will keep you guessing."

—*Dr. Albert J. Munk*

"*Circle of Doors* was very well written and reminded me of The DaVinci Code. It should be made into a movie."

—*Joe M.*

"I found *Circle of Doors* to be not only intriguing, but also very descriptive and a fun read. It stimulates consideration of what may be possible within scientific realms, spiritual planes and the human potential."

—*Valerie B.*

"*Circle of Doors* was very refreshing. I devour books and found it to be different from anything I have ever read. I enjoyed it as a fun read and found its principles to be thought provoking and true. It is not often an author allows me to use my imagination and bends my mind at the same time."

—*Kevin Whittington*

"I made a big mistake in starting to read (*Circle of Doors*) with a deadline looming to get my own book finished. It was a great ride with a beautiful ending. You made the characters seem so real. It really captured my interest. Great job."

—*Nancy J. Miles*
Author of In Good Taste

INTRODUCTION

Circle of Doors had remained a secret for almost five years until just before publishing. Only my immediate family and a few close friends knew about the project. For a true entrepreneur, stepping outside conformity, taking risks and embracing atypical ambition is a normal way of life. But sometimes life can nudge you in directions so different from even a path of thinly disguised normality, that prudence suggests a quiet road.

In the midst of running a thriving business, the intensely focused interest that had fueled my professional ambitions since childhood literally vanished overnight. I woke one morning to the strange realization that a lifetime of direction was simply gone. It was as if someone had reached into my soul and taken it all from me while I slept.

Several empty and confusing months went by while I tried to find reason and understanding in what had happened. I struggled to complete existing business projects and kept waiting for the missing interest to return. It never did. Then one night I experienced an incredibly vivid and unusually organized dream, and the next night the conclusion of that same dream. My wife suggested that I write the experience down and while doing so, felt impressed and compelled to detail and expound upon what I had seen. One thing led to another and a new ambition was born.

With a certain amount of previous writing experience and a newfound fervor, my first novel was underway. After a few months of hard work, I eagerly went back to read what had been penned. It was disappointing. The story wasn't just poorly written, it was weak and devoid of the feeling and depth I had originally experienced. Despondent, I deleted everything and stopped writing, becoming lost in self-doubt. I knew I was a decent writer, and the events that had inspired this new journey had not come about by coincidence or chance—of that I was sure. *So what was wrong?*

With the voices silent once again, introspection found my answer; I had become so single-minded about making this new endeavor successful that I was writing only what I thought people wanted to hear. The *real* story from within the dream had been carelessly run over by selfish ambition. It was time to pause and search for understanding that only comes from beyond one's self. Inspiration comes *through* you, not *from* you. That's something I've known most of my life, but had momentarily forgotten.

The *desire* to work had never left. So with my businesses now all but extinct, I sought honest direction. That spring and for part of that summer, I did nothing but work on our property clearing brush, moving dirt, terracing slopes, building walkways and retaining walls...and listening. I built fences, mowed lawns, planted trees, grasses, flower gardens...and listened. As I worked, the waiting story began to emerge in ideas, concepts, characters, plots, and purpose. True direction and motivation were coming together. It was all becoming clearer. The doubts were gone.

Professional writing advice was sought. I studied the works of others and started the journey over. *This* time everything was different. Many times the ideas that came were so powerful that I would became emotionally overwhelmed and had to stop because of flowing tears. Other times the ideas would simply come so fast that it was almost impossible to keep up. Weeks turned into months, then into years...

Circle of Doors is much more than just a story about adventure and mystery, it's about all of us. It's a testament to strength, purpose, conviction, hope, justice, love, and endless possibility. Many times our greatest accomplishments are met with the greatest challenges, but nothing of real and lasting value is ever easily achieved. Every choice we make continues to mold our character, and those who always reach for what is more worthwhile will always find themselves in some way better and stronger for their efforts. It is my hope that this work conveys at least some of those values.

When we begin to understand who we really are, then we can begin to understand what is truly possible. Greatness is within us all if we will only encourage the desire to search, to learn without prejudice, find the patience to understand, and develop convictions that endure. And sometimes finding direction can even be as simple as just closing the doors, and listening...

To my family

And to you who choose to see
with no disguise

CIRCLE OF DOORS

A NOVEL BY

RANSE PARKER

hb Hampton & Beck

CIRCLE OF DOORS is a work of fiction. Names, characters, places and incidents are the product of the author's imagination or are used fictitiously. Any resemblance to actual events, locales, or persons, living or dead, is entirely coincidental.

CIRCLE OF DOORS

Copyright © 2007 by Ranse Parker
Eye photo, cover art, design and layout by Ranse Parker.
Galaxy photo credit: Hubble Heritage Team (AURA/STScI/NASA/ESA)
Earth photo credit: NASA
www.spacetelescope.org - www.hubblesite.org - www.nasa.gov

Published by Hampton & Beck
PO Box 1008
Layton, UT 84041

Visit the website at WWW.CIRCLEOFDOORS.COM for more information.

ISBN-13: 978-0-9800738-0-5
ISBN-10: 0-9800738-0-4

Library of Congress Cataloging-in-Publication Data: Pending

First printed in paperback June 2007
First commercial print in paperback October 2007
Second print September 2008

Printed in the United States of America

CONTENTS

PROLOGUE

ONE — Rain 5

TWO — Impossible Possibilities 22

THREE — Shafan 41

FOUR — Mirrors 54

FIVE — Secrets 82

SIX — White Dresses 102

SEVEN — Vertigo 119

EIGHT — Vision of a Dream 132

NINE — The Henry Effect 147

TEN — River of Shadows 173

ELEVEN — Revelations 188

TWELVE — Echo of Lilies 216

THIRTEEN — Hands of Fate 247

FOURTEEN — Providence 281

FIFTEEN — Incursion 303

SIXTEEN — Land of Mist & Light 315

SEVENTEEN — Das Heim von Oma 332

EIGHTEEN — Shattered Glass 348

NINETEEN — Power of Souls 364

TWENTY — Traitors & Nobles 380

TWENTY-ONE — Heart of Fear 385

TWENTY-TWO — Détente 415

TWENTY-THREE — State of Grace 425

EPILOGUE 435

"If people are good only because they fear punishment,

and hope for reward,

then we are a sorry lot indeed."

- Albert Einstein

PROLOGUE

MASSIVE BOLTS OF LIGHTNING crisscrossed a turbulent sky, occasionally striking the horizon ahead of the large Egyptian galley. Ear-splitting thunder pounded the ship as it heaved and fell in the outer wake of the storm's merciless fury and unyielding authority. Frequent flashes of brilliant white light illuminated strained faces, many filled with fear as rowers and crew endured this deadly dance in twilight at the edge of imminent peril. A light, cold rain began to fall.

"We are going to die!" the man's friend exclaimed frightened.

"Do not be afraid. You will not die today," the man replied sedately as he sat strangely calm, but pensive—both of them huddled in meager garments near the bow of the ship.

The last words of instruction from the man's beloved counselor were resonating in his mind with absolute clarity. The charge of protecting the sacred vessel contained in the heavy leather satchel now secured around his shoulder and resting on his lap was an honor beyond description, and carried with it a consequence few could imagine. For such an honorable and important task, the ship the man had been instructed to procure seemed inadequate. *This* ship, the one *he* had chosen, was certainly a more worthy choice for such a paramount journey. It was a decision made in a moment of arrogance that would soon find itself lost in his counselor's prophetic wisdom—for that wisdom was not simply in the choice of a worthy sailing vessel, but also of its crew.

With the final revelation received, the man's convictions began to waiver. Weight of choice would come to bear when the captain and two of his crewmen approached from aft in the murky light.

"We can wait here no longer. This storm is like nothing I have ever seen before. We should take leave of it immediately," the captain said loudly.

"I now know where our destination lies," the man replied as he stood.

"And where is that?"

Hesitantly the man raised his hand and pointed toward the storm. "*In there.*"

The captain and his crewmen looked at the storm, then back at the man. "What kind of riddle is this?" the captain asked.

"We must journey into the Heart of Fear. *That* is our destination."

The captain stared at the man in disbelief, at the storm again, then burst out laughing. "Have you gone mad? No one could survive such a thing!"

"Yes we will. What I carry with me is of God. He will protect us. This *is* our destiny."

"Death may be *your* destiny, but it is not mine. And if your god has told you to go in there, *he doesn't like you much*," the captain mocked while his two crewman laughed nervously.

The man knew how his words must have sounded, even though they were true. His commission was clear and somehow he had to make this captain understand. "I will show you," he said confidently as he unstrapped the satchel to carefully remove the sacred vessel and present it for the captain. "Gaze upon it and *see* the Power of God."

The captain looked at the stone vessel, as did the two crewmen. They saw nothing more than what was possible for them to see. The man had only confirmed his own delusions.

"When I agreed to this voyage, there was no talk of gods or endangering my ship and crew for any such foolishness."

"*It is not foolishness*," the man rebuked sharply, carefully placing the heavy vessel back into the leather satchel. "*This* is why I am here. God *will* protect us. This you must understand." But the vessel had not manifested itself to the men as it had to others. *Why?*

"Your words are deception and would cause us all to perish," the captain said irritated before instructing a crewman to prepare the ship to return to port.

The man knew the sacred vessel could never go back. It had to be hidden from those who sought its power. "We *will be* protected," he insisted. "What I carry with me *is* of God. It *is* the truth. You *must* believe me!"

The captain shook his head at the man's audacity. "Sit down and say no more. I will deal with you later."

"Wait! Money! I have more money," the man pleaded. "You can take it all…all of it. *Please*, we must complete our journey."

"And what would your money or all the gold in Egypt buy me if I am lying dead at the bottom of this sea? *Your* journey is over. Now sit down and do not anger me further," the captain demanded before turning to leave.

The man's frustration welled. His destiny awaited and he was *not* going to let this insignificant heathen keep him from completing his God's work. "But I have already paid you! You *must* do as I say! *I command it!*" the man shouted, lunging forward to grab the captain's shoulder and turn him around. One of the crewmen quickly pushed the man back.

The captain turned, stepped toward the man and glared at him. "On *this* ship, *I* am your god, and *you* are nothing. I will not risk my life or the lives of my crew for your insanity. *Secure them!*" he barked before walking away.

"*No! You must hear my words and understand!*" the man shouted in futility. The captain would hear no more.

One of the crewmen was already holding his friend and the other had grabbed the man's wrist. Angered at the insolence, the man wildly swung his arms, knocking the crewman away before bolting backward toward the very bow of the ship. The startled crewman hesitated and the man took those precious few seconds to climb over the cargo hold and out under the masthead that overlooked the primitive and angry sea.

"Come down from there!" the crewmen shouted to the man just out of his reach. His friend could see the determination and desperate frustration dimly reflected in the man's face. No one could now absolve him of the choices he had made. He had failed his counselor *and* his God, and understood the price of an irrevocable obligation.

The tempest in the storm beckoned with unworldly glory and inexorable power, but destiny was lost. In hopeless silence, and with frantic resolve, the man released his precarious grip on the ship to clutch the heavy satchel tightly to his chest, and fell to the surface where he quickly sank into the deep, cold and dark water.

CHAPTER ONE

Rain

WATER RUSHED UP THE shoreline and flowed out slowly to be overrun by other approaching waves in an endless ballet. Rachel was chasing Allison back and forth across the warm sandy beach. The girls laughed and giggled when Allison would challenge the rolling water then run from it when it caught up to her and splashed her skinny little legs.

He loved their long, golden-blond hair that flitted and danced as they ran and played in the mild coastal air. He couldn't have been happier—smiling and looking on from the shade of his large beach umbrella. This was a beautiful place and he had a beautiful family.

"Ethan," Rachel shouted from behind him. He stood and walked across a freshly mowed dark green lawn to where they were working in a flower garden. Allison had collected a small bouquet and held it in her hands. She looked adorable in her white garden hat and work gloves that matched her mother's.

"Do you like them?" she asked, holding the flowers up for inspection.

"I think they're beautiful, just like you," he said smiling and tapping the brim of her hat. She giggled and ran to the house to find a vase.

Ethan sat down on the grass near his wife. Rachel loved flowers. Her printed dress and large garden hat made her blend in when she kneeled amidst the many groups of Asters, Daisies, Zinnias, Mums and other plants in the massive beds that were scattered about their large property. Because of his wife, their home and yard was the envy of the neighborhood, and he couldn't have been prouder. Everything was perfect.

She put her arm around him and they kissed when he heard the faint melodic notes of her piano coming from the house. He followed the sound down the hallway and around the corner through the dining room to the music room where she was playing one of his favorite compositions. He sat quietly on the loveseat behind her baby grand and listened. He had heard few people play with such feeling and conviction. Her compositions were like stories that would lift you up on invisible strings and caress you as you flowed through their emotional discourse—pulled along, rising and falling in harmony with the notes and chords. She was an incredibly gifted woman. Many times he wondered how he had been so lucky to find her.

As he sat and listened, relishing in his melodic journey, something hit him on the cheek. He slapped at it—an insect maybe. Then there was another, and another. They were becoming more frequent. But as he wiped his face and looked at his hand, there was nothing there.

The piano started making strange and confusing guttural noises that were ugly and foreboding. Rachel ignored them, or couldn't hear them. The intrusive sound was beginning to drown out the piano's natural tones. He called her name. She didn't respond.

Now he was shouting, but his voice was empty. The rumbling slowly escalated to a roar and suddenly he found himself standing in the middle of a street in a downpour. His wife and daughter were on a nearby sidewalk getting ready to step off the curb onto the rain soaked asphalt. Rachel was holding a small umbrella, trying to protect them both from the deluge. Allison was holding a bag with a new pair of jeans her mother had just purchased for her. They moved in slow motion.

Rachel looked both ways and nudged her daughter. They stepped off the curb. Ethan panicked and began shouting at them. Once again there was no sound from his voice—no way to warn his family. He knew what was coming and screamed their names again and again, trying to run to protect them. But a familiar and callous invisible force would not allow it. He fought it with every ounce of his being. He couldn't break free. He was helpless.

Rachel was hunched over keeping the umbrella close to Allison. They were smiling—amused at the moment. Then they both looked up at him and waved as if to say 'goodbye.' His silent screams would go unheard—his efforts in vain. He threw his head down into his hands and buried his face to hide.

"No! No! No!" he silently shouted over and over as everything went black and silent. Then in the darkness he heard real screams. They were his. Abruptly he awoke and opened his eyes to find himself lying in grass. He had fallen asleep again. It was another dream, just another hellish dream. What could he have possibly done in his life to deserve this? No one should have to live like this.

The cemetery was peaceful as he looked around—quiet with only faint sounds of chirping birds and distant city life on the air. The low sun made long shadows on the small hill where Ethan sat next to a large white granite headstone with the inscription 'Rachel Allison Grey, Beloved Mother and Wife, Daughter of God.' The headstone was wide with a space for *his* name when the time came. Whenever that would be, it wouldn't be soon enough. In the shadow of Rachel's headstone was another—smaller, but of the same fine granite with the inscription 'Allison Amber Grey, A Child of God and Forever a Light in our Hearts.'

Every Saturday he would stop at the local flower shop to bring them a fresh bouquet on Sunday. The lady at the shop would make a different arrangement for him every week. Early spring flowers complimented the beautiful white stone today. He always took a couple of flowers from Rachel's bouquet and laid them in front of Allison's headstone. Today though, she had received a special treat—her very own arrangement. It was the least he could do for her since she would be turning ten years old the day after tomorrow.

He loved his family more than life itself and had visited every Sunday since the accident almost a year ago, regardless of the weather. There wasn't much left of what qualified as his life anyway, so what else was there to do? The bitterness and anger he now embraced had driven away most of his friends and the others were just too busy to worry about a distraught, middle aged man who didn't want their help or company anyway. While softly caressing one of the flowers, he spoke softly to the ground. "Sorry I fell asleep again. I'm so tired..."

People would come and go—visiting their departed loved ones on the peaceful hill. Occasionally they would watch Ethan curiously from a distance while he sat and talked to the ground, sometimes for hours.

Closing his eyes would take him to another place where he could see his family splashing in the swimming pool, or maybe chasing each other with the hose, or eating dinner on the patio. He saw Rachel standing to the side of Allison at their new baby grand piano. Allison was trying to spread her little fingers to reach all the notes in the chord her mom was teaching her. He smiled as Rachel sat on the edge of their bed in her long white nightgown—a yellowish gold sheen reflecting off her beautiful long blond hair. She was slowly running a brush through its length.

The sun was setting into twilight and an evening chill was slowly replacing the warmth of the day. But he didn't want to leave just yet. She was his companion and he wanted to spend as much time with her as possible. As he picked and twiddled blades of grass between his fingers, loneliness overwhelmed him—emptiness led to tears. "I miss you," he said quietly, reaching out to run his fingers along the edge of her name. "I wish you could talk to me."

Wiping his face, his eyes moved to the inscription on Allison's headstone—'Forever a Light in Our Hearts.' "Not anymore," he said with contempt, but instantly regretted the remark. "I'm sorry…I'm sorry," he said embarrassed, lowering his head. "I better go."

His legs were stiff and he struggled to stand, holding on to Rachel's headstone for support. He leaned over and kissed the hard surface. The warmth of the granite startled him and sudden flashes of her face passed briefly through his mind. Remembering those small details was one of the good things he could hold on to. But afterward, the feelings always seemed to turn hollow when the longing for that which he could no longer have would find him in its grim reality. "I'll see you next week Rachel. Bye bye Allison."

His mind churned in thought as he drove away from the cemetery. They were random silly thoughts like Rachel sorting laundry, complaining about the socks not getting clean, or stopping by to get the occasional ice cream—preoccupying, distracting thoughts of being happy. He didn't notice the stop sign until the other car was right in front of him. Tires squealed and his old, heavy Sunday transportation slid to a stop only narrowly avoiding the other vehicle.

"*Idiot!*" the man shouted out his window before continuing on. Breathing hard, Ethan's heart was pounding and his hands shook. Thoughts were no longer pleasant. *Idiot indeed,* he thought while trying to start the stalled car. Someone honked at him while he sat in the middle of the intersection waiting for the ancient piece of junk to come back to life. Finally, the other car drove around him and honked again, long and loud.

"*Shove it you moron!*" Ethan shouted angrily. The big engine finally caught, sputtered and roared to life.

Embarrassment, along with intense frustration and pent-up anger suddenly erupted into full-blown rage. He floored the gas, popped the clutch and blindly accelerated forward in a violent ensemble of squealing tires, smoke and noise. *I hate people! I hate them!* his thoughts screamed as he blipped the throttle and yanked the shifter hard into second gear. The immense torque caused the car to drift and slide dangerously sideways—white tire smoke still pouring from the back end. He didn't care. *Pathetic! Your whole damn life is a joke!* the thoughts shouted.

He jammed the shifter into third. Other vehicles were passed as if standing still. The speedometer needle was rapidly approaching one hundred. The raging engine harmonized his thoughts in angry noise and fury. The car rolled and pitched perilously on the uneven rural road, flirting with the natural laws of physics. He didn't care. He'd had enough.

Maybe he'd get lucky and a truck would pull out in front of him. Maybe a tire would go and his life would end in a glorious concert of spinning, smashing, flying metal. He slammed the shifter into fourth and stomped the accelerator back to the floor. An approaching car quickly moved off to the side and blared its horn to warn of the boy on the bicycle scrambling to get out of the way. Ethan scarcely noticed. The world around him was becoming a blur. Everything was blending into everything else with no point of reference, no definition, no purpose—just like his life.

One-twenty... Another intersection approached. Maybe *this* is where it would end. Maybe someone would be merciful. The intersection passed at one-twenty five. Maybe he'd just drift into the upcoming overpass support. Quick and easy. *Just move the wheel...just a little. That's all it will take. Come on... You can do it. This is what you want.* His mind was convinced, but his hands wouldn't intentionally cross that line. He rested them on his legs and tried to close his eyes—tried to give his life to fate.

Suddenly there was a loud *'BANG'* and the car jerked. The engine started misfiring with a horrible clacking sound and the car shook and shuddered violently. Startled, he instinctively grabbed the wheel, let off the gas and applied the brakes to keep from losing control. Something had broken. The once beautifully engineered and powerful machine coasted by the overpass at a little under a hundred, and slowing. *Unbelievable.* Even the fates wouldn't grant him mercy today.

The engine still ran, barely. Limping home at thirty miles an hour was certainly not fast enough to escape any local law enforcement that might have been notified of his rampage. Actually, all anyone would have to do now is follow the huge plume of blue smoke coming from the right-side tail pipe, or maybe the trail of oil on the road. So far, it seemed no one had done anything. Only the occasional passerby would give him a questioning stare. Apparently no one *really* cared.

The clanking noise from the crippled engine warned everyone within a half mile of his approach. Finally home, he turned up the long driveway, coaxed the car into the third bay and lowered the door behind it. The wheezing engine sputtered, jerked a few times and seized. He leaned back in the seat to sit alone in the quiet calm of the garage, listening to the creaking and clicking of the exhaust along with a warbled hissing coming from somewhere around the overheated, steaming and smoking engine.

The smell of hot antifreeze and burning oil was becoming intolerable. Still, he just sat—leaning his head against the steering wheel and slamming his fist into it, and again. *What was the point? When would it end? When?* He looked over at Rachel's car still sitting where it had been parked since the accident. It was dusty but untarnished. Sometimes he could almost see her sitting in it smiling at him and waving.

It was a bland little car, but she liked it and refused to let him get her something nicer. Oh, she probably would have driven whatever he would have bought for her. Still, it was *her* car and he respected her choices, most of the time. Then the light on the garage door opener timed out and the garage went dark. Darkness was a familiar place. At least there, no one can see you cry.

The house was quiet as always until he found his friend the television. It only picked up a few stations. The bill for the satellite was probably there somewhere, or maybe in the landfill. PBS came in pretty good. The signal was a little fuzzy since the house was on the opposite side of a hill way out of town. Some show about penguins was on. Thrilling. Maybe he'd live-it-up with a gourmet dinner of fish sticks.

Another exquisite day had come to an end. But before heading upstairs, there was one last thing to do. Rachel's baby grand was center-stage in its own venue that Ethan had arranged just for her. Every night that he hadn't fallen asleep on the couch or someplace else, he would listen to one of the many original compositions she had recorded. Sometimes he would even doze-off on the small wicker loveseat as he became absorbed in her vicarious solace.

Tonight he sat on the piano bench and selected an arrangement from the small screen above the keyboard to the right of the music desk. Her ability to compose and play music was one of those talents that always amazed him, especially since he had no real musical or artistic talents of his own. It was truly a unique and wonderful gift to be able to take thoughts, pictures and emotions from your mind and translate them into harmonious sounds that when shared could create sweeping emotion in the hearts and minds of others. The fact that such a gift would be taken from him and from those fortunate enough to have shared in it was just another impetus that fueled animosity and inflamed his soul.

Their large bedroom was at the end of the hall upstairs. Allison's was at the other end. Sometimes thoughts of his mortal existence and the lives he could no longer share would take him there to contemplate. In their bedroom, Rachel's picture sat proudly on the nightstand next to the lamp where she could keep him company as he slept. It didn't always ward-off the nightmares, but it was comforting to be the last thing he saw before closing his eyes.

He looked at it so often that every curve of her face had been memorized. All he would have to do is close his eyes to see her again—the slight squint when she smiled—her hair, always with a scent of berries. Sometimes he would take the books she liked to read and just hold them. He could imagine her hands around them and would gently caress the covers, desperately trying to find that warm and familiar touch he longed so much to know again. She was his life—his happiness.

Her joyfulness, and that of his daughter filled their home with purpose and a love he didn't really understand or appreciate until they were gone. He could still see their pictures, listen to his wife's music, hold her books... But the house was still empty, the rooms still dark, and the voices still silent. Despair was his new companion. Sleep was the only place of occasional escape. Even there his dreams would sometimes betray his desires and anguish would become visualized in exaggerated detail, denying him the unconscious peace he so desperately sought.

It wasn't always his wife and daughter he would think about though. Tonight while he sat on the large bed they used to share, his thoughts were only of himself as he took the nine-millimeter pistol from the bottom drawer and laid it to the side of him. At that moment he wasn't thinking about how Rachel would adamantly disapprove of having a gun in the bedroom, let alone him owning one at all. Instead, he was wondering whether or not he would finally have the guts to end the relentless torment that plagued what was left of his life. *It's easy*, or so he kept trying to convince himself.

But actions can betray thoughts. It wouldn't be over until he could reach that unequivocal point when his will to exist would become less than that of his fear of dying. It was that overwhelming fear of the unknown in death, and his innate instinct to survive that kept him from ever raising the gun to his head—the same instinct that kept him from turning the steering wheel, even just a little. If there was some other way, he wished he could find it. The longing to once again feel his wife's love, warmth and compassion was so intense that the instinct to stay alive was fading a little more each day. Lines were beginning to blur.

The next morning found him asleep, fully dressed and rolled up in their fluffy yellow comforter. The warm morning sun bathed the bedroom in bright, invigorating light. Fortunately he had been spared the unpleasant experience of watching his family die again. As a matter of fact, he remembered nothing of his dreams as he slowly awoke, squinting and turning away from the light that brightly lit the large room. With the realization of another happy, sunny day, he pulled the covers up over his head.

He didn't want to shower, and hadn't since Saturday. *It doesn't really matter* he thought as he rolled to the side of the bed and slowly sat up. He hadn't shaved in two or three months or had a haircut in three or four either.

Trying to adjust to the room's intense illumination was a daily annoyance. Rachel liked everything bright and cheery, which was reflected in the lightly colored walls, white trim, bright curtains and large, colorful rug on the wood floor. The room had no consideration for his feelings and seemed to mock him every time he awoke there in its warm, sunny glow. But that's the way she liked it, so that's the way it stayed. Clothes were piled in a basket in the laundry room. They'd get washed when he ran out of things to wear.

The milk was still sour and the cereal still stale. He had intended to stop at the store on the way home. It slipped his mind. The bread was gone and there just simply wasn't anything else to eat for breakfast. Maybe a frozen dinner. Well, maybe not. A spoonful of peanut butter maybe? Then he remembered there was dehydrated milk. That's just like real milk when you add water, right?

After reading the directions, he had now proudly produced a small container of white liquid that should work just fine in cereal. He filled his bowl with some generic round oats and poured his new milk over them. Then sitting down at the small breakfast table, he chewed a spoonful and looked out the French doors. A sneer formed as the unique flavor hit his tongue. It was awful. *Maybe more sugar would help.* He poured another spoonful into the bowl and stirred while choking down the first attempt. Unfortunately the second attempt just tasted like stale, overly sweetened bits of cardboard in nasty flavored white water.

Shaking his head in disgust, he dropped the spoon back into the bowl and was contemplating whether or not to spit the rest out into the sink when a cold chill slithered through his spine. It made the hair on the back of his neck bristle like the fur on a frightened cat. He stopped in mid chew and quickly glanced around the room with his eyes. Frozen in place, he listened intently, but heard nothing except the low hum of the refrigerator. *Something* had set off his internal alarm. It reminded him of the unnerving feeling he had had just before the incident at the lab.

Quickly he finished chewing and swallowed hard. Scanning the room briefly revealed nothing out of the ordinary. He turned and surveyed the room. There was nothing behind him and everything was still quiet. It didn't make any sense. Then as he turned forward again, a strange purling noise began, a low vibration in the air... Then it hit.

Suddenly his sight became blurred and the air shook. The room began bending and curving, shifting and sliding. Objects distorted and twisted in rippling prismatic diffractions. *What was happening!* An unknown force had completely engulfed him in rolling waves of liquid colored light that pulled shapes into a whorl of moving, contorted images. He reached out to grab the table to stabilize himself and saw his arms bending and twisting like rubber. The reality of his world was gone.

The loss of reference caused him to sway at the mercy of shifting waves of energy and sound. He could hear strange and incoherent voices that seemed to come from everywhere. They became clear for just a moment and he thought he recognized those beautiful intonations of his family all around him. His mind was slipping. He held the table intensely and closed his eyes. It didn't help. What was happening was more than just visual trickery. It was somehow real. Then several seconds later it abruptly ended.

The sounds of his racing heart and rapid breathing boomed in the quiet aftermath. His ears were ringing. He kept his eyes closed, grimacing at the thought of what he might find. Slowly he opened his eyes just wide enough to see his shaking legs and the edge of the table. Cautiously he looked to one side, then the other, then behind him, leery of what might be lurking there. Everything *seemed* normal. He started to raise his head and that's when out of the corner of an eye he glimpsed something— something that hadn't been there before.

Full-scale panic induced temporary paralysis. Shock held him in the chair just long enough to glimpse a small black shiny object not more than three feet away resting in the middle of the table. His chest was tightening with fear. His mind told him to do one last thing when his body finally took over—*RUN.*

Lunging backwards, the chair and his body both hit the floor. He flipped over onto his hands and knees and flailed for traction like a Terrier on tile. Sprinting down the hall and upstairs to the bedroom, he retrieved the pistol from the bottom drawer and ran to the outer doors leading to the upper deck. As he frantically pulled open the door, Mutters ran in. Startled, he pointed the gun at the unconcerned tabby. "Stupid cat," he said harshly under his breath while moving to the door to look out.

There was no one in the back yard and no one on the hill above him that he could see. Everything was quiet. He ran down the back steps of the deck, jumped over the last landing to the ground and ran around the house to the side of the garage. Holding the pistol down to his side, he looked around the corner then moved slowly along the outside wall to make his way to the front of the house.

"Morning Ethan," a distant cheerful voice announced. Surprised, Ethan looked across the yard to see his neighbor, Mr. Hendricks, weeding around the back of some of his plants. What a time to run into him. "What ya chasin'?" he then asked loudly, standing into view.

"Uh...wasps," Ethan replied, turning his eyes to the front of the property.

"Wasps? *With a pistol?*" Mr. Hendricks asked bewildered.

Ethan looked down at the big black semi-auto in plain view of his neighbor. "Brilliant," he said irritated under his breath. "Uh... it's a squirt-gun. Just giving them a sporting chance."

Mr. Hendricks stared at Ethan blankly, trying to understand the empty logic. "Okay," he finally responded, dropping the strange conversation to go back to his work. Ethan rolled his eyes and shook his head. He hated lying about anything. But really, what was he going to say?

He looked around to the front of the garage again. Of course there was no one there now that his neighbor had so kindly announced his presence. He cautiously walked around the front of the house, looking behind trees and down at the road as he crossed to the far side of the property and around to the back again. He crept up onto the patio and looked around the corner of the French doors into the kitchen where Mutters was at her food dish. The little black object was still on the table. A shiver went through him. Shock had been replaced by paranoia and confusion.

Someone had to have been here, he thought while making his way back around to the front of the house, looking everything over again. This time he stopped and checked the front door...it was locked. All the garage doors were down and secure. He put the pistol in the back of his waistband and covered it with his shirt before checking the side door to the garage. It was locked. He knew the bedroom door had been locked as was the kitchen patio door. All the windows were also closed and secure.

"Mr. Hendricks, did you see anyone over here this morning, besides me?"

Mr. Hendricks stood up slowly and walked toward him. "No, no don't think so. Been out for about an hour and a half. Haven't seen anyone. Is there a problem?"

"Nah, just wondering."

"Is that why you had the gun? I thought maybe the neighbor's mutt was over there doing its business in your yard again. Course, I'm not sure how you'd be able to tell..." he commented, looking toward the overgrown lawn. "You can shoot the little butt-sniffer if you want. Won't bother me none."

"Okay, well, thanks." Ethan started back to the house.

"Hey, I can help you get that yard spruced up and maybe get rid of those weeds too if you'd like. Wouldn't be any problem."

"No, that's fine, but I appreciate the offer," Ethan blindly responded with his thoughts elsewhere.

Mr. Hendricks seemed a little dejected. "Well...okay. If you need anything just let me know."

"I will. Thanks"

"By the way, that's quite the castaway thing you got going on there with the hair and all. Oh, got some wasp spray too if you run out of ammo."

"Great, thanks," Ethan replied, still distracted. Mr. Hendricks snorted, shook his head and went back to his weeding.

After moving around to the back of the house and out of his neighbor's view, Ethan pulled out the pistol and started to make his way back up the stairs to the bedroom. After checking the bathroom, he started a methodical search of every room in the house. He looked in every closet, under every bed, even in the showers. Moving downstairs he started farthest away from the kitchen and checked those rooms—the garage, mudroom, closets, bathroom, Rachel's music room, his office, every room in the house until arriving back at the kitchen.

As he peered around the doorway, he could see that the object was still on the table in addition to the sugar and cereal bowls and the box of oat cereal that apparently had also panicked and tried to escape, but with less success. It lay lifeless on its side, innards strewn about the table and floor. Nothing more seemed to have happened and nothing else was disturbed or out of place. His analytical thought process would be of little value to him now because whatever happened here had no physically viable explanation. The object couldn't have caused the distortion because it wasn't there when the phenomenon started and it seemed that no one else was around. "This is absurd," he said aloud, looking into the family room, then into the kitchen again.

He walked cautiously toward the table, constantly glancing around the room, watching and listening for anything strange. Now within a few feet of the object he could see it was of similar design to a small mobile phone or pocket global and had a glossy black appearance over its curved surface. One end was slightly convex and the other concave with the top gently curved across its width being about a half-inch thick in the center and a quarter-inch on the outside edges. It was a little less than two inches wide and three inches or so long with symmetrically curved, parallel lines on top at the convex end. It looked like a cover or door.

In the center of the door was a semi-transparent circle and in the center of the object itself was a square translucent area—a display maybe. Below that, near what appeared to be the bottom, was a thin silver line that transected the surface glass across the object's width. At the very bottom right hand corner was the word *Filo*. As he looked closely, he could see the object was worn with rub marks and light scratches as if someone had routinely handled it.

Mutters was washing her paws and her bell made a repetitive tinkling sound. It was little distraction to Ethan as he sat near the table, trying to find coherence to the new and strange questions that had no readily apparent answers. The device wasn't unlike many others he was familiar with. Though its arrival was strange, unexplainable as of yet and frightening, the device didn't seem threatening, and it didn't seem to be active.

Could it be that someone was singling him out because of the work he used to be involved with, or was this something completely different? But why would someone target him when he had nothing to do with that kind of work anymore? There had to be an explanation.

Digging around in one of the drawers produced a pair of long handled plastic tongs. The object was carefully clamped, gently turned over and set back down on the table. There was writing on the underside, oddly typical of what a manufacturer might put on a mass-produced product. 'FILO SEKI' was inscribed in small white print along with other numbers—probably manufacturing information. This was hardly something a group with clandestine motives would produce, unless it was intended to disguise the device's true nature of course.

Like a piece of hazardous waste, he picked up the device with the tongs again and carefully carried it to his office where it could be studied more closely. Had it been found on the ground somewhere, or even on his porch, it likely would have garnered more simple curiosity than paranoid suspicion. But since it arrived in the manner it had...

With the device now gently placed on his desk, space was cleared off on the long workbench and an old portable computer was plugged in and turned on. He had also thought about fingerprints. That was outside his scope of expertise however, and there was no way he was going to contact anyone until he knew what was going on.

Several pieces of equipment previously used for various projects related to his electronic and scientific study were stacked in the office closet. It was actually more of a hobby, or so he kept telling Rachel when she accused him of working too much. Buried at the bottom under boxes, manuals and other equipment was the multi-spectrum signal analyzer. The old bulky unit along with its test box was retrieved and moved to the bench. The test cables were connected and the data cable attached to the portable computer. After finding the correct program, he opened the top of the test box, picked up the device with the tongs, lowered it in and closed the lid.

The analyzer was designed to monitor, classify and document radiological activity. The program would display the energy signatures based on known classifications. Specifically, and before proceeding further, Ethan was hoping to determine if the device was emitting any particular energy patterns that would indicate what its purpose might be. And with the push of a button, the test began.

He watched the monitor carefully as one possible classification displayed fairly quickly—a low-level and stable electrochemical energy signature. Probably just a power cell. Then another classification of a high frequency receiver circuit came up. Now *that* was interesting, though still not uncommon. He leaned back in his chair and watched the monitor for a while longer. Nothing else came up. Running the test for a couple hours might still bring up sleeper systems that could only be detected with time so he decided to let the program run and go clean up the kitchen.

An hour or so had passed and several trips to the office found no anomalies or new energy signatures in the device. Finally, he sat back down in the chair to let his mind become fully engaged in a self-sustaining flurry of rampant conjecture. Anyone who really knew him or his work would know he would eventually figure out what this device was. So what was the point of the Hollywood special effects cloak-and-dagger crap?

It had now been well over an hour and the program had recorded no additional energy signatures. He ended the program and opened the test box. With a certain degree of displaced courage, he reached in and grabbed the device. There was nothing strange about the way it felt, other than those sensations physically manifested by mentally induced anxiety. Nevertheless, it was removed and set on the bench without delay.

Now in front of the GlobalNet terminal, Ethan ran through his login sequence, brought up a search screen and entered 'filo.' The system displayed several matches but as he read through each one, none referred even remotely to a company or any similarly related product or device. He entered 'filo seki.' Again, nothing.

He stared at the screen while drumming his fingers on the bench, then brought up a new screen and entered a new password on the SAN or Secure Access Network. Normally this wasn't a place he would go, but it was only medium-level security and wasn't really monitored that closely anyway. His rights had never been removed after his former employer's haste to close-shop. Unfortunately even an extended search there provided no additional pertinent information.

"So what are you and where did you come from?" he said as he picked up the device, looked it over again and set it on his desk near the soft illumination of a lamp. Studying its small and elegant design, and feeling its smooth glassy texture revealed no obvious purpose. But as he ran his fingers over the worn surfaces, a vague sense of ownership began to emerge—a feeling somehow familiar yet fleeting—like a memory just out of reach, or images just out of view.

While resting his chin in one hand, he continued to run his fingers thoughtfully over the surface of the device. Its ambiguous nature was beginning to project an impression of something less hostile and more inviting. Tactile sensations became more than the culmination of pragmatic observation. A silent prompting from a place beyond conscious thought caused him to touch both ends of the silver metal bar simultaneously, resulting in an illumination of the object. He had found the 'on' switch.

Chapter Two

Impossible Possibilities

STARTLED AT THE OBJECT'S sudden proclamation of life, Ethan jerked his hand back and moved his face away from the device while it briefly emitted a soft high-pitched whine that quickly ramped out of hearing range. He rolled back against the workbench to keep a safe distance from whatever was happening. The device made another steady high-pitched sound and a small door on the top at the back started tilting upward, pointing toward him. Now even more startled, he jumped out of his chair and moved several feet away to the side while keeping his eyes trained on the device. The door stopped tilting at about a seventy-degree angle.

A floating video screen then appeared in the air directly above and behind the device. "Whoa," he blurted out as an animated image of 'FILO SEKI' was displayed briefly, changing to a scene of cows grazing in a field. He had never seen any kind of remote projection this advanced before. With guarded, childlike curiosity, he moved closer to study the image then circled the desk with admiration as he listened to the soft sounds of mooing and cowbells and chirping birds coming from the device.

The image itself seemed to be projected from within the top of the angled door and the floating screen was so thin you could barely see it when you stood to its side. The back of the image appeared as a dark gray matte made of some kind of energy and was almost completely opaque, making a stable contrasting surface for the image on the front. *"Incredible,"* he exclaimed as he moved full circle back around to his chair.

The picture was vivid and fascinating—Holsteins grazing in a rolling field with white fences and scattered trees with a big red barn on a hillside in the distance under a low brilliant sun. The colors and clarity were extraordinary in their hues of reddish orange and purplish blue over bright green pastures. Even the dimensional sounds of chirping birds seemed to be projected from around the twelve inch high by seventeen inch wide floating screen. He just sat and stared like a mesmerized child.

At the bottom left of the image over a strip of black were the words 'Chronological Playback Mode Enabled 401 Records.' On the right was what appeared to be the incorrect date and time. Next to it was 'Time Synchronization Unavailable.'

He picked up a pen and carefully poked it into the floating image. The area above the pen was disrupted and as he moved it downward toward the device, the disrupted area above it became larger. He shook his head in amazement and moved the pen across and up and down and twirled it around in the image. After a moment he set the pen down and looked closer at the top of the device.

The middle section appeared to be an information screen with command words displayed. 'Mode Select' and 'Play' were currently showing in small white letters against a black background. He looked up at the screen and read the message in the corner, then down at 'Play' and realized the device must be a visual terminal of some kind.

So, the real moment of discovery now seemed to be at hand. He looked at the strange device for a moment and tried to prepare himself in some way for whatever he was about to experience. Reaching out hesitantly, he touched the thin silver bar below the word 'Play'. *"Please say your name,"* a professional sounding female voice said as the message 'Unrecognized User' was displayed.

"Umm," Ethan stammered.

"*Name not recognized. Please say your name.*" He became flustered and froze. "*Please say your name,*" the female voice insisted. He sat motionless and waited. "*Session ended. Goodbye.*" The floating screen disappeared, the projector door retracted and the device went dark. With a sigh of relief, Ethan let out a long held breath and slumped back in the chair.

His balance used to be his work and family. When those were taken from him, realities of the real world were overshadowed with fear and anxiety created from within until it became his new balance and new reality. This is where his thoughts sought refuge when an always-present doubt and suspicion began to question where the technology to produce such a device could have possibly come from, and what had actually transpired to make it seem to magically appear. How was *any* of this possible? It was simply more food to feed a growing neurotic psychosis.

Rachel had a list from her church with all the neighbors' phone numbers stuck to the inside cover of the phone book in the kitchen. She was always good about organization—something Ethan always appreciated. He opened the book and found the listing for Craig & Lynette Kensington who lived down the hill across the road. He hadn't spoken to them for several months. That's what sometimes happens when you alienate people by telling them 'you don't want their help, thank you,' and mean it. Only in a sincere desire for understanding will the outward search for truth begin to emanate inward. Even a seemingly insignificant phone call can form the first steps on a course to acceptance and resolution.

Ethan dialed the number. It rang a few times, then a young child answered. "Hello?"

"Hi. Is your mom or dad there?"

"Yes......"

"Can I talk to one of them, please?"

"Okay." The receiver rustled and became muffled as a little boy yelled to his mom that she was wanted on the phone. Then another reply that he didn't know who it was because it was 'private'—the byproduct of calling from an unlisted number. "May I ask who is calling?"

"Ethan Grey." Another moment of muffled conversation and rustling...

"Ethan, this is Lynette."

"Hi Lynette. I was wondering if...umm... How are you doing?"

"We're doing fine," she replied a little surprised.

"Well, I was just wondering if, uh, maybe you or your husband or maybe one of your kids have seen anyone around the house recently? Maybe this morning? Someone in a car or van or something parked someplace near here you didn't recognize?"

There was a short pause. "No, can't say that I have, and the older ones aren't here. Is something wrong?"

"No. Well...I'm not sure. I was just checking to see if someone was around doing work on the power systems maybe or if you just saw somebody outside."

"Not that I'm aware of," she replied in a questioning tone.

"Okay, thank you."

"Wait, Ethan?"

"Yes."

"I still owe you for the last time Rachel brought me the flowers."

He had to stop and think for a minute what she was talking about. "Oh yeah. No, it's no big deal. Don't worry about it."

"No, it's important to me. A debt is a debt and it's been bothering me ever since...well, for a while."

"You don't have to."

"I know, but I want to. It's important to me. I'll come by sometime, if that would be okay."

"Uh...sure. That should be all right."

"Great. Thank you."

Well that didn't help, he thought, standing and looking around the kitchen. Maybe one more walk around the property and house was in order after first checking to make sure things in the office hadn't changed.

This time he observed the world outside a little more intently as he slowly walked the property, still looking for something that would lend to an explanation. As he walked through the back yard, his attention was at the top of the hill a quarter mile or so behind the house. Sometimes you could see children or day-hikers through the trees as they made their way around the nearby pond on the other side. Allison and her friends used to love to go play there, which always made him just a little nervous. Mr. Hendricks wasn't in his yard anymore and the lot on the other side of the house was still vacant even though someone had purchased it several years ago. He walked along the edge of that property—there was nothing there—only overgrowth.

Across the road was the Kensington house. It was older than the others in the area having been passed down to a son after the father passed away. They still farmed a small portion of the original land below the house and had sold everything above it in one-acre parcels to pay for medical bills for one of their children who had developed a degenerative bone disease. There was also a quaint little orchard where people would sometimes come to pick apples, apricots and peaches. A large shop was located a few hundred feet behind the house with farm machinery around it.

While walking across the front yard, he turned and looked up at his family's house. He remembered the first time he brought Rachel here to see it when it was for sale. Her eyes got real big as it came into view from down the road. She said it was too nice and probably too expensive. Except for his work at the lab and what had happened to him there, not telling her where most of his money had actually come from was probably the only other secret he had ever kept from her. It wasn't dishonest, he told himself, but there was still something about the way it had all transpired that kept even him from wanting to know too many details. Regardless, it allowed him to give his family something wonderful and to him that's what really mattered at the time.

A long forgotten sense of intrigue was beginning to resurface. The ingrained interest and desire to investigate and work in his scientific domain had been a benefit to his professional career, and was also part of what drove him to dabble in it at home. But after his work had been suppressed and then with the accident, those interests were displaced in abjection which became the standard in his degraded state of mind. However, the strange and portentous little black device had brought back a small spark of dormant enthusiasm. With that, he went back to his office and sat down.

He rolled up to the desk and rested his hands in front of him. After taking just a second to try and clear his mind, he then touched the ends of the silver bar. The device started up just as before. He looked over the screen and lower display carefully, then touched the silver bar below 'Play'. The device responded as it did previously and asked for a name. After a deep cleansing breath, he replied, "Ethan Grey." The screen displayed 'Recognition in Progress' and the female voice asked,

"Ethan Grey. Is this correct?"

"Yes." There was a very brief pause then the screen displayed 'User Accepted' and it changed to show five rows of what appeared to be file names. The female voice then began.

"Thank you, Ethan Grey. You are now authorized for sequential playback of all records. Press play or say play next record."

Ethan leaned back in the chair, rested his hand over his mouth and stared at the screen. There were no more doubts that someone had intended for him to find or view something on this device. But who, and why? Anticipation and apprehension were engaged in an exuberant rumba while he looked over what appeared to be file entries or listings. They started with 'SJP Visual Record 1' and ended with 'SJP Visual Record 124' with the last line simply showing 'Next.' After each file name there was also another number that was probably the file or record creation date, but the dates didn't make any sense.

Ethan quickly grabbed a notebook and mechanical pencil out of a side drawer, flipped the notebook to a clean page and set it on the desk by his right hand. Then delicately he touched the silver bar below 'Play'. The device responded as the screen displayed 'SJP Visual Record 1 Selected for Playback' and the female voice stated, *"Playback of record one."*

The picture on the screen changed to that of a little girl with long blond hair, smiling as she looked ahead. "Like this Daddy?" she said as she turned her head and looked up.

A voice of what sounded like an older man just off screen responded, "Yep. Just look here and talk. Then we'll play it back so you can see yourself."

The little girl turned back again and giggled, "This is weird."

"It might seem kind of strange at first, but after you record yourself a few times, it'll be fun. Do you see this red word that says recording?"

"Uh huh. And there's me in the little box at the bottom. Right there," she said pointing.

"That means it's recording right now. If it isn't recording, you'll see the word 'waiting' in green instead of the word 'recording' in red. Okay?"

"Okay," the little girl responded, "but what do I say?"

"Anything you want. How about...your name and what today is."

"My name is Sara and today is my birthday!" The little girl smiled and giggled shyly, looking back up at her father.

"That's right and how old are you today?"

"I'm ten."

"Yes you are, and what did you get for your birthday?"

Sara looked up in deep thought, held up her hands, put her right forefinger on the inside of her left forefinger and started to count, "Ummmm...Melissa got me a purse. Jessica got me a poster...ummm. Matt got me a game..."

"And what did your Mom and I get you?"

"Wellll...Mom got me some clothes and new shoes...and the SkatePed!"

"Yes and what else?" A hand appeared from the side of her head and a finger pointed toward the screen.

"Oh yeah! You got me a Filo!"

"And what can you do with it?"

"I can record myself, play music and movies and games and talk to my friends!"

"And you can call us if you need to, too, right?"

Sara gave a big positive nod. "Right!"

"Okay. Let's stop it and see what you look like."

"Okay." Sara leaned toward the camera lens so her head looked really big. "I push stop, right?"

"Right."

"Right here?

"Yep."

The image switched back to the list of records and the female voice announced, *"End of record one. Press play or say play next record."*

"Well, that was…interesting," Ethan said out loud as he sat back in his chair, confused. After a moment he touched 'Play' again.

"Playback of record two."

"Hello everybody!" Sara was smiling and waving at the screen. There where several girls around her who appeared to be about her age. They were scrunched in close, smiling and fidgeting. Sara pointed to each girl and they individually waved at the screen as she said their names. "This is Kelsey, Janette, Ashley, Clarissa and Alicia. I finally got one."

"When we get home we'll have to link them up and talk," Clarissa said.

"But I don't have one," Kelsey exclaimed in a pouting tone.

"Well, tell your parents to get you one," Clarissa replied.

"Yeah like that'll happen. I had to save all summer just to get a stupid SkatePed."

"Come over to my house, we'll use mine," Ashley responded.

"Okay"

Alicia was making faces at the screen.

"So now what do you want to do?" Sara asked.

"How about we sing Happy Birthday?" Clarissa suggested. Everyone agreed. She raised her hand. "Ready, go!"

"Happy birthday to you, happy birthday to you, happy birthday dear Sara uh uh, happy birthday to you!" The girls laughed and clapped.

"Let's see it!" Janette exclaimed.

"Okay," Sara replied as she reached toward the screen and the image disappeared.

"End of record two. Press play or say play next record."

Ethan laughed to himself as he tried to figure out why anyone would want him to see a ten year old girl's birthday party with her giggly, silly friends. It made no sense at all.

"Playback of record three."
This time Sara and her friends were dancing to music. It looked like a beach party the way they were jumping and swinging their arms. Occasionally one of them would dance in front of the screen, then someone would bump them out of the way and dance there themselves. This went on for several minutes until Sara danced toward the screen and shut off the recorder.
"End of record three. Press play or say play next record."

"Playback of record four."
"Hi. So Dad says that when I want to remember things, I should say them here so someday when I'm older I can remember what it was like. It's kind of strange to talk to no one. Mom always makes fun of Dad when he does it. Well I'm going to bed so goodnight. Oh, Dad told me a joke. Why do cows wear cowbells? Because their horns don't work," she said as she smiled and waved then turned off the recorder.

Over the next several hours, Ethan continued to watch as the little girl would record entries about all kinds of things; mostly just adolescent jabber about what she did that day, or silly banter with her friends and her sometimes obnoxious little brother. There were several entries of simple information that just seemed to be there because she had promised her father she'd record something from time to time.
The frequency of the entries varied from every day to once every couple weeks or less. Entries that tended to be more inane began to lessen and there became large gaps between some entries, at least according to the variance in the dates on the records. An attempt to skip ahead only brought an error stating that the option was not allowed. He was going to have to watch every single entry in order.
For her eleventh birthday, she got a kitten she named Frisky and there were several entries shortly thereafter with her and the

cat—cat in a box, cat with string, cat on the bed, cat on the sofa, cat eating food, cat sleeping, cat playing with a ball—apparently she liked the cat. Sometimes she would also carry the device around and record her Mom and Dad doing things around the house or outside. She never did say their names and Ethan didn't recognize them. By that evening he had watched sixty-two records and intermittently observed about two years of this little girl's childhood. Still there was nothing in the records to explain why the device was left with him or what its real purpose could possibly be.

It was getting dark, he was getting really hungry and still didn't have any milk or anything decent to eat for breakfast in the morning. Before leaving the office, he looked at the device sitting on his desk then went back, picked it up and looked around for a safe place where no one would look for it—just in case. A couple of old sport-jackets hung in the closet with some other old clothes so he slipped the device into the inside pocket of one of the uglier ones. It was a safe bet no one would want to look there.

He arrived back home after treating himself to a fast food delicacy and picking up a few groceries. The device was retrieved and put in the top drawer next to his wife's books when he retired to bed. It had been a strange, but not entirely unpleasant day. There were a lot of questions that would be pondered for some time as he lay in bed gazing at the picture of his wife. Her sweet face and warm smile blurred his focused thoughts. He began to slowly drift into the evening void, and fell asleep.

The next morning as the sun's glorious light once again lit up their bedroom, Ethan rolled away in his usual manner and continued to slumber in a state of transition until his eyes opened wide at the realization that the device had not been another incoherent dream. He sat up and opened the top drawer. It was there, right where he had left it.

Anxious to start watching more of the records, Ethan poured some real milk on fresh cereal and instinctively started toward the kitchen table to sit down. He stopped and looked around warily as the event of the previous morning went through his mind.

Without further thought, he immediately turned around and headed to the office.

"Playback of record sixty-three."

"Hello, it's me again. Dad got the new job he was trying for. He says it will be more secure than the one he has now. I kind of like the one he has now. He says this new one is going to take a little more of his time away from home, but it should allow us to do more things. I'm not sure what he means exactly. Maybe he's talking about making more money. Maybe that's what he means. He's excited and happy so that's good, I guess.

"There are people still pushing him to be part of that National Civil...whatever-it-is. He says they're a bunch of punks. They kind of scare me. Some of the people from my school are moving away. They think it's safer farther outside the cities. I like it here. I hope we don't have to move." Sara stared off to the side briefly then waved. "Goodnight."

Her entries were becoming more thoughtful and more specific as she matured. He could see the subtle changes in her face. She was growing up. Of course it's easier to notice those things when you can see two years worth of change in a day. With the cereal gone, he set the bowl to the edge of the desk and played the next dozen or so records until an odd one got his attention.

"Playback of record seventy-nine."

"Hi." Sara paused for a long time like she had something important to say, but wasn't sure how to say it. "After school today, something really strange happened. I'm not sure I want to say exactly what it was right now because someone might see this." She was staring off to the side again, apparently thinking about whatever it was. She caught herself and looked back at the recorder. "Maybe someday." The recording ended.

Ethan jotted down a couple notes before continuing and by noon had watched another thirty-three records. Sara's thoughts and the tone of her messages were changing. She was beginning to talk more about the nature of people and issues of society and things that seemed pretty heady for a now thirteen-year-old girl. Then again, he didn't know how a thirteen-year old really thought because he had been robbed of the privilege of raising a daughter to that age.

There were a few more regular entries then he noticed a large gap, almost three months. Even though the dates were incorrect, they seemed to be consistent in their progression. The date on the next record would indicate that it was recorded a little over four years from the first entry. This means Sara would now be just over fourteen years old.

"Playback of record one hundred-thirteen."

Ethan immediately noticed the background behind Sara was different than what he usually saw of her bedroom wall. *She* looked different too. There was no sparkle in her eyes and her face seemed drained of spirit. As she looked out at him from behind the screen, he could see something was terribly wrong. After a few moments the emotion began to show. She was fighting it—trying to keep composure. Whatever it was slowly overpowered her and tears began to flow. She completely broke down. Embarrassed at the outburst, she awkwardly shut off the recorder.

Even though Ethan still didn't know who this little girl really was, he had come to know her through this device and to see her like this was very difficult. He remembered when Allison would become upset or cry because of something that had happened. At least he was able to comfort her. All he could do here was watch.

"Playback of record one hundred-fourteen."

Sara was sitting in the same place as before, only this time she was holding a fuzzy tan stuffed animal under her arms. Her expression was very sober and she had red, puffy eyes. "Okay. Ty and I are at my Aunt Hailey and Uncle Mitch's house." She took a deep breath then let it out. "About three months ago...actually it was a week before my birthday, April twelfth, Mom and Dad were at a dinner for Dad's company in town when a bomb in a dumpster went off next to the building they were in. I was told that they were both killed instantly. Thirty-six other people died too. I don't understand how someone could do something like that," she said angrily. "My mom and dad never did anything mean to anyone." She broke down momentarily and reached toward the screen, then stopped as she regained her self-control. "People said that the new company Dad was working for was developing a medication that would stop a person from being addicted to certain kinds of illegal drugs. They think it was the people who sell the drugs that did it.

"Uncle Mike and Aunt Hailey are really nice and we even have our own rooms here since my cousins moved out. I'm worried about Ty. It's summer so we don't have to go back to school for a while, but meeting new friends is hard. They take us to church so we met some people there and I still know Michelle from when we would visit before, but Ty doesn't really know very many people here his age. He's changed and seems to get upset easily and loses control when he gets frustrated. He doesn't seem to like anything anymore. I don't know what to do for him.

"Aunt Hailey said she'll stay home with us, at least until school starts." Sara started to cry again. "I really miss Mom and Dad. I miss talking to them." She lowered her head and wiped her face with the sleeves of her shirt. "I don't know what to do," she said through flowing tears. After taking a moment to compose herself once again, she continued. "Our house just sold. Uncle Mitch said we could keep anything we wanted, but they needed to sell the house to pay-off the mortgage. Whatever Mom and Dad have saved and what we get for the house will go to Ty and me in a trust fund.

"They're real good people. Frisky ran away though. They have a dog named Shorty and when Frisky saw her, she got all scared and ran and Shorty chased her like dogs do I guess. We never found her. They said cats don't usually bother her so maybe I can get another one someday." Sara looked away cuddling the stuffed animal and stared blankly in deep thought. After a moment, she looked back at the screen. "Guess that's all."

Regardless of how Ethan had tried to shut out the rest of the world and live in his own misery, the tears in his eyes had now manifested the empathy he felt for someone else's suffering. At that moment, he had come face to face with the defining reality of another's anguish. He looked at the screen and the next record, but couldn't bring himself to watch anymore. The impenetrable little world he had lived in for so long was no longer his alone. This little girl, now a young woman, and he both shared something all too familiar even though they were decades apart in age and had never actually met. For most, grief will fade with the passing of time, but it can thrive if held prisoner in the boundaries of a mind. He knew how she must feel and it was more than he could bear. To know that this young woman and her brother were experiencing what he himself had been going through gave him no comfort. He turned the device off and left the room. There would be no more reminders of misery today.

Another month had passed in Ethan's life as summer approached and he tried half-heartedly to keep up with the lawn and property. Mr. Hendricks still offered to help, Ethan still declined. When possible, his wife's piano serenades would still precede retiring for the night. Interestingly though, the bottom drawer of the nightstand had remained closed.

A few days ago found him at record three hundred eighty-three where Sara talked about her sixteenth birthday. Her brother was doing okay although he did tend to get into trouble once in a while. Nothing big, but Uncle Mitch had to put his thumb on him a few times. Sara bought a car and quite often ended up being a chauffer for Ty. She didn't seem to mind too much though relating the fact that he *was* the only brother she had.

The record entries became less frequent with one every few weeks or so. All things considered, Sara was getting along fairly well. Both Ty and she were attending church with their aunt and uncle and making friends at school. She spoke often of her mom and dad and was beginning to talk about gaining an understanding of knowledge regarding our existence and starting to see things in what could be described as an almost metaphysical sense. She seemed to be referring to something more than a simple understanding of religious principles. However, exactly what those were remained untold. She had also decided to officially join her aunt and uncle's church which, oddly enough, was the aunt and uncle's church which, oddly enough, was the same one Rachel belonged to. Certain aspects of *his* life and Sara's, as documented in the journal, were strangely coincidental.

She had recently turned seventeen and was excited about having a summer job working for the city in the arts and recreation department. She was also starting her senior year of high school that fall. It was early that following spring when her last record entries would then take on a strange new context and set a new course for Ethan's life.

"Playback of record three hundred ninety-six."

Sara was sitting with her long hair in a braid pulled around and resting in front of her shoulder. Her left arm was resting on the desk with her chin in her right hand. She didn't look upset, but seemed serious. "Today in World Government we got assigned research projects. I really hate those things. They take *way* too much time." There was a long pause. She seemed to be in deep thought. Her fingers were drumming her chin as she continued to stare off screen then leaned back in her chair and folded her arms. "Something very strange is going on." There was another long pause. "My assignment is to research the Asian Apocalypse and how it affected the world political climate and the United States in particular. I've read about other historical events, but for some reason when we talk about this one, something just doesn't seem right. Even when I was younger and Dad would mention it or I'd see those documentaries, I got kind of a strange feeling then too. It's hard to explain. I still can't really explain it." She took another long pause. "I know it happened twenty-eight years ago but it's like...there's something wrong with it, you know? It's like...I don't know." Clearly she was frustrated. She looked off screen again then leaned forward and looked directly at the camera.

"Okay. When I've studied other things in history, let's see, like the conflicts in the Middle East or the other wars—some of the disasters, earthquakes and stuff like that, I realize and understand what caused them and I know they happened for a reason. They may not have been good things, but they happened and they're a part of history. When I read about the Asian Apocalypse there is something different about it, like it shouldn't be a part of history. I know that sounds strange but that's the only way I know how to explain it. It feels out of place, like it shouldn't be there.

"I know this doesn't make any sense and I certainly wouldn't tell anyone else how I feel, but there *has* to be a reason why I feel this way. I just don't know what it is. I know I'm different, and that could have something to do with it. I'm not sure what to do. It's really bugging me so maybe I'll see if Ms. Lechman will give me a different topic. I don't know. Maybe it's just another freaky Friday in Saraville, or so my little brother likes to remind me. At least that little twerp's *mostly* normal, even if he does keep asking me to check out the girls for him to see which ones are the *bad* ones, the little horn-dog. I'll keep you posted," she said animatedly before shutting off the recorder.

In his mind, Ethan turned the pages of history trying to think if he had ever heard of something called an Asian Apocalypse. He hadn't, and a quick check on GlobalNet also produced nothing. Then the indicated date on the device, and the one on this last record plus Sara's statement about 'twenty-eight years ago' started the calculator in his head. If the numbers after the file listings *were* date codes, then the last several entries were all within a week of each other and within two weeks of the current active date shown on the device. Curiosity harbored instinctual skepticism as he wrote down the year of the last listed record entry and subtracted twenty-eight. The result was a date about two years away.

He looked at the number, then back at the device and the screen. His thoughts were arriving at an impossible conclusion and there was no way he was going to even consider *that* possibility. "*No, no, no, no,*" he said shaking his head as he stood up and started pacing the floor in his office. The part of him that understood the simple logic of deductive reasoning fought a contested battle with that of perceived common sense; a scientific indefinability that often leaves a trail of dissension among its postulators. That's because anything that cannot unequivocally be proven untrue may have at least *some* truth to it, regardless of personal beliefs or ideology. This was a place he dreaded and always avoided like the plague. Nevertheless, here he was.

"Playback of record three hundred ninety-seven."

"Hello," Sara said laughing in a slightly anxious manner before her expression turned more serious. "Oh boy, here we go." She cleared her throat. "It's been an interesting few days. First of all I want you to know, whoever you are, that if our places were switched and you heard what I'm about to say, I'd probably think you were crazy. Anyway, I'm just going to say exactly what I think and you can decide for yourself.

"There are some things about me that I don't quite understand yet. Other people don't see things the same way I sometimes do, at least that I know of. I haven't told my aunt and uncle about it either. Ty knows a little bit but just thinks I'm weird. Whatever. He's a good kid though. Still has a big mouth so I haven't told him too much."

Sara took a long pause to think. "Mom and Dad knew I was different. We never really talked about it much. It was kind of awkward. Whatever it is though seems to be changing or getting stronger. I was in the library this afternoon watching a short documentary on the Asian Apocalypse and something really interesting happened. Well, let me back up a little. This is kind of strange to talk about so, um…okay.

"When I was younger, sometimes I would see this weird glow around people. I didn't really know what it was. Sometimes I could see a light around them and as I got older it started to change. One time I tried to explain to Dad that I could tell who was good or nice and who wasn't. I think that kind of worried him so we didn't really talk about it again. What I mean is there are good people and there are not so good people. Sometimes I can tell who is who because there is a color, sort of, that people have around them.

"Okay, there was this kid once, when I was twelve I think, named Gregory Hawthorne. He was a real jerk. He was a bully and had a foul mouth. I think he used to steal beer and stuff too—he and his friends he always hung around with. I just didn't like him and tried to stay away from him. He never really bothered me much but one day after school they started following Kelly and me home. He started talking to us and...and being real disgusting and stuff. I tried to ignore him but he just kept talking and trying to impress us. Kelly told him we weren't interested and to get lost. Then he put his arm around my waist and that was it.

"I remember turning around and looking him in the face and yelling at him telling him to leave us alone. I looked right at him. Suddenly I could feel his darkness and anger and frustration, loneliness. I had never felt such a cold and strange feeling so strong like that before. I could actually see those feelings and what kind of person he was. It was like there was a color around him and through him. It was a dark color—mostly darkish gray with purple. He just stood there, and I stood there staring at him. He swore at me and they walked away, but this color stayed with him. I could see his friend had a color too. It wasn't as dark—more purplish with green. It scared me because these colors were so clear and so plain.

"I watched them walk away and Kelly grabbed my arm. I looked at her and she had a white color with shades of a whole bunch of other colors, but mostly white. We started walking again and as I looked around I could see colors in all the trees and flowers and even the grass on the lawns, and the other people. Then it sort of faded out and everything looked normal again.

"It was almost like I could see the soul or the spirit of living things. You know what I mean? I asked Kelly if she ever saw colors around things and she just laughed and said no. I didn't say anything about it again to her either. She thought it was really cool how I stood up to that Hawthorne kid though. He called me a few not-so-nice names after that, but never really bugged me too much."

Sara let out a deep sigh and continued. "When Mom and Dad were killed I felt like I was going to die. Everyone around me was so sad, and I was sad. It seemed like every time someone would come to see me I couldn't help but feel their own sadness along with my own and it was just more than I could stand sometimes." Tears began to form and run down her cheeks. Her mouth started to quiver. Wiping tears, she took a few moments and composed herself.

"I found a documentary about the Apocalypse. When I was watching it I had this incredible feeling that something about it was wrong. I know that there are evil people out there and sometimes wars and stuff like that happen and I can understand that, but there is something different about this. I honestly don't think it was supposed to happen.

"When they would show pictures of the cities that were gone, I felt like they should still be there. The millions of people who died shouldn't have. I can't single out a reason for it. It's so overwhelming that I can't stop thinking about it. When they would talk about the World Alliance forming a strategic balance of power to stand up to the United States, I just kept thinking to myself, no, this shouldn't have happened. It was a mistake."

She looked around the room and gathered her thoughts. "This energy wave... No one has ever even been able to recreate such a thing of any kind. Even today everyone still says that they have nothing even remotely capable of causing that kind of very specific destruction and no one has ever figured out what it really was. I believe them. Everyone in this documentary seemed to be truly puzzled by the whole thing. Many people thought it was some doomsday weapon that went off by accident. Some thought it was aliens or mythical gods ravaging the earth. Some thought God was evoking his punishment. That isn't true this time. I know that, but there always has to be someone to blame for everything and the world blamed us. I finally realized that many of the horrible things that happened to the U.S. since then were because of the hatred other people had for us.

"I don't think it was our fault, and I don't think it was a weapon either. I'm sorry it isn't clearer, but that's it, it's just wrong. I guess what I think now really doesn't matter though does it? It happened a long time ago." She smiled and shook her head. "I don't know. I just wanted someone else to know how I felt I guess. Anyway, I copied the documentary to the Filo and I'm going to set it up so it plays next so you can see it if you haven't already. It's kind of old." Sara turned the recorder off.

"Playback of record three hundred ninety-eight..."

CHAPTER THREE

Shafan

T HE SCREEN WAS BLACK as violin music started to play. 'A Deveraux Production' faded in and out then an image of a mostly flat and shiny charred landscape came on the screen. There were no trees or vegetation of any kind. A professional male voice began to narrate. "It is known by many names; The Asian Apocalypse, Wrath of Nusku, Shafan, Phlogiston and even Armageddon. Whatever its name, it is recognized as the single most devastating and mysterious documented event to have ever occurred in mankind's recorded history." A short musical interlude started as various scenes were shown. The narrator continued. "It was a cold and partly cloudy afternoon that November third about two hundred kilometers west of Balkhash, Kazakhstan—an area once been used by the former Soviet Union's military testing and development program. With its declaration of sovereignty in nineteen-ninety and recognized independence from the Soviet Union in nineteen ninety-one, Kazakhstan began an uphill journey to build a self-sustaining independent State and government.

"Paramount to this journey was redefining its industries to shift many government-controlled segments to the private sector and focus on mining and oil production. With this shifting of priorities, many of the large military installations used in the previous decade had either been dismantled or abandoned due to obsolescence or the high cost of maintenance. Smaller and more localized military forces became the standard. In this remote area, one such antiquated military installation once used to detect long-range missile attack and invading aircraft was deactivated and sold to a private buyer. The documents for this transaction have since become lost. However, at exactly ten hours thirty-eight minutes and eleven seconds Greenwich Mean Time, this location would become ground-zero for an event that would forever change our world.

"From this point, an energy detonation radiated outward in a circular pattern at a speed of approximately one thousand kilometers per second. Then, with a precision never encountered before, it abruptly dispersed and subsequently vanished completely. In one-point-nine seconds, six countries were completely decimated. Forty-six major cities, five hundred and sixty-one towns and settlements and two hundred eighty-nine point two million people disappeared off the face of the earth." Maps and animations were then displayed on the screen. "The energy wave took on a semi-spherical pattern as it traveled just under thirty-two kilometers upward into the stratosphere with an almost perfectly symmetrical radius at ground level. Its total encompassing diameter was three thousand six hundred seventy-four kilometers.

"The front of the energy wave traveled north four hundred kilometers past the city of Yekaterinburg to stop eighty-eight kilometers past Krasnoyarsk in the Russian Federation. To the east, it passed six hundred thirty kilometers into Western Mongolia and one thousand seventy-one kilometers into Western China. The farthest city south to be destroyed was Ludhiana, India. In neighboring Pakistan, Multan was the farthest city west to be destroyed. Half the city of Quetta survived as did part of the city of Gorgan in Iran. Barry Duncan of the International Geological Society has been studying ground-zero inside what has been aptly named 'The Dead Zone.'"

An older, balding man with a thin peppered gray beard was standing on the smooth terrain. He spoke with a slight English accent. "Nothing was spared in the path of the incomprehensible energy wave that was believed to have originated at this point. A crater two-point-four kilometers deep and nineteen-point-seven kilometers wide marks the believed point of origin. It doesn't look like a typical blast crater. As you can see, the bottom slopes up at a consistent rate as it moves outward, like a steady force flowed upward as it moved away from the center. The crater is almost perfectly symmetrical around its perimeter and you can actually walk or even drive partway into the crater as we did.

"An artificial lake has been steadily forming here as rain and water from other areas slowly flow into its depression. All bodies of water within the blast area were originally depleted down to nineteen-point-eight meters below the surface outside the crater's boundary. Exposed bodies of water less than this depth completely disappeared within the event radius. The Caspian Sea was most affected, wherein about eighty percent of its total area fell victim to the energy. As the water evaporated, or was consumed in the east end, the higher level of water remaining to the west flowed toward the east creating a tidal wave. Eventually the sea settled twelve meters below what was once average. Even today, the overall water level is still slightly below normal.

"The deadly effects on all living things in the path of the energy wave were total. Nothing living survived. All vegetation and most infrastructures such as buildings, even ones made primarily of stone or concrete and steel, are gone. Not destroyed as in a conventional blast, but simply gone as if something scooped them from the earth. Only very large rock formations and the mountains themselves survived this total devastation. The rugged mountains of Western China and the Tien Shan look as if they've been melted with a blast torch. About five meters of ridgeline along these high mountain peaks appears to have been dissolved or burned away.

"The ground everywhere within the radius of the event is smooth except where subsequent cracking has occurred. Dirt can be seen under the hard crust through these cracks that in some places seem to run endlessly in all directions. In many areas the surface has a glassy appearance, formed as minerals within the top layers were super-heated to form a hard, smooth covering. To form a crust of this type the temperature at ground level must have reached into the thousands of degrees Celsius. Strangely enough, satellite imagery and atmospheric monitoring stations located just outside the edge of the event recorded close to normal temperatures.

"During the actual dispersal of the energy wave, there was no radioactive residue or any unnatural substance of any kind left on any surfaces that we have been able to detect. This would indicate that the extreme temperatures experienced within the event radius were somehow constrained to only the area within the event, or were produced by a source still completely outside our currently understood and accepted sciences. As you can see here, the landscape is slowly recovering as vegetation once again begins to grow through slivery breaks in this sterile surface—glimpses of a defiant, living world still hidden beneath."

The narrator began again. "Immediately following the dissipation of the event, strong winds of hurricane velocity began to blow inward into the event area. Although not conclusively verified, it is theorized that a portion of the molecules within the air itself were removed causing a massive depressurization. Vince Eubank, Professor of Atmospheric Sciences at Boroughs University explains..."

The scene switched to a man in a college classroom setting. Weather maps and large video screens with moving cloud and weather models could be seen in the background. "Subsequent weather events associated with the energy wave of the Asian Apocalypse are of a scale never before seen in verifiable recorded history. One of these phenomena was the apparent depressurization of the area inside the event.

"Depressurization occurs when air molecules are made significantly less dense in a given area, or are removed to another area altogether. High and low pressures as we know them from naturally occurring weather events are typically caused by an area of higher density air moving to an area of lower density air as they try to balance, or equalize pressure. These naturally occurring shifts in air density produce storms and wind. In all cases, the air molecules are simply flowing from one point to another.

"What was observed during the Asian Apocalypse was a massive flow of air into the event area from all directions outside the event boundaries. This would indicate that a very large-scale depressurization occurred. However, for this to be possible it would have been necessary for air within the area to be rapidly pressurized to a localized point or removed to another location outside the event perimeter. Neither incidence was observed or is even possible to such a scale. A popular theory is that a part of the air molecules themselves were somehow consumed by the energy wave leaving the atmosphere substantially less dense and resulting in super low pressure. This theory has its problems as well.

"Air is made up of molecules; specifically seventy-eight percent nitrogen, twenty-one percent oxygen and one percent argon and other gases. These molecules have a specific atomic structure that together form the air we breathe. Molecules cannot be completely destroyed in the sense that they could somehow be made to no longer exist in any form and therefore create empty space. They can only be displaced or their atomic structure changed to another form, just as heated water turns to a gas and is visible as vapor. Therefore, if a portion of the air molecules *had* been changed at the atomic level, there should have been a detectable residual effect.

"Later readings from weather drones sent into the area indicated lower than normal levels of oxygen and nitrogen in the atmosphere, which would support the hypothesis that the energy wave somehow depleted those molecules. Unfortunately, no residual energy trace from such a molecular conversion was ever detected. This leads to only more questions as to how a portion of the air within this area could have been removed or displaced with no post indicators.

"No monitoring stations survived within the event, although several stations near the event boundary did detect a substantial drop in atmospheric pressure as the air began to move inward toward the point of origin.

"A super low-pressure area, similar to that experienced near the base of tornados, was detectable for several kilometers away from the event outer wall. As a result, many with breathing ailments or respiratory problems literally died from asphyxiation.

"Deaths due to high winds and other weather related causes were reported in areas up to one hundred thirty kilometers from the event boundary. Those unfortunate enough to be caught outside a solid structure were sucked into the event area and killed by blunt force trauma, mostly a result of mobile debris.

"Winds reaching over three hundred kilometers per hour rushed toward the event center causing massive tornados and dry lighting storms of epic proportions. These violent weather events continued within The Dead Zone for approximately sixteen hours before they began to settle. Generally high winds continued for several days until the atmospheric pressures began to stabilize.

"Weather formations and jet stream patterns have been affected over the entire planet to varying degrees, particularly in areas within two thousand kilometers of the event boundary. Even three years later abnormal weather patterns can still be observed in many parts of Europe and Asia where heating, due to a lack of vegetation, frequently causes unusual atmospheric destabilizations."

The narrator started again as scenes of destruction were shown. "The corresponding analysis of infrastructure and vegetation at the event boundary lends as much to its mystery as the event itself. The land and everything living and growing in this area was either burned smooth or completely destroyed up to a definitive point. A vertical line perpendicular to the ground divides the devastation from the initially unscathed. At this point a surgically precise separation is observed—even in high mountainous regions covered with trees. The snow-pack in some areas up to four and a half meters deep was cut smoothly and had no evidence of melting or heating more than inches away from the edge of the event. In the cities of Quetta, Pakistan and Gorgan, Iran, this dividing line at the event wall is where some of the most baffling consequences have occurred. Dr. William Smythe of the British Science Consortium has been studying these areas..."

"Here in Quetta, Pakistan, a little more than half the city fell victim to what the locals are calling Shafan. Those who were outside the event when it occurred and caught a glimpse of the energy wave say it appeared to be a wall of bright fluorescent green followed by a blinding white light. Those who did not see it approach believed it had appeared spontaneously. Many initially saw the front of the energy wave several hundred miles away because it extended so high above the earth. The dissipation of the energy at the edge of the event was marked by an intense white light that left many temporarily blinded before it disappeared immediately afterward.

"The entire event lasted only about two seconds before the winds began. People on the unaffected side of this energy wave say they initially felt nothing. The only sensory indication of the event in addition to the blinding light was what most reported as a brief and very high pitched sizzling or crackling sound. Another interesting point is the lack of a shock wave or concussion wave that would normally precede a large explosion or physical mass moving at a high rate of speed. This is in direct contrast to what occurs during the detonation of any conventional weapon.

"Now granted, there is almost nothing about this event that we can say we honestly understand as of yet, and I think it's fair to say that for many of us in the scientific community, the more we study the effects of this so called energy wave or energy pulse, the more questions that arise. In one example, trees on the edge of the event that were partially exposed directly to the energy and not toppled by subsequent winds are still growing today. This, despite the fact that in some cases up to half the tree may be missing.

"Here in town we can see this same strange phenomenon where structures are simply cut in half and left exposed. Objects or items that would normally ignite by an open flame, such as curtains, furniture and clothing, were burned in pieces, but did not catch fire. To the best of our knowledge, no fires were ignited by the energy wave itself. As you can see here, the edge of this structure appears to have been heated on the surface with no indications of heating past the point of effect.

"At one fueling depot, exposed fuel lines were severed by the energy wave. An observer, fortunate to have survived, stated that the ensuing fire that occurred here was actually caused by sparks dropping from a dissected lighting assembly over the pumping station and not from the energy wave itself. There are similar descriptions from literally every location around the entire circumference of the event from those who were fortunate enough to witness Shafan, and survive."

Narrator: "In the wake of this incomprehensible devastation, even survival was bittersweet for some. This Pakistani man was asleep on a cot when the energy wave hit."

The man began to tell his story while an un-credited voice translated. "I was at my sister and her husband's house resting on a cot when the light and noise woke me. When I opened my eyes, their home in front of me was gone—like it had been cut away with a giant blade. The wind started and I tried to run to the back of the house and that's when I realized this foot was gone here and my leg gone here. I fell to the floor and crawled to a corner. Part of the house fell on me and I was stuck under a wall for two days. It was very hard to breath and my left arm was broken. People came and found me after the winds went away."

Narrator: "Few who actually came into contact with the energy wave survived. Most were badly deformed and died shortly afterward. What kind of energy dispersion could possibly possess attributes to cause such a wide variety of specific conditions? Over seventy images of the actual event were documented." A picture showing a satellite view of a region of Earth was displayed. A sudden flash of greenish white light erupted from a point on the surface moving outward in a rapidly expanding dome. Then it disappeared. The area inside the dome was black with no clouds or discernable features.

As he watched the screen, the blood drained from Ethan's face. Images of a moment from his past had suddenly exploded into his mind. He had seen this energy wave before.

The narrator continued to talk about the various video images that came from satellites, video recorders, news crews, GlobalNet cameras and other sources that happened to be recording as the disaster struck. The images were displayed in a continuous barrage with foreboding string music accompaniment. Some images were recordings of just the flash of light while other fixed cameras recorded well into the stage of high wind before losing their picture. The images on the screen pounded on the doors of his mind while memories from the past were quickly sought, pulled to the surface and run through a rapid cycle of comparisons and evaluations.

Dr. Smythe returned. "As you can see from this satellite image the energy starts at this point here. When we play the images slowly, you can see that when the dome reaches the lower stratosphere at about thirty-six kilometers, it begins to dissipate. This pattern would indicate that the energy was either directed outward or was fueled by air molecules that become much less prevalent as you travel upward through the atmosphere. You can also see that the leading edge maintains this height of about thirty-six kilometers as it travels outward until it reaches one thousand eight hundred thirty-seven kilometers and abruptly stops.

"The area inside the event is now black and void of clouds. As we speed the images up, you can see the cloud formations outside and around the event begin to flow inward as the areas attempt to balance their different atmospheric pressures.

"An infrared satellite image of this area also detected no anomalous readings during the event even though we know that extremely high levels of some kind of heat must have been present. Shortly afterward however, you can see here where the infrared signature near the center of the affected area begins to change as ultraviolet radiation, normally filtered by the atmosphere, begins to heat the surface.

"Temperatures reached over two hundred-ten degrees Celsius before the air was gradually replaced and circulated causing temperatures to decrease. Had the energy wave traveled farther into our atmosphere, even fifty-kilometers instead of the measured thirty-six, the effect on the global climate and long-term atmospheric damage would have been substantially greater with the possibility of tens of millions in additional weather related deaths.

"The process of scientific discovery involves studying the effects and interactions between nature and the subject of that we wish to learn about. To understand geological formations for instance, we look to the ground that gives us a blueprint into the past. It is not dissimilar to what a detective might do to solve a crime. We look for post incidental evidence and study that evidence to piece together a puzzle that will hopefully allow us to construct a correlated history into events that have transpired.

"In the case of the Asian Apocalypse we have minimal residual artifact to work with. The depleted atmosphere and very thin layer of heated surface material is all we have to work with. But a thorough analysis of these areas produced no traces of any unnatural compound or element. Additionally there was no trace of any elemental fission process and no unnatural residual radiation. There was no concussion wave to indicate a physical movement of matter and no detection of anomalous electromagnetic properties or changes in the earth's magnetic field. And although remote seismic stations recorded a strong vibration during the event, no initial tremor or ground disturbance was recorded to indicate a detonating catalyst.

"Any kind of energy we currently understand that is capable of producing a known and measurable effect will also produce a noticeable byproduct. This Asian energy wave has left absolutely none. We can only hypothesize that it is simply a form of energy yet unknown to our sciences.

"Some even speculate it could be what is classified as TDE or Theoretical Dimensional Energy. The TDE concept suggests that a 'transitional energy' exists that is capable of moving between dimensions, therefore interacting in our physical environment only to shift completely into another dimension that is undetectable to us. Of course, we presently have no way to prove such a theory. However, based on what we have all observed I think it's safe to say that any theoretically possible explanation cannot be dismissed until definitive evidence is found to the contrary.

"The fact is, there is no known science that currently exists to either create or control, or even explain the event that has taken place in Central Asia. This is one of those phenomena that will be continuously studied for as long as it remains a mystery."

Narrator: "The world reaction that followed was as varied as the cultures in its population. All nations and countries were astonished and appalled at the devastation and loss of life. Those with the available resources inundated the affected areas around and within The Dead Zone to assist in search and rescue as well as humanitarian aide, clean up and eventual rebuilding.

"As the world began to see and experience the horrible destruction and death, there were many who sought retribution on behalf of those who had suffered. It was widely believed and understood by civilized nations that no country or government possessed the knowledge, capability or even the desire to inflict such a precise and grand scale cataclysmic devastation. Even so, there would be those under the rallying-cry of perceived genocide who would use the opportunity to bring together those willing to ingratiate themselves in the propaganda of fighting evil and rise up against a common foe—the United States of America.

"Within weeks attacks began on those providing aid in the regions outside The Dead Zone with skirmishes against workers and between armed rebels and American and allied defense forces. Many of the third-world countries and others devoted to seeking justice formed the World Alliance that proclaimed the United States as the instigator of the Asian Apocalypse. This new Alliance was responsible for acts of terrorism on several continents against targets with U.S. affiliation. Within the United States, covert terrorist cells began to form within its borders and initiated attacks that would bring about severe restrictions on many of the country's freedoms.

"The United States found itself fighting enemies on several fronts. Civil unrest led to the formation of independent military style organizations committed to suppressing the terrorist threat and weeding out individuals believed to be sympathetic with inland terrorist groups. Although initially well intended, tensions began to rise between these civil organizations and sanctioned law enforcement agencies. In many parts of the country, chaos ensued and it became necessary for the government to establish a military presence in urban areas to discourage actions by these rogue justice groups, many of which were comprised primarily of restless and opportunistic, gun wielding thugs.

"For many years the United States and its allies would defend freedom and work to protect its citizens. Not only from those outside its borders, but many times from within. Some of the restrictions imposed during those years of unrest still exist to-day—a constant reminder of this dark time in our world history.

"With the support of neighboring nations, including the United States, many areas of The Dead Zone have since been renovated and replanted with native grasses, foliage and trees. As melting mountain snow and rainfall continuously create new streams and rivers, new grasses and plant life begin to grow through the cracks in an arid and sterile surface. Nature's never-ending evolutionary process continues to slowly move forward in transforming this region of Asia back to its once diverse and beautiful landscape.

"The dark shadow cast over our world that November will never be forgotten—a history brought about by one of the most fantastic and dreadful mysteries of all time. Whether unimaginable horrors conjured from the dark unconscious, or magnificence challenging the feral depths of imagination, we stand in awe, and become a changed people." The record ended.

The connotations and implications ran rampant through Ethan's mind as he pulled fidgety fingers through a scraggly, long beard. A part of him tried to hold firm to the belief that this was still just a manufactured story, while another reminded him that nothing had been proven untrue, *yet*. Only three records remained.

"Playback of record three hundred ninety-nine."

"Last night I had the strangest dream. I was walking through a field of grass and flowers alone on a small hill when I saw a woman standing near the top. I walked up to her. She smiled and said, 'Choose to see with no disguise. Open your heart and open your eyes.' Then I found myself standing in a dimly lit corner of a very large room with bright lights and machines near the center. The machines were making a strange noise and there was a man standing in front of them covering his ears. He turned and looked at me. He seemed surprised, and scared. Then I woke up. Pretty strange, huh?

"I also feel like something else is happening to me. The life around me is becoming brighter. It's almost like I'm beginning to see the essence of living things—more than what I could before. Weird, I know. I'm not sure what it means." She took a long pause. "Hopefully I'll figure it out."

The date on the next record showed it was four days later and the last entry seven days after that.

"Playback of record four hundred."
Sara seemed content and had a pleasant smile. "I know who those people were in my dream. I'm beginning to understand how it all ties together." The record ended.

With one record left, Ethan knew this was the one that would have to tie it all up. This was what he had been waiting for—the end of the story. He was ready, and with cautious enthusiasm pressed 'Play.'

"Playback of record four hundred one."
Sara was outside sitting on the ground in front of the camera with her legs crossed. Behind her were lots of trees, like a forest with mountains in the distance and a bright blue sky above. She looked beautiful with the sunlight reflecting off her hair—loose and flowing over one shoulder with her face radiating a peaceful inner countenance. She spoke with incredible insight and intelligence for someone her age. Then with her final words and a radiant smile, she ended the record.

Ethan stared at the screen, then dropped his head and banged it on the desk several times. *That's it? That's all?* he asked incredulously, staring and waiting in frustrated bewilderment. "There has to be more than that. *Come on!*"
"Request not recognized. Please—"
"Oh shut up," he said turning the chair sideways to stare at the wall.

CHAPTER FOUR

Mirrors

FOR THE NEXT THREE days Ethan pondered Sara's journal as he tried to tie it all together. There was now no denying that somehow, someone knew about what had happened at the lab. Why else would he have received this information? But that was impossible. He had told no one. *No one.* What could Sara have possibly figured out that made him a part of all this?

There were also no *real* historical records to verify any of the events chronicled in the journal. Of course GlobalNet was so diluted with erroneous garbage that it was sometimes impossible to separate legitimate information from the mindless disseminations of lunatics and conspiracy theorists. But even with that there should have been something. How do you prove or disprove something that has no basis in fact?

It was early morning as Ethan looked at the ceiling from the couch in his office where he had fallen asleep the night before. The device was still sitting inconspicuously on the desk where it didn't really look out of place anymore. His eyes moved to the picture of Rachel and Allison. He looked at it briefly then got up, walked over, picked it up off the desk and returned to the small couch where he proceeded to study the faces of his wife and daughter. Gently he ran his fingers over the glass as if to feel a presence that might somehow emanate from their smiles. He desperately wanted inspiration. "I'm losing it, aren't I?" was the question asked as he gazed at them. An answer wasn't really expected—it *was* just a photograph. It hadn't worked the other hundred or so times either.

The picture was returned to the desk and as he walked to the kitchen, a nostril full of something rancid permeated the air. *What is that smell? Is that me?* He lowered his head to an armpit and took a whiff. "Oh!" he exclaimed as he quickly moved his head back. Several days without a shower had taken its toll. Regardless, food was still the priority. Opening the fridge revealed that apparently shopping had *not* been a priority for some time. He was going to have to go to a store or to a drive-in or somewhere, but not like this.

Now freshly showered, presentable attire had to be found. It took awhile to locate a not too seriously wrinkled shirt. At least he was now clean and dressed. Strange, it was the first time in several months that there seemed to be a feeling of direction to his life again. It was barely perceptible, but for some reason going out this time didn't seem like such a drag. He wasn't really happy, just...okay, which was still acceptable.

The destination wasn't necessarily preplanned that morning. Maybe he'd go to a real grocery store in town. Every other food-run had typically been late at night to the closest open 'Quick Mart' or snack-laden gas station.

Being out this early was strange and exhilarating. Merging into traffic reminded him that this was the same route he used to take to work. Thoughts of the lab then crept in as he recounted experiences and pictured the facility and his colleagues before their deaths. More memories began to surface and thoughts focused on the last project his team was working on together.

There was talk that the client had paid a one hundred million dollar deposit to establish the contract. A contract fee wasn't unusual, although that amount was a little larger than most—*if* the rumors were to be believed. They didn't know who the client was or any other specifics, only that the entire project was secret and the small test sample they were given was only a minute portion of more that existed somewhere. At the time none of it really seemed out of the ordinary since secrecy and discretion were always standard procedure.

Each of the families of the deceased employees had received a sizeable settlement as incentive to keep quiet and accept the accident as a terrible tragedy and nothing more. He had always been a little suspicious of the unexplained coincidences that started the day before, and then there was the visit from the Director.

Now it seemed with this strange journal that someone might be trying to tell him something about what he saw there. If he was going to find any answers regarding what really happened and who was involved, the bartered silence would have to be broken and those buried questions resurrected. Even with little to lose, thoughts of stirring up the past were not all that intriguing.

As Ethan thought intently, trying to find cohesion to some of the clues and questions, the intended exit passed and was now miles behind him. "Brilliant," he said to himself sarcastically. 'Lakewood Blvd' was just ahead so he quickly moved to the right lane and took the off ramp. This area was unfamiliar to him. At least it was nice and had several small malls with grocery stores. Since he was already there, he picked one at random and went in.

Looking almost domesticated with his shopping cart, he strolled up and down the aisles looking for the usual smattering of easy-to-fix meals. It's astounding how many different foods can be frozen or canned. Is there any other kind?

There seemed to be a lot of women in the store with very young children—not something he usually saw during his runs at midnight. Some children were apparently there against their will as they protested and demanded to buy this and that while others just screamed to be set free. It was a strange world this time of morning.

Finding the frozen foods took a few minutes, but now their familiar offerings were there in front of him, displayed far and wide for his perusal. While looking over the many varieties of potatoes, vegetables, chicken and fish, he glanced down the row of freezer doors to catch a glimpse of a woman's face as she passed the end of the aisle. Suddenly, memories were stirred and they churned while he stood motionless, waiting for a connection that never came. *I know her from somewhere,* he thought.

Leaving the still mostly empty cart, he swiftly and casually walked to the end of the aisle and looked in the direction the woman had been walking. Several people were going about their shopping. Her face wasn't among them. Quickly he walked along the end of the aisles and briefly peered down each one. Then halfway down one of them...there she was, turned partly away from him, carrying a hand-basket and looking at a jar of something. Ethan stopped and just kind of stared at her, hoping to catch another glimpse of the face he couldn't quite place. She turned and glanced up at him. Their eyes met.

Startled, Ethan was suddenly struck with embarrassment. A hasty retreat was in order, but then he realized it might look too obvious so a box was quickly pulled from the shelf and scanned intently for nothing in particular. After a moment he casually looked up again. She was gone. His eyes rolled at the feeling of stupidity when a memory suddenly connected the face.

In his mind's eye he saw the woman at the funeral services—she was a friend of Rachel's. He had only met her a few times in the past fifteen years or so, but that was her—he was sure of it. Her name was Alex...something. Last he remembered she was married and living several states away. This *couldn't* be the same woman, *could it?* It seemed pretty unlikely, although it would sure be interesting to talk to one of Rachel's friends.

He walked to the end of the aisle and didn't see her anywhere. Walking along the other side of the store found her rounding the far end of another aisle. It was like cat and mouse. Unknown to him though, the prey was aware of its stalker.

As he turned up the aisle where she was last seen, she was gone again. *Man, talk about elusive. Maybe this isn't such a good idea,* he thought as he continued walking. Just because this woman might be a friend of his wife didn't really mean anything, and didn't change anything. So that was enough and this time when he didn't see her anywhere at the end of the store, he started making his way back to frozen foods.

In contemplation, and with his head lowered, he walked back down the aisle toward his shopping cart when another cart blocked his path. He moved to go around it, but the cart moved in front of him. Confused he looked up to see its driver was a large burly man with big, bare tattooed arms and a shiny skull earring dangling from a pierced ear. Startled and silent, Ethan just looked at the man who glared at him with an evil sneer. Then it spoke. "You got a problem, Sport?"

"Me?" Ethan said has he gingerly pointed to himself.

"Yeah, you. The nice lady says you're following her around. So what's your problem?"

"Problem? I don't have a problem. Oh, you mean the lady with the dark hair. I mean…I don't mean she's a problem. I know her. Well…I think I know her."

"Maybe you better get lost."

"Actually I was just thinking about doing that."

"Maybe you need some help, too."

"No, no, I'm sure I can handle it, thank you. But I really do think I know her. That was all I wanted to find out."

"Look buddy, you better beat it before—"

"Please, if she says she doesn't know me then I'm out of here, right away lost, very gone. Okay?"

The man took a long look at Ethan. With a forceful sigh he pointed his finger and replied, "Okay, but if she doesn't know you… What's your name?"

"Ethan Grey. My wife is Rachel Grey."

"Don't go anywhere," Burly Man grunted as he left his cart in front of Ethan and disappeared around the end of the aisle.

Ethan's emotions were mixed with fear and curiosity. He had managed to avoid talking to 'friends' for a long time just so he wouldn't have to keep responding to that same annoying question over and over and over, even if they *were* just being polite. Maybe if this really was Alex, it might be okay to talk to one of Rachel's *real* friends—as long as he didn't get pummeled first. He remembered Rachel said that distance and work had kept them from doing much together, but she had still spoken highly of Alex.

Just then Burly Man came back with the woman walking behind him. He pushed his cart to the side of the aisle as Ethan watched nervously. The woman stood to his side and looked at Ethan. His tenuous emotional stability was not well hidden.

"You say you're Ethan Grey?" she asked.

"Yes. Are you Alex?"

"Could be, but I don't recognize you. What was your daughter's name?"

He didn't like hearing 'was' associated with his family. "Her name is Allison," Ethan said as he tried to smile, but ended up glancing around embarrassed as Burly Man folded his arms, waiting for the signal to melee. He then continued. "At the funeral you told me that Rachel once offered to teach you how to play, but you declined because you didn't want to put her through that much pain and anguish."

Alex slowly started to smile then turned to Burly Man. "It's all right, I know him. Thank you for your help."

"You bet, anytime," Burly Man responded as he took his cart and stared Ethan down in passing.

"I didn't recognize you at all. You look...different." That was her polite way of saying he looked like crap. It was probably true though. Funny, until that moment, he hadn't really cared. "How are you doing?"

Ugh. There was that question. He started to reply with the standard response, but then paused to think about how it had been asked. The cadence of her voice was different than that of the rehearsed inquiries he usually received. She might really be sincere in wanting to know how he was doing. The instinctual defensive animosity was pushed aside for just a moment as he looked at the floor and thought about the consequences of an honest answer. He was reluctant to say how he really felt, but didn't want to lie to his wife's friend either.

"It's uh...it's been hard."

"I'll bet." There was a brief, awkward silence. "You haven't eaten yet this morning have you?"

"Well, no... How did you know that?"

"I can hear your stomach from clear over here. There's a decent little place to eat just up the street a couple blocks. Let's go grab some breakfast. It would be nice to catch up."

The concept seemed almost foreign to him. It took some effort not to automatically reject the offer and retreat to the shadows of obscurity. But she was friendly, and she *was* one of Rachel's good friends.

"Well I uh...I suppose. I'm not really dressed for the occasion."

"That's alright. I don't think a tie and jacket are required." Her comment was followed up with a smile.

"Okay." he responded, grinning modestly. "What about your groceries?"

"They'll wait."

Ethan followed her as they left the store and walked to her car. "What *was* the story with that guy anyway," he asked.

"After the third time I saw you checking me out I got a little concerned and asked him to ask you what you were doing. You don't exactly fit the Mr. Rogers persona with the hair and all you know."

"Who was he?"

"I don't know."

"You mean you didn't know him?"

"Never seen him before."

Ethan was surprised by her boldness. "You asked a total stranger to confront me."

"He looked okay. Usually I'm a fairly good judge of character. Plus the name 'Molly' tattooed on his arm gave me the impression he was probably decent to women. I figured it was a safe bet."

"So you thought he looked safer than I did?"

"Nothing personal."

"Molly could be his pit-bull you know."

"Maybe," Alex replied as they approached her car.

"Well, I am sorry about the way I look. It just seems to be easier to look at this face in the mirror than the other one. The other one had a family. This one is just...somebody else." Alex discretely watched him as he stood by the passenger door, waiting for her to unlock the car. It was difficult to remember what he really looked like under all that hair. She could vaguely see his face on an old Christmas card and from the service—still only vaguely.

She was enjoying this impromptu reunion, but Ethan was feeling out of place and wasn't very talkative during the short drive.

The restaurant was one of those little family diners that serves breakfast anytime. The waitress seated them in a booth by a window. "Something to drink?" she asked.

"How about uh, chocolate milk," Ethan replied. The waitress turned to Alex who found his choice of drink amusing. He looked more like someone who would prefer whiskey from a brown paper bag.

"And for you?"

"Orange juice, please."

"Alright, I'll be right back."

"Thank you," Alex responded.

Ethan picked up his menu. "I get the impression you've been here before."

"Yeah, I kind of like this place."

"I'm not used to being out this early," he added, looking outside and squinting at the bright sunshine.

Alex looked at him with a puzzled expression. "It's ten thirty in the morning—an hour and a half before noon. Most people don't consider *this* early." Ethan lowered his menu. Of course she had no idea what his life was really like—the frequent sleepless nights and depression. He tried to remember that. Still, deep within, animosity and frustration quietly simmered.

"Like I said, things have been a little difficult. Some people may not handle certain situations as well as others."

Alex was a little embarrassed and leaned back in her seat as Ethan looked out the window. "I'm sorry, I didn't mean to sound callous," she offered. "It's just that I feel like I know you from what Rachel used to tell me."

"What did she tell you?"

"Well, she said you were very intelligent."

"That's good."

"She always said good things about you."

"That's just because she was too nice to be honest."

"No, I think she was really happy and I suspect you and Allison were a big part of that." Ethan stared at the table as the faces of his wife and daughter passed through his mind. Alex let him daydream for a few moments. "So why were you following me around in the store like that?"

Ethan sighed and shook his head. "That was embarrassing. When I saw you I knew I had seen you from someplace before. It just took awhile to figure out from where. Then you sent that nice young man to talk to me."

"Yeah, sorry about that. If you look at it from *my* point of view though, you have to admit that being followed around like that *was* a little creepy."

"You mean having *me* follow you around was creepy."

"Well... Have you moved? Last I heard you were still near Copper Valley," she redirected.

"Yeah, we're still there."

Alex stared at him for a second before responding. "We?" she asked somewhat puzzled.

Ethan looked up at her in surprise when he realized what he had said. "Uh, me and the cat. You know."

"I see. That's quite a ways from here, isn't it?"

"Yeah that's another good story. Started thinking about things and didn't realize where I was going until I was here—kind of daydreaming. Not a good thing to do when you're driving."

"I don't know, we may not have met otherwise," Alex said with a slightly suggestive smile. Ethan wasn't entirely sure, but that response seemed a little forward for someone who was married.

The waitress approached the table and set the drinks down. Ethan quickly looked at his menu.

"What can I get for you?" she asked Alex.

"I'll have the Country Omelet."

"And for you sir?"

Ethan turned the menu toward the waitress and pointed to an item. "I'll have this pancake special thingy."

"How would you like your eggs?"

"Scrambled."

"Okay. Anything else I can get for you?"

"No, that's all, thank you," Alex replied.

"I'll bring out your orders when they're ready." The waitress took the menus and left.

Ethan then attempted to take charge of the conversation. "So you seem to know a little about me, but all I know about you is that you used to teach math at Wilhelm."

"Still do—summer break."

"Well then you're a lot farther from home than I am. What brings you clear out here?"

Alex took a drink of her orange juice then set it down. "My brother lives out here."

"Oh, so you and your family visiting?"

"No, just me."

"Taking some 'me' time then."

"The 'me' time is permanent. I'm divorced."

"Oh, sorry."

"It was inevitable. I married a power monger. He was a wonderful man nine years ago, then his priorities changed and I became insignificant to his megalomaniacal career ambitions. What's worse is I think the kind of person he became is the person he really was. Somehow, I think what I saw in him originally was a façade. It seemed like the more he conquered the more he changed until he became emperor and my contribution to our marriage was trivial at best. He didn't need me anymore and really didn't even want me. His new mistress was wealth and power. You know what I mean?"

Ethan was somewhat uncomfortable being the recipient of so much personal information from someone he didn't really know *that* well. "Are you doing okay now?"

"It's been handled. We didn't have any children so I'm okay." Ethan knew that wasn't entirely true. No one is just 'okay' after a traumatic personal experience like that. It never completely goes away. You have to learn to accept it or you end up hiding in your house and alienating the rest of the world.

Fortunately the waitress returned to head-off any awkward silence. "Here you go. One Country Omelet and one House Pancake Special, eggs scrambled. Is there anything else I can get for you?"

"That was fast," Ethan commented.

"Looks fine, thank you," Alex replied.

Ethan picked up the syrup and poured a healthy layer of blue-berry on his pancakes. Alex sat staring at her omelet.

Ethan put the syrup down and looked at her. "This was a good idea," he said. She didn't respond and had that glazed look in her eyes. "This was a good idea," he repeated a little more deliberately while motioning to his plate.

"Yes...yes it was," she said smiling after realizing he was talking to her.

Both of them were quiet for a time as Alex methodically speared small vegetables and Ethan shoveled away. Having eaten about half the omelet, Alex set her fork down and put her hands in her lap. "I apologize if I was a little too forward."

"You don't need to apologize."

"No, you don't understand. I think I misread the situation."

"What do you mean?"

"When Rachel died it was a serious wake-up-call for me. I thought about what my then-husband would have done if *I* had died. I don't think the jerk would have been too overly concerned at all." Ethan stopped eating and set his fork down. "Do you know what it feels like to believe you have no value as a human being? I think it's probably one of the most demoralizing things a person can ever experience. Sure, my brother and his family are really nice and I know they love me, but it isn't the same. In the store when I found out who you really were, I was excited. I know who you are because of Rachel. It seemed like fate brought us together. I mean, what are the chances we would be at the same place at the same time so far away from our homes. That's pretty incredible."

"Alex, I can appreciate the fact that you've had some difficult times, but at least you still have some family. I have nothing. My parents are long gone, I have no living siblings and I never really got along with Rachel's parents. I don't think you can really understand what it feels like to have a perfect life one moment and then have it ripped away from you the next. You don't get time to prepare and you don't see it coming. Then in the blink of an eye, you're completely alone. Everyone is always sympathetic and sorry for you. That doesn't change anything though. You're still alone."

"I see," Alex said soberly, looking at her plate. "I guess we have something in common then, don't we?"

Ethan took a moment to ponder. "Yeah, I guess we might."

"Come on, you have to admit that us running into each other this morning was pretty interesting. You're a scientist, what are the odds?"

"Interesting, yes, I'll go that far. But if you're implying that this coincidental meeting is some kind of cosmic fate or destiny, *I don't think so.*"

"Ah, the cynical side of Ethan Grey. Well then, that and the Charles Manson look should keep you in pretty good company," she said a little bitingly.

"You always this reserved with people you invite to breakfast?"

Alex realized her response was just as cynical. She started to smile as she looked down, took her napkin, folded it in fourths and set it on the table to the side of her plate. She looked up at Ethan and held out her hand. "Hi. I'm Alexandria Zavalla. My friends call me Alex."

Ethan pushed aside his simmering animosity to recognize her sincerity in wanting to give friendship a chance. Maybe sarcasm was just one of those ugly byproducts of being hurt and alone. He sighed and took her hand. "Hi Alex. Ethan Grey"

"Nice to meet you, Mr. Grey. Shall we go?"

"Sure. I'll get the check."

Ethan climbed into the car and they headed out of the small parking lot and back down the street to the grocery store. "What kind of math do you teach?"

"Statistics mostly. Sometimes I assist another professor with his Universal Dynamics class."

"That's impressive. Understanding that level of math and theory is no small feat."

"Well, it seems like everyone has their little niche. I can't sew a shirt to save my life, but I can analyze a hundred pages of data without breaking a sweat. It's just what I do."

"Do you like teaching?"

"Yeah, for the most part. How about you? What do you do now?"

"Oh, been retired for a while."

"Retired? You're too young to be retired aren't you?"

"You might say it was warranted by the circumstances."

"Well that must be nice."

"It's okay. I'm surprised Rachel didn't tell you. I was retired before the um...the accident."

"No, she never mentioned that. But even retired people have to do something; whittle wood, fish, go to dinner at four in the afternoon?"

Ethan laughed. "No, I don't fish. Just some, well, let's just say I have some personal projects I'm working on."

"Fair enough. Here we are." They were back at the grocery store parking lot.

"I'm curious about this other professor. What is Universal Dynamics?"

"It's a course related to Theology that emphasizes personal awareness and how you can become 'one with the universe.'"

"More cynicism?"

"Let's just say I don't necessarily buy into all of it. But the Professor is a good friend and I try to be respectful." Alex pulled into a parking stall and shut off the engine. "Are you going to finish your shopping?"

"Nah, I think I'll just head back to my own neighborhood."

"Kind of ruined it for you, huh?"

"No, it was fine. I'd just feel more comfortable where things are more familiar. That's all. What's the name of the professor who does the Universal Dynamics stuff?"

"Dr. Samuel Greenhagen. Why?"

"Just curious." Ethan opened the door and climbed out. Alex did the same. "Oh wait," she said as she set her purse on the hood and dug around to finally pulling out a blank piece of paper. "I'll put my mobile on the back just in case you decide you might want someone to talk to. Do you mind if I get yours?"

"I don't have one."

"You don't have a phone?"

"I don't have a mobile."

"I thought everyone had a mobile."

"Don't really have much use for one. I think it's in a drawer somewhere."

"I'm sure I still have your home number. Is it the same?"

"Should be."

Alex handed the piece of paper to Ethan. "It really has been nice seeing you again."

"You too."

Alex locked her car and started back toward the store. Ethan walked to his car, but had to look back one more time. Alex turned at the same time and waved again. He waved and smiled, climbed into the car and watched her as she walked through the doors. *Hmm.*

As Ethan drove up to his house with two bags of groceries from a local store, he carefully surveyed the neighborhood for the usual 'something that didn't look right.' But everything looked fine. As a matter of fact, since the device had arrived, everything else had become fairly normal. That in itself was kind of strange.

Now he had some real food in the house and after putting the groceries away, took one of the big Granny Smith apples and headed to the office. He took a quick look to make sure the device was still where it had been hidden, then sat in the chair and rolled it over to the GlobalNet terminal.

It was just curiosity again and after a brief log-in sequence to the SAN, he selected a 'Search by Name' option and typed in 'Alexandria Zavalla, Virginia.' The terminal searched for a few seconds as he took another bite of apple. A listing came up for a woman, seventy-one years old. Unless Alex was the successful test subject of a cellular regeneration experiment, this wasn't her. The other names under Zavalla didn't match either. Then it occurred to him that her address must be in Rachel's little purple address book. It was in the desk in the family room. He had tried to get her to put everything in the computer but she preferred to hand-write her friends' information because she said it was "more personal."

Ethan approached the roll-top desk and stopped as his mind's eye saw his wife sitting in the wooden chair going through their bills. His conscious thoughts were lost in fond memories. He gazed at her imaginary image and let the feelings of the past overwhelm him. He forgot what he was there for. As her image faded away and he found himself standing alone in the dead quiet room, his senses returned and he opened the desk to gently remove the address book from its neatly organized location.

Back in the office he carefully thumbed through the small book. There was an entry under Zavalla, but it looked old. *Of course, she said she was divorced.* So was Zavalla her married name or maiden name? He started in the A's and looked at every entry for one with the first name of Alex or Alexandria. As the names under 'S' were read he came across Derric and Alex Stanovich in Massachusetts. This time he entered 'Derric Stanovich, Massachusetts' and a full screen of information appeared.

He eagerly read through the slew of various corporate ownerships and executive level associations. "Busy, busy," he said to himself. He cleared the entry and typed in 'Alexandria Stanovich, Massachusetts.' The screen displayed one entry that was a short blurb of Derric Stanovich and must have been old because it simply listed Alex as Derric's wife. Quite a contrast. He then typed in 'Alex Stanovich, Virginia.' Two people came up and they were both male. That was odd. Her information shouldn't be this elusive. Next, he brought up the information for Wilhelm University. Under a listing for 'Faculty Members,' he searched for Alex Stanovich and Zavalla, but found neither. In the department search under Statistics programs the names of two instructors came up; Michael Jehaus and Alex Fullerman. Something didn't jive.

Next he looked for a Universal Dynamics class. It was there with an instructor 'Professor Samuel Greenhagen.' That was credible. So why would there be no record of Alex with the last name she had given him? Was it a mistake...or something else?

Ethan wasn't the most patient person in the world and his curiosity seldom waned with time. Later that night while looking at the paper with her number on it for the fourth time, he decided it was time to call.

On the third ring a female voice answered. "Hello?"

"Hello. Is this Alex?"

"Yes it is."

"This is Ethan."

"Ethan," Alex said surprised, "I wasn't expecting to hear from you so soon. Actually, I wasn't really expecting to hear from you at all."

"I was just thinking about this morning and feel like I owe you a little better conversation, if I can find one."

Alex laughed politely. "That's okay. I wasn't exactly in best form myself. Did you have something in mind?"

"Well, it's a little late for me, being past four and all, but what about meeting for dinner?"

"Actually I just ate with my brother's family. I wouldn't mind dessert though."

"I can do dessert. Do you know of any good places up there?"

"There's a little ice cream shop not far from where we met this morning. But won't that be a lot of driving twice in one day?"

"It really isn't that far and I don't mind."

With plans made, Ethan washed his hands and prepared to leave. But as he looked up at the stranger in the mirror, the façade began to crumble. The beard and scraggly hair *did* make him look like someone he really wasn't. He leaned over on the counter and looked down at the sink. How long was he going to keep this up? He had to stop hiding sometime. Maybe now was as good a time as any.

The trimmers had to be in the bathroom closet somewhere and when they were finally located, the cord was missing. Scissors where certainly more primitive, but did the job as large hunks of beard fell into the sink. What was left was removed with a good old-fashioned razor. Several agonizing minutes later the job was finished. Now the face in the mirror was a new stranger—not quite himself, not exactly who he was before. The haircut would have to wait until later.

Alex had been sitting in her car for about fifteen minutes when Ethan finally pulled in. He saw her a few spaces down and waved to her as he walked in front of her. She stared briefly, not sure who he was, then stuck her head out the window. "Ethan?"

"Ms. Zavalla."

"Man, you look different. What made you decide to do that?"

"I suppose being myself again didn't seem so bad. Plus it bothered me a little that you didn't recognize me."

Alex got out of her car. "Well, you're half-way there."

"Yeah, still have the hair to do. The urge to clean this up hit me just before I left. Sorry I'm late."

"It's okay. I would have given you another five minutes."

The ice cream shop was an old fashioned drive-in with a few seats inside and a group of tables outside. There were a couple hours of daylight left and a lot of people were taking advantage of the warm evening.

Alex led Ethan to the order window where they looked at the menu for a minute before she ordered. "I'd like a single scoop of rocky road in a waffle cone please."

"I'll take a small chocolate chip shake."

After receiving their order they moved to an outside table and sat down. Alex licked and nibbled her cone as Ethan tried to get some of the super thick shake through the straw. Cheeks were strained, the straw was sucked flat—it just wasn't working.

Alex watched in amusement as he struggled with the defiant dessert. "You want a spoon?"

"I suppose," he replied annoyed.

"I'll get you one," she said as she started to get up.

"No, no, that's fine. I'll get it." Ethan turned to pull his leg over the seat and grimaced when his knee banged the underside of the table.

Alex put her hand on his shoulder, squeezed and pushed on it slightly. "No really, just stay there and I'll get you one." She then walked to the window and retrieved a plastic spoon.

When her hand was on his shoulder, a feeling went through him he hadn't felt in a very long time. It was the unmistakable sensation of a woman's touch—a warm feeling of concern and caring that can be experienced in even unintentional moments. As brief and simple as it was, it was still a little uncomfortable. Alex brought back the spoon, handed it to him then sat back down.

He didn't look up. "Thank you."

"You're welcome."

Now with something to actually eat the shake with, Ethan removed the lid and inserted the spoon. The thick ice cream emerged from the cup, sticking to the plastic utensil in a large blob that trailed as he lifted it into the air. "I'd like to know who decided that milk shakes should be so thick that you have to eat them with a spoon. If I wanted a cup full of ice cream, I would have just ordered a cup full of ice cream. Why do they even bother to stick a straw in it? For effect?" Alex grinned as she licked her cone in a circle around the outside.

"You know, they used to call them *milk shakes* because you put milk and ice cream in a container and shook it. That's what the straw is supposed to be for." Perturbed, he dropped the giant glob back into the cup and pushed it away, shaking his head. "You seem to like yours," he commented to Alex.

"I *love* rocky-road," she replied taking a few more good licks. "So why did you really decide to call me?"

"I just thought I was maybe a little offish this morning—could have been nicer."

"Uh huh. Is that the only reason?"

"Well...maybe you could clarify something for me." Alex looked at him apprehensively. "Something doesn't make sense and I was just wondering what it meant." He reached into his pocket and pulled out the faculty member page printed from the Wilhelm site. He unfolded it and slid it over to her. She looked down at the paper while continuing to eat the cone more slowly. When she saw the circled faculty names under her department, she knew what he wanted to know.

"So, you've gone from checking me out to checking up on me. Should I be flattered?" Ethan fidgeted a little, but didn't say anything. Then with her free hand she pushed the paper back to him and stood. He watched, wondering what she was going to do. "Let's go for a walk," she suggested. Ethan grabbed the paper, folded it up and put it in his pocket while he stood to follow.

"What exactly do you want to know?" she asked when he finally caught up to her.

"Since I don't really know you that well and Rachel did, I just thought I'd...uh...do some homework. The last name you gave me wasn't on the list at the University. It just raised some questions."

They walked a moment in silence as Alex kept slowly working on the cone. "Can I trust you?"

"Of course," Ethan said without hesitation. There was another moment of silence. She was being fairly guarded about something.

"You have to promise to keep this to yourself. It's really nobody else's business and I'll tell you only as a friend. Okay?"

"Sure, okay."

"Alex Fullerman, the name on your list, that's me. The divorce wasn't exactly typical. We didn't just have a falling out or agree to irreconcilable differences. Derric became abusive and I was the focus of his aggression during the last couple years. It was just small stuff at first, but as time went on his personality really started to change. Sometimes it was just words, sometimes he would shove me around and slap me. It got progressively worse. It was like I told you, he changed from the person I thought I knew.

"It got to the point where I couldn't take it anymore. He had already threatened me a few times not to 'do anything stupid.' This was a person who had become connected everywhere, and everyone respected his authority. He threatened to do things to me or my family if I ever tried to leave him. It was crazy. He developed this personality that had to have total control over everything, including me. I wanted to leave—I wanted to tell someone, but I was afraid what he might do. It was horrible and I think he would have made good on his threats. No one knew, not even Rachel. I didn't want to involve her in my private little hell.

"It seemed the only option was to either kill him, or myself. It would have been tough for him to do anything to me after that, right?" She looked over at him with a forced grin from her morbid humor. He wasn't smiling. Her words had hit just a little too close to home.

She tossed the rest of her cone behind some bushes and continued. "I couldn't bring myself to do either one. That's just not who I am. Then a strange thing happened; I ran into a person I hadn't seen in over ten years. The professor I mentioned? It was him—saw him outside a convention center in North Carolina.

"Before I met Derric I was attending a little university there where the Professor taught Foreign Studies. He was really nice and always treated me with respect. When he found out I was going to have to drop out of school because I couldn't handle the tuition, studying and working full time, he came to my rescue like I was one of his own children. His wife was really nice too and they let me stay in an extra bedroom for free. It was like I became one of the family. He used his position at the university to get me discounted tuition and I stayed with them for about a year until he moved back to his estate and returned to Wilhelm. That's around the time I met Rachel.

"Just before the divorce, if you can call it that, Derric and I had flown to the convention. The Professor happened to be there on some other business. His hair was grayer and he looked a little older, but he still had the same goatee. He was very happy to see me and, of course, wanted to know about my life and what I was up to." Alex cleared her throat to keep the emotions under control. "This man was like a father to me, but I was afraid to say anything. I just told him that things could be better and he asked if that's what the bruises on my face were about. I had forgotten that a few days before, Derric was in one of his moods and had shoved me out of his way. I hit the side of my face on a shelf. It wasn't bad, but still noticeable.

"When I looked in the Professor's eyes I knew he could see the pain I was hiding. Somehow his fatherly instinct just knew and that was it. I lost it and spilled my guts. We went over and sat on a bench and I told him everything. Then he told me that if I wanted to be free of Derric for good to meet him back in front of the convention center in an hour. There would be a silver limo waiting to pick me up. I had no idea what to expect, but I trusted him.

"The limo was there just like he said it would be. I remember the windows in the back were blacked out. You couldn't see out or in at all when they were turned on. Funny I remember that. Then the Professor asked me what I *really* wanted. I told him I just wanted to leave and get away from Derric and have nothing to do with him or anything he was connected with ever again. He looked at me with that fatherly smile and told me it could be arranged.

"At first I thought the worst, like he'd have him killed or something. He told me that he believed people were basically good, only sometimes they seem to forget and need to be reminded that consequences will always find those who abuse others. Derric was certainly one of those. Then he asked me if I was sure this is what I wanted to do. It was pretty scary because I didn't really want anything bad to happen to Derric, but I didn't want to hurt anymore either, you know? I just wanted to be free. He told me it would be fine and not to worry anymore. And that was it. It was done.

"He got out and the driver took me to this huge house somewhere west of town, best I could tell, where I stayed for two days. I still don't know where it was. That's how I remember the windows were blacked out. Everything I needed was there. I was told not to make any calls or talk with anyone. A few days later he came back, sat me down and told me that everything was okay. He said that Derric and his people would never bother me again. I was assured they weren't dead, but was also told not to inquire about details. That was part of the deal.

"He set me up with an apartment and got me a teaching position at the university. The different last name was to make a break to any obvious past associations. No one really cared about Derric's former wife anyway. It was just a precaution I guess. A lot of my personal information was removed from public records as well. The Professor must have connections somewhere because no one has bothered me at all since all this happened. I don't even get credit card applications unless they're addressed to 'resident.' Whatever he did was pretty thorough.

"So now I live alone, teach math under a name that isn't even mine, and I'm watched over by a man with more influence than I care to honestly understand. At least I'm not getting beat-up anymore. That's a good thing. So does that answer your question?" she concluded.

Ethan hadn't expected such an involved answer. It was a lot to take in. "Yes, it does," he finally replied solemnly.

"Good. Now it's your turn."

Ethan stopped walking. Alex stopped a few feet ahead and turned around. "Tell me something about you. It doesn't have to be personal. Just something."

"We should be heading back." Ethan turned around and started walking slowly, allowing Alex to catch up.

"Now come on. I answered *your* question, now you give me something."

"I don't have anything worth telling."

"*Oh please.* I don't believe that for a second."

The one interesting subject he had was so strange that any normal person would think that his crops had a few too many circles. And this professor sounded like he had his hands in some very powerful and possibly questionable pockets. It takes high-level connections to make personal information disappear from public records and systems like GlobalNet and the SAN. The man's affiliation with Alex made Ethan wonder whether or not he wanted a friend that close to those kinds of people. He'd been associated with their type before, and wasn't really interested in doing so again. "So what kind of professional relationship do you have with this Professor now?"

"Just work with him at the University. That's all. Occasionally he and his wife invite me over for dinner and we visit."

"You get involved with any of his other interests?"

"To be honest, they're none of my business and I keep it that way. Now quit stalling. Come on."

They walked for a while, then Ethan stopped. Maybe it wouldn't be such a big deal. He really had nothing left to lose and it might be interesting to see what someone else thought. And Alex did seem pretty intelligent. She stopped and waited for him.

"Do you have an open mind?" he asked.

"Depends on the subject. Try me," Alex replied as they started walking again.

"This isn't just personal, this is something you *really* can't tell anyone about, or it might come back to bite me sometime."

"Well now I don't want you to tell me something that might get you in trouble or anything."

"If you just keep it to yourself there shouldn't be a problem, I don't think. Just so you understand."

"Okay. I understand."

"You're sure?" Alex glared at him. "Okay. I've been dealing with some issues for a while. No surprise there. Like you, there was a point where I wasn't sure what I was going to do. Then this video diary sort of uh...shows up."

Ethan continued with his story, hitting the highlights of what the journal entailed with Sara's records, the confusing date codes and the documentary of the 'non-existent' historical event. Alex listened intently until he was finished. "So how's that for bizarre?" he then concluded.

"You win. I can't top that," she said, pausing to think. "You really have this thing at your house?"

"Yes, I do." Alex grabbed his arm and stopped walking, then turned to him with a look of excitable curiosity.

"Do you think I could see it?" That one he didn't see coming.

"What, are you kidding? You really believed all that?"

Her expression changed from fascination to dejection. "You mean...it isn't true? You just made it all up?" she said baiting the hook.

"No, actually I didn't. Which is what makes it even *more* ridiculous."

"So you really *do* have this video journal?"

"Well...yes, I do."

"Well...then my inquiry still stands."

He looked at her, thinking about the possible consequences, and then tossed them all out. "You know what? Fine, maybe you can tell *me* what's going on," he said as they started to walk again, "because honestly I'm not sure what to believe anymore." When he realized the commitment he had just made, paranoia returned. His demons had found him once again. "Uh, but I'll have to call you." *What's wrong with me?*

Alex was clearly disappointed by his sudden change of attitude. "Look, I'm leaving to go back home in two days. You've got that long to decide."

"Two days. I'll call you—I will." She could tell he was fighting something personal and there was no point in laboring the issue. Two days or two months, he'd call if and when he was ready.

The perceived conspiracy behind the journal just didn't carry the weight it once did. There was still something very strange about it, but explaining it to Alex brought on a different feeling, one he couldn't quite yet define. As he sat and stared at the device in the middle of his desk, the stories and pictures and Sara's voice filled his mind. Maybe something would click—a new correlation or revelation or something, *anything*.

A realization of sorts did come in that for most of that day his thoughts had not been on his family as they usually were, but were instead on Alex and other things, and he felt ashamed. Suddenly an inquisitive 'meow' came from the floor by his feet and it startled him. It was the cat. "Hello fur-ball," he said indifferently. Mutters walked to Ethan's foot and nonchalantly rubbed her side on his ankle, wrapping her tail around his shin as she walked by and stopped. Ethan leaned over and looked at her. As he did, she turned to look at him and sat down.

He had never really looked at her closely before—pets just weren't a big part of his life. As he looked carefully at her face, he was surprised by the detailed texture of her fur and coloring. Her whiskers and the intricate stripes complimented gorgeous big greenish-blue eyes. She seemed to be patiently waiting for him. He put his hand down to the side of her face. She sniffed at his fingers then rubbed her face against his hand. He gently put his hand on her head and stroked the fur down to her back a few times. Mutters responded by closing her eyes and lifting her head to push on his hand. She almost seemed to smile.

"I've been kind of a jerk, haven't I?" he commented. "I bet the neighbors have been nicer to you than I have. Allison wouldn't appreciate that much, would she?" He petted her for a moment longer, then leaned back in his chair. Thoughts became random and images began to flow in an eddy that spiraled into a realm of strange imagination. His mind wandered past the edge of consciousness and into the boundless world of dreams.

The next morning arrived quite rudely to the sound of the phone ringing on the desk. He was covered up on the couch again in the office. It must have been too much to go all the way upstairs after waking up in the chair in the middle of the night. Still groggy, he picked up the phone, not bothering to look at the display. "Hello?"

"Good morning sir, I'm calling on behalf of the Association to Promote Well-being in your area. Are you familiar with our organization sir?"

Sitting at the end of the couch, Ethan closed his eyes and squeezed his forehead with his hand. "No."

"Well, sir, if I might take just a moment of your time to explain what our—"

"You know what?" Ethan said cutting him off sharply. "You can start promoting *my* well-being by not calling here again." He then dropped the receiver on the floor and rubbed his eyes and face a few more times before looking at the clock. It was almost 9:30 A.M. Once again it was a nightmare free evening. He was on a roll.

Then came the recollection of last night, meeting Alex and some of the things they had talked about. He had a choice to make. Meeting her *was*, admittedly, an interesting experience and it seemed neither of them were strangers to personal trial. *Small world*, he thought as he picked the receiver up off the floor and put it back on the cradle. A picture of Rachel and Allison was next to it on the desk. Guilt came over him as he looked at their faces while thinking of Alex. He would stay loyal to his wife in every possible way and pushed the thoughts of Alex aside to go on with the mediocrities of the day.

Several hours later after a shower and some lunch, he remembered today was garbage pickup. The big green can wasn't that full even after a couple weeks. But the summer sun and food remnants had created an odiferous cocktail of which the flies had become quite fond. After opening the door to the little fenced area where the can was kept, he dumped in what was left from the house, tipped the can on its wheels and headed down the long driveway to the road.

There were a couple of children playing in the Kensington's front yard. Their house looked nice and well kept. Frequently they would be out mowing, weeding, painting—it was always something. They seemed happy. Sundays on his way to the cemetery he would often see them dressed up on their way to church, just like Rachel and Allison used to do.

The little Kensington girl would come over to play with Allison. He could still see them sitting on the front steps in the warm sun, eating Popsicles as they slurped trying to keep the flavored ice from dripping. Dancing and singing—they had a lot of fun. Mrs. Kensington used to bring over vegetables from her garden. Rachel would give her some of her cut flowers in exchange for whatever was in season. Ethan smiled at the pleasant thoughts.

After setting the waste container to the side of the driveway by the road, he walked over to the mailbox and removed a small stack of mail. A lot of it was probably junk so he stood near the upwind side of the garbage can and flipped open the lid. One by one he looked at the letters and determined their fate. Envelopes with his wife's name on them were *never* thrown away and were in fact all kept in a special place in the house. Letters with applications or personal information were shredded.

Carefully he read the names as the letters were sorted with the selected ones unceremoniously tossed into the garbage; Mr. Ethon Gray, Resident, Ethan Grey, Ms. Rachel Grey...

Time suddenly stopped as he saw the letter with his wife's name on it go over the lip and disappear into the garbage can. He lunged forward, pulling the edge of the can down and grabbing the letter from the rotting pile of trash. The letter itself probably meant nothing, but what had just happened meant everything. His mind began to spin.

When his family was taken from him he made a vow to never forget them and never dishonor their memory. Through the hellish torment he kept his wife with him in every aspect of his life that he could possibly imagine. Anything less than a total devotion to what they were as a family, and to her as his wife, was a betrayal of his oath. But trying to maintain the mortal existence of something that had been taken from mortality was a futile battle with time.

The progressive nature of our existence constantly moves us forward, and in its wake we must let go of the past, or become lost in its future. No man's soul was as full of feeling, or heart so full of loving memories as was Ethan's. His past was his life—

where everything good once lived—where *they* lived. But change is inevitable. Sometimes what we think we want is irrelevant to what we need. Regardless of our willingness to accept, understand or prepare for our conditions, we still move forward. *Time is the master by which all things must pass.*

As he held the letters and started walking up the long driveway toward their home, a cold and disturbing reality came over him. He looked around and like a slap in the face, there was a sudden awareness of how neglected he had allowed everything to become. Small weeds and wild grasses were growing between cobblestones in the driveway and were everywhere in the overgrown and sickly looking lawn. Large weeds had overtaken flowerbeds. Flowers that used to flow out of several hanging baskets on the front porch were long dead. Paint around the garage doors was faded and peeling.

The delusive and selfish existence where Rachel and Allison still shared his life was beginning to fade. At that moment, every ugly thing around him became his reality—his *real* world, suddenly and painfully visible for all to see.

After entering the side door of the house, he walked straight to Rachel's piano and sat down. He lifted the keyboard cover and turned on the control console to listen to his favorite composition. The piano began to play the symphony of music he held so dear to his heart. He listened to the notes intently, desperately trying to picture Rachel's hands and fingers moving along the keys—she wasn't there.

He lightly rested his fingers over the keys as they played, feeling each one as it dropped and rose again. He strained to find the once familiar solace in her music and closed his eyes to listen to every note, every cadence as he had done so many times before while searching for that warm and safe place. He could feel the keys, and hear the notes in their beautiful melody...but she wasn't there.

He opened his eyes to the stark realization that this was no longer about her, but was now about him. Her music and memories would no longer provide refuge for him to hide from reality.

The indifference shown to everyone offering friendship, the unkind words and ill feelings, those turned away in spite—*this* was his *true* reality. The consequences of everything he had so carelessly abandoned were no longer in the shadows. Time had callously removed the mask from his life.

Rachel loved Ethan as a devoted wife would, but memories alone can only sustain a superficial world. The bitter realizations cut through his soul, and listening to the music of the woman who meant everything in the world to him now only magnified the grief that could no longer be ignored. He began to weep. It wasn't about purging anger or searching for pity, it was about truth, it was about finally facing his fears. This long and dark journey had seen its course and was nearing its end.

As the music finished its serenade and the piano once again became silent, the emotions that had been bottled up inside for so long were finally set free. The darkness that had been holding him prisoner in hopelessness and despair began to flow from him in a torrent that would continue until his body writhed and ached in pain. He would never forget the wonderful memories of his family, but could finally see that those memories alone could not replace the people who still existed in his life. Rachel knew this, and she would finally be set free. He could finally let her go.

Still wiping tears from his face, he placed his fingers gently on the keys and slid them softly over the surfaces to feel their smooth texture and quiet elegance one last time. Then with a peaceful reverence, he slowly lowered the cover over the keyboard, and said goodbye.

CHAPTER FIVE

Secrets

THE LADY ON THE other end of the phone was borderline hostile. Ethan couldn't blame her. "I know and it was my fault completely. I've had some...issues to deal with lately and some things just got misplaced. My yard is a mess and I really need you guys to come help me out."

"Mr. Grey, the invoice for the last two times our crew was there hasn't been paid yet. One of our people even came to your house and left a letter in your door. We finally sent the bill to collections."

"I'm really sorry. It was just a misunderstanding. How about if I pay the past due and whatever penalties I owe and give you the next month in advance. Would that do it?"

"That would be acceptable as long as it was paid by credit card or cash."

"I'll give you cash. How soon can your guys be here?"

"Let me check...it looks like next Tuesday."

"Next Tuesday? You mean almost a whole week from now?"

"That would be next Tuesday, yes."

"There's no way you can be here sooner?"

"No sir."

Ethan paused as he thought it over. "Well, I guess I don't have much choice do I?"

"You can have someone else do it."

"You mean…you want me to go to someone else?"

"No, I'm just saying that if you need it done sooner than next Tuesday, you'll have to find somebody else. We have a full schedule and just can't get there any sooner." A whole week. That was a long time to be reminded of his ignorance. Well, there *was* Mr. Hendricks…

"Okay. Will you have your guys get the weeds out of the flowerbeds, too?"

"Sure. That's extra. And I'll need advanced payment on that as well, given the situation."

"No problem."

Ethan finished the arrangements and hung up the phone. A whole week Oh well, he had no one to blame but himself. No doubt there were probably going to be a lot of things he was going to have to 'make right.' The yard was just the beginning.

It was the second day. If he was going to let Alex in on his little mystery, today was his last chance. As frustrating as it was to admit, he knew there would be no answers at all if he didn't do something, regardless of how illogical or ambiguous it all seemed.

"Hello Ethan. How are you doing?"

"I'm okay. I've been giving the situation a lot of thought…"

"The situation?"

"You know, what we talked about the other night. I've thought it over and if you're still interested I'd like you to take a look at it and tell me what you think."

"Sure I'm still interested. What time?"

"Anytime is fine."

"Well then how about this afternoon. Say around 2 P.M.?"

Ethan quickly ran through his mental schedule. It was blank. "That should be fine." He then gave her directions to his house.

"That's about an hour's drive from here, right?" she estimated.

"Sounds about right."

"You know I have to admit, I didn't think you would call back. This is twice you've surprised me."

"That's good, I guess."

"What made you change your mind?"

Ethan sighed. "Let's just say I realized that trying to figure this out alone is going to be difficult. It's out of my league."

"Out of *your* league? You're a scientist. I thought you knew everything."

"Funny, but no. I usually deal in a more quantitative environment. I don't even know where to start with this one."

"Well then I'm not sure *I'll* be of much use."

"Anything will be better than where I am now. If nothing else at least you can give me your opinion."

"Fair enough. I'll be there around two."

"Okay. Drive safe."

A properly presentable house suddenly became a priority. The appearance of mental instability with the story of a futuristic journal in addition to looking like a Woodstock hippy reject just wasn't going to cut it anymore. It was time to start redeeming himself. The yard was a lost cause and needed professional help. The inside he could manage. Panic-mode was initiated and a whirlwind of cleaning began. It was going to be a busy few hours.

❈ ❈ ❈

As Alex entered the onramp to the interstate, she began to wonder about her own sanity. She was going to visit the widower husband of her deceased friend to discuss something that any half-thinking person would run away from. Rachel always expressed what a good person Ethan was so even as strange as things looked on the surface, she'd give him the benefit of the doubt, for now. His personal situation was clearly very difficult, which could make anyone act strangely. It happened to her—it can happen to anyone.

The story of the journal sounded preposterous, yet almost too detailed and elaborate to be completely made up. *A journal from the future?* She giggled out loud at the thought. Ethan was either on to something utterly fantastic, or had become a master at disguising total dementia. Either way, she sure knew how to pick 'em.

Ethan's directions were good as she found her way into the rural neighborhood where he lived. She studied the numbers on the mailboxes carefully until arriving at the one matching his address. The house was a bit of a surprise. It was huge—a beautiful two story country home on a gentle hillside set back off the road several hundred feet or so with a three car garage. It was almost color with dark red speckled brick, white trim, green shutters and a black shingle roof.

An inviting wraparound front porch was the backdrop for tattered shrubs and a lawn that looked like a herd of sheep should be grazing on it. A lot of money and care had been put into this place at one point. Now its upkeep looked all but nonexistent. The sprawling yard was full of weeds and tall yellowing grass. Large borders and flowerbeds were unkempt and overgrown. The scene was full of strange contrasts.

She pulled forward to verify the address on the large brick mailbox; 1355 Dyerwood Road. This was it. The beautiful house looked defiant standing amidst the neglected landscape as she pulled into the turnaround next to the garage and parked by the sidewalk that led to the front porch. The first thing she noticed after closing the car door was how quiet it was. There was no noise from cars or traffic. There *was* a curious whirring sound coming from the garage, however. A smile of satisfaction came to her when she recognized it as a central vacuum. He was cleaning for her. That was sweet.

Weeds were everywhere and she couldn't help but notice the six planters hanging from the porch, all with short dead stumps of once beautiful flowers poking out from the top. The view from the porch over a sparsely populated valley was beautiful.

She walked up the steps to the front door and rang the doorbell. After a couple seconds, the whirring stopped. It was almost eerily quiet. There was the faint sound of a tinkling bell from inside, then footsteps. The door opened.

"Hello," Alex said smiling.

"Took me a minute to remember what that 'ding-dong' sound was. Come in. Did you find the place okay?"

"Yeah, I did." Mutters walked in front of Ethan and looked up at Alex.

"Ooh she's pretty. Is it a she?"

"Yeah that's Mutters, Allison's cat."

"Mutters. That's an interesting name."

"Allison named her. When she was a kitten, she used to make these funny little sounds when she purred. It sounded like she was muttering so Allison named her Mutters."

"That's funny. Is she friendly?"

"Very. She's a cat that's more like a dog. I forgot that she runs to the door whenever the doorbell rings."

"Seriously?"

"Yep."

"Can I pet her?"

"Sure. She loves attention. You may get a little hairy though."

Alex knelt down and held out her hand. "Hi Mutters." Mutters put up her tail and sniffed at Alex's fingers, then rubbed her head against her hand.

"See what I mean."

"She's a sweet kitty."

"Come on in. Let's get you away from that yard." Ethan backed up, holding the door as Alex came in and Mutters ran out. "I forgot to warn you about the place. The whole maintenance thing kind of got out of hand. I have some people coming to take care of it."

"It's a beautiful place," Alex said as she followed Ethan into the foyer.

"It used to be."

"Still is. It just needs a little love and attention."

"Yeah that's been in short supply around here for a while. Would you like a drink? I've got uh..." Ethan grimaced as he realized he missed another item on the mental checklist. "I guess I've got water, milk or some really, *really* old pop. I could make some orange juice."

Alex smiled. "Water's fine." Ethan headed to the kitchen and Alex followed.

"Directions okay?"

"They were great. Very detailed. I drove right here."

"Good. Details are kind of a thing with me." He opened the dishwasher and took out a glass, then paused. "Well, except for the yard...and the house."

"It's fine, don't worry about it." He held the glass under the ice dispenser in the door then under the water dispenser and handed the glass to Alex.

"I'm afraid this is about as fancy as I get at the moment."

She took a sip. "Tastes like water."

"Remember when I asked you if you had an open mind?" Ethan pointed at the breakfast table. "That's where it appeared." Alex looked at the table then back at Ethan. "I was sitting there eating a bowl of cereal. Then all of the sudden the room starts doing *'the wave.'* I hear my dead family speaking, the walls disappear a couple of times and presto, there it was. Nothing more has happened since." Alex kept the glass to her lips, partially to hide her startled expression as she stared at him. "I thought it was prudent to skip those details the other night. Didn't want you to think I was *crazy* or anything," Ethan said as he waved his hands in the air and smiled facetiously with big eyes.

Alex gulped some water then set the glass on the counter. "Okay," she said a little concerned.

"That's one mystery. You ready to see what you came for?"

"I think so."

"It's in the office."

Alex followed him as he walked through the dining room to the hallway. At the hallway Ethan stopped and turned to face her. "I keep it hidden. If you wouldn't mind just stay here for a minute while I get it. You understand don't you?"

"Sure." He walked down the hallway and disappeared around the corner.

What the heck had she gotten herself into? If trust is earned, then Ethan was definitely on a strange road to get there. She turned around and looked back into the dining room. They had some nice things. As she looked around she noticed the doorway leading into the piano room. Curious, she walked over and peeked in. It was dark. Sliding her hand along the inside wall of the room found the light switch. As her hand passed over it the room lit up in a soft glow.

Rachel's beautiful glossy black baby grand piano sat at an angle in the middle of the room on a hardwood floor. There was a white wicker loveseat at the back of the room and two white wicker chairs off to the side. In front of the loveseat was a small colorful rug. The walls were a light rust color with large pictures on three of them. Alex noticed another slide switch to the side of the light switch. Pushing up on the slider illuminated the walls and pictures with carefully placed spotlights.

There were tall dried flower arrangements in each of the far corners and a large detailed arrangement on the wall to her left highlighted by another light. As her eyes scanned the room, she could almost feel Rachel's presence. It was warm and friendly. She knew though that it would not be appropriate for her to go in, at least not without being invited.

Half composed sheets of music rested on the music stand and top of the piano. It looked like they could have been the last things Rachel was working on, or maybe playing. There was a graceful, but sad feeling to the room.

Then she heard Ethan's distant voice. "Alex?" Startled, she hurriedly fumbled the switches to shut off the lights.

"In the dining room!" Quickly she walked across the floor and stopped as Ethan came around the corner. "Nice room," she said looking around innocently.

"Thank you. Ready for the dog and pony show?"

"Sure."

"Follow me." They walked around a corner and down the hallway to the office. "Here we are."

There was a large desk with an office chair and a smaller chair to its side. The desk was clean with only a picture, a lamp and a small, shiny black object resting in the middle. That must be it. On her right was a small sofa with a pillow and wrinkled blanket. Behind the desk was a long counter with a computer, data terminal and other devices she didn't recognize. Above the counter were shelves filled with books and models and other interesting trinkets. To her left was a closet and on the far wall a large window with closed wood blinds.

"Have a seat," Ethan said as he rolled the office chair back for her to sit down. Alex studied the object intently as she walked around the desk and sat in the huge leather chair that over-whelmed her small frame. Ethan sat in a small side chair next to her.

With her hands clasped together in her lap, she leaned forward to get a closer look. "That's it?"

"Yep, that's it."

"It's smaller than I was expecting."

"You can pick it up. So far it seems harmless."

"So far?"

"Well, it hasn't infused me with any mutating alien DNA or beamed me to another planet...as far as I know."

"And you don't think this is a hoax of some type?"

"I'm not sure what to think." Ethan touched the ends of the silver bar and the device lit up. As the screen appeared and the image formed, Alex leaned back, astonished. Ethan smiled as he saw the look on her face.

"Yeah, that's what I thought the first time I saw it."

"That's incredible," Alex said intrigued, leaning forward again.

"Yes it is. Near as I can tell there's a projector back here that emits a low-level energy beam creating an interwoven screen of thousands of polarized points. The separate colors are carried to each point that in turn creates a full image. No one I'm familiar with has technology even *remotely* this advanced yet."

"If you say so. Wow," Alex said as she slowly reached out to touch the screen.

"You'll feel a very slight electric charge."

When her finger touched the image, she quickly pulled it back. "Ooh, it tingles. It can't hurt you, can it?"

"I don't think so." Ethan touched the bar and entered the playback mode. "Here it shows there are four hundred and one entries. At first it would only let me play them from first to last in order. After I played the last entry, it let me go back and play them at random. Here's something else interesting. It says 'Time Synchronization Unavailable,' and here's the current date it shows. I think it is supposed to pick up a timing reference like personal phones and other devices do."

Alex thought about it. "Maybe one doesn't exist yet. Is that possible?"

Ethan was impressed by her intuitive response. "Well, I'm not willing to go that far just yet. You ready to meet Sara?"

Alex looked up at Ethan and gave him a devilish grin. "Absolutely."

"Okay. Most of the records involve Sara's personal life. I'm going to playback the last five records where all the pertinent information is. They should give you a pretty good idea of what's going on. Here we go."

Ethan pressed 'Play' and the female voice started. "*Select record for playback.*"

"Three hundred ninety-seven," Ethan responded.

"Playback of record three hundred ninety-seven."
"Hello."

Alex watched and listened intently as Sara described her strange ability and her feelings about the Asian Apocalypse. At the end of the record, she leaned back in the chair while still staring at the screen. "That is totally bizarre." She then turned and looked at Ethan. "That is just totally bizarre."

"That's nothing. The next one is a half hour long and the last ones are just as strange."

Alex turned back toward the screen, then back to Ethan. "Do you know her last name?"

"No"

"Where she lives?"

"Once she mentioned a place called Summer Falls, but I don't know what State and that was before her parents were killed. I found over seventy references to Summer Falls in the United States. It didn't help."

"And in all those records she never mentions her last name."

"Nope."

"That's strange. A journal without a last name."

"I'm curious about something," Ethan interjected. "Speak into it and say 'play record three hundred ninety-eight.'"

Alex leaned over toward the device. "Play record three hundred ninety-eight."

The device responded. *"You are not an authorized user."*

Ethan leaned back in his chair. "She did this on purpose. Somehow she knew who I was. I've been watching this girl grow up and I feel like I know her—like she's like a part of my family." Ethan paused as he reached out and straightened the lamp on the desk. "I still don't have any idea who she is. Anyway, here's the long one. Play record three hundred ninety-eight."

"Playback of record three hundred ninety-eight."
The documentary started. When it was completed, Alex was even more stunned. "It's like watching a science fiction movie of some kind. It seems so real."

"Yeah, I know and here's the next bombshell; several years ago I had an experience at work where I saw something incredibly strange. It was kind of like what happened in the kitchen when this thing arrived, but different. What I saw looked exactly like that energy wave. It was bright green at the front, trailing white and made a sizzling sound *exactly* like this documentary describes."

"What was it?"

"That's the big question. I don't know what it was and I never saw it again."

"Wait, I'm a little confused. You saw it, but you don't know what it was? Did anyone else see it?"

"No. I'm pretty sure only I saw it."

Alex thought about his answer, looked back at the screen and pointed to it. "Well then how did she know that you—"

"Exactly!" Ethan interrupted, pointing his finger at her. "*I* don't even know for sure what I saw. So how did someone know to send me this thing with a documentary describing the *exact* same energy wave no one else has ever seen? Now can you see why I'm padded-room material?"

"Well, maybe you weren't the only one who saw this...energy wave and you just don't know it."

"Not likely."

"Why not?"

Ethan distinctly heard the lid come off the can of worms. He smiled with his lips closed and sighed. "That's a whole different story but trust me, I saw it."

"Well, then this makes no sense of any kind."

"Ya think?" he replied a little sarcastically.

Alex just ignored it. "Show me more."

"Playback of record three hundred ninety-nine."

"Last night I had the strangest dream. I was walking through a field of grass..."

"Playback of record four hundred."

"I know who those people were in my dream and I'm beginning to understand how it all ties together..."

"That was short. Does she ever say who these people are?"

"No, and her demeanor has totally changed. Did you sense that?"

"A little, I guess. Is this the last one?"

"Yup, this is it."

"Playback of record four hundred-one."

"I've come to understand many wonderful and incredible things—more than I could have dreamed. I've discovered the boundaries that hold us to this physical world and I can now see through the essence of time. It's magnificent—different from how I thought it would be.

"The feelings and misgivings I have about those events from the past are being formed from a place I can't describe, but I am aware of it, and I'm not alone in its knowledge. There are forces in this universe that are beautiful and sometimes difficult to comprehend. Still, we must live by the knowledge we receive and walk our own paths. *My* path is my own and it leads to places I could not have imagined. *Our* paths are all unique, but not dissimilar or unfamiliar.

"The light of truth is timeless and endless. Still, we must *choose* to live by it. And even with what I now understand and know to be true, it is still only *my* truth. Each of us must find for ourselves that which is most important.

"We search for the same answers and want the same things. Yet there are those who choose to run in shadows. Their truths are hidden in lies and their answers found in darkness. *They* are the ones who seek to deceive and who will suffer at the hands of truth.

"When you see disparity, don't turn away or be ashamed to look into his eyes. What is sometimes hidden behind that which turns us away is many times what we are actually searching for. *This* is where your journey begins.

"You may not always understand everything you see. That doesn't mean it isn't a truth. True understanding can only be found with true desire. Be patient, and always remember that you are never alone. None of us is ever really alone. Even I am with you now." Sara smiled as she looked down in thought, then looked out from the screen. "Journey well."

"End of record four hundred one."

"Wow. How old is this young woman?"

"At this point I think she's seventeen."

"That is astounding. Did you see the glow she had around her?"

"A glow?"

"Yeah. A white glow, like an aura."

Ethan shook his head. "No, I didn't see that."

Alex leaned back in the chair and rested her chin on her hand while she continued looking at the screen. "Is it possible that this could be just what it appears to be? I know it *seems* impossible, but yet..." Ethan stood up and walked to the window, pushed up a couple of the slats and looked outside.

"I mean, if you just watch it and listen to it with no predisposition, there's nothing that gives you the feeling it isn't real. It gives me chills. And when she says 'you,' do you get the impression she isn't just generalizing?"

"Do you realize what you're implying?"

"Yeah, I think so." Ethan looked at her briefly, then turned back to the window. She continued. "Alright, let's forget supposition for a minute and figure out what's factual. This thing really exists because, here it is and...and..."

Ethan dropped the slats and turned back toward her. "And that's it. There are no names, no locations, nothing definitive.

The device registry doesn't show up anywhere, the manufacturer doesn't exist, nothing."

"Okay. The dates from the records would indicate this event would happen when?"

"Supposedly a little less than two years from now."

Alex started drumming her fingernails loudly on the desk. They must have been connected to the wheels spinning in her head. "Didn't that documentary say the energy thing started in an old military facility of some kind?"

"Yes, it did."

"So why don't we see if this place exists? At least that might be something."

Ethan was a little hesitant to tell her that he had already done some investigation in that regard. With her enthusiasm, it might be like throwing gas on a candle. "It does appear that there may be an old long-range radar military facility around there some-where."

"Really?"

"Don't have any details though."

"There really is one there? Like this documentary talked about?" Alex said, trying to make sure she heard him correctly.

Ethan saw the fuel heading for the flame. "Yes, one is sup-posed to exist around there somewhere."

"Well then, that seems like a logical place to start."

"And what exactly do you have in mind?"

"We should go there. Doesn't that make sense? It's the one tangible clue we have."

Ethan looked at her with a subtle 'have you lost your mind' expression. "You want to fly half-way around the world to look at an old military site? What good is that going to do? What do you think you're going to find?"

"More than we will sitting here."

"And what's this 'we' stuff?"

"Ethan, you've got one of the most incredible mysteries here I've ever seen and besides, *you* invited me here to help you figure this out, right? Or was I just an excuse to clean your house?" She pointed at the device and continued. "I think this thing was sent to you for a reason and the clues are in it. If you want to know why this is happening, you're going to have to go find the answers and you're going to take me with you."

With his hands still in his pockets, Ethan slowly walked back to the small chair to the side of Alex and sat down. He sighed, and thought briefly. "Do you remember what you said about your professor friend having the kind of influence and connections you didn't necessarily want to know more about? I used to work with people like that. Not directly most of the time, but the projects I worked on were classified and I know they weren't just for the mainstream military. We didn't ask questions. We received our assignments and did the work. Your professor friend is probably a choirboy compared to many of those people. They have very long memories and very long arms and if any of them are involved with any of this, we could disappear without a second thought."

"But what kind of motive would someone like that have to do something like this? That doesn't make any sense to me. It has to be something else." She was right and basically he was just grasping at excuses to try to prolong the inevitable.

"Just jumping on a plane and going over there wouldn't exactly be a prudent first step. We'd have to find out exactly where this building is, who owns it and any other pertinent details. I seriously doubt we could get permission to see it anyway."

"I'll bet I could get the information," Alex said confidently. Ethan started looking around at the floor.

"What are you doing?" she asked.

"Looking for your marbles."

"Oh fine then. Can you get the information?"

"If someone I used to work with *is* involved in this, they might know I was snooping around. That would *not* be a smart thing for me to do."

"I'm sure Professor Greenhagen could get it."

"And *that would* be a smart idea? What will you say when he starts asking questions? You can't tell him anything."

"We *have* to do something."

"*We* don't have to do anything," Ethan said with a certain finality.

"Then let's make a deal. I won't tell the Professor what it's for—I won't even mention your name. If I can get the information and we find out this place is really there, then we go check it out. What do you say? Is that fair?"

Ethan thought it over. "Do you really understand what the risks could be? I have no idea where this will lead if it leads anywhere."

"I volunteer. I want to do this." She was, if anything, determined.

"He probably won't even consider it without wanting to know exactly what it's for."

"I won't tell him anything you don't want me to. If he'll do it, great. If he won't, then we'll figure out something else. Do we have a deal?"

This was the defining moment and a decision he didn't want to regret, if that was possible. "Okay, you've got a deal.

"Yes!" Alex shouted, throwing her arms in the air as Ethan flinched and moved his head away. "Sorry. It'll probably be sometime next week. I'll let you know as soon as I find out something. Oh, if I need to send you something should I use the old Global-Net address?"

"No, I have a different one now." Ethan pulled his notebook from the top drawer, ripped off a blank page and wrote the address on it along with the site location details from the journal. "Remember, don't mention a thing about this to anyone, and if you decide to send me something over the Net, don't say anything specific. You never know who might be sniffing."

"Got it." Ethan handed her the paper with the address as she stood to leave.

At the front door, she stopped. "This is really something, isn't it?"

"Just remember what we talked about," Ethan reminded.

"Don't worry. I'll let you know as soon as I find something and by the way, the house looks great," she said as she enthusiastically bounded down the steps to the sidewalk and to her car.

"Thank you," Ethan replied. She waved a last time before heading down the long driveway to the road. He waved back and watched her until she disappeared out of view.

Standing on the porch, he took a moment to look across the valley at the distant houses and wondered what those people must be doing—probably simple things that families do. He missed doing those things with *his* family. It was strange fate that brought him to this point, and he was afraid it was only going to get stranger.

He didn't mention that he had watched the last few records several times and it *did* seem as though Sara was talking directly to him. Her perplexing messages had been buzzing in his thoughts ever since he first saw and heard them. Was this really all for him? What was he supposed to do with all this information?

How he wished he could talk with Rachel. She always listened and seemed to have the right things to say—even when it may not have been what he wanted to hear. None of this seemed logical *or* fair. He hated being alone and hated being the subject of something so ridiculously cryptic. It was unlikely Alex was actually going to get any useful information anyway. Still, he *had* made a deal. If she came through, he'd keep his word.

☀ ☀ ☀

Visiting her brother was nice, but it was the last thing on Alex's mind when she arrived home at her townhouse. It wasn't long before making the call was the only thing she could think about. The long drive had given her some ideas of how to present her request. It was going to be awkward, but there was no way she was going to let this opportunity go.

"Hello?"

"Hello Mrs. Greenhagen, this is Alex."

"Well hello, dear. How are you doing?"

"I'm doing just fine, thank you. Is the Professor home?"

"Yes, he is. Let me get him." Alex paced back and forth by the counter. The Professor had done so much for her in the past that it was almost embarrassing to ask for something so unusual—especially since she couldn't tell him what it was really for.

"Alexandria…"

"Hello, Professor."

"Did you have a good visit with your brother?"

"Yes I did. I trust you're doing well?"

"I'm warm, regular and mostly pain free. Can't ask for much more than that at my age."

"Glad to hear it."

"What can I do for you?"

"I have a favor to ask."

"Sure, how can I help?"

"Well, I'd like to stop by and ask you in person if you wouldn't mind."

"I should be here most of the day. When would you like to meet?"

"Whenever it's convenient for you."

"How does eleven-thirty sound. You can stay for lunch. I'm sure Margene would be happy to see you."

"That would be nice, thank you."

"See you then."

He is such a nice man, Alex thought as she hung up the phone. This was *not* going to be easy.

The Greenhagens lived in a nice neighborhood that looked and felt like old money. It was full of large, gracious homes on sprawling estates built in the early nineteen hundreds. Theirs was a U-shaped two-story with lots of stone and old-world charm.

After a few moments Mrs. Greenhagen opened the door and produced a big smile when she saw Alex. "Hello, dear! Come in, come in!" As Alex walked through the door, Mrs. Greenhagen gave her a warm hug. "So nice to see you. You look like you're doing well."

"I'm doing fine, thank you." She held Alex by the arm and walked her into the family room. "I'll tell Samuel you're here. We're having chicken pasta salad. I hope you like it."

"Everything you make is always wonderful."

"Oh, you're too kind," Mrs. Greenhagen said as she left and returned a minute later with the Professor.

"Good morning, Alex," the Professor said as he gave her a quick hug then escorted her to the greeting room. Mrs. Greenhagen announced that lunch would be ready in about fifteen minutes, then went back into the kitchen. "So, everything's okay?"

Alex smiled. "Yes, everything's fine."

"You worried me a little with your phone call."

"It's nothing. I just feel bad asking you for anything."

"Please. It does an old man good to do something for a friend. What do you need?"

"Well, sir, I need to find out if there's an old Russian radar facility at a certain location in Kazakhstan. It's for a project I'm working on with a friend."

"A radar facility in Kazakhstan... That's an odd request. Does this friend have a name?"

"Ethan. He was married to a friend of mine who was killed in an accident a few years ago. I ran into him again down by my brother's house and we started talking."

The Professor may have been into his senior years, but his intellect was tack-sharp. The simple fact that Alex hadn't offered a last name meant she didn't want him to know who this friend really was. Hardly a criminal submission—strange behavior for her nevertheless.

He leaned back in his chair and garnered a questioning look. "What kind of project is this?"

Alex hesitated. "We're working on something that I can't really be too specific about. I kind of made a bet with him and if there really is a radar facility where I think there is, then I win. At this point that's really all there is to it."

She *was* hiding something. "You'd tell me if you were in trouble wouldn't you? There's no coercion or anything like that going on?"

"Oh, no sir. He's just been through a lot and is fairly private and I respect that. I'm just helping him out."

"What kind of information do you need? Photos, history..."

"Anything would be fine. Just so I can prove it's there."

"You understand I don't usually do things like this without knowing the whole story. Getting specific intel on a foreign military facility, even an old one, may still draw some unwanted attention."

"Well, sir, I don't want you to do anything that will cause problems."

"No problems. The request is just a little out of the ordinary. If anything odd comes up though, you may have to tell me who your friend really is and what you're up to."

Ethan would pull the plug in a heartbeat if he had heard that. However, the slim chance of something unforeseen happening was a risk she was willing to take. "I understand."

"Give me just a minute," the Professor said as he left the room briefly to return with a small notepad and pen. "So, we're looking for an old military radar facility in Kazakhstan. Where in Kazakhstan exactly? It's a big area."

"About two hundred and twenty kilometers west of the city of Balkhash."

The Professor wrote down the information and studied it briefly. "That's it?"

"Yes, sir."

"Very good then. I'll see what I can find. It will take me a few days."

"Great."

Professor Greenhagen set the notepad down on the coffee table. Alex could tell he wasn't all that comfortable with so few details. It was difficult trying to keep the promise of one friend while not risking the trust of another. "I really appreciate this and everything else you've done for me."

"I'm happy to do it for you, Alex. Just *please* be careful. You've been through a lot and I certainly don't want to see you go down any of those roads again."

"Me either, but Ethan really is a good man."

"Even good men sometimes carry unseen burdens. You can end up sharing them if you're not careful. Just keep your wits about you. Emotions can confuse even the best of intentions."

"Oh I have no intention of muddying our relationship with emotion." It was a well-intended statement, even though she knew that emotion can never be completely suppressed in any relationship. Simple friendship or otherwise, inherent risks are always present.

"Well then, I wish you the best with your friend," the Professor said as they stood. He put his arm around her and gave her a friendly squeeze around the shoulder as they walked into the kitchen.

This favor would just add to the long list of debts owed him that she knew could probably never all be repaid. The Professor knew this as well. But keeping score was never a criterion of their friendship, and never would be.

CHAPTER SIX

White Dresses

IT HAD BEEN AWHILE since his last hair cut. It felt strange, and pleasant to have a woman running her fingers through his hair. Afterward, there was a quick stop at the local store for a few supplies, then home. A very small part of the life he used to know was slowly coming back, although there was still a certain emptiness that always lingered not far away.

Even though he maintained a great deal of skepticism, there was also a fleeting sense of responsibility associated with the journal and with Sara's prophetic words. It was just impossible to grasp an understanding of something shrouded in so much ambiguity. Part of him was hopeful that Alex would come through with some definitive information. Another part hoped it would all go away. One moment the direction was clear, and then the next...

As the houses passed, his attention was drawn to a large grouping of flowers in a field to his right. He hadn't noticed them there before and had driven home this way often. They were almost luminescent in their brilliant yellow and white coloring and appeared to glow making everything else around them monochromatic. The world shifted into slow motion...then a flash.

Rachel and Allison were suddenly there. They were wearing matching white dresses and Rachel had a large white garden hat with a big yellow bow. They were both smiling and waving at him. The colors were magnificent. They seemed so close...so real—their tender faces and warm smiles highlighted by the sun. He wanted to believe...

A jolt through the steering wheel instantly sent the vision away. Startled, he turned his head to look forward. He was off the road and running on the right shoulder. It was too late to miss the mailbox on its large wooden post. The post caught the edge of the front fender and the mailbox smashed into the passenger side windshield. The right side mirror broke from its mount and the mailbox vaulted into the air, then landed in the grass on the side of the road.

A heavy twist of the wheel and hard braking sent the car sliding across the road toward the other shoulder. An overcorrection then sent the back-end swinging wildly as it tried to snap around. Another hard correction swung the car around again. It was like wrestling a mad pig in mud. Finally, he regained control and got the car pointed the right direction, stopping to the side of the road.

He could hardly breathe and his heart was pounding so hard it hurt—his hands clamped to the steering wheel like vice-grips. There was only a splintered stub where the mailbox used to be and skid marks all over the road. The outside mirror was gone and the windshield was a mess. It was an embarrassing and frightening experience. A car crested the hill ahead of him so he quickly drove off before somebody could figure out what had happened.

Not long afterward, his conscience began to weigh in. Taking out someone's mailbox then leaving the scene was cowardly and not very neighborly. Technically it was vandalism—destruction of property. He had no idea who lived there, but should have gone back to apologize and at least offer to pay for the damage. That would have been the right thing to do. 'Sorry I ran over your mailbox. I was distracted by my dead wife and daughter picking glowing flowers in the field next to your house.'

With the getaway vehicle now hidden safely out of sight in the garage, he got out to inspect the damage. The headlight was cracked and there were scratches and scuffs all the way up the side from the bumper to the back door. The mirror was hanging by wires and resting against the side. The wind whipping it around was probably the repetitive thumping sound he kept hearing. There were deep scratches on the windshield pillar and the whole passenger side of the windshield was shattered. *How stupid can you be?* he thought. The small bag of groceries was strewn all over the back seat and floor as well. They were put back in the bag and taken to the kitchen where he sat on a bar stool and just stared at the counter.

The feelings of idiocy were replaced by bewilderment—the image of his wife and daughter standing in a field of flowers. What cruel trick was his mind playing on him? Had he fallen asleep? A waking dream? He closed his eyes to see if they would return when a horribly distressing realization came; it was Monday, yesterday was Sunday. He had completely forgotten.

Hurriedly he threw the perishables in the refrigerator, stuffed some in the freezer, left the rest on the counter and ran back to the garage. As he started down the steps, he stopped. The old Challenger wouldn't be going anywhere for quite some time and he couldn't take *his* car with it looking like that. Without a doubt the police had been alerted and a countywide manhunt was already underway.

Rachel's car was the only one left undamaged. He looked back and forth between his and hers and finally climbed into hers and shut the door. The smell of the interior hit him. It was pleasant and triggered a whole host of other memories and images—a surreal moment that lost him for a time. He pushed the garage door opener and turned the key. The engine struggled on a weak battery, then finally started.

Forgetting Sunday was unforgivable. How could he let something so important, something he'd been doing faithfully every week for so long just slip his mind? Even walking into the floral shop on a day other than Saturday didn't feel right as he looked around for the lady who usually had the arrangement prepared for him. She wasn't there.

"May I help you?" a young woman asked.

"Yes. Do you have an arrangement for Grey?"

"I believe I saw that one this morning. Let me go check." She walked into the back of the shop out of sight. Ethan stood and looked around at all the different flowers on display. It seemed most of them had been in his arrangements at one time or another, even though he didn't know most of their names. Then while starting to thumb through an order book on the counter, there was a picture of the same flowers from the field. A strange sensation came over him.

The young woman returned from the back with a large arrangement and set it on the counter. She looked carefully at the note stuck on the side of the vase. "This says 'Ethan Grey on account.'" She looked up at him. "Do you want this on your account?"

"Yes, please."

"You must do a lot of business with us," the young woman said smiling. Ethan was distracted and didn't respond. "Here you go. Anything else I can do for you?"

"Actually there is." Ethan pointed to the picture in the book. "What are these really big flowers called?"

The young woman turned the book sideways and looked where he was he pointing. "Those are lilies—probably a Star Gazer or some other oriental hybrid."

"I think my wife has some in our garden. They have an incredible fragrance."

"If she does then you should start seeing them bloom in about six weeks."

"Six weeks?"

"This variety typically blooms later in the summer depending on the climate. Some of the Asiatic varieties are starting to bloom now, but they're usually smaller and aren't nearly as fragrant."

"I see."

"Is there anything else then?"

"No, that's all. Thank you," Ethan said as he picked up the arrangement.

"You're welcome. Have a nice day."

Opening the back driver side door, he carefully placed the arrangement on the floor, wedging it between the seats. He was sure Rachel had some of those same lilies in her flowerbeds. It was hard to recall. So if they aren't going to bloom for over a month, then it *was* all imagined. Therapy was inevitable.

It was a short distance from the car to the two graves. He pulled out the two nicest flowers in the arrangement and placed them at the base of Allison's headstone. Then he placed the arrangement next to Rachel's name and sat on the ground. "Hi ladies. I'm really sorry I missed you both yesterday. It's been a strange couple of weeks. I just got caught up in this journal thing and forgot. I am *really* sorry." He took a long pause and picked a blade of grass to twiddle with it. "I met your friend Alex earlier this week. She's interesting to say the least. I hope you didn't mind her coming to visit the other day. Since you knew her, it seemed okay to show her the journal. She thinks it could be real. I'm still not convinced."

He looked down and watched the grass spin between his fingers. "Why does everything have to be so hard to understand? I mean, I don't mind figuring things out, that's what I do. But I don't like not knowing where to look for the answers. I never felt like this when you were here. You seemed to make it all work. Everything just seemed to..."

Ethan plucked another blade of grass and started pulling off small pieces, tossing them into the air. "So you and Allison certainly surprised me earlier today. Can't say I was expecting *that*. I don't suppose you'd uh...be willing to let me in on what's going on here would you? Just a hint maybe? Is it really all in my head? Well, I mean of course it's all in my head..."

He pulled another blade of grass and continued. "Are you trying to tell me something?" There was another long pause. "Screwed up the car. Took-out somebody's mailbox then ran like a punk kid. I sure feel stupid. Sorry Allison. I know I'm not supposed to say that.

"Did you know about all this stuff that happened to Alex? I feel really bad for her, especially after what you and I had. What would it be like to be married to someone you thought you really knew only to have them turn out to be someone completely different? Someone mean and callous. I can't even imagine. So I hope you don't mind I've been talking with her. Her enthusiasm about everything is a little hard to get used to and seems a bit reckless. Maybe I shouldn't have gotten her involved. I don't know. I had to tell somebody though. Well, besides you."

Sounds on the air were different—a little distracting. The droning of traffic, cars honking, construction machinery... The subtle sounds he was used to were hard to define within the chaotic murmur of life. It was normal people going about their business on the first day of a busy workweek—a world away from Sundays when the air was more reverent and people rested and visited loved ones.

Today he was completely alone among the departed. "You know, I would have gladly traded places with you two. I would have. I hope you know that." Those old feelings he had tried to lock away were pushing through and he could feel them starting to strain his emotional stability. "Well, I guess I better get going," he said as he stood and brushed off his pants. Thoughts of a seemingly distant past skirted his memories as he gently slid his hand across the top of his wife's headstone. "Bye sweetheart. Bye Allison. I'll be on time next week. I promise."

Now a few miles from home, Ethan came to the intersection where he could either go the short way past the imaginary flowers and very real mailbox, or go the long way around and avoid the whole thing. For some reason it was a tasking decision. He felt incredibly guilty, even though he had no idea who the people were. But sometimes curiosity can be strong motivation. Besides, it was his wife's car. No one would be the wiser.

He was understandably apprehensive as he made his way up the narrow country road. Returning to the scene of the crime so soon after it had been committed was a foolish criminal indulgence. Any half-thinking vandal knows that. There was another car a few hundred feet behind him so he couldn't go too slowly. He kept glancing to his right. The anticipation was unnerving. He knew there would be nothing there. Yet somehow…maybe…

Then it came into view—a field of weeds and grass. That was it, nothing more. The scattered pieces of accidental mayhem had been cleaned up off the road and shoulder. The tattered mailbox was now resting on the ground next to the splintered post base sticking out of the gravel. He saw an older gentleman pushing a wheelbarrow down his driveway toward the house. The man had been out cleaning up the mess made by some inconsiderate imbecile. Ethan just shook his head. Could he feel any worse today? Someday he was going to make that right.

❄ ❄ ❄

It was cold and dark and beginning to rain. There seemed to be no one around, anywhere. He stood and peered into the blackness and began shouting, "Hello? Hello?" There was no response as the rain steadily became heavier. He tried to shield his eyes from the huge, stinging drops and turned around slowly, looking for anyone else. There was only emptiness.

He hated rain. Its roar and ever increasing ferocity was now pounding down and collecting around his feet. He ran to find shelter, but there was nowhere to run. Everywhere was nowhere, and the same.

The relentless rain steadily increased its crushing onslaught. He sluggishly walked through the water now up to his knees. Louder and louder, the large drops began to combine into choking falls that roared onto the water all around him and continued to rise.

Desperately he tried to find someone to help, but there was no one else there. It was almost impossible to see now. He could hardly open his eyes or breathe and he gasped for every breath as the water continued to rise.

Now at his neck, the falling water worked steadily to push him under. It pressed hard against his chest. He tried to scream. It was impossible to find enough air to carry a panicked cry. He began choking and gasping. There was no compassion—no mercy here. He flailed his arms against a cruel, invisible and uncaring enemy. His breath began to fade…

'Ding-dong, ding…dong.'

Expelled from the darkness, face wet with sweat, Ethan blinked rapidly and looked at the ceiling of their bedroom. It took a moment to understand what was going on. The doorbell chimed again. It was early, or at least it seemed early and he wasn't expecting anyone that he could remember. Climbing out of bed, he put on his slippers and retrieved his robe from the hook in the bathroom.

Then there was a knock at the door. He walked down the stairs and into the foyer. Mutters was already waiting impatiently and meowed at him as he approached. "Yeah I know," he said as he looked through one of the sidelights. There was a man with a clipboard just starting to walk away. Ethan wasn't sure who it was. He unlocked and opened the door.

The man heard the door and stopped at the bottom of the steps and turned around. "Good morning. I'm with Sunny Hills Landscaping."

Ethan had to kick-start his memory. "Oh right. It must be Tuesday."

"Yes, sir. It's Tuesday."

"Okay. I guess you know what to do."

"Yes, sir. It says I'm supposed to pick up a payment before we get started."

"Right, right. Come in. I'll go get it." Ethan went to retrieve the payment as Mutters purred and paced back and forth in front of the man. Two visitors in one week. What a treat.

Ethan returned with an envelope. "Here you go. Just apply whatever's extra to the account."

The man took the envelope, thumbed through the bills, made a note on the clipboard and clipped the envelope to it. "Looks good. Now, we used to come here to mow, trim and fertilize, which is what we're supposed to do today. It also says you would like us to kill some weeds and tidy up some of your bedding areas. Is that correct?"

"I just need you to do whatever it takes to get this place looking good again. You'll need to check the sprinkler system too."

The man looked around briefly at the property and responded smiling, "Guess I'll be able to get the wife that new living room set, eh?" Ethan looked at him puzzled. "Sorry, bad joke. We'll get'r done. Just remember that after we apply the fertilizer it will take at least a week or more for the lawn to start greening up."

"That's alright, I expected as much. Just go ahead and start and I'll come out pretty soon."

"Sounds good," the man said as he headed back out the door and started shouting instructions to the others sitting on the edge of the trailer.

Ethan put on some clothes, gobbled a cinnamon roll and poured some orange juice. Before heading outside though he would check GlobalNet for messages. The terminal was already on so he clicked a key to activate the screen. No messages. He thought Alex would have sent him something by now.

A well-tanned young man was operating an elaborate riding mower, a young woman was running a trimmer and another person was cleaning out one of the many flowerbeds. The man he spoke to at the door was checking a valve box for the sprinklers near the driveway.

"How bad is it?" Ethan asked.

"Once we get through with the yard and beds, we'll test the system. Is the controller in the garage?"

"Yeah, I'll open it up for you."

"What about the garden area out back?"

"Just kill it off."

"Okay. Did you realize you have a lot of really nice plants and flowers growing in these beds? You just can't see 'em for the weeds. After we get 'em cleaned out, we could put some mulch in there and they'd look pretty nice again."

"Yeah…yeah, that'd be good."

After about three hours of hard work, the landscape crew had made a huge difference before breaking for lunch. The color of the lawn was seriously anemic, but at least it was short and flat again. Most of the weeds were gone. The rest had been sprayed instead of pulled. It still looked a hundred times better and gave him a good feeling. It was even enough incentive to start cleaning out the garage and think about painting the trim.

Lunch was sounding good and it was time to check for messages again. Anxiously he activated the screen. No messages. There was a subtle sigh of disappointment.

It was now Wednesday and there was still no word from Alex. Cleaning was the only distraction that kept his mind occupied—that and blather from the radio. Maybe he'd get started on the trim. Maybe he'd have breakfast—monumental decisions for this early hour.

The cool morning air was slowly warming as he opened all the garage doors to let the light in. It was now easy to see what needed to be done. They weren't packrats by any means so there wasn't a lot of stuff to organize, but everything was covered in a visible layer of dirt and dead bugs. Ah, country living.

With the two drivable cars now pulled out on the driveway, Ethan took all the miscellaneous boxes and equipment and started ferrying them outside. This was only the second time the garage had been cleaned since they had moved there.

An hour or so later while two years worth of dirt was being swept into a pile, he noticed someone walking up the driveway. As the person got closer, he could see it was Mrs. Kensington from across the road. She was carrying a box, so he walked out by the cars to meet her.

"Good morning, Ethan."

"Mrs. Kensington."

"I saw you up here while I was baking so I thought you might like a rhubarb pie," she said as she handed over the box. "There's also a bottle of jam and two bottles of homemade salsa."

"This is really nice. You did all of these this morning?"

She laughed. "Oh heavens, no. I did the jam and salsa last fall and the pie yesterday. You know us, lots of kids, lots of food. I'm always, picking, baking, canning something."

"It's very nice. Thank you."

"You're welcome."

Mrs. Kensington was a pleasant woman. She was a few years older than Ethan and personified his idea of a farmer's wife. She reminded him a little of his grandmother—somewhat utilitarian in her role as mother and homesteader. Mrs. Kensington and her family had been nothing but friendly to Ethan and his family since they had moved there.

"I didn't mean to interrupt your work."

"You're fine. I've got all day to do this."

"Then would you have a minute?"

"Sure. Would you like to come in?"

"This is fine out here. Thanks."

Ethan realized she didn't feel comfortable being alone with another man. There were definitely no issues and the notion seemed a little old fashioned, but he would certainly respect her principles. The chairs on the porch were still covered with dirt.

"It isn't much, but how about a couple lawn chairs."

"That would be fine," she replied. Ethan grabbed two of them, banged off the dirt, wiped them down and set them just inside the garage in the shade.

Mrs. Kensington sat down. "You were sure busy yesterday. The place looks good."

"It was about time, wasn't it?"

"Oh I didn't mean to imply—"

"I know you didn't," Ethan interrupted. "It was getting pretty bad and just time to do something about it."

"Well, it does look nice. We should have offered to help more."

"Lots of people offered, I just wasn't interested, you know?"

"I do. I miss her too. It's strange not to see her outside working and I miss our exchanges. It was especially hard for Krissie to understand why Allison left. Ethan, I just want you to know that I do understand what you're going through, and want to let you know that you really do have friends who care. Healing can be difficult and sometimes it takes a long time. But with faith and prayer and the support of friends, it *can* be done."

Here we go. This was the kind of stuff he used to hear Rachel and her church friends talk about all the time, and the same kind of stuff he just wasn't interested in listening to. She *had* brought him a box of goodies though, so at least he should try to be polite. Mrs. Kensington also seemed a little uncomfortable in wanting to express thoughts that might not be well received.

From not long after the services until only recently, Ethan had made it a point to isolate himself from everything and everyone. He knew he had alienated a lot of people and needed to work at changing his attitude. Regardless, touchy-feely conversations were not on his list of comfortable activities to explore.

Mrs. Kensington could sense his discomfort, and being a little embarrassed and nervous started to get up. "You know, I should probably go."

"Did you know that except for a couple brief chats with Mr. Hendricks, in the last six months you're one of only a few people who have had enough nerve to actually come here and talk to me?"

"I'm really sorry Ethan."

"No, no, no, that's not what I mean. I mean most people don't *want* to talk to me anymore. Why would they? You treat them like dirt, you get what you deserve."

Mrs. Kensington sat back down. "No, Ethan, you don't deserve that. I don't think anyone really deserves to feel that way. I just wanted you to know that we all think you're a good person and that I understand what you're going through."

Ethan looked around with a slight sneer on his face. He had heard that last part from everyone a few too many times and wondered just how many of those people who said it really did know what it was like. "No offense, but I don't think a person can really understand something like this until it happens to them."

Mrs. Kensington looked down and wiped a small smudge of dirt from her knee. "You're absolutely right, Ethan. When I was a little girl, my family lived just outside a small town called Brooke, Missouri. I had two older brothers and two sisters—one older and one younger. We struggled. My dad worked for an agricultural supply company and Mom took care of us. My oldest brother Daniel was just out of high school and was working trying to save enough money to go to college. My other brother Jesse was seventeen and my older sister Jacqueline was fifteen. She was kind of a...free spirit you might say.

"She was always getting into arguments with Mom about staying out late, and the kind of people she hung around with among other things. Even though I never saw her do it, I knew Jacky drank because sometimes I could smell it on her. When Mom would find out, she'd ground her for a week, which just made Jacky furious.

"One night after a shouting match with Mom, I remember she paced back and forth in our bedroom ranting about how no one understood and how Mom hated her and how she wished she had never been born. I guess she had had enough and climbed out the window and left. It was dark and I remember going to the window and calling her name, asking her to come back. She just kept walking like none of it meant anything to her anymore. I'd seen her get mad before, but not like this. I sat in the room for a long time thinking about telling Mom, but I was only seven and didn't want to get in trouble. So I just stayed in the room and waited.

"I remember Dad coming in and waking me up, wondering if I knew where Jacky was. I told him I didn't know. They looked everywhere then started calling people. Dad drove around for a long time but they couldn't find her. The next morning we got a call from the local police that a neighbor about three miles away had found her floating in a pond where the kids would sometimes go to swim. They said it looked like she had drunk so much that she had passed out and fell into the water and drowned. That may have been what happened, but we never found out for sure.

"My father seemed to understand about life and death and choice and learned to cope with it. Unfortunately, my mother never really did. She blamed herself for not doing more and never forgave herself for what she believed was her fault. I thought it was my fault. For a long time I thought if I had just told Mom when Jacky left, she wouldn't have died.

"Can you imagine what it was like to be that young and think you were responsible for your sister's death? Dad tried to explain to me that death was a part of life and that it doesn't always happen in the way we think it should. Our inability to understand it only affects our ability to cope with it, and changes nothing else.

"One of my brothers died because of a drunk driver. My father died of cancer. One of my good friends was killed in a car accident and there were times when I would sit in the hospital room wondering if I was watching one of my own children leave me as well. I'm no stranger to death so with all due respect,

Ethan, I *do* understand, and I know Rachel understood because she was my friend."

Ethan's confidence in his obstinacy was shattered. The pedestal from where he proclaimed his defiance was crumbling beneath him. He couldn't really say for sure what *he* understood because right now he didn't really know. There *was one* thing... "And I suppose this 'understanding' has to do with the all-powerful God of Oz who compassionately and mercifully watches over and blesses all those in His kingdom."

Mrs. Kensington smiled. "If you're referring to *the* God, *our* God, then yes, it does—*everything* does," she said resolutely. "But no one's going to convince you of that. That's something you'll have to figure out for yourself." Seemed he had heard a young woman recently say something similar.

He sat silent and slowly shook his head. Mrs. Kensington continued. "Ethan, I know you didn't believe the same things Rachel did, but have you ever considered prayer?" He snorted and garnered a sarcastic smile, looked away and didn't say anything. "It's just a thought. You might be surprised." He still didn't respond. "Well, I better get back to work. I'm sorry if I've said too much," she concluded, holding out her hand.

Ethan stood and shook it. "No, you're fine. I should probably bite my tongue more often. You can take your goodies back if you want."

Mrs. Kensington smiled. "They're a gift, not a bribe. I hope you like them."

"I'm sure I will. Thank you."

"You're welcome," she said before turning to head down the long driveway back to her home. Ethan took the box to the kitchen and set it on the counter as he thought about what she had said.

It was now Thursday afternoon and he was almost done painting the trim around the garage doors. They were looking pretty good. The property was starting to look like someone actually lived there—maybe even someone who cared.

After cleaning the brushes and stowing the materials, he went back to the office to check for messages. If Alex hadn't sent a message or called by that evening, then he'd call her. Hesitantly he turned on the screen and there it was, one message—'From: Alex Fullerman.'

With reserved excitement he rolled the office chair over and sat down. The message read:

'I think you're going to find this interesting. Copy the attached program and run it on your other system. You must run the attached program and enter the password in lower case letters to decrypt the information. The password is who you introduced me to when I was there. Call me after you see it. Alex.'

Who did I introduce her to? he wondered while he flashed the message and program to his other system. After it loaded and ran, the screen displayed a field to enter a password. He thought back to that day. Sara was the only person Alex saw when she was there so he typed in 'sarah.' It didn't work. He tried 'sara.' It still didn't work. He tried *his* name. That didn't work either. She must have done something wrong.

He leaned back in the chair and thought about what he may have missed when from somewhere in the hallway came the tinkling of Mutter's collar as she scratched it. *Clever...very clever*, he thought as he laughed to himself and typed in 'mutters.' The program opened and text appeared followed by images. The text read:

'Hah! I was right. Here are several pictures showing a radar facility exactly where you said it should be. It was decommissioned and sold to a private company. That's all the information I have for now, but it's enough. You better start packing! Alex'

So it would seem. The image was a particularly clear aerial view of the facility. To the right side of the picture were buildings that looked to be about twenty-five feet high, twenty-five feet wide and about two hundred feet long according to the scale at the bottom. The buildings formed an 'L' shape connecting at a corner point and running along two sides. There were places along the outside of the buildings where it looked like antenna systems had been located, now removed. Behind and in the center of the 'L' shaped structures were one small and one large square building. All of the structures were low in height and of a basic box design. There was one road that led to the edge of the facility.

He was impressed that she got such a detailed photo, and *that's* what bothered him. This level of detail could have only come from an agency satellite. That meant the Professor probably pulled some strings with some of *those* people. Maybe it wasn't really a big deal…maybe.

☀ ☀ ☀

Even though the idea of the journal and what it could mean was incredibly intriguing, Alex still had a curriculum to prepare for the fall semester. It was hard to concentrate on schedules and course outlines when there seemed to be something so much more important out there. Her mind would frequently wander to the possibility of a journal from a time ahead of our own. As she tried to imagine how that could somehow be possible, the ringing of her mobile phone interrupted the daydream. She picked it up and looked at the display. It was Ethan. Her pulse quickened in anticipation.

"Hi Ethan."

"Hi Alex. I'd ask how you're doing, but I suspect I already know."

"Ask me anyway."

"How are you doing?"

"I'm just *peachy*, thank you. You got my message."

"I did. Very interesting."

"It is, isn't it? So now what?"

"You didn't say anything did you?"

"Your secret's still safe, if that's what you're asking."

"It is."

"I told you I wouldn't say anything and I didn't."

"I know, it's just that in order for this guy to have procured what he did means he knows somebody who knows people in places where people who don't want their lives under a micro-scope shouldn't go. You know what I mean?"

"Uh…"

"He makes me nervous."

"I still think you're worrying too much." There was silence. "So, when do you want to leave?" There was more silence. "Hello?"

"Yeah I'm here. Just…thinking."

"We made a deal you know."

"I know, I know. I just never really thought I'd have to make good on it."

"In other words you didn't really take me seriously."

"Well, kind of… No."

"Bet you won't make that mistake again. Don't worry. I'll plan everything. What do you think, two weeks?"

"You're really going to make me go through with this."

"Of course."

There was a heavy sigh from the other end. "Alright. I'll tell my staff to reschedule all my meetings."

Alex laughed. "Okay, you do that."

"What about you? Don't you have obligations?

"I can delegate. It shouldn't be a problem. When I have a trip itinerary I'll give you a call, but just plan on about two weeks from now. Okay?"

"Alright."

"I'm excited!"

"Yeah."

"Talk to you soon."

"Bye."

Ethan rested the receiver in his lap, leaned back in his chair and stared blankly at the wall of his dimly lit office. It was like he was sitting behind the wheel, but someone else was driving. *"What…have I done?"* he said out loud, shaking his head in disbe-lief before hanging up the phone.

CHAPTER SEVEN

Vertigo

THE AIR WAS HUMID that evening and storms threatened in the skies over Dulles. Ethan was staring out the side window of the taxi as it neared its destination. This was one of those days to just stay home, crank up the fireplace and watch a good movie or read a good book. His warm imaginary scene included someone else though. Otherwise the thought of sitting alone was empty and cold—just like this.

Alex reached over and pushed on his shoulder. "Hey, you okay?"

Startled, Ethan turned to look at her and forced a weak smile. "Yeah, I'm fine," he said as he turned back toward the window and continued to stare at the depressing weather.

"It's supposed to be nicer around Balkhash."

Ethan looked at her with surprise. "You thought to check the weather in Kazakhstan?"

"Well, kind of. I was just curious and maybe a little excited to see what it was like there." Ethan pursed his lips and nodded then turned back to the window again. They were almost there.

After loading the luggage on a carrier, they both headed for the terminal. Lines were long and Ethan's anxiety was less than subtle. The wait didn't bother Alex. For her the anticipation of the trip made all the pre-boarding issues bearable. Unfortunately, Ethan wasn't looking forward to any of it.

The solitude he had chosen for his lifestyle, and his basic personality made him overly sensitive to noise and the chaotic nature of places like this. The long flight, switching planes at Frankfurt, the puddle-jumper from Almaty to Balkhash were *not* things he would intentionally do for fun. His emotions were like a pendulum swinging from one extreme to the other. In one moment, excitement about possibilities. In the next, an overwhelming urge to run and hide.

After what seemed like hours, they finally boarded the plane and found their seats. Ethan finished stowing his small bag in the overhead then took the window seat as Alex sat in the middle of the three-wide arrangement. The aisle seat was still vacant. She noticed Ethan looking out the window again like he was in the taxi. It wasn't just interest in the weather, it was the same look people get when they would rather be anywhere but where they are.

"Are you sure you're okay? You've been awfully quiet," Alex asked.

"I'm still fine," Ethan said as he continued to stare out the window.

"You're a lousy liar." He turned to look at her as she continued. "Come on, share. You afraid of flying? Afraid of *me* maybe?"

Ethan chuckled and leaned back in his seat. "Hardly."

"Then what is it? You've been like this since we got in the taxi."

Ethan looked across the aisle and sat up to see who was ahead and behind them, then leaned over to Alex and spoke in a quiet, stern tone. "I don't like this cloak and dagger bull. Pretending to be someone I'm not is just going to screw things up. I'm not sure I can do this."

Alex leaned over toward him and spoke softly. "It's going to be fine. We're just going to look at the site. The cover is just in case we get asked questions. That's all." She sat back briefly then leaned toward him again. "You didn't say anything about this earlier. Why is it bothering you so much now?"

"I don't know. I guess it's because we're actually on the plane now. I'm not good at trying to be someone I'm not. Misleading people or lying about who I am just isn't something I'm comfortable with."

"Oh come on, you expect me to believe that you've *never* told somebody something that wasn't true?"

"Well…not like you want me to do."

"Maybe a little fib here or a little white lie there. Weren't you ever asked, 'does this make me look fat?'" Can you honestly tell me you never lied about that one?" Ethan rolled his head down and looked over and up at her. Alex then realized to whom she had inadvertently referred. "Right, bad example. But come on, no one's perfect."

"Of course not. I just don't like to lie."

"How about when someone asks how you're doing? Can you tell me that every time you say 'fine' that it's the truth?"

"That's different and you know it."

"How?"

"It just is. No one really cares how you feel when they ask you that. It's just a pleasantry—a formality."

"I care." Ethan was taken off guard by the sincerity of her comment. He started to look back over at her, but didn't dare. Any possible feelings of that nature were in another can of worms he definitely wanted to keep closed. "It's just pretend—like you're a kid again. You're going to pretend to be someone else. That's all."

"If you say so."

Alex reached over and lightly shook Ethan's shoulder as they started to descend into Frankfurt. "Ethan." He was sound asleep against the pillow. She shook him again. "Ethan," she said a little louder. He opened his eyes and looked around, trying to figure out where he was. "Good morning. We're coming into Frankfurt in a few minutes."

"Ugh. Morning? Already? Nothing like a good night's sleep," he said sarcastically while yawning and stretching.

The airport was busy. Their particular terminal wasn't overly crowded though. They both collected their small carry-ons and found a reasonably out-of-the-way corner of the concourse to wait for the connection to Almaty. Ethan was quiet as he leaned his head against the back of the chair and closed his eyes.

After about ten minutes of sitting in silence, Alex couldn't take it anymore and stood up. "Do you want something to eat? I can get us a snack or a drink or something."

"I'm dreaming of eating," Ethan responded sluggishly.

"Well I'm going to get me something anyway."

"Maybe a water then, if you don't mind."

"Just water?" Ethan nodded his head. "Okay. Be back in a minute," she said as she headed out of the waiting area.

Ethan listened to the sounds of the people who continuously flowed in and out of the concourse. Business people, vacationers, families... He opened his eyes to watch them. You could kind of tell which ones were which by the way they dressed and acted. He studied their faces—some showed a simple business calm, others confused and lost. Some in a hurry—worried about something.

People are strange, he thought. Everyone running around like ants in a maze—scurrying to meet deadlines, trying to figure out where to go, what to do. Going to see new things, make big plans. It almost seemed silly sometimes.

Suddenly, the concourse changed. All the people were different. Startled, Ethan sat up and it changed again. He turned to look out the large glass windows—it was dark outside! He blinked and it was light again. People would disappear then different people would reappear. The room would blur and images would superimpose and change again. He grabbed the chair and strained to keep focus. His legs...*they were someone else's!* There was a dress, then shorts and sandals. Everything was shifting in a dream-like haze—back and forth.

Hunching over slightly, he took his arms and folded them against his stomach to try and ease the queasiness. Looking up at the dizzying and continual change of scenes and faces, he caught a glimpse of one that seemed to stand out—a man in a dark, long coat, walking onto an escalator. He didn't recognize him at all, but his image was distinctive. Then the crowd shifted and the man was gone—melted away into a sea of new faces.

He closed his eyes to try and stop the bizarre illusions that had overcome him, but the images were still there, now in his mind…shifting, fading, spinning, twisting, floating, falling… Suddenly they shot away as if launched backward from a slingshot. Everything around him was a blur of motion. It almost seemed like he was going backward in time with the rest of reality passing forward around him.

The incredibly abrupt change of perspective and severe rush of vertigo was more then he could take. He forced his eyes open and found himself hunched over in his seat, grunting and staring at the floor. He was breathing hard, his stomach felt sick. Tossing his cookies here would be most undignified. After a few long, deep breaths, he sat back in the chair and was able to regain a certain degree of dignity. It had happened again—just like at the lab. What was it and why here? What was the connection?

He looked around to see if his little episode had caught any unwanted attention. Everyone was still scurrying about their business—unaware or just unconcerned about most everything else, including him. Thankfully, whatever it was seemed to have passed.

"Hey buddy, you okay?" Still gingerly holding his weak stomach, Ethan looked to his left to see where the voice had come from. Apparently he *had* caught someone's attention.

He was a large man, mid thirties, dressed casually, sitting several chairs away on the row of seats facing the opposite direction behind him. Ethan sat up and forced a smile. "I'm fine, thanks. Airplane food."

The man smiled back and extended his hand over the chairs. "Gotcha. My name's Zach."

Ethan unfolded his right arm and slowly leaned over the empty seats to shake hands. "Ethan."

"Nice to meet you, Ethan. I heard you talking to the lady earlier. Going to Almaty huh?"

"No, Balkhash. Well, Almaty then Balkhash."

"Ah, Balkhash. First time?"

"Yeah," Ethan replied as he took another long slow breath and let it out. The queasiness was going away.

"I've been there a few times. You should like it. It's an interesting little place. You from the U.S.?" Ethan nodded his head. "Me too. Cleveland. You?"

"Uh…Virginia."

"Yeah, nice place. I sell automobile parts. When cars break, people need parts," the man said, then laughed at himself. Ethan just smiled and nodded in acknowledgement. "So what do *you* do?"

This is where the weak smile got weaker. Time to lie, or pretend. He knew what he was *supposed* to say. "I'm a…uh… We're…"

"Independent journalists," Alex remarked as she handed a bottle of water to Ethan. "Sorry it took so long. I'm Alex."

"Zach Gonzales," the man said, standing halfway to acknowledge her. Alex sat down next to Ethan on the far side. "So, is this a married team?" the man asked. Alex waited for Ethan's response. He had managed to get the bottle to his lips and kept it there so he wouldn't have to say anything else.

"No, just colleagues." Ethan then lowered the bottle. Alex casually turned toward him and gave him 'a look' while opening her pretzels.

"So what do you guys do? Report on stuff, write stories…?"

"Sometimes we receive assignments for magazines. This trip we're doing some independent research on a story we're following."

"Really. That sounds interesting. Mind if I ask what the story is?"

"Well, we can't really say—competition and all. You know how it is."

"Gotcha." A boarding call for Kabul came over the public address system. "That's me," Zach said as he grabbed his bag and stood. "Nice to meet you both. Good luck on the story." He then motioned to Ethan. "Watch that airline food." And with a cheesy grin, he waved and walked away. They both waved back.

"Why did he say that?" Alex asked. Ethan just shrugged his shoulders and took another drink. She stared at him suspiciously.

"Thanks for the water," he offered.

"You're welcome. It looks like we should be boarding in about twenty-five minutes." A few pretzels later, she had to ask. "So what exactly *were* you going to tell him?"

"Apparently nothing. I couldn't spit anything out."

"Guess that career in the CIA just isn't an option huh?"

"No," Ethan responded dryly.

"Well, that's alright. The world could probably use more guys like you anyway."

"You mean bi-polar reclusive obsessive-compulsive?" Ethan quipped.

Alex grinned. "No...well maybe a little. I mean honest people. It's just funny how sometimes people you think you know end up strangers while strangers can become friends. Of course, if I hadn't known you from before, I probably would have let the guy at the store work you over."

After a few minutes, Ethan got up and walked to the nearby windows to watch what he could see of the busy air traffic and people outside. Alex left him alone and just slid down in her chair to rest her head, and kept munching.

As he looked out at the parked planes, the image of the man he saw earlier came back. That face. *Who was he?* He strained to make out the details in his mind—they just weren't clear enough. And the vision—kind of like the one at the lab.

What the heck is going on? If Alex knew about this stuff she'd probably run like a scalded monkey. No, actually she'd probably want to study the manifestations to extrapolate a correlation of relational phenomenon to...

Ethan slowly rolled forward on his feet, leaned his forehead against the glass, let out a deep sigh and just stared. Then a very unpleasant thought came. What if there *was* something physically wrong with him that was causing all this weird stuff—a brain tumor or developing neurological disorder or something. The thought filled him with dread and he stood up straight. He hadn't been to a doctor in years. Weird visions...depression and mood swings... It didn't explain everything, but *could* explain a lot. *Great, just one more thing,* he thought before going back to sit down.

"Only a couple left. You want one?" Alex offered.

He looked at the bag for a second then reached in and took out a pretzel. "Thanks."

"You're welcome."

It was about a half hour into the flight and all Ethan could think about was 'brain tumor.' Could that really be possible, or was he just reaching for answers? It was still a frightening thought and confusing as well because at one point not long ago, death was what he thought he wanted. Now it didn't seem so appealing.

As he pondered, guilt came over him for the way he had been acting. Alex was excited about this trip. She was trying to be friendly and nice. His reactions to her enthusiasm were always distant or indifferent—even belligerent at times. Trying to make *her* feel bad because of *his* inadequacies, or lack of confidence, was childish.

He wondered if that was the same thing Rachel had put up with for so long. All *she* ever wanted was for him to become a better person. But sometimes all he could remember was being sarcastic about her ideas and beliefs. What was he so afraid of?

The landing at Almaty was uneventful. A small commuter plane flew them to the Balkhash airport where they took a taxi to the hotel in town. The long flight east had accelerated time and it was early evening when they finally arrived. As they exited the taxi, Ethan stopped and looked around. "This is strange."

"What's strange?"

"I'm ready for breakfast and most of these people are probably done with dinner."

"I suspect you'll get used to it about the time we leave," she commented as she adjusted the bag over her shoulder and walked toward the hotel doors.

Alex set her bag down at the check-in counter. "Hi. Reservation for Fullerman," she announced.

The clerk typed the name into the terminal. "One moment please," he said in fairly clear English. Ethan was distracted and stood back, looking around at the spacious and nicely furnished main foyer.

"You have rooms four twenty-two and four thirty-seven. Here are your room keys." The clerk then placed a hotel guide on the counter for Alex to see. "The elevator is over there, the restaurant is here and open all hours. The pool area is here and there is an exercise room here next to the pool. Enjoy your stay and please let us know if there is anything we can do for you."

"Thank you," Alex replied.

"That was efficient," Ethan said as they started walking toward the elevator.

"The Professor likes to be efficient," she remarked.

"The Professor arranged all this?" Ethan asked with some apprehension.

"It was easier this way. We'll settle up with him later."

"Humph."

"What can I say? He likes me."

The bellman pulled the luggage cart onto the elevator and pressed the button for the fourth-floor.

"Speaking of the Professor..." Alex said as she removed a global from her bag, "I need to let him know we're here. Then let's get something to eat after we get our bags unpacked."

Ethan looked at the global with an uneasy feeling. He hadn't seen one in a while, but knew her having one couldn't be good. "That's an interesting phone. Mind if I see?"

"No. It's pretty cute really." Cute wasn't a term he usually associated with this device. "It's a phone plus it does all kinds of other things. Most of them I don't understand."

"Humph," Ethan grunted again as the elevator stopped and the doors opened.

"The Professor gave it to me. He said it's more secure than a regular mobile phone."

"Of that I have no doubt," Ethan said annoyed. Alex sensed his sudden change of mood, but didn't know what the problem was.

As they walked off the elevator, Alex pulled Ethan's key-card out of the folder and handed it to him, then started toward her room.

"Hang on just a minute," Ethan said as he held the card against the sensor that unlocked the door. "There's something I want to ask you. Thank you," he then said to the bellman who was dismissed with a tip. Ethan pushed open the door and carried part of the luggage in, then came back and got the rest.

"What exactly is this—"

"Wait." Ethan interrupted as he set the rest of the bags down.

"What—" she started to ask again when he quickly exaggerated a motion of his finger to his lips and widened his eyes. He gently took the global from her hand, set it on the dresser and motioned her back out into the hallway. She was obviously perplexed at his strange behavior. "What was that about?"

"I'll tell you in a minute," he replied as he walked down the hall, looking into each open room. He found a door that lead to a small balcony above the pool and located an empty table away from other people. "Have a seat," he said as he pulled out a chair for her and sat down next to it. She walked to the side of the chair and stood looking at him with her arms folded. "Just sit. Please." She did, but kept her arms folded and her guard up. "Did you, by any chance, have that global with you when you came to my house?"

Alex thought for a moment. "You mean when you showed me the journal?"

"Yeah."

"No. Well, maybe. I don't remember. Why?"

"Ah man," Ethan said irritated as he leaned back in the chair and looked away.

"Why? What does that matter?"

He didn't respond, then looked her square in the eyes. "Listen, this is really important. I need you to try to remember if you had it with you when you came to the house. Do you usually keep it in your purse?"

"Most of the time, unless it's charging in the kitchen or in the car."

"Try to remember. *Did you have it with you?*" Ethan was becoming more insistent and it was making Alex more irritable.

"I don't know, I don't remember. Why is it such a big deal?"

"Because that global your buddy the Professor gave you is not your run-of-the-mill, mall-kiosk mobile phone. What he gave you is issued by those same organizations I told you I wanted nothing to do with."

"Oh what so now I'm a spy?"

Ethan dropped his head in frustration. "No, you don't get it. This thing is designed to gather information. The microphone and camera can be activated remotely so someone else anywhere in the world can listen to everything you say and see everything you do and you wouldn't be the wiser unless you knew how to disable it. It has an intuitively invasive retrieval and reporting capability that sniffs other systems in close proximity and mirrors the information. It has a global mapping translator so most likely the Professor knows *exactly* where you are and, yes, it's secure because it uses a system the public doesn't even have access to.

"He probably has the itineraries and personal information of everyone with a PDA, laptop and mobile phone you were ever within ten feet of. He probably even knew everything about Happy The Salesman at the Frankfurt Airport within thirty seconds of when we sat down. And the worst part is, apparently 'Grandpa' never told you any of this so how can I trust you if you don't even know what's really going on? He could have heard everything we talked about that day. This is a nightmare," Ethan concluded, leaning back and rubbing his forehead.

Alex sat somewhat annoyed at the verbal assault and worked to keep her senses, then responded calmly. "Look, I don't know everything about what's going on. All I know is that he has always treated me well and has never done anything *ever* to make me question his intentions. If that thing does what you say it does then I'm sure he's just trying to watch out for me."

"It doesn't bother you that he can listen to every conversation you have? What about the other people you know? Don't you think *they* might care that every time you talk to them on this thing that someone else might be listening? And you honestly don't think they would mind that someone else could be covertly copying and viewing all the information from their personal devices every time you're with them? Wake up Alex. Your personal savior is probably a lot more involved with that crap than *either* of us wants to know. And *that* is something I want *nothing* to do with."

"Oh please, don't blow a vein. You don't know if he can really do *any* of this. You're just speculating. "

"*Alex...*" Ethan responded with gritted teeth. He took a deep, slow breath and continued. "I used to work for people who designed this kind of stuff and I know *exactly* what it can do. The people who use these things are the same people who make other people disappear. I've seen it happen. Have you ever *really* stopped to think about who this Professor could actually be involved with? Do you have *any* idea of what he does aside from teaching, and making you his favorite adopted daughter? What do you think he really did to get your ex-husband to leave you alone—drop him a 'please get lost' card?

"Besides his university credentials, he isn't listed anywhere—no official Government records, no tax records, nothing. How does a person do that, Alex? You can't be average Joe Citizen and not have an official history somewhere. It just isn't possible...unless you're connected to people who can erase your past. This is getting out of control. I only agreed to this trip because I trusted you. But how can I trust you if you trust someone like that?"

Alex thought, then leaned forward and calmly rested her arms on the table. "You worry too much. Come on," she replied before standing to walk away. Ethan threw his hands in the air and dropped them on his lap. How could she be so naïve?

As he reluctantly followed her down the hall, he still wanted her to understand his points. They *were* valid and he knew what he was talking about. Somehow he had to get through to her. "Alex, I just don't think you understand what this guy could really be involved with."

She abruptly stopped, turned around, stepped right up into his face and spoke with determination. "Look, I'm a college math teacher. I live alone, I have pet fish. He doesn't care what I do on my own time *or* what you do at all. So get a grip and let me get my luggage, please." She continued to glare at him for a second longer before turning and continuing down the hall.

If ever there was a time when he felt like a whipped puppy, that was it. There was no doubt she could defend her point of view. It was something Ethan would remember and respect from that point forward.

She waited while he took out his key-card and unlocked the door. She then stopped at the door on her way out after gathering up her things. "Let me know if you want to get something to eat, otherwise I'll see you in the morning." That was all she said.

Several blouses went on hangers and the rest of her attire stayed in the suitcase. After checking out a few features in the room, she walked to the window to stand and look outside. It was disappointing that things had already become so tenuous. She knew Ethan was still dealing with personal issues and she had even tried to prepare herself for the fact that he might not always be the best company. That eventuality, although not unexpected, was still difficult to accept. She hoped he could find his true character because the answers they searched for were probably buried deep within questions only he would understand.

CHAPTER EIGHT

Vision of a Dream

ALEX KNOCKED QUIETLY ON the door to Ethan's room, trying not to wake other guests. It was fairly early, about 6 A.M. The trip to the site would be long so she wanted to make sure they met the driver on time. Again she gently knocked. The television could be heard faintly. This time she knocked a little harder.

The door opened and Ethan stuck his head around it. "Hello," he said, trying not to drool toothpaste.

"Morning," Alex replied. Ethan held the door open allowing her to enter, then went back to the bathroom. "Looks like you're ready to roll. Sleep okay?" she asked.

"It's really only 9 P.M. yesterday, you know. Last night was just a nap. I finally went down to breakfast a couple of hours ago."

"This time change has really screwed you up, hasn't it?"

"To say the least. And what about you?"

"I'm managing. Lay there for a while, finally fell asleep then woke up about an hour ago. I'd like to get something decent to eat before we leave so I'll go to the restaurant and maybe meet you in the lobby in a half hour?"

"That'll work."

Alex turned and started toward the door then stopped. "You can come with me if you want."

"No thanks, I still need to clean up and finish getting dressed."

"Alright," she said a little disappointed. "We okay with everything?"

"I guess." Not the vote of confidence she was hoping for.

Ethan was sitting on one of the big chairs in the center of the main lobby when Alex walked up.

"What are you reading?" she asked.

"Some travel magazine. I think it was written by someone here and translated into English. The phrasing and word usage is off. Pretty entertaining."

"Got everything?"

"I think so," he replied as he put the magazine down and stood.

Alex started walking to the hotel door. "He should be here any time."

"Who are we looking for?"

"I'm not really sure. The Professor just said someone would meet us here to take us to the site."

Moments later a dirty, red four-door sedan pulled up to the curb with some other vehicles and a man stepped out to briefly scan the people on the sidewalk. While taking a piece of paper out of his shirt pocket, he walked around the front of the car to the curb. "Feel-or-man?" the driver said with a heavy accent. Ethan snickered.

"That's us," Alex replied. Saying nothing else, the driver waved his hand, motioning them to get in as he walked back around to the driver's side.

"Friendly," Ethan commented quietly before they both climbed into the back seat. The man started the car and they sped away into traffic.

"Do you know exactly where we're going?" Alex asked the driver. The driver handed back a piece of paper with a crudely drawn map showing a route west out of the city to a point marked by two Russian words in a box.

"I'm oozing with confidence," Ethan commented quietly.

"The location looks about right so I think we'll be okay."

Ethan leaned over the front seat and tapped his finger on the paper. "How long till we get there? How much time?" The driver held up four fingers.

"Four hours?" The driver nodded his head, took the paper and set it down next to him.

"I didn't even bring anything to read," Ethan commented, looking around.

"We could always talk."

"Yeah, because I do that so well," he replied with a sarcastic grin.

Ethan grabbed the side of his forehead and rubbed it after it bounced off the side window glass a second, and then a third time. He opened his eyes, took a deep breath and looked around to see the driver and Alex both bouncing around as well.

"Morning," Alex said. "Enjoy your nap?"

"Man I guess. Where are we?"

"Right here," she said as she showed him the display on the global with a real-time map of the roads and their position. "Relative to the site, we should be about forty minutes away." She also had a paper map on her lap, folded to display the local area. "See? Here *we* are and here is where the site is supposed to be."

Ethan looked at the global then over at Alex. "So, I guess you know how to use it after all, huh?"

"After last night I decided to try and be a little more honest with you. I don't know about some of this other stuff you were talking about, but I know how to see where I am. The Professor did tell me a long time ago that if I ever got into any serious trouble and couldn't call out, to push these three buttons simultaneously for three seconds and it will send out an emergency call for help and show my location. I hope you aren't too mad at me."

"No, not really I suppose. I probably went a little overboard."

"If we're going to really trust each other, we need to be as honest as possible so I'm sorry and next time I'll try to be more understanding."

"Well, I'll try to mellow a little, if that's possible." Then he pointed to the global. "Just don't hold these two buttons and push this one five times."

"Why?"

"It activates a micro-chemical explosive that sprays an acid inside the case melting the circuit board and components. It can also be activated remotely. Bet you didn't know that."

"No...I didn't," she replied, nervously eyeing the global.

"You probably don't have anything to worry about though, unless they discover you're working for the other side."

"I'll keep that in mind."

The terrain outside was mostly flat with a few rolling hills sparsely covered with grass. The dirt road was narrow and rough with large potholes full of water. The driver would slow to go around them, sometimes running two wheels off the shoulder, which was a little nerve-wracking considering that ponds of water straddled the sides of the road.

As they came around the backside of a hill, the driver pointed to another one about three miles away and said his second profound statement of the trip, "There." Ethan and Alex both leaned toward the center and over the front seat to look through the bug-splattered windshield where the driver was pointing. On a hill in the distance was what looked like a small group of buildings.

"Good!" Alex replied enthusiastically as she patted the driver on the shoulder and leaned back to look at the map on the global. "Isn't this exciting?" Ethan just watched the hill and tried not to encourage her.

They came to a small gate over a cattle guard from which a five-strand barbed wire fence extended in both directions. A large sign was posted on the gate with two smaller signs posted on the fence on either side. The small signs were also spaced about every three sections on the fence for as far as you could see.

The driver stopped the car abruptly just before the gate, opened the door and jumped out before Ethan could ask what the signs said. Alex quickly pulled a camera out of her bag and took several pictures. The driver walked up to the gate, pulled out a key and inserted it into one of several locks hanging on a large chain.

"He has a key." Ethan said in a curious and somewhat concerned tone.

"Looks like it," Alex replied unconcerned. The driver opened the gate, came back to the car and pulled it forward far enough to close the gate behind them.

"What do the signs say?" Ethan asked the driver as he climbed back in.

"Not to worry. No one here."

Ethan sat back and leaned over to Alex. "Yeah, no need for concern. I'm sure you'll make a great wife for one of the prison directors. Me they'll just shoot."

Alex grinned and leaned over almost uncomfortably close to his ear. "You worry too much," she whispered softly.

"*You* don't worry enough," he replied matter-of-factly.

The buildings disappeared out of sight as the road wound its way up the hill in a slow ascent. Alex continued to eagerly watch for them to reappear as they climbed, then Ethan spotted a clearing on the side of the road inward toward the hill. A huge door appeared to be set in to the hill behind tall overgrowth.

"Wait. What's that?" Ethan asked while pointing.

The driver stopped. "Machine entrance." Alex took a picture of the door then the driver started forward again.

The entire facility came into view when the car crested the top of the hill. Long, low straight buildings defined its perimeter with a partially dismantled tower near the center. Between two of the buildings at the edge of the complex was a very large chain-link gate about twenty feet wide with old razor wire looping across the top. The same large sign from the gate at the bottom of the hill was posted on both sides of this gate.

"Okay," the driver said as he stopped the car near the gate and shut off the engine. He held the ring of keys over the back of the seat. Alex took them eagerly. "Forty-five minutes. No more. We leave, forty-five minutes," the driver said, showing his watch and tapping it with his finger.

"Okay. Thank you," Alex replied, grabbing her bag and opening the door.

"Whoa, whoa wait a minute," Ethan said, scrambling out of the other side to catch Alex who was already halfway to the gate. "Are you nuts? We could get into serious trouble for this—like *real* prison."

Alex was sorting through keys trying to find the correct one for the old lock. She ignored Ethan's pleas for reason. "You want to help me find the right key?"

"*No* I'm not going to help you. Why do you think this place has razor wire and giant red signs?"

Alex tried a key then leaned back briefly to look at one of the signs. "Can't read Russian. Sorry."

"I am *not* going in there," Ethan said in disgust and started walking back to the car.

A little miffed, Alex pulled the key out and turned around. "*Why* are you such a wuss?"

"Why are you such a twelve-year-old?" he rebutted. Realizing the commotion they were making, Ethan looked at the driver who had lowered his newspaper to see what was going on. The driver tapped his watch again and went back to his paper.

"What did you think we were going to do when we got here?" Alex asked in a slightly calmer tone. "Just say 'yup, here it is' then go home? What would be the point of that?"

"At least we'd stay out of prison."

"*No one's going to prison,*" Alex said irritably, turning back to work on the lock again.

This whole thing was too organized and she was way too casual about it. That and the keys could only mean one thing; the Professor. He didn't just arrange the ride, he must have arranged a little self-guided tour as well. "Ah man..." Ethan said, swinging his head in frustration. He walked back toward Alex who had managed to find the right key, remove the lock and open the gate far enough to walk through.

As he got close to her and was about to speak, she pressed her finger to his lips and looked into his eyes. "You worry too much. You need to trust me."

"You could have told me this part had been arranged you know."

"Could have, but that would have been too easy."

"I like easy."

"My point exactly." Ethan said nothing more and in an exaggerated wave of his arm, bowed and motioned her to lead the way. "Thank you," she said politely.

The satellite photo was unfolded and examined. "So, it looks like we're over here. What do you think is in these buildings around the outside?"

"Well, they were probably full of transmitter equipment when this place was active. The control center would most likely be underground somewhere."

"So we need to find a way underground."

"What exactly do you think we're going to find here anyway?" Ethan asked.

"You tell me. Maybe there's something you might recognize or find familiar."

"I don't see how. Everything familiar to me is eight thousand miles away."

"Come on, let's go look over there," Alex said pointing to a structure in the center of the compound that was about three feet high and looked to be made of concrete. As they approached, they noticed a stair railing to the side of the structure leading down. At the bottom of the stairs, well below ground level, was a large steel door.

"There you go," Ethan said as Alex walked to the edge of the stairs and looked around. Carefully she started down the steps, surveying each one as Ethan followed. "Watch for snakes," he added.

"Oh, thanks," she quipped.

"I'm not kidding," he replied quite serious.

Alex stopped and looked around nervously, then huffed out a breath. "Maybe *you* should lead."

"Nooo, you're doing fine," he said with a fiendish grin.

At the lower landing Alex studied the door and the lock carefully, then pulled out the ring of keys and started looking for one that might fit. Ethan was standing behind her and reached out, grabbed the handle and pulled. The heavy spring-loaded door opened. "Somebody forgot to lock up," he noted. Alex just shook her head and put the keys back in her pocket.

Ethan slowly opened the door to expose a heavy matting of webs in a very dimly lit vestibule with another door about four feet in. "I don't suppose you have flashlights?"

"Of course," she said before pulling two small high intensity lights from her fanny pack and handing one to Ethan.

To the side of the inside door was a small sign with an electrical box below it that probably used to be an access reader or keypad. The corners of the vestibule were full of spider webs and the floor was covered with the exoskeletons of bugs and insects and even a few rodent carcasses. There was a light fixture on the ceiling and a switch on the wall. Ethan reached in and flipped the switch a couple times...nothing happened. "Figures," he said and stepped past Alex to grab the handle on the inside door, giving it a tug. "Well, guess I was wrong. They did lock up."

Alex pulled the ring of keys from her pocket and started trying them while continuously flipping her flashlight upward and around to illuminate the webs. "I doubt they're man eating. You want me to do that?"

"No, I got it," she said defensively. After trying three different keys, the fourth slid in and with a firm twist, the lock unlatched and the bolt slid back.

The key was removed and she pulled on the heavy steel door. Ethan held his flashlight above her head as they both walked slowly into the cold, empty room. The room was about twenty feet square with another steel door in the wall to the left. A small sign was mounted on the wall to the right side of the door above an electrical box with naked wires hanging out of it—similar to the second entry door. In the far wall there were two large vents and several large electrical conduits poking through the floor that ran to open boxes attached to the wall on the right. Something appeared to have been bolted there at one time.

Four open light fixtures with wire covers were attached to the ceiling and conduit ran to light switches at the entry and far doors. Ethan flipped the two inside switches a couple of times while Alex made her way to the other door.

"It's unlocked," she said in a quiet voice before cautiously pulling the door open and directing her flashlight up and down to reveal a stairwell that led down and to the right. Ethan followed her and was looking around in the stairwell when he saw another light switch on the inside stairwell wall and clicked it up and down a few times. "It looks like there are two more levels down here," her voice echoed while she peered over the edge of the railing. Then without hesitation, she started down the stairs. Ethan followed a few steps behind.

At the next landing was another door. This one was unlocked as well and inside was a hallway that led to several small rooms on the left and a larger room on the right. On the wall to the right of the door to the large room were a couple of signs in Russian. "Interesting," she said as she pulled out her camera and backed up against the hallway wall to take a picture.

Ethan was in one of the small rooms then came out into the hallway. "I think these were sleeping quarters," he commented.

"Look at this door," Alex said after the camera flashed. "It looks like a high security area of some sort." Ethan walked in front of her and opened the door. He looked around in the room with the flashlight, then clicked the light switches on the inside wall a few times.

"Why do you keep doing that?" she asked, shining the flashlight toward his face.

"Hey, do you mind?" he said as he quickly closed his eyes, wincing at the blinding light. "Thanks. Now I'll be seeing spots."

"Sorry," she said after lowering her flashlight.

"I don't know, just checking to see if any of them work I guess." After blinking a few times to get his sight back, he continued looking around the room. There were numerous electrical boxes on the walls and lots of conduit. The floor had several areas where it looked like consoles had once been secured. "Looks like this was probably a control room—maybe where they operated the facility from."

"Well, let's see what's downstairs," Alex said, holding the door open.

The door at the bottom of the stairwell had no signs around it, or box for a keypad. It did have a small enclosure attached high on the wall that looked like an industrial speaker with two unmarked buttons on the front at the bottom. Above it was another small box. Alex pulled the handle on the door—it was locked. She pulled out the ring of keys and started trying them as Ethan held her flashlight.

"Here we go," she said after the second key slid into the lock and was turned. The door still wouldn't open. She turned the key again and looked between the door and the frame to see the dead-bolt slide back out of the way, but the door was still being held closed by something.

"Crap!" she shouted, grabbing the handle and pulling on it in desperation, her voice reverberating in the tall concrete stairwell. "Now what do we do?" Ethan said nothing and just stood holding the light steady on the door lock. "Ethan?"

He handed the flashlight to her and moved her hand so the light would illuminate the boxes on the wall near the top of the door. Reaching up, he opened the top box to reveal a small panel with some buttons and an inoperative digital readout. He then pushed on the upper left portion of the panel which caused it to pop open. Attached to two clips behind the panel was a small copper and silver colored rod with a black round rubber ball on one end. He removed the rod and held it by the rubber ball while counting the small holes in the red metal cover on the lower box. Then he inserted the rod into one of them and pushed the left button. A loud '*clack*' came from the door causing Alex to jump, fumbling the flashlight.

Ethan grabbed the door handle and pulled the door open as Alex picked up the light and pointed it at Ethan. He then re-moved the rod, put it back in the clips, closed the panel and the front cover. As he walked through the door, he turned to his right and flipped two switches that energized a series of lights over a huge three-story room below them. It was at least a hundred twenty-five feet across.

Alex cautiously followed him onto the small metal landing where they both stood and looked down. "Now this is interesting," Ethan said with negligible emotion.

Alex was both shocked and confused. "How did you know to do that?" she asked. He didn't respond. She pushed his arm. He bobbled, and then slowly turned to look at her. "How did you know to do that? That thing with the door?"

Ethan looked at her in the pinkish colored light, then looked back at the door, then back to her. A puzzled look came over him as he looked back at the door again and at her again as if he didn't understand. "I don't know."

"Don't play games with me. That's not funny."

"Really, I don't know. I just...I just knew what to do. It was like a memory, like I'd watched somebody do it before, or something."

"How is *that* possible?" Alex asked tensely.

Ethan realized he had just revealed one of the strange attributes afflicting his otherwise stellar psychology. "I uh...hey, at least we got in," he said as he forced an empty smile and looked around, knowing he couldn't really explain it.

"Ethan, that's really creepy." He just shrugged his shoulders and held his empty grin.

A long set of wide metal stairs to their left led straight down to the floor while to the right was a walkway that turned and followed the wall to what appeared to be an observation room about halfway across. "I'll bet that goes to that equipment door we saw on the way up," Ethan said as he pointed to a large tunnel on the far side of the floor. "How much time do we have?"

"About twenty-five minutes, then we need to head back up."

"Well then, up, or down?" Ethan said motioning to the room at the end of the walkway, then down to the floor.

"Up, but you go first."

Ethan turned off his flashlight, put it in his back pocket and headed down the metal catwalk. There were tarps covering several good-sized objects and other pieces of construction machinery scattered about in different areas of the large, open room. He twisted the knob, pulled open the unlocked door and turned on the light.

The room was about twenty feet wide and fifteen feet deep with several large, angled windows to the left that formed a continuous span across the full width of the room. It afforded an unobstructed view of most of the room below. There was a door at the back corner of the room that Alex went to investigate. Otherwise the room was empty, except for the typical conduit and evidence of previously mounted equipment. "Nothing," she replied as she started walking back toward him.

Ethan turned to look out the large windows and was startled by what he now saw. In front of him were two men facing the windows, sitting in chairs at a wide control console with terminals and several video displays. Each one of the men wore a small headset and similar white lab coats. The man on the left was looking intently at one of the data terminal displays in front of him while the other watched a large flat video screen in the upper right corner of the room. Ethan looked over the console and out the windows at the floor below.

There were several pieces of equipment in the middle of the room spread around in a half circle on a low raised platform. Another man, also in a white lab coat, was standing near its center, taking readings with a small handheld device. About fifteen feet to his left was another row of equipment with cables running on the floor toward the platform. Suspended a few feet above the center of the platform was what he recognized as a targeting chamber. It had three distinct ports to which accelerators were attached and the encircling equipment was connected. He looked up at the image on the large display. It was a close-up view of the targeting chamber at the center of the platform.

He strained to make out details when the man at the left of the console pushed a button and began speaking, "Zwei minuten bis zu aktiverung. Alle personen müssen den raum sofort verlassen." The voice echoed back faintly from the other side of the glass and the man standing at the platform immediately turned and walked away. Then a man behind and to the side of him spoke. Ethan turned and started to look up to see who the man was when his attention was turned back to the men at the console as they started conversing back and forth verifying data. He couldn't understand what they were saying, but when he looked down at one of the small screens it was displaying a precision timing event currently at one minute fifty seconds and counting down.

"Oh no," he said out loud.

"What?" came a female voice from behind him. He turned to look at Alex briefly, then back toward the windows only to find that everything was gone. The room was empty, just as it was when they first entered. The floor area outside the windows was also empty. "Hey, you're not going weird on me again are you?"

He quickly forced a smile. "No. Let's go see what's downstairs."

Alex stepped off the last stair and onto the floor of the huge open room. "We don't have much time left."

"Then how about you see what's in those crates over there and I'll look under these tarps."

"Okay," Alex replied before heading to some crates on the far side of the room. "It appears to be equipment of some kind," she shouted after inspecting them.

"Same thing here," Ethan shouted toward her. Then as he looked back toward the crate, it was gone. He was now staring at a large power generator. To his right was the platform full of equipment he had previously seen from the room above. There was a loudspeaker booming from the ceiling. It echoed heavily.

"Zehn sekunden bis zu aktivierung. Neun...acht...sieben..." The equipment started to buzz and squeal as it charged. Confused, Ethan looked around frantically. *It was the countdown.* Panic-stricken, he started to run, darting one way then another, only to stop when he realized there would be no place to run to—nowhere to hide.

Scared and frustrated, he looked up at the control room windows that were now covered. No doubt a shield to protect the occupants from whatever inadvertent scattered energy might be produced by this insane experiment.

Even though he didn't want to believe it, he knew what he was about to witness. In a few moments the blending of an artificially induced reaction was going to trigger an inconceivable power, and for over a thousand miles in every direction, every living creature, all life of every kind was about to be wiped from the face of the earth. These men were about to plunge the world into a darkness not seen for centuries, and cause one of the greatest world conflicts ever known.

He reached out to disconnect a power cable on one of the large generator units, but his hand passed through it. It didn't make sense. This was impossible. Still, somehow, someway, he was here at the point of origin—forced to watch the birth of annihilation, and there was *nothing* he or anyone else could do to stop it.

"*...sechs...fünf...*" *This is impossible. Why would anyone want to do this?* The equipment was ramping to an almost deafening level while emitters charged to perform their duty.

"*...vier...drei...zwei...*" the voice continued above the scream of the equipment. Ethan turned and covered his ears in a vain attempt to dampen the sounds and to shield himself when something caught his eye. Standing in the dimly lit corner of the room was a pretty young girl with long blond hair. She was looking at him strangely...

"*...eins...*" Ethan pushed his hands hard against his ears and closed his eyes tightly. He tried not to listen, but after a moment realized the only sound he could now hear was his own groaning from the grimaced anticipation of inevitable destruction.

With trepidation, he slowly opened his eyes to darkness—total and complete darkness. It was done. Everything was gone. "*No! No!*" he screamed as he clenched his fists and fell to his knees in the nothingness.

"Ethan!" Alex's voice shattered the dark. He looked up to see her holding his shoulders. She was looking directly at him. The terror on his face startled her. He instinctively grabbed her and held on trying to understand if *she* was real. "Ethan, it's okay."

He was trembling and breathing erratically. "Get me out of here...please," he said quietly in a broken and distressed voice.

"Okay, come on," she replied, helping him to his feet.

The driver was standing by the gate as they approached. "Must go! End of time!" he said motioning them to move along. "You lock doors?" he asked as Alex came closer.

"Yes."

He held out his hand. "Keys?" Alex pulled the ring of keys from her pocket and handed them to him as she walked past, leading Ethan by the arm. The driver watched them walk by, then closed and locked the gate while they climbed into the back of the sedan. Ethan immediately leaned forward and hid his face in his hands. Alex had her hand on his shoulder, unsure what else to do.

The driver got in the car and they started back down the road off the hill. Alex knew Ethan had experienced something traumatic and didn't want to pressure him for an explanation, even though she was very curious and concerned.

They made their way back down the road to the lower gate. Ethan kept his face hidden—disturbed about what he had seen. Alex gingerly rubbed his shoulder reassuringly to let him know it was okay.

He kept to himself the rest of the way back to Balkhash and said nothing. She occasionally took out the map or global to fill her time. When he was ready to tell her what happened, hopefully he would.

CHAPTER NINE

The Henry Effect

ALEX THANKED THE DRIVER as they got out of the car in front of the hotel. He stuck his hand out the window, waved and sped away.

"Ah, it's good to be home," Alex remarked jovially, trying to encourage Ethan's spirit. Usually he always had some smart comment to impart. Not this time.

At the door to his room, he held the key-card near the lock. It beeped and the lock clicked. He didn't open the door though and turned to Alex instead. "I'm sorry."

"There's nothing to be sorry for," she replied. There was a long pause as a female guest exited the room next to them and walked passed. "Are you going to be all right?"

"You know, I'm not sure. This whole thing is just... I'll talk with you a little later. Okay?"

She really didn't want to leave him alone, but didn't want to impose either. "Ethan, I'll do anything I can. Come get me if you want to talk. Alright?"

"Okay, thanks," he said with a forced grin, briefly glancing up at her before unlocking the door again.

The small sofa was beginning to lose its comfort after an hour of sitting and listening to the faint muffled sounds of the foreign city outside. It wasn't unlike being home visiting the cemetery—listening to the sounds of life flirt with each other on a willing wind. Similar, but not quite the same.

Being here in a strange country, the isolation of encroaching madness, the visions, the impossible questions... The darkness and emptiness, the nothingness felt in that one instant from the vision was overwhelming. He looked up at the window that separated him from the outside world. He didn't want to be alone anymore. He needed to be with other people—to feel life—to fill the emptiness.

The streets were busy as people made their way to destinations of importance. Everyone seemed to have a place to go, a schedule to keep. For many, time was an adversary, always nipping at their heels, causing them to hop or skip in a frantic race to find more of what was allocated. For a precious few it was an ally. Planning and knowledge facilitated understanding that allowed for a sure and steady pace in their race against rats. He watched and wondered where they might be going—homes, jobs, appointments, friends, husbands...a wife and family maybe.

Ahead was a large community square with a tall fountain at its center, water spilling over its sides into a surrounding pool. Hundreds of people traversed over the intricate stone designs, many in narrow lines like ants following a leader, making their way to a mass transit system somewhere. He was intrigued by the large open space, elaborate buildings, statues and trees. The essence of life was everywhere.

The fountain seemed to be a popular gathering place for many different types of people. Gray-haired men sat and talked while children ran around its edge to the dismay of some older and wiser. Even in the chaos of noise from voice and machinery, some could still hide themselves away in a world of their own to sit on an old wood and metal park bench, knees pulled up close as they read a favorite book.

Ethan stood in the middle of the square not far from the fountain and looked around. He wondered about these people and what their individual or combined ambitions might be—what they must believe in, how they perceive *their* lives. What would they do if they knew their existence was about to end? How would *they* react? How many would run in panic and fear? How many would stand and accept death either bravely or otherwise? He watched them and looked in their faces as they passed, knowing that whatever terrible fears or courageous convictions they held within them, either to cherish in strength or to despise in ignorance, were theirs alone.

The vision of his own extinction scared him senseless and had him cowering like a frightened child. He had already discovered that his fear of the unknown in death was greater than his ability to terminate his own life. And when he found himself faced with what he perceived as the end, it didn't matter what he thought, or how brave he might be, or how scared, how intelligent, how prepared, how wealthy... There was *nothing* that gave him comfort in that moment. *But if nothing, then what?*

He wondered if Rachel's beliefs helped her when her moment of inevitability came. She seemed so sure about her convictions. Maybe he should have listened. But does anyone really know truth? Or is truth simply what is perceived by those wanting to believe something badly enough? Maybe she was right about all of it—maybe not. How does anyone really know?

People continued to stream by and Ethan continued to wonder if any of them understood any *real* truth, or even knew where to find it. If you only learn the defining truth about life at it's end, then what is the point of its journey? There had to be something more. The inner deliberation was only making him more frustrated. There were no answers here, only more questions.

Continuing across the square brought him to a quaint little street with interesting stores and vendors. Even though he couldn't read most of the signs or understand most of the people, these people and this place didn't seem that different from his own a half world away. Just being around them was comforting in an odd sense.

The very uniqueness that makes us all different is exactly what binds us all together, regardless of where we live, what language we speak or what we believe. Everything is different everywhere and exactly the same. It was a confusing preponderance of thought that continued as he walked along the sidewalk in the crowd of strangers.

About halfway back to the hotel, a man sitting alone on the curb caught his attention. His clothes were worn and old, which seemed to complement his beard and long hair. It was curious how he just sat there as the rest of the world walked by, keeping stride in their agendas.

Ethan stopped on the far side of the sidewalk near a storefront and watched the man. He appeared to be destitute. Ethan wondered if the man might have a family somewhere, and what could have happened to bring him here? He didn't seem to be doing anything—just sitting. No one to meet, maybe not even a purpose for living. It was sad.

Slowly, Ethan started to walk away when a second later he stopped inexplicably and turned back to look at the man again. His mind wandered to a time not so long ago when *he* probably didn't look much different and no doubt felt similar. He was all too familiar with disparity. At least he had a nice house and friends. Well, one or two friends at least, and caring neighbors. This man appeared to have nothing. As the man turned to look down the sidewalk in Ethan's direction, Ethan quickly turned away, not wanting to make eye contact. He was ashamed to acknowledge the man's presence. Then Sara's words rang clear in his mind. Could this be the disparity she told him not to turn away from?

Waiting for a few moments to find courage, he then walked over to the man and sat down on the curb beside him. Neither looked at the other, then finally Ethan spoke. "I don't suppose you know a young lady named Sara do you? Long blond hair, has a brother named Ty? Lives someplace called Summer Falls? A little eccentric maybe?" Ethan looked over at the man who was still looking ahead. "Yeah, didn't think so. Probably can't understand a word I'm saying either," he mumbled, turning his head back toward the street. *Now what?*

There was a strange feeling about this man. Not threatening, but odd like he was out of place or didn't belong there. A minute or so of silence went by as they both sat bereft, gazing blankly at the blur of moving traffic. Suddenly, the man spoke. "What are you searching for?" he boldly asked, maintaining his apathetic demeanor.

Startled, Ethan turned and looked at him. "I'm...not sure what you mean."

"You're here because you're searching for something. What are you searching for?"

Ethan was caught off-guard and stammered trying to think what the man was really asking. Only one answer came to mind... "The truth."

The man smiled, reached into his pocket and pulled out a small piece of tan folded parchment and handed it to Ethan. Ethan took it, then looked up at the man who was now looking at him. The man's eyes were crystal clear blue and sharp. There was no disparity or sadness behind them. Instead, they projected strength and power in radiating clarity.

"What is this?" Ethan asked respectfully.

"A stone for your path," the man said before he stood and offered his hand. Ethan looked at it, took it and stood. "When you seek, you shall find. Journey well."

The man then let go of Ethan's hand and stepped onto the sidewalk to disappear into the crowd of moving people. Ethan watched until he could no longer distinguish the man from the others, then unfolded the parchment to see what it was. There was writing on it, but it was nothing he recognized. Puzzled, he looked around, then folded the parchment back in half and slipped it into a pocket where he held on to it while making his way back to the hotel.

It was time to tell Alex everything. He knew deep down past the Laura Croft personality that she was honestly sincere about trying to discover the truth just as he was. And if you really thought about it, she seemed to be about the best kind of friend a person could ask for. It was just that if any of these bizarre visions were to become public knowledge, any professional credibility he might otherwise be able to retain would likely dissolve into oblivion.

Ethan knocked softly on Alex's door. She opened it.
"Hi. Mind if I come in?"

"No, of course not. I was just reading some stuff I picked up in the gift shop. Here, sit down," she said as she motioned to a chair at a small table next to the sofa. She cleared off a couple of magazines and her purse and put them on the bed as Ethan sat down. He stared at the table in deep thought, trying to organize the many things that needed to be said.

"I got some drinks from downstairs. One might be a strawberry banana something."

"Might be?" Ethan said as he looked up at her.

"Can't read Russian, remember? But I'm pretty sure it's bananas and strawberries on the front. Haven't tried one yet. Wanna be a guinea pig?"

"Sure, why not," Ethan replied solemnly. Alex took one of the drinks from the small refrigerator and handed it to him. "Thanks."

"You're welcome." He shook the bottle, unscrewed the lid and took a drink. After sitting down, Alex put her elbow on the table and rested her chin in her hand She appeared somewhat tired. "Quite a day, wouldn't you say?"

"Definitely," he replied as he took another drink and held the bottle out in front of him to examine it. "Not bad," he said nodding.

"Good. The Professor says 'hello.'" Ethan noticed the global sitting on the nightstand next to the bed and wondered what all she may have told him. Casually she turned to see what he was looking at, then looked back at him with her eyes. He didn't say anything, and didn't have to.

She walked over to the nightstand, picked up the global, removed the back cover, popped out the battery and set the pieces down spread out so Ethan could clearly see it was inoperative. Then she came back and sat down.

"What did you tell him?"

"That we checked the place out and it was interesting. He didn't ask anything more, I didn't tell him anything else."

Ethan let out a sigh. "Thank you." Alex leaned toward him and smiled.

"I told you, you can trust me."

"Yeah, I know. It's just that things started out strange and now they're just…off the scale." Alex looked down and started playing with her fingernails. Ethan could tell she wanted to ask what was going on and was trying hard to be patient—giving *him* the opportunity to share what he thought was important.

He took another drink, swallowed and cleared his throat. "There are things I've kept secret for good reason. Not only for personal reasons but also because some of it's classified and I believe the people I used to work for may have in the past employed, shall we say, extreme measures to keep them that way. Do you understand what this means? If I tell you what I know then *you* could be at risk as well. That's one reason why I'm so leery of your professor friend. We *cannot* risk taking any unnecessary chances.

"I never *ever* told Rachel about our projects. She knew where I was working and knew the work was classified. That was it. The problem is, I think what's happening now is somehow related to one of those projects. In fairness to you though, you need to understand the risks. This whole thing is just getting stranger and I don't want anything to happen to you."

"I can appreciate your reservations, but I'm a big girl, Ethan, and coming here *was* my idea. So don't worry, I'll be fine."

"Are you sure? You can still say no."

"Do you *really* want me to say that after we've come this far?"

He let out a sigh and looked down at the table. "We tell the Professor *only* what's absolutely necessary, and *only* if I approve it. Okay?"

"That's fair."

Ethan took another drink, cleared his throat and started. "The lab I used to work at was run by a private organization. This was the kind of facility where even branches of the Government would bring their projects because they didn't want their own people to know what was going on. It was sometimes jokingly referred to as Area-51 East.

"My team worked in a special group called DED, or Dense Energy Development. Our work was for various contract customers—mostly government stuff, but not always ours. My team specialized in atomic bonding and conversion, primarily working with exotic elements to form stable self-sustaining power sources.

"The last project we contracted was Class-5, which meant only our team of four was even briefed and allowed to work on it. We seldom knew who our customers actually were and it didn't really matter anyway as far as the work itself was concerned. This time though, I would have liked to have known.

"We were to break down an unknown element and isolate its matrix. The procedure was common, but the sample was like nothing we had ever seen before. It was a crystalline-like compound that resembled grains of salt or sugar and had a unique energy signature we couldn't identify.

"The sample was broken down to a point where we should have been able to isolate and identify its atomic structure. The bizarre thing is, it didn't seem to have one. Even at what would have been classified as the subatomic level, where we can identify individual molecular particles, it still appeared to be a dense mass of some kind. As far as I'm aware, this has never been seen before in the constraints of our known sciences.

"You see, every natural element can be broken down to its elementary particles. Everything in our universe is made up of these particles in their different organizational states that form all matter as we know it. *This* sample exhibited characteristics that we could only speculate might be a massive matrix comprised of a yet unknown elemental particle or particles. We named the sample Element Zero until we could figure out something more definitive.

"This is one of those discoveries that would have resonated throughout the scientific world and facilitated intense study at all levels of theory unparalleled in modern science. The problem was, we couldn't share what we had found with anyone—not even other scientists. The biggest discovery of our careers and it was part of a secret project that would remain secret. You can't *even* imagine what it was like knowing what we knew and having to keep it to ourselves. We thought about trying to find out where the sample came from originally, but no one wanted to risk the consequences.

"We kept working on it, using the standard array of bombardment and acceleration techniques to try to initiate a change or reaction of some kind. It almost seemed inert, which we knew wasn't possible because of its energy signature.

"Then we decided to try a highly destructive test using an instrument called the Henry Wave Accelerator, or HWA. It was built by one of the teams in our organization and produces a very high-power, short burst of cascading parasitic energy oscillations that will literally vibrate atoms apart. This accelerator amplifies the parasitic and harmonic interactions in a self-perpetuation that theoretically produces strong harmonic wavelengths smaller than we're physically capable of measuring."

Ethan realized Alex's eyes were glazing over. "Sorry, I'll try to get to the point. So when we used the HWA, the atoms would sometimes reorganize, but usually just broke apart becoming unstable. However, there were some instances when a certain number of the resulting subatomic particles couldn't be accounted for afterward. Their changed state wasn't detectable by any visible reaction. So it was theorized that they might be breaking down into the even smaller particles that we think could make up the elementary particles themselves. We called this vanishing particle phenomenon the Henry Effect. The problem is, since no one has actually documented or even detected these smaller particles, it's still just a theory.

"If you really think about it, all matter is theoretically dividable down to smaller portions and those portions dividable again and so on until the only limitation we encounter is our ability to continue to physically divide and measure the results. One researcher even posits that the Henry Effect could be the particles changing dimensional states by shifting into what's theorized as sub-space. That's probably similar to what the TDE or Theoretical Dimensional Energy was they talked about in the documentary from the journal. I suppose anything is possible.

"My focus is in the specific sciences where I don't have to be concerned so much with conjecture and speculation. I have to admit though that even I was interested in trying to figure out what Element Zero actually was. The most likely theory, in my opinion, was that we could be looking at a large stable matrix of sub-elemental material. At any rate, we were hoping a test with the HWA might give us some kind of definable reaction we could document and work with. It was one of our last available standard tests before we needed to start looking at options we hadn't thought up yet. Are you following all this?"

"For the most part…I think."

"Good. There were some other projects going on while the HWA was being readied for the test on the sample scheduled for the following day. I was in the control room working on setting up some test parameters. That's when it happened."

Ethan stopped as images of the events he was about to relate began to form in his mind. "I was sitting at one of the consoles going over some notes. I distinctly remember looking at the pad when this really weird feeling came over me—like what happened just before the journal showed up. Then the notepad was gone. It was just gone and the mechanical pencil I was holding in my hand had disappeared. It was really confusing and when I looked up, the whole test area was different. There was equipment and people in the room that weren't there the moment before. Then everything became double exposed, like looking at two overlapping images. They began to distort and fade, then reappear at random.

"I became dizzy and nauseous as the images just kept shifting and changing. I saw things and events that I'm pretty sure had already happened years ago. Then there would be equipment and people I didn't recognize at all. At one point I think I even saw construction workers in the room—possibly when the place was first being built.

"The clocks on the wall and their times kept changing. Then the clocks were gone—then back again. My head was spinning and it was all I could do to keep from falling out of the chair. Then I heard a loud sizzling sound and saw a brilliant white-green flash, then nothing—absolute nothing. It was pitch black. I couldn't see anything, feel anything, sense anything. That moment was the most terrified I think I'd ever been in my life, although what happened at the site today gave it a good run for its money."

Ethan took a deep breath and another drink. "Then I felt a hand on my shoulder and everything came back. It was one of the guys on my team. I remember him asking me if I was all right, then running down the hall to the bathroom where I swear I threw up everything from the past week. It felt like everything inside was being twisted back and forth and sometimes my vision would distort and blur. They wanted me to go to the hospital, but I convinced them to just call Rachel instead. She picked me up at the outer gate and drove me home. I stayed in bed the rest of the day and that next morning.

"The accelerator test went on as scheduled and just before noon, while lying there dead to the world, I was suddenly fine. I felt fine again. The queasiness went away and my vision came back, just like that. I waited for about an hour then Rachel drove me back to the lab because I was anxious to find out what happened with the test.

"When I got to the gate there were two security vehicles blocking the entrance and several military guards. The lab itself was about a half mile past the gate and a few hundred feet below ground next to the administration building. I asked one of the guards what was going on. They just told me no one was being allowed in.

"The gate officer knew me and told me there had been some kind of explosion at the lab and everyone was going home after a briefing. He didn't know anything more and nobody else was even available to confirm anything. I tried to make some calls into the facility and hung around for a while, but finally Rachel and I just went back home.

"That night I called two of the other guys at their houses. I was told they hadn't come home yet, which didn't sound right. Later that day I received a call from one of the administrators. They knew I wasn't there when the accident occurred and just told me not to talk to anyone and that someone would contact me later. The next day I get a call that someone would be coming out to the house. That was my first clue that something really strange was going on because they would never send someone to your home otherwise.

"The Director himself shows up later with two 'associates.' Luckily, Rachel and Allison where both gone somewhere. I had only met this Director a couple times before and he *seemed* decent enough, but to have him in the house was weird to say the least. The two guys with him looked like bodyguards. One of them stood behind the Director and the other behind me the whole time. Our very comfortable home did *not* feel all that comfortable while they were there.

"The Director told me there had been an accident and the lab had been destroyed. But there was something in the way he said it that made me wonder if there might be more to it than that. He didn't volunteer anything else and I got the distinct impression I shouldn't ask. What was left of the facility was apparently gutted and the hole filled in. The entire operation was shut down along with all current and future projects. That meant that the last moments of my illustrious career there were spent puking in a toilet. Glorious, don't you think?"

"You could be dead," Alex offered.

"Yeah, there is that I suppose. So anyway, that was it. The worst part was when he told me that no one in the lower facility had survived. That meant I was the only one still alive who had worked at the lab. I was in shock. Twenty-two people were killed in the lower facility and four in the upper building.

"The really strange thing though is later I found out that some of the people from the upper facility were found on the ground between the two buildings along with glass and debris. You see, that doesn't make any sense. An explosion in the lab, or the lower facility should have forced objects in the upper building away from the blast, not toward it. You see what I'm saying? It's backwards. Instead of the debris moving away from the explosion, it was moving toward it. I think that explosion was something else.

"Do you remember the descriptions of what happened in the area of the so-called Asian Apocalypse immediately after it occurred? What happened to the air outside the event area?"

Alex thought for a minute. "It was all sucked into the middle."

"Exactly. If all or most of the air is suddenly removed from a localized area at a rapid enough rate, it would be just like a bomb going off only in reverse. Everything from outside is sucked into that area. I think what happened at the lab is the same thing. And the flash of light I saw during…whatever it was I experienced the day before the explosion looked *exactly* like the thing from the journal. I've never seen anything like it any place else. Plus, there were no reports of anyone hearing an explosion. Now can you see why I didn't want to say anything?"

"Yeah, I guess I can. What happened with the men at your house?"

"The Director said he was in a unique situation and wanted to give me a chance, then he slid this piece of paper in front of me. Basically it was a confidentiality agreement, but not like one I'd ever seen before and not even remotely similar to the one I signed when I started working there. This one was short and just stated that I had to keep confidential all information related to the lab and the projects. In addition though, I was restricted from using *any* of the knowledge gained from working there, for any future purposes. In effect, I was no longer allowed to work in the scientific field I had been in for the past twenty years. It was ludicrous. Nobody does that.

"Then he slides another paper over to me and says that if I sign the agreement, a certain sum of money would be placed in a certain bank account in my name—'to keep me and my family comfortable' was how I think he put it. It was a lot of money with a few more zeros than I was used to seeing. The scary thing that didn't really sink-in until later was the fact that he didn't give me any other options. I don't think there were any, if you know what I mean. So I signed the thing and tried to forget I ever had a career.

"It was one of the only times I can remember not being entirely truthful with Rachel. I told her the company had decided to shut down and the money was a severance—I just never said how much. She was a little upset that I hadn't told her what was going on until it was over. As always, she forgave me. Most of the money went into investments and as time went on, the impression was that I had become some sort of closet financial genius. I never said anything to the contrary.

"About six months after that, I couldn't help but start wondering what really happened at the lab. It wasn't coincidence we were working on this unidentifiable sample and the accident occurs the same day as the Wave Accelerator test. But I was concerned what might happen to me or Rachel or Allison if someone found out I was asking questions. I also thought it was strange that no one asked *me* any questions. It was like they had already concluded what had happened and just wanted it all to be forgotten.

"It wasn't long afterward when Rachel noticed an obituary for a brother of one of the scientists I used to work with. Apparently he was killed in an auto accident. We went to the parent's home after the service and when the mother found out I used to work at the lab with her son, she pulled me into the kitchen and told me she didn't think his death was an accident.

"The brother had been suspicious of the circumstances surrounding the death and started asking a lot of questions. Officially, the police report stated that the son had been drinking and ran his vehicle off the road and down an embankment into a lake where he drowned. But a discredited witness thought she saw a large, dark colored vehicle run the guy off the road. His mother said he hardly ever drank either.

"I think someone shut him up, permanently. That was pretty sobering and it scared the curiosity right out of me so that was it, I was done. Rachel and I planned our future, we moved to the new house and then two years later, I lost them anyway."

Alex was afraid to ask the question that had come to mind, but she couldn't help herself. "You don't suppose…"

Ethan knew what she was thinking. "That their accident wasn't an accident? No, I don't think so. That stupid kid was just a stupid kid. Besides, I hadn't said anything to anyone yet so there would have been no motive."

Ethan calmly took another drink and set the container down and looked at Alex. She appeared a little overwhelmed with all the information. He continued anyway. "In the radar facility I had a similar experience to the first one at the lab. It was a lot clearer and more intense this time though. I saw equipment on the floor in the middle of the big room. I think at least one of the pieces was another version of our Wave Accelerator. There were several men there and I think one of them was counting; acht, sieben…"

"Sounds German," Alex offered.

"I think I was watching the triggering point of the event described in the journal. The accelerator fired, then nothingness.

Just as I had seen before—absolutely nothing." Ethan stared at the almost empty bottle. "I think that what supposedly causes this 'Asian Apocalypse' is that same element from the lab." There was silence while he pondered and stared. "Well anyway..." He then grabbed the bottle, leaned back in the chair, took a last drink, set it back on the table and folded his arms. "That's good stuff. So...what do you think now?"

Alex sat quietly, then responded, "Wow." Ethan waited for more, but Alex just sat there staring at nothing as her mind raced.

"Yeah. At one point I think I saw Sara standing in the corner of the room too. You know, Sara from the journal?" he added, shaking his head and chuckling to himself.

So was she going to be polite about it? Or just tell him bluntly that his geese had all gone south for a long winter? He waited, then grabbed the bottle off the table and held it.

"*It's you,*" Alex said before turning to look at him.

"What's me?"

"*You* are the key to this whole thing. It's all about *you,*" she said enthusiastically while beaming a huge smile.

His sarcastic grin quickly melted. "What do you mean by that exactly?" he said nervously.

"Think about it. You're the only one who worked on that project at your lab and survived that explosion because of a vision, or whatever it was, the day before it happened, right? Then you have another vision at the very place where this other explosion is supposed to occur. We come here and go to that site because of a journal that this girl Sara sent to *you,* and you think you saw her there. *You're* it. *You're* the focal point of this whole thing," she continued as she pointed her finger at him, then stood and started pacing.

"You actually believe I've been...somehow singled out in all this?"

Alex ignored him and kept pacing. "We need to find out who brought that sample to your lab," she suggested eagerly.

Ethan slowly leaned forward, set the empty bottle back on the table and put his hands over his face. "Did you not hear the part about what happened to the guy who was asking too many questions? I am *not* Indiana Jones," he said in a muffled voice between his palms.

Alex sat back down moved the empty bottle so she could look at him. "Who's Indiana Jones?" He moved a couple fingers and looked at her with one eye. She was serious. He covered his face again and shook his head as she continued. "Look, I admit there are a lot of *really* bizarre things going on here, but we still need more answers. *Nothing* has really changed."

Ethan lowered his hands and leaned back in the chair. "Speaking of bizarre..." He removed the folded parchment from his pocket and set it on the table in front of her.

"What is it?"

"You tell me."

She unfolded it and studied the writing. "Looks like hieroglyphics or something. It isn't Russian, I don't think. Where did it come from?"

Ethan paused then let out a long sigh. "A guy sitting on a curb gave it to me."

"Are you serious? Who was he?"

"I have absolutely no idea. He seemed to know who I was though."

"Well that's really—"

"Of course it is," he interrupted. "What isn't?"

"We're going to need some help with this."

"Let me guess, *the Professor?*"

"You know, he's not such a bad guy and does have a lot of resources. I'll bet he could tell us what this says."

"Well then let's just hope it doesn't say anything that can get us in trouble. Put that thing back together and let's give him a call." Alex reassembled the global, turned it on then dialed. "Just tell him we're sending a picture with some writing on it. Don't tell him where it came from, okay?"

"Alright," she replied.

While waiting for the Professor to answer, Ethan walked to the dresser and set the parchment under a lamp. The Professor answered and spoke with Alex briefly, then she handed the global to Ethan. He took a picture of the parchment, sent it and handed the unit back to Alex. She then acknowledged the Professor's receipt of the picture and disconnected.

"What did he say?"

"He said he thought it was a version of old Arabic and would get right on it. He'll call back when he has something."

"Arabic...Arabic... That isn't common around here, is it?"

"I don't know. Not one of my areas of expertise."

"I don't think it is."

"You know, today's been pretty...umm..." Alex was searching for a tactful description, "...informative. Why don't we take a break and just go enjoy the rest of tonight, do something fun. Go see some sites, maybe find a nice place for dinner."

Why not. It didn't sound bad, all things considered. "Sure, we could do that. But I really thought you might want to keep your distance after all this. Have me committed, maybe."

"It's way out there, I'll admit. But you haven't lied have you?"

"No."

"Had any inclinations to use Maxwell's silver hammer?"

"Don't think so."

"Then I'm probably safe. How about I come by in about an hour?"

When he opened the door, the sight of the woman standing there briefly derailed his train of thought. She was wearing a cream colored knit mid-length dress with matching shoes and long jacket. Modest gold earrings peeked out from behind beautiful flowing dark hair and a thin, long gold necklace adorned her neck. She looked elegant. Realizing he was staring, he quickly tried to recover. "Uh, am I underdressed?"

"No, you look fine. I'm not *overdressed* am I?" she asked as she looked down at her dress and shoes. "It's the only nice thing I have with me."

"No, you look great."

As they walked through the lobby, Alex stopped at the front desk to ask the clerk where a good restaurant might be located within walking distance. Alex really was pretty. Her typically conservative attire didn't usually accentuate her womanly attributes. Maybe she did that on purpose. He couldn't help but watch her walk as she came toward him—although he did try to be discreet about it. He felt compelled to let her know how nice she really looked, but the chains of guilt rattled at the idea. It could tear those lines between friendship and other feelings.

"He says there's a nice café type restaurant down the street about a half kilometer on the other side not far past a square with a fountain. He also said there's a cultural center near there that might have some interesting things to see. What do you think?"

"Sounds good."

The fountain was still a popular attraction at the square, although most of the younger children and older gentleman had retired to other venues. The square was now inhabited by a different group of people. There were small crowds of young men and women talking and laughing while another group was gathered around two men; one playing a Balalaika and the other a typical guitar.

Families were crossing the square heading to their various places of interest as Ethan and Alex headed toward the restaurant. The overhead lights that illuminated the darkness created an air of intimacy that made Ethan feel just a little uncomfortable. Alex seemed right at home, enjoying the romantic mood with its young people and their joyous enthusiasm. She had a happy nature about her, always looking for the good in people and wanting to explore and discover. Much like someone else he used to know.

The restaurant was pleasant and busy with only a few open tables. Their table was close to a window near the front, which allowed for a good view outside. It wasn't a high-end restaurant by any means, but nice nevertheless.

"So how's your steak?" Alex asked before taking a drink.

"Pretty good. Looks like you're really enjoying your...whatever that is."

"It's delicious," she said taking another mouthful. Ethan was a little surprised at the ferocity of her appetite. He watched her eat for a moment then inconspicuously shook his head and took another modest bite of his salad. "So Ethan, how did you and Rachel first meet?"

"It was at a restaurant, kind of like this one. She was on a date. I was too, actually."

"You were on a date with someone else?"

"Yeah, as a matter of fact I was. As I remember it, the girl I was with was nice, but we weren't exactly hitting it off. She was having more fun talking to the other people we were with. Then I saw Rachel. She was gorgeous."

"That she was," Alex added supportingly.

"She was sitting with her date and some friends a few tables away. I remember she looked over at me and smiled in a passing glance. After that I knew I had to meet her. It took me awhile to find out who she was. After I got her name I sort of arranged a meeting through the real estate company she was working for."

"I remember her telling me that," Alex commented.

"She was doing pretty well at the time, as I recall. It was a little awkward when she found out I was just interested in *her* and not in what she was selling. She'd been dating this other guy and was pretty interested in him, so I was surprised when she called me a few weeks later. Seemed her boyfriend wasn't meeting her expectations and I guess she must have forgiven me for my misguided meeting arrangement."

"She thought it was sweet," Alex added. "I told her I thought you were probably a stalker. She was impressed that you went to that much trouble just to meet her."

"You told her you thought I was a stalker? Thanks a lot. Had you known her long?"

"Not really. We became roommates after the Professor moved. She moved out about a year and a half after that. We kept in touch."

Ethan set his silverware down. "So you already knew how we met."

"Only the last part."

"And you really thought I was a stalker?"

"Hey, I just called 'em as I saw 'em," she said shrugging her shoulders.

"Well, now you know how perfectly normal I turned out to be," Ethan said as he rolled his eyes and took a drink.

"I was at your wedding you know. I met you there. Do you remember?"

"That was some time ago and...kind of a blur," Ethan stammered. "Sorry."

"I suppose I am somewhat forgettable. So, she told me one time her parents weren't really happy about her marrying someone outside of their faith. Did that ever bother you?"

"A little. Her parents were always 'polite' and they supported Rachel and told her it was her decision. You could tell they weren't warm to the idea though. I always felt awkward around them and I think they would talk about certain *things* just to antagonize me. She married me anyway though, didn't she?" Ethan picked up his silverware and started eating again.

"Yes, she did," Alex responded in a slightly disagreeable tone. Ethan wasn't listening that closely and didn't catch the intonation. "Did that make it difficult when she would go to church?"

"A little. I went a few times. It seemed kind of strange, you know? It just wasn't for me. So why all the questions?"

Alex let out a deep sigh and took a drink of her water. "She'd send me mail once in while to share her thoughts, concerns. You know, girl stuff."

"Girl stuff huh?"

"Eighteen years is a long time to be friends. Sometimes it's nice to talk to someone else besides your parents."

"Or your husband?"

"I suppose...sometimes," Alex responded sheepishly while poking at her food. Ethan could tell she had inadvertently brought up something that was more than just a passing thought. He didn't want to get too involved in this kind of discussion and just kept nibbling at his dinner. Then she started again. "I joined her church after the divorce."

"You mean Rachel's church?" Ethan asked surprised.

"It made a lot of sense to me—answered a lot of questions."

He shook his head in disbelief. "What made you decide to do a silly thing like that?"

"Your wife." Ethan stopped chewing momentarily, then started again without looking up. Alex continued. "I was pretty lost after my marriage ended. I started thinking about what I was going to do, what life really meant to me. My brother helped me quite a bit but Rachel was the one who seemed to really have it all together. She understood what life was about. It was only a few months before the accident. I called her and she was just so nice and gave me the real direction I needed."

"She did seem to be good at helping people," Ethan remarked quietly.

"Yeah, she really was. So how come *you* never listened to her?"

Ethan scrunched his brow at the biting question. "Now what's that supposed to mean?"

"Well, I don't want to get *too* personal. I just don't understand how you could have been with her for so long and not really understand what you had. It took a serious crisis in my life for me to figure out what I was missing. I mean, I know you miss her, I know that. But, I get the impression you never understood just how incredibly insightful she really was. You never really appreciated what you had."

"Are we still talking about me?" Ethan asked cautiously.

"So many incredible things are a part of your life, and you take them for granted. Even today, you thought I was just going to arbitrarily dismiss your stories as psychobabble, didn't you? The way you described it all to me was kind of like, here it is, there you go, whatever. I think you were just looking for me to give you an affirmation of your own insecurities—wanting *me* to believe you're as nuts as you think you are. Something incredible is happening to you and you keep trying to ignore it. Delusional psychosis, schizophrenia maybe? Or just plain fear."

"Is this the *fun* part of the evening or did I miss something?"

Ethan's remark made her stop and think. "You're right. I'm sorry."

"Why do you really care to understand me anyway? Does it really matter that much?"

"Do you *really* want to know?"

"Why not, since you're already in it waist-deep and most of these people probably can't understand what you're saying anyway."

Alex was calm. She pushed her plate forward and rested her arms on the edge of the table. "Rachel really loved you, but it frustrated her that you were so stubborn and that you automatically dismiss everything that isn't an absolute. Early on she believed you would eventually come around to see the truth in what she believed. Now I didn't talk with her a lot during the few years before the accident, but I got the impression you never did really try to understand her, and now I can kind of see why. You still have no real direction, no convictions. You just seem to exist with no real purpose. What you have in the moment seems to be all you have as a whole. This...*quest* we're on is one example. *You* are the center of something that is just absolutely astounding, but you can't see it, or refuse to see it, which is probably more accurate.

Do you think it's just coincidence or by total chance that you met one of your wife's old friends and now we're together thousands of miles away trying to sort out this mystery? Something wonderful is happening and you keep trying to find reasons not to believe it.

Now just speaking from a woman's point of view here, ok? It's a little hard to understand why one of the most talented, beautiful, caring and gracious people I've ever known would marry someone who may be intelligent, yes, but who can also be so incredibly indifferent as well. It's as if you purposefully limit your understanding so you won't have to live up to the expectations you might actually be capable of achieving. You're not convincing me, and I don't think you'll ever really convince yourself, even if you pretend the rest of your life." Ethan listened patiently, trying not to read too much into it.

Alex paused for a minute then caught her second wind. "It's that rigid scientific ideology isn't it? The absolutes I kept hearing about—empirical reasoning is the only valuable component to rational thought. Sound familiar? You've put a ceiling over your head so low you're always looking down. Are you going to go through the rest of your life like this? When are you going to step outside and look up and around? I'll even bet you're one of those people who believes that life, as we know it, began in a pond of magical goo somewhere. Am I right?"

"Well, can you say with all sincerity that you actually believe an all-powerful magical super-being created the universe and all of us? Come on…"

"It wasn't just him, but alright. Did you ever have a moment when you took a real heart-felt look at Rachel or Allison and wondered how they could be so perfect? Did you ever really look at their faces, see their smiles or really look into their eyes? Did you ever listen to her play and not wonder where such incredible talent honestly comes from?" Ethan wasn't going to admit it, but there had been occasions when he had done *exactly* that, and wondered those same things.

He kept silent. Alex was ready for more. She started shaking her finger at him, squinted her eyes and said, "I think we need some good-old primordial sex. What do you think?" Ethan looked up at her suspiciously.

Alex stood and moved her plate and chair from across the table to sit next to him. She took her fork and a portion of Ethan's salad and potatoes and mixed them together with some of the food on her plate. "Let's see, a little acidity…" She added some steak-sauce and stirred some more. "And how about a little sugar? We want him sweet, right?" A small packet of sugar was opened and dumped onto the mix. She stirred while quietly humming some sort of unintelligible tune. *"Voilà!"* she then declared. "Now all we need to spawn creation is…*the spark of life,*" she continued in a melodramatic fashion before reaching into her small purse to remove a stun gun.

Making sure her point was being made, she held the stun gun up close to Ethan's face and discharged it. It made long blue-white sparks and a loud repetitive snapping sound that caught the attention of everyone in the restaurant. Ethan quickly leaned back in his chair. Alex put the stun gun near her 'pool of goo' and discharged it a few times. Then she put her hand on Ethan's shoulder and gave him a big smile. "Congratulations. In a hundred million years or so you *might* have a happy, healthy baby boy."

She put the stun gun back in her bag, leaned back in her chair and smiled at him. He didn't say anything. No doubt in shock from being the unwilling participant in her impromptu performance that still had the undivided attention of most of the restaurant patrons. She leaned forward and looked directly at him. "Now, how much sense does *that* make?"

"*You are* nuts, you know that?" Ethan said a little concerned.

"Yeah, but it's a good kind of nuts," she replied mischievously.

The waitress cautiously approached the table. "Is the meal okay?" she asked in her heavy accent.

"Just fine, thank you," Alex replied.

"Would you like some dessert?"

"*Nooo,* I think we're ready for the check," Ethan replied anxiously.

"Actually, I would like a piece of that kind of pie that lady is having over there," Alex said as she pointed to a nearby table. The waitress said its name then left to retrieve a serving. Ethan just looked at Alex and wondered, seriously, what he had gotten himself into. "It just looked good. Besides, I thought it might be interesting to try for a girl." Ethan rolled his eyes and tried to hide his sarcastic grin as he rested his head against his thumb and forefinger to look away. Alex just smiled. He had taken it all pretty well she thought.

On the way back to the hotel, Alex didn't revisit the conversations from the restaurant. She figured Ethan had been tortured enough for one day. He didn't say anything at all, not wanting to tempt another appearance by Mrs. Hyde. Oddly enough, he wasn't really upset either. Maybe it was because he was too confused to focus or maybe thoughts of his family had once again filled his mind. Whatever it was, at least they weren't engaged in more sharp dialogue.

"I was a little hard on you, wasn't I?" Alex said as they strolled along the sidewalk.

"Oh, I probably deserved it," Ethan responded quietly.

"Sometimes I guess I just go a little overboard."

"Ya think?" Ethan said in a humorous, and slightly sarcastic tone.

"Fine, okay. I guess maybe I get kind of passionate about some things." Ethan kept quiet. "Hey, there's nothing wrong with being passionate," she added, in response to his silence.

"No, no, I agree. As long as no one gets hurt."

They both walked quietly for a time. Alex started to giggle and Ethan started to giggle as well. "Did you see that old lady with the red hair? I'll bet they find a brick on her chair when she leaves," Alex remarked.

"I don't think it was just her. That whole table was scoping an exit strategy." Then Ethan started to laugh out loud. "I'm surprised the waitress was as calm as she was. That was quite a show you put on." They both laughed some more.

"You know Alex, I have to admit, you seem to be doing quite well considering all you've been through. You're a very confident person and you should be proud of that."

"Funny. I thought you probably found me more annoying than anything."

"Well, I guess I'm just not used to your unique personality yet. No, really. It's just pretty amazing that you seem to have dealt with it all so well."

"That's nice of you to say. I don't feel quite as healed as you may seem to think I am though."

"Could have fooled me."

"After I finally got away from Derric, it took quite a while to overcome the constant fear—partly fear of *him*, but just fear. I was afraid of everything. I know you're not sure about Professor Greenhagen but he really did take me in like a daughter and gave me hope and a safe place to live and work and I'll always be grateful to him. Even with that though, I had no real personal anchor.

"I felt lost and that's when I kind of started asking questions and looking for answers. Rachel always seemed strong and sure of herself. After a while I finally decided I had to rise above the fear and self doubt and go forward. It was either that or self-destruct. I feel very fortunate to have good friends because it all could have turned out so different.

"I haven't told anyone else this, but there are times when I'm walking out to my car or going into my house that I have this horrible flash of my ex-husband lunging at me with a knife. I can see the hatred in his face. Sometimes it's just so clear that it really, really scares me. I'll walk toward a dark room and the anxiety becomes so bad that I can't even go in to turn on the lights without getting a flashlight first to see what's there. I know what panic and fear feel like so you're not the only one with a few 'issues.'"

"But if you really feel like that how come you still live alone and don't have a roommate or something?" Ethan asked.

"I don't think it would be fair to make someone else live with my emotional baggage."

"Can't say that doesn't sound familiar."

"I don't know, maybe he's not really a threat at all and I'm just paranoid. In a screwed up sort of way, I'd like to think I was important enough to him that he still thinks about me once in a while. The more likely reality is that he's long since forgotten that I ever existed, which in my case would be for the best anyway." Ethan instinctively put his hand on her shoulder to comfort her. "No, no, don't feel sorry for me. I'm fine, really." He put his hand back in his pocket. "We are quite a pair though, aren't we?" she said looking over at him and smiling.

"That we are," he replied.

After returning to the hotel, Ethan had only sat down for a few minutes when there was a knock at his door. It was Alex and she had her global. "The Professor just called. He said your writing was old Ottoman Turkish Script—hasn't been used since around nineteen thirty. He's sending text of the full message and said it was a person's name and a location in Southern Turkey. It's a farming area of some sort and a man matching the name on the parchment does have an address there. Does this make any sense to you?"

"Not in the slightest."

"Well then, what do you want to do?"

What else could he do? They were here to find answers and this was just one more question. "Turkey huh?" Alex began to smile.

CHAPTER TEN

River of Shadows

BEDRI WAS STANDING IN front of the passenger side back door of the Mercedes Traveler as the old twin-engine plane rolled to a stop near the end of the runway. Ethan grimaced and ducked his head to his shoulder as he exited behind the idling engines kicking up dirt from the runway. Alex followed behind him and stood waiting for their luggage to be unloaded. Bedri stepped forward and extended his hand. "You must be Alex!" he said with a heavy accent.

"I am!" she shouted.

"And you must be Ethan!"

"That's right!"

"Welcome to Turkey! I am Bedri!" he shouted over the engine noise. He grabbed the suitcase being handed to Alex and started toward the Traveler. "I trust you had a good flight?"

"Yes, we did," Alex replied as Ethan took his own suitcase and bag. Bedri walked to the back of the Traveler, opened the door, set Alex's luggage inside then headed to the front to open the door for her.

"Thank you," she said before he closed her door. Ethan set his luggage in back and closed the tailgate while Bedri ran around to the driver side to climb in. Alex watched as three men unloaded several boxes of supplies then closed the door on the plane. Ethan was just climbing in and had barely closed his door when the plane's engines throttled up and it turned, spewing a huge cloud of dust behind it that partially engulfed the vehicle. "He's in a hurry," Alex noted.

"Yes-yes, time is money," Bedri replied as he entered a couple commands on the navigation unit. "The man you wish to speak to, he lives near a cotton farm about twenty-five minutes from here. Do you wish to go straight there?"

"Yes, that would be fine," Alex replied. He put the vehicle in gear and drove to the end of the small dirt access road, then turned onto a wider road and headed west.

"Isn't Alex a man's name? It's a good thing you were not a man. I would not have been able to know which one of you was which. I figure since you are a woman, it would not be likely you would be called Ethan unless that is a woman's name also. Is it a woman's name also?"

"Um…no, not that I'm aware of," Alex replied as she glanced at Ethan in the back seat.

"That is good. That would be very confusing."

"Yeah, I guess it could be. How do you know Professor Greenhagen?"

"Oh I do not know the man. I was told to pick you up and take you to the farm and to the hotel. That is all."

It was quiet in the Traveler the rest of the way until the navigation unit made an indication to turn right onto a side road. "The people here keep to themselves. I don't know how friendly they will be," Bedri informed them as they continued up the narrow road paralleled by huge open fields of tall bushy plants.

"So we should keep an eye out for the ones with pitch forks?" Ethan mused.

"No, guns," Bedri corrected. Ethan's countenance quickly sobered. Bedri then pointed to a small group of houses and outbuildings in the distance surrounded by immense fields. "It is probably over there." Ethan leaned forward to see where he was pointing.

There were several buildings that looked like shops for machinery and two homes with two others farther away. You could feel the mix of anticipation and anxiety growing as they stopped at the first house. "I'll see if this is it," Bedri said as he jumped out. They watched him walk to the house where he knocked on the old wood door. It opened slightly and an older woman cautiously looked through the slit. The two spoke briefly then the woman stepped out onto the small landing and pointed farther down the road. Bedri thanked her and came back to the vehicle.

"She says he lives at the end of the road."

"Good." Alex replied.

She turned to look at Ethan who was visibly nervous. "Hey, no sweat," Alex joked, trying to lighten his mood.

"Yes-yes, no sweat," Bedri added. It didn't help.

Time seemed to slow as the thousands of rows of plants streamed by in an endless, hypnotic blur. The landscape was vast and full of simple, yet appealing detail. Tan brush-speckled bluffs stood low above the sprawling fields of green while distant mountains peeked through variations in the terrain. The land behind them seemed to disappear into clouds at the edge of the horizon.

They were approaching the dwelling. Ethan studied the small, attractive home intently as they pulled up in front and stopped. The scene was oddly normal, even anticlimactic, lacking the sinister pitch-fork wielding nomadic presence he had preconceived.

Without hesitation, Bedri jumped out and started walking toward the house. Ethan and Alex exited the Traveler more slowly. They both stood to the side of the passenger front fender while Bedri confidently walked up to the door and knocked.

"This is really gnawing at you, isn't it?" Alex said as she looked into Ethan's nervous face.

"I'm not a big fan of gun-wielding farmers," he replied as Bedri waited for someone to answer.

"You know he was just kidding. I think."

Bedri knocked on the door again. "Merhaba!" he shouted, then began walking toward one of the barns.

"Well this doesn't look very promising," Ethan remarked. He put his hand above his eyes to shield them from the sun and looked around. Bedri was by the barn, still shouting. "Maybe *that's* him," Ethan then commented. Alex turned to see where he was looking. A pickup was coming toward them about a half mile away at the end of one of the large fields. Bedri noticed it as well and they all watched it approach ahead of a low cloud of trailing dust. Finally, it pulled up to the side of the barn and stopped. The dust cloud thinned and floated through the yard.

The man driving the pickup eyed them all suspiciously through his open window. Slowly he opened the door and climbed out, followed by a young boy and girl. A very old man started climbing out on the other side.

"Merhaba," Bedri said to the younger man, waving in a friendly gesture. They began to converse but were some distance away. All that could be distinguished in the quiet foreign dialogue was the word 'Americans.' The older man had a walking-stick and used it to make his way slowly toward the house. The children both stood by the younger man who appeared to be their father.

The younger man nodded a few times then looked at Ethan and Alex as Bedri continued to explain what they were doing there. Then Bedri motioned for them. The man bent down to his children and told them something before they ran to the house.

"This is Hazzar Yenen," Bedri announced as Ethan and Alex smiled politely. He had a friendly and full face that was dusty and tan from work.

"Hello. I'm Alex Fullerman and this is Ethan Grey."

"Hello," Hazzar said as he tried to wipe the dust off his hand before shaking theirs. "To what do I owe a visit of travelers from such a distant land?" His English was surprisingly articulate. No one said anything as Hazzar waited for a reply. Ethan thought Alex was going to do the talking and Alex was waiting for Ethan.

She nudged him encouragingly. "It's *your* message."

"Well…we have a bit of a mystery on our hands. While visiting Kazakhstan, a man in Balkhash gave this to me." He pulled out the folded parchment and handed it to Hazzar. Hazzar opened it carefully.

"The old language," he said surprised. "Who was this man who gave it to you?"

Ethan looked over at Alex briefly. "That's part of the mystery. We don't know who he was and this was all he gave me. We were hoping it might mean something to you."

Hazzar studied the parchment carefully, then shook his head. "I don't know why someone would write my name and the name of this valley in the old language." He paused. "Unless this is about my father. Come in and I will ask him."

The inside of the house was well-kept and had the appearance of a woman's touch. Nicely framed pictures adorned papered walls and small trinkets rested in glass displays. The furniture was common and modest, but in good condition.

"May I offer you water?" Hazzar asked generally.

"That would be great, thank you," Alex replied. He left the room and everyone sat quietly and looked around. The children sat on the floor near the doorway where Hazzar had exited. They were intrigued by the strangers and studied them carefully.

"Is that you guys?" Ethan said as he pointed to one of the pictures on the wall. The children looked up at the picture and giggled. Hazzar then returned carrying several clear containers of water and passed them out.

"The water from the well is not very good. We have to buy our water to drink." He noticed the children staring at the strangers. "Go, go," he said as he motioned them to leave, which they did. "Please permit me a moment while I talk with my father."

Several minutes passed, then Hazzar returned. "My father would like to speak to you. He says he has a story he wishes to share. I respect him very much, but he is ninety-three years of age and sometimes his stories are difficult to believe."

"Well then he's in good company today, isn't he?" Ethan quipped to Alex.

"He seemed excited when I showed him the writing. I think he recognized it. Please, follow me."

Hazzar walked out of the small room and everyone stood to follow him—Alex first, then Bedri and Ethan. They walked by a small kitchen and out a back door to a patio. There was a fire-pit with backless wooden benches and a large umbrella that provided shade where the shadow from the house fell short.

Hazzar's father was sitting in a wooden chair and the children played around an old faded and rusty car partially sunken into the ground some distance away. Ethan noticed the old man was holding the parchment in his hand as he sat down across from him on the other side of the fire-pit. Hazzar sat next to his father and Bedri sat next to Alex who then moved to sit on the other side of Ethan.

"My father understands English but cannot speak it very well. I will translate." There was a long silence while Hazzar's father stared at the parchment. Then he began speaking in a somewhat raspy voice in his native language.

"I wrote this to a friend when I was sixteen years of age. My father and mother led humble lives here and we needed money so I chose to help them by traveling to Syria to work for a wealthy European man. He was digging up a lost city. We would dig and dig and dig and haul out barrels of dirt for days and days. We started finding things in the dirt—bowls and tools, bones of animals. For months we dug and took things out of the ground.

"The European man had workers who would take the things we had found and study them. They were looking for something. We found a vault made of stones. It was sealed and had no entrance. We told the men about the vault and they made a hole in the wall to go in, then sent us away for the day. I was curious and stayed away not far, hiding behind the large machines.

"The men took from the room many rolls of writings bound in hides. They were scrolls put there by people who used to live in the city. The workers took them to a tent and left them there for the night until the European man could come to see them. I wanted to know what was in the scrolls, but I knew it would never be allowed.

"That night I snuck past the sleeping workers in their tent and took two of the scrolls to hide in the old city and look at them. Much of the writing was in Hebrew, which I could read because my father had taught me well.

"The first scroll spoke of the history of people of many lands and there were pictures drawn of many things.. The second was about the people of Egypt and about a man who lived among the people. His name was Hitaat and it was said he had with him the Power of God.

"He was greatly respected of the people and had a knowledge of matters that others did not possess. He knew the order of the universe, the stars and of other worlds. He understood a great many things and possessed great powers to move the earth and cause the elements to heed his commands. He taught the people and showed them many marvelous things, but did not rule over them. Instead he lived among them and was never challenged because of his authority. He taught the people architecture and how to cut and move great stones with the ease of cutting and moving a staff of wood.

"One of his powers was known as Judgment Fire. The people feared it most of all. When a man was subjected to this power, all thoughts of the mind and character of the soul would be washed with a white flame and from it no man could hide. The sinful man would be wrought with a death transforming his body to the dust from which he came. His spirit was taken to dwell with others of its kind. The man was then no more.

"When Hitaat was nearing the end of his life, the people had become jealous of the power that he possessed and in his old age they sought to take it from him. The people had become so corrupt and wicked that the power was to be removed from their presence. It was written that the Fire was then removed from the man and secretly contained in a stone vessel filled with crystal sand. The vessel was to be hidden only to be brought forth again for the judgment of man at the Last Days. The vessel was called the Power of Souls.

"There was more, but the night was giving way and I knew I would be severely punished if I was found. I bound the writings up again and took them back to the tent to replace them from where I had taken them. The next night I had planned to take the scrolls again, but the European man came in a truck with another man. I hid behind the tent and listened as they talked in a strange language. I think the other man could read the scrolls and they stayed in the tent for many hours. I knew they were talking about the man in Egypt and the Judgment Fire and the vessel. They were excited and gathered all the scrolls and went away.

"We stayed at the old city for another season and continued to work. We never found anything more that was of value to the men. I made friends there and gave this very parchment to Tariq, a boy my age who was like my brother. I never knew what became of him.

"Many years later I was in Africa working on irrigation systems when I saw the European man again. He was traveling on a road with many trucks and he passed no farther away from me than you." The old man pointed to where Ethan was sitting. "I remember his face and I looked into his eyes. They were cold and dark. I knew this man was evil and had no goodness in him. I wanted to know what the man was doing, but was afraid. Never had a dark presence been so strong around me. It was as though the devil himself had looked into my soul. I never saw that man again—if he really was a man."

Hazzar's father stopped speaking and stared at the fire-pit. Everyone exchanged glances of curiosity, wondering what the other must be thinking. Then the old man looked up at Ethan. Ethan caught his eye and an uncomfortable feeling came over him. The old man then opened his eyes wide, held up his walking-stick and pointed it at Ethan. With authority he spoke in poor English. "*You know.*" Ethan leaned back surprised as everyone else stared at him. The old man then reared back and started to laugh showing several gaps from missing teeth.

Again he spoke in his native language and held up the parchment. "You were brought here to me because you are looking for that man." He then said something to Hazzar and Hazzar pulled a half burned stick from the fire pit and handed it to him.

On the gray colored brick by his feet, the old man drew a circle with curved lines emanating from all around it. The inside of the circle was scraped with the stick to fill it with black char, then the old man tossed the stick back into the pit with the others.

"For all my life I have wondered why I have seen such a thing. Now I know. In the shadow of evil I saw this—a Black Sun. If you follow this, you will find him."

Hazzar's father slowly stood and walked over to Ethan who also stood. The old man held out the parchment in his gnarled hand to offer it back to Ethan.

Ethan looked at it, gently cupped his hand over the old man's and said, "It belongs to you."

The old man looked into Ethan's face with hazy eyes. He smiled again, took the parchment, gripped his walking-stick and began making his way back to the house.

Everyone was quiet and just watched Hazzar's father walk slowly away until Ethan let out a sigh and walked around the fire pit to look at the drawing on the bricks.

"We had heard stories our whole lives, but this is the first time I've heard of this," Hazzar said almost apologetically as Ethan sat down to look at the drawing.

As he studied the crude picture, he suddenly found himself looking at carpet. The bricks were gone. From a leather chair he now faced a large, glass desk in front of a wall of windows in an office somewhere. It was two or three stories up, according to the view. Strangely, there was no fear with this inexplicable and sudden change of temporal venue. This was more like a dream—one that he knew wasn't real.

Something behind him seemed to be calling his attention—a dark suit jacket hanging pristinely on a hanger from an arm of a metal coat tree near the door. He got up and walked to it, his eyes drawn to a small glossy black half sphere about a quarter inch round attached to the left lapel.

It was strangely inviting as a milky blackness twisted and rolled inside it, swirling in a hypnotic dance. It felt dark and was beautiful and intoxicating. The longer he gazed into it the more it enticed and pulled him until it began to fill his whole mind. It melted and flowed in its alluring current and spun into an ever-enveloping river of desire that caressed and coaxed him to feel its power and lose himself in its insatiable hunger. Then in an instant he was back, looking at the picture on the ground.

Alex was still watching him when he looked up and caught her eyes. "You back with us?" she asked. He looked at her a little confused, then back at the ground.

"This European man my father spoke of couldn't possibly still be alive. Who do you think this man is?" Hazzar asked.

"I really have no idea," Ethan replied. The two men sat silent as they both looked at the drawing, then Ethan finally stood. "Well, I guess we should be going. Thank you for everything, and please let your father know we appreciated him talking with us."

"I will. I think he enjoyed the visit. It was quite interesting," Hazzar commented.

Alex took a picture of the drawing with the global before they all walked around the house and back to the vehicle.

"Thanks again. It was nice to meet you," Alex said to Hazzar as Bedri opened the rear door for her.

"You as well."

Hazzar's children ran out to stand by him before they all waved. Bedri then turned the Traveler around and headed up the narrow road. "That was strange, yes?" he commented, looking in the mirror.

"How long until we get to the hotel?" Ethan asked.

"About forty minutes."

"Have you heard of any of that story before?" Alex asked.

"No, but..."

"What."

"I'm not sure. We should probably discuss this later," he said, inconspicuously motioning toward Bedri. She understood.

"Thank you very much, Bedri," Alex said as he pulled her luggage from the back and carried it to a hotel cart.

"You are welcome," he responded happily. Ethan pulled his own luggage from the back, walked to the cart and set it down.

"Will there be anything else?" Bedri asked.

"I think we've got it from here," Ethan quickly responded.

"Then I wish you a good day, yes," Bedri said before heading back to his vehicle and driving away.

"Sooo I get the impression you and Bedri aren't going to be pen pals?" Alex jested. Ethan rolled his eyes.

"Not even if hell freezes over, yes-yes?" he said smiling sarcastically.

"He treated *me* well."

"That's just because you're a very attractive woman and he likes you. If you were a guy, I suspect it would have been different." Alex looked down and smiled. He had just said she was attractive—*very* attractive at that. It may have been a Freudian slip, but he still said it and she could have hung him out to dry with it. Maybe this one she'd just keep for herself.

After checking into the hotel, they went next door to an eclectic little outside eatery for lunch. Alex was still waiting for Ethan to volunteer whatever new information was hiding in that unique mind of his.

Being with him was fascinating and exciting. Sometimes it bothered her though that she always seemed to be at his mercy for details. Learning about his work at the lab and now Hazzar's father's stories, along with everything else, was like walking the side of a hill with an ever-increasing slope. It was a great view, but how long could she keep her footing?

Ethan was always completely up front about his reservations regarding the unknown, which to her, sometimes made him appear weak. She preferred to be a little less transparent and wasn't really too worried about the unknown anyway. The spiritual knowledge she understood helped her deal with that aspect of things, although being with Ethan was sure giving her sensibilities a workout.

"So what did you think about Hazzar's father?" Ethan asked.

"A pretty wild story. What do you think he meant by finding a black sun?"

"I'm not sure. I've never heard of a black sun before, but something else happened."

"When you zoned out? You were totally gone for a minute."

"I think I was seeing the office of the director for the company where I used to work."

"You mean the lab?"

"Yeah. Well no. Actually his office was in the adjacent building. I had only been in it once so the memory is pretty vague. I felt a very powerful and beautiful darkness that was addictive. I could feel the emotion, but they weren't *my* feelings, if that makes any sense. I think this black sun has something to do with the Director."

"Do you know where he is now?"

"No. After the incident with my colleague's brother I tried not to even think about thinking about it."

"What was this director's name?" Ethan looked at the table while searching his thoughts.

"Chamberlain. Yeah, Tom Chamberlain."

"Do you want me to ask Professor Greenhagen what he can find?"

"Does he really mind doing that kind of stuff?"

"He loves it. Mysteries are a huge enjoyment for him."

"So *that's* why you two get along so well." Alex just smiled and shrugged her shoulders. "Should we also see what he can find out about digs in Syria around the time Hazzar's father claims to have been there? That would have been what, about seventy-seven years ago? Let's just keep it at that for now. I think we've had enough excitement for one trip."

Several hours later she received the call as they were walking through a crowded nearby market. They quickly ducked into a side street to hear what information the Professor had to convey. Alex set her global for speakerphone.

"I found a couple of interesting things," the Professor started. "During the time period you mentioned, there were two listed archeological projects in Syria matching your description of a buried city. One was being funded by a British Museum and the other by a group originally believed to be associated with a European Preservation Consortium.

There is some controversy on this one. Seems the project was shut down after accusations of theft led to the discovery that the Consortium was actually a group of investors and not the preservation society they claimed to be."

"Any names?" Alex asked.

"None that were legitimate. This group was definitely up to something. But according to records, no one officially figured out what they were up to exactly. There are some follow-up articles—most are just speculation. Now, for this other guy... From the information you gave me, I have a Thomas K. Chamberlain, former president of Aridel Systec, died last year in a boating accident in Indonesia. That's about it. Anything else?" Ethan and Alex looked at each other.

"No, that was all," Alex responded.

"So when you get back you'll have to fill me in on your travels. It sounds like you've been busy."

"That we have. Thank you and we'll see you when we get back."

"Very good then." The connection dropped.

"He's dead. Hmm," Ethan remarked solemnly.

"Sorry," Alex offered.

"It wasn't like I knew him all that well. But still…"

The flight home was scheduled to depart late the following morning. That evening had been pleasant, although it was exhausting to navigate all the images and thoughts that were continually running through his mind like a looping video playing over and over and over. The thought of going to sleep was even a little disconcerting with all the new experiences to feed the dreams.

That night found him standing in an open desert, alone with nothing around him for as far as he could see—just lots and lots of sand. There was a ringing sound. He turned to see a single tall cactus behind him. It was ringing like a telephone. He walked up to it and it rang again. One of the giant arms was shaped like the handset of a phone, but it was covered with long thorns. There was no way to answer it.

It just kept ringing, and it was a *strange* ring. He walked around the cactus and looked at it, frustrated. *Why would someone make a phone you couldn't answer?* It kept ringing and ringing. His desert world then partially faded enough for him to realize that the incessant ringing was actually coming from the nightstand.

Reaching in the direction of the sound, he fumbled for the receiver and pulled it over to him, holding it loosely to his ear. His mind said 'hello,' his mouth said nothing. "Ethan?" *Funny, that sounded like Alex. I didn't see her here anywhere.* "Ethan!" came a shout through the receiver that snapped him out of his sandy slumber.

"Yes…what…what is it?" he replied half mumbling.

"Are you awake now?"

"Yeah…I think so."

"We need to leave." He heard what she said. It just didn't register. "Ethan, we need to leave, now."

"Why? It's like…two something."

"Professor Greenhagen just called. He said someone knows you're here."

"That doesn't make any sense. *Who* knows?"

"Something about Eve. I don't know, just get packed. We have seats on a plane leaving in about two hours. I've already called for a taxi."

"Alright," he said fumbling for the light switch, "just give me a few minutes."

"I'll be there in five." *'Click'*

Ethan had 'that look' on his face again when he opened the door. It was the same one she had already seen a few times before when something was bothering him—something more than just being awakened in the middle of the night.

"Do you need some help?" she asked.

"No. I didn't even pull anything out last night." He collected his bags and they headed for the courtyard. His silence was incriminating.

"You know, it's okay to tell me what you're thinking, or do you *prefer* to play this cat and mouse game all the time?"

"I tell you things."

"Only after I twist your arm. Like now, something's got you bothered. You don't always have to protect me you know. I'm a big girl." She was smart too, but sometimes it just didn't seem necessary to tell her everything. Like the fact that when he finally became mostly coherent, 'EVE' started to sink in. It wasn't just the biblical name for the first woman on Earth, it was an acronym for 'Eyes Everywhere.'

During the cold war, the U.S. Government began various secret programs to tap into the flow of information between the Soviet Union and Cuba. It started by simple eavesdropping of communications using local listening devices by spies or well-placed operatives with the pilfering of mail or courier based paper transport. As technology progressed, the methods were improved with the development of remote electronic listening devices and photographs from high altitude reconnaissance aircraft.

The ever-increasing perceivable threats to American freedom facilitated a rampant development of more sophisticated and invasive information gathering methods, including high-resolution satellite imagery and tracking. The proliferation of GlobalNet, paperless money and wireless devices necessitated the continual expansion of an information web that spans the globe and keeps growing. Millions of networked cameras, commerce points, industrial systems and integrated databases allow almost limitless access to our personal lives by those with the authority and knowledge to use them.

Ethan may have been paranoid, but it wasn't without merit. He knew that even the typical mobile carried by Average Joe or Jane was just another method of gathering information. There was good reason why he didn't use a mobile phone and almost never used plastic money. It was unlikely the Professor would mention EVE without good reason. It was a wake-up call that their quest for answers had not gone completely unnoticed. He was now a 'person of interest' to someone.

CHAPTER ELEVEN

Revelations

A LIMOUSINE WAS WAITING FOR them at the loading zone as they came out of the terminal. The driver took their bags and opened the trunk. It was good to be back in the States. Alex climbed in while Ethan stood for a moment and looked around. When he started to get in, he realized someone was sitting in the rear seat, and it wasn't Alex.

He paused and looked up to see an older gray-haired man with a goatee and a bit of a scowl. He hadn't seen Alex give the Professor a quick hug before sitting in a rear-facing seat across from him. Although he had never been formally introduced to the man, there was little doubt who he was. It was an awkward moment when Ethan sat down next to Alex and tried to act casual.

"Ethan Grey, I presume," the Professor said, politely extending his hand in greeting. Ethan accepted. "How was your flight?" he then asked Alex before Ethan could respond.

"It was okay. Long, but we survived."

"And did you find what you were looking for?"

"Well," Alex replied, unsure of what she should or shouldn't say, "I think Ethan is the one who should probably tell you how it went."

"Ah, so it comes back to Mr. Grey," the Professor said sporting a smug inflection. Ethan was starting to become visibly uncomfortable. "Ethan, are you good friends with Alex?"

Ethan suddenly felt like a teenager about to be grilled by his date's father. "Well, I uh—"

"No doubt Alex has told you something about our relationship," the Professor interrupted. "If so, then you know she's like a daughter to me, and I protect her like my own. Now *you*, on the other hand, I don't know from Adam. What you do on your own time is your own business. But when your business involves her, it involves me."

Alex looked at Ethan and gave him the raised eyebrow, which confused him. She seemed to be making light of a situation he saw no humor in whatsoever.

"So when I find out you're being tracked by someone deep in the mud, it gets my attention," the Professor added.

Alex sobered-up quickly. "So someone really was following us?"

"*Him*, more precisely. There's a network out there with a database full of names and information. It employs various methods of relational identification and various levels of interpretation depending on who's being watched and by whom. Yesterday afternoon I was notified that Mr. Grey here had activated someone's watch criteria and that an alert had been sent out. It was a low priority alert. Nevertheless, someone wants to know what you're up to." The Professor leaned forward. "Any idea who that might be?"

"No," Ethan responded hesitantly.

"You're sure. Maybe a former employer?" the Professor asked, squinting out the corner of his eye.

"He's dead...which you already know."

"What about someone else in the company?"

"I don't know."

"What about the people in your department. Someone else you may have worked with?"

"There's no one left. I think you know that too."

"Yes, well, it doesn't hurt to ask. No associations with any other *questionable* people since then?"

"Just you." The Professor and Ethan were staring at each other. Now Alex was becoming a little uncomfortable. Then an almost imperceptible smile came to the Professor and he leaned back in the seat.

"Once a person is put on the list they usually stay on the list until someone takes them off. *You're* still on it."

Ethan thought about the lab and wondered if someone really could still be interested in what he was doing, or maybe Chamberlain did it when they were still at Aridel. Maybe that agreement he signed carried more weight than he realized.

"Any idea at all who could have put him on the list or who the alert went to?" Alex asked.

"Not at this point. All we have is that the last node traced was in Europe. The department entity where the alert was initially set up has an authorization attached to it that requires a higher level of access that I didn't want to pursue at the time. Even then, it would probably lead to a dead-end—same with the alert destination. It would be difficult to verify exactly where it went or who received it without people asking questions."

"How was it activated? No one even knew we were there," Alex commented.

"Bedri. I knew there was a reason I didn't like that little insect," Ethan grumbled.

"No, it wasn't Bedri. I handled that arrangement personally. A low level priority is usually a print scan or credit card verification. Did you use any personal credit cards?"

"No."

"Then it was probably a print scan—a scanner in the elevator of a hotel, a phone or on a door somewhere. People are pushing buttons and opening doors all day long. You push a button with your thumb or forefinger, your print is scanned and compared and if it matches someone in the database, presto."

"And you know all this...how?" Ethan asked incredulously.

"I make it my business to know things, Mr. Grey. That's why I did a little research on you. I know where your former place of employment was, what kind of work they used to do and I know you were the only survivor of a highly suspicious explosion that closed the operation down. It was only prudent to put your name out there to see if it showed up somewhere and sure enough...

"And by the way, you're welcome for the heads-up in Turkey. So unless you're willing to tell me what's really going on, my association with this little excursion of yours is going to end, right now."

"Professor, we really didn't have any idea anything like this was going on before we left," Alex explained. "There are some things we discovered on this trip that could potentially be extremely important. But it's up to Ethan to decide what he wants to do. I'd like to discuss it with him before we do anything else."

"Don't take too long. Wheels are in motion."

"We won't," she replied.

As the limousine pulled away, Ethan watched it momentarily, then turned to Alex who was standing to the side of him looking at her townhouse.

"Hope you have some waders and shovels," he said.

She looked at him puzzled. "Why?"

"Because I think we really stepped in it." She looked down, then back to her townhouse and let out a sigh.

Inside, Ethan set his bags in the front room and sat down on the couch. Alex set her luggage by the island in the kitchen. She came back in the front room and sat in a large chair to the side of the couch. Ethan slouched down and leaned his head on the back cushion. Neither one of them said anything for several minutes.

"Does this really change anything?" Alex then said as she stared at the wall.

"It does for me." There were another few moments of silence.

"Don't you think if someone was really going to do something, they would have done it by now? I mean think about it. Your name being on this list just means someone was interested in knowing where you went. You went on a vacation. That's all."

"And trespassed on a Russian military installation. Let's not forget that little detail."

"We had keys. Besides, it was abandoned. And aberrations don't count. It was still abandoned," she added. "Seriously, *nothing* has really changed. We still need to get to the bottom of this."

"But how deep is this going to go before we decide it isn't worth the risk anymore? These people play for keeps, remember?"

"*What people?* You keep saying that. Your former boss is dead and you've kept to yourself since then so why would somebody be tracking you now? That makes no sense. I think your name was put on that list when you still worked at that lab and it was just never removed."

"Then why was the alert sent to *Europe*?" Ethan questioned.

Alex looked at him for a second, then back at the wall. "I don't know. I still don't think anything has really changed. We can't slam on the brakes every time something like this comes up. We just need to decide to go forward no matter what and figure this thing out. Come on, be a man," she said jokingly. "I'll promise to stick with you, through better or worse, sickness and health until—"

"That's not *even* funny."

"Look, we're partners, right?"

Ethan grabbed a pillow, covered his face and pushed his head back into the cushion. "Don't you ever quit?" he said with a muffled voice.

There was a brief pause. "Mmm, no." He sat silent. "Fine. Go take a shower. You'll come around. There's an extra bedroom and bath down the hall. I'll see if I can scrounge up something for us to eat."

Alex got up, grabbed her bags and headed upstairs. Ethan stayed on the sofa for a few minutes then got his bags and went to get cleaned up.

Her extra bedroom was nice. He felt a little strange showering in another woman's house even though Alex *was* just an acquaintance—maybe a friend. As he stood and let the hot water wash over him, he closed his eyes and tried to think of nothing important. That didn't last long.

The outcome of the internal deliberation was actually known before it began; Alex was right. In the grand scheme of things little had actually changed. But they were definitely entering unknown territory and the proverbial fog was only getting thicker.

"I defrosted some ham for sandwiches or I have some frozen entrées," Alex said when Ethan came into the kitchen.

"You're fast."

"You're slow."

"It was a very warm shower and a sandwich would be great, thank you. I don't care to ever see frozen dinners again." Alex grinned at the comment. "I've given it some thought and…I guess you're right. As long as there are still questions, I have to keep searching."

"*We* have to keep searching."

"Okay, *we*. But I'm not like you. You're kind of that 'hell-bent with your hair on fire' type and I'm not, so you have to promise to keep the flames down. Okay?"

"Mayonnaise?"

"Sure."

"Mustard?"

"No."

"Thanks."

"For what?"

"The compliment. Can't say anyone's ever described me quite like that before. Tell you what, I'll try to keep my hair under control if you promise not to dive in the grass every time we encounter a problem." Ethan just looked at her, knowing she was being funny, but still serious. "Hey, you need me as much as I need you."

"I know…okay."

"You mean 'okay' as in it's a deal 'okay?'"

"Just try not to overdo it."

"Shake on it."

Ethan put out his hand. Alex grabbed it and held on. "Good. Now you're really serious, right? Because I haven't exactly seen the steel backbone side of you yet. No backing out?"

"No backing out."

"Okay…okay," Alex said smiling and letting go. "Here's your sandwich." She set the plate in front of him.

"Thank you," Ethan replied before picking it up and taking a big bite.

"So, what do you think we should do next?" Alex asked, knowing he couldn't answer with his mouth full. "Okay, we need to find out where this element came from, right?" Still chewing, Ethan nodded. Alex turned around and stepped to the kitchen sink to look out the small window as she thought. Then after a moment, she turned to face him, leaning back against the sink with her arms folded. "Is it possible that someone else from that company you used to work for might be doing this? Someone you don't even know about?"

Ethan set the sandwich down and swallowed. "I suppose, but I wouldn't know who."

Alex started slowly pacing back and forth. "I think we should just tell the Professor everything."

"You *can't* be serious. I thought we'd been over this."

"It would seem we really don't have a lot of other choices, do we? We're still going to need his help."

"Alright. For the moment let's just forget about his connections and say we go talk to him. 'Hey Professor, Ethan here has a journal from the future that says a cataclysmic energy wave caused by unidentifiable matter is going to destroy half of Asia.' What do you think he's going say...honestly?"

"Well, first I wouldn't say it quite like that. And second I'm sure he can help us find out more about this European man, or this black sun thing. You won't have to tell him every single detail, just the important stuff."

"The problem is he'll want to know *every single detail* and I'm not willing to go that far."

"Then what *are* you willing to do?" He couldn't answer. He wasn't even sure of that himself. "These people who know other people you keep mentioning. A lot of them are the good guys you know." That was probably true. But, it didn't tell him on which side of the fence the Professor's herd was grazing. But he *had* to make some decisions, and again, she was probably right. "Let's just talk to him. You tell him only what you want to discuss and we'll go from there. I think you'll find that he can be a valuable resource once you level with him. Look what he's done so far." He couldn't argue with that either. It still didn't ease his reservations about the man.

It was decided that Alex would talk to the Professor first and impart a little more pertinent information to see what his reaction would be. She didn't mention anything about Ethan's personal revelations, the journal, or the specifics about Element Zero.

The Professor, in turn, expressed his concerns that her new friend seemed to be hiding something and that his credibility was highly suspect. However, mentioning the black sun and possible connections to Ethan's former employer seriously piqued his interest and produced an onslaught of questions. The Professor then agreed that a meeting with all of them was in order. He set up a time to meet at his home.

Ethan didn't say much on the way there. To him, this meeting ranked right up there with going in for an invasive colonoscopy. His first introduction to the Professor had been less than pleasant and there was no guarantee that this meeting would be any less so.

"It's only a few more miles," Alex said as they crisscrossed streets and neighborhoods.

They turned off a wide, secluded street and drove through a large open gate flanked by rock walls partially covered in thick leafy vines. Passing through the gate revealed an old stone driveway that twisted around several large trees through a huge, green yard to reveal a stately, well-cared-for two-story home. Alex pulled her car around and parked it at the edge of the driveway.

"Your Professor friend seems to do well for himself," Ethan commented while climbing out of the car.

"Yeah, he does all right," Alex responded as they approached the tall recessed entry with large wooden double doors. Alex pushed the button and the doorbell chimed a melodic tune.

"Are we supposed to bow or curtsey or something?" Ethan asked with a grin.

Alex rolled her eyes and the door opened. "Hello, Mrs. Greenhagen," she said with a smile.

"Well hello, dear," Mrs. Greenhagen replied happily, holding out her hand to offer Alex in. "It's nice to see you again. I hear you've been traveling."

"Yes, I have. This is my friend, Ethan Grey. Ethan, this is Mrs. Greenhagen."

"It's nice to meet you," Ethan said politely.

"Oh, you are a big handsome fella aren't you?" she said while shaking his hand. Ethan smiled like a kid. "Come in, come in," she said warmly, leading Ethan by the hand. "Samuel said you would be stopping by. He's in his study if you want to just go on back. I'm working on some pictures in the guest room if you need anything."

"Okay, thank you," Alex replied.

"It was nice to meet you, Nathan."

"It was nice to meet you too, Mrs. Greenhagen," Ethan responded.

"She got your name wrong," Alex commented after they were a certain distance away.

"She's a nice lady. No big deal."

"The study is this way," Alex said as they turned and walked through a large gathering room. Ethan could see out the back windows into a beautifully manicured courtyard with rose bushes and fountains and formal sitting areas. They walked down several very wide steps to a landing where there was another set of wooden double doors to the right. Alex knocked on one of the doors in a broken rhythm.

"*Come in!*" a reverberating voice said from the other side. Alex twisted the old antique knob and pushed in on the massive door.

Alex walked in first and Ethan followed, stopping just inside. "*Holy...*" he said under his breath, standing in astonishment of the huge two-story wood room. It was at least fifty feet long and thirty feet wide with a planked cherry wood floor. A beautiful, large round oriental rug was sprawled out before them. A large antique desk sat behind it in the middle of the room. Behind the desk were several tall bookcases filled with books, papers, pamphlets and other literature.

On the sides of the room were desks and tables with maps and models of the solar system and various small and unique antique machines of different kinds from various eras and places. Long curtains covered columns of windows that stretched from a few feet off the floor to the ceiling on both sides of the room. An enormous circular black iron chandelier hung from the center of the ceiling to provide a warm yellowish light that was accented by hues of green, red and blue from a round stained glass window set high in the center of the far wall over the bookcases.

Ethan leaned over to Alex and whispered, "And I thought *my* office was nice."

Professor Greenhagen and a tall, middle-aged woman with short reddish-brown hair were sitting at a large round table on the left side of the room, apparently just finishing a discussion.

The Professor stood to greet them. "Alex, Ethan, I'd like you to meet Ms. Rianna Benoit." Ms. Benoit also stood, smiled and looked at them over a set of reading glasses perched low on her nose. "Alex Fullerman and Ethan Grey," the Professor announced.

"Nice to meet you both," Ms. Benoit said, shaking their hands.

"I asked Ms. Benoit here because she has some information I think you two need to hear. Let's get started." The Professor motioned for Ethan and Alex to sit across the table from them. "Rianna is a specialist in cultural affairs and history and also has an interest in, shall we say, less mainstream organizations."

"I investigate cults and secret societies," Ms. Benoit stated.

The Professor continued, "One of the organizations we've been jointly keeping tabs on is a group known as the Order of the Black Sun. As I understand it, you two talked to a man in Turkey who mentioned a black sun and you think there might be some other connections and a possible threat. Is that correct?"

"A threat?" Ethan said, looking over at Alex.

"I just said there could maybe, possibly be something going on. That's all."

She wanted Ethan to handle the questions so he would feel comfortable in what they would discuss, but his first response was already defensive. He wasn't expecting the meeting to be so formal with another 'guest' present—not what he was expecting at all.

The Professor could see Ethan's hesitation. He calmly removed his glasses, set them on the table and clasped his hands together. "You used to have high-level clearance at a private research facility some time ago, did you not?" he asked Ethan.

"Yes." And the fact that he knew all this was still a little unsettling.

"Then I can understand your reservations about sharing information in this group, especially with me. You should know, however, that Ms. Benoit has classified clearance privileges higher than yours and at more than one agency, and personally I've been around long enough to know how to keep things discreet. Now, I'm not sure you two know this, but you may have stumbled onto something a lot bigger than either of you realize and I think it's *very* important that we work as a team and share information on this. Hopefully you can help us, and I'm sure we can help you.

Ethan, you need to understand, we aren't the enemy here. But there is a real one out there, more ruthless than you could imagine, and whether you know it or not, you're knocking on their front door." Alex got a cold chill. Ethan thought for a second, and looked over at Alex.

"Alright," he replied.

"Very good then," the Professor said as he put on his glasses and leaned back to look at the notes in front of him. "We think your former employer might have been a member of the Black Sun." The Professor referenced a paper on the table. "Then there's this; one of the known members of the Order owns several different businesses in various parts of Europe. One of these companies is run by a Russian industrialist who likes to buy old military assets which includes...anyone?"

"The radar facility," Alex offered.

"Bingo," the Professor said, pointing his finger at her.

"Did you know this before we left?" Ethan asked.

"No, I didn't. After the alert surfaced I decided to dig a little deeper and that's when this came to light. You know, you two have really stepped in it." Alex and Ethan both looked at each other.

"Could be coincidence, couldn't it?" Ethan commented unconvincingly.

"What do you think?" the Professor replied bluntly.

Ethan looked down and swept a piece of lint off the table. "I think we could use those shovels," he said quietly, looking over at Alex.

The Professor leaned back in his chair. "You two need to hear what this organization is really about." He motioned for Ms. Benoit to begin.

"This society maintains an almost imperceptible level of public visibility. It also has a long history and formidable resources.

"It's believed they idolize an antediluvian figure that represents an absolute purity of anti-light—a Black Sun. We believe this is a mythological reference to the polar opposite of the power of light and may actually reference the symbolism of a black hole. When you look into a black hole you see nothing because its gravitational pull is so strong it absorbs all other energies, including light itself. Light cannot escape its grasp and therefore is the essence of absolute darkness or dark power."

Ms. Benoit opened a folder she had earlier pulled from a black leather attaché bag and slid a photo across the table. "This was drawn by a man about seventy years ago who was a member of the Order." She leaned across the table and with a pen in her hand, pointed to the picture and began to explain. "Here at the top is the head, which is the Black Sun. Around the perimeter are the sunrays. Notice how they emanate inward and not outward. And see how they all curve one direction? That's usually indicative of a continual or endless cycle." The sun face of the idol looked eerily similar to the one Hazzar's father had drawn on the ground. "The mouth is large and open, which could mean intimidation or a representation of consumption. You'll probably recognize this," she said pointing to a medallion hanging around the neck of the idol.

"It looks kind of like a Swastika," Alex offered.

"Correct. It's one of the oldest symbols known to man and is evident in findings of many early cultures. It means good luck, health, happiness, good fortune and other similar references. Even the Boy Scouts and certain branches of the United States Armed Forces once wore patches with the Swastika before World War II. It may have even been incorporated into early solar calendars.

"Unfortunately most of us know its common connection with the Nazis of the Second World War. It was adulterated by the Nazi party and used as a symbol of their power and control, so most people still associate it with that stigma. However, the Nazi's usually displayed it in a diamond rotation whereas the original Swastika was typically oriented to a square, like this one.

"What it symbolizes here isn't really known for sure. *My* opinion is that it represents credibility or security and good fortune of the people as projected by the godhead, which is dominant over it. But it could be a deception.

"Here you have the hands outstretched with the palms up. In the left hand stands the body of man, symbolized by these three straight lines. In the right is the spirit of man, symbolized by three wavy lines. You see how the body of man and his spirit are being held near the Swastika medallion below the mouth of the Black Sun god? I have a theory.

"The order is made up primarily of incredibly wealthy businessmen from all over the world. These men are deliberate, loyal, quiet, patient and *very* powerful. Most of them stick to legitimate operations, although a few are under regular scrutiny by various agencies for questionable associations and business practices. The interesting thing is that in the past many of them have pooled their money to make huge acquisitions under new company identities. Our theory is...well, my theory at least, is they're methodically building empires and gaining control of major industries all over the world in preparation for something.

"The most visible member of this organization is a henchman of sorts." Ms. Benoit pulled several more pictures out of the folder. "His name is Pancros, which is an English variation of the ancient Greek word Pankratios. The name means All Power and was once used as a reference to Christ, so you can guess what kind of psychological podium this guy works from.

"He travels a lot. We've seen him in Africa, various parts of Europe, China, Australia, South America, England, the U.S. and a few other smaller countries. Unfortunately, there just isn't enough manpower to follow him everywhere. He could be setting up business ventures, recruitment... Whatever he's doing, I suspect his primary goal is to continue building their operation.

"The most intriguing thing about this person is that we believe he has no fingerprints. There have been cases where an agent has followed him and scanned specific items he's held—a glass for instance. We found only smudges. It appears he is either wearing some sort of covering over his fingers, or his fingerprints were removed somehow. There's a story supposedly told within the organization about a man who would 'come forth' having been born of darkness with no identity, and who will lead those worthy of his audience into greatness. I prefer not to speculate on that one.

"It's believed that Pancros reports to someone called the Priest. We have no pictures or records of this person and no one has actually seen him. We're not even sure he's real. One theory is that he exists only as an icon to give the illusion of a mythical leader who is all-powerful and untouchable—maybe a manifestation of the Black Sun god himself. If this is true, then this Pancros might actually be the organization's leader.

"He's often seen near a large estate outside Bremen, Germany." She slid another picture across the table. Ethan picked it up to look at it. "Although the group has estates all over the world, we think the operation is based here. He always travels with an entourage of three; usually one driver or pilot and two guards. His favorite local methods of travel are a custom limo and helicopter. He also frequently uses one of several private jets owned by various members and companies of the organization.

"Right now, the Order has as much economic and reserve political power as many industrialized countries. At the rate they're expanding, if at some point in the future they decide to exercise control in those industries, their influence would shake the stability of every respective nation. Basically, they will have the resources to dominate entire societies and mold the political climate of the entire planet."

"Like what Hitler or Stalin and people like that try to do," Alex commented.

"Well, sort of. Those men were dictators and egomaniacal. Their tactics were more intimidation and fear—always a show of force. With Hitler for instance, if you couldn't be lured into allegiance by the grandeur of idealistic Aryan purity or German pride and heritage, they would resort to intimidation. A gun in your face, or the cold-blooded killing of someone you love can be strong motivation.

"The Order, as a whole, is just as malicious. However, their tactics are disciplined more in stealth and patience. It's like the difference between being poked with a tiny poisonous thorn versus being blown up in a car bomb. One is an act of egomania that screams 'look at me,' and usually causes a public outcry that demands justice for its victims. It's highly visible. When someone dies quietly in their sleep or in a hospital room, or maybe in a car accident or from a drug overdose, many times the general public never hears about it, and there is seldom an investigation. Same result, completely different tactics and public responses.

"The Black Sun projects altruism while quietly shaping the world to its will. Everyone focuses on the 'flash and bang' so no one is watching what goes on in the shadows. It takes a great deal of self-discipline to control societies in this manner and it's extremely effective. That's what makes this group so dangerous.

"Here's how I think it works. Let's say you're a political leader, or part of the leadership in a province or state somewhere. The winter is especially harsh. You need a constant supply of heating oil or coal or gas and you depend on constant shipments of food and trade to fulfill the peoples' needs. If the shipments are slowed or stop altogether, people begin to panic. They demand help from their leaders. You need to fix the problem. Maybe your leadership is even threatened. Someone offers you a solution and you make a deal to keep the commodities flowing. The Order controls the oil, the food, the transportation. If you're dependent on someone else for those commodities, and you want to stay in power, you'll do just about anything to keep control. And if you don't fall in line, you're incidentally replaced by someone who will.

"If you control what the people need to survive, then you control the people. I think that's what this organization is working up to. They're patiently gaining control over the world's economies while the people are in turn given security in knowing those resources will always be available to them. People seldom question where something comes from as long as it's always there to provide for their needs.

"Their simplicity and discipline are almost genius. Most of the so-called terrorists or other groups with agendas want the world to see their cause. It's about force—to show everyone who they are—to shock the average person into submission. Eventually, submission turns to fear, fear turns to anger and then the people rise up to overcome their oppressors.

"The Order doesn't want to instill fear. They want to provide security, which they own, by patiently and silently extending their grasp over the very resources that shape societies all over the world. And those societies have no idea what's going on. Even our own Government is so preoccupied with *bigger* issues that they aren't taking this threat seriously. The sad thing is, I think you're looking at only two of a handful of people who understand what's really happening out there."

"Rianna's theories met with some skepticism when they were presented to certain Government interests," Professor Greenhagen added. "Although one agency has since made some effort to investigate aspects of the Black Sun, their focus was shifted to other more pressing matters. So, effectively they've tabled our concerns. Interpol and a couple other foreign security agencies showed a little interest at one time, but they have their own problems to deal with as well."

There was a long and heavy silence among them. The Professor had heard the same presentation several times before, so it was nothing new to him. Alex was overwhelmed and Ethan was caught up in the feeling of an all-consuming, dark and foreboding, beautiful power. It was the same feeling he had in Turkey while looking at the lapel pin in his vision.

"Do you have other pictures?" Ethan asked. Ms. Benoit looked at the Professor who nodded his head.

She opened the folder and sorted out a small stack of photos, then slid them across the table. "Some of these are pretty old, some are newer." Ethan carefully looked at the first picture, handed it to Alex, then the next and so on. "I have pictures of some of the members, their properties, other assets…"

Ethan looked over the pictures carefully, then saw a face that looked familiar. He studied it, and an image from the Frankfurt Airport surfaced. The man in the picture was the same man he had seen going up the escalator in the 'episode' experienced there. But why would he focus on a man from the Order he had never seen before? "Who's this guy?" Ethan asked Ms. Benoit while holding up the picture.

"Wang Li. He owns several shipping companies in China. Why? Have you seen him before?"

"I'm not sure. He just looks kind of familiar," Ethan remarked, not wanting to dig himself an unnecessary hole. As each picture was examined, another familiar face presented itself. Ethan held that picture up. "Who's this one?"

"Richard Grayson. He operates a communications products manufacturing company called Ireon in Hamburg, Germany."

"Is the date on this photo correct?"

"Yes, it is."

Ethan turned the picture around to look at it again, then chuckled to himself. "Chamberlain isn't dead."

Ms. Benoit and the Professor looked at each other, confused. "Why do you say that?" Ms. Benoit asked.

"Because, this is him."

"Are you sure? It isn't a very good photo."

"It's good enough. He's missing the satan-beard, but I'm pretty sure your Grayson is my Chamberlain." The Professor stroked his goatee.

"You seem pretty sure. Did you know him fairly well?" Ms. Benoit asked while starting to rustle through her papers.

"Well, no, but—"

"Then how are you so sure it's him?" The Professor interjected.

Ethan started to fidget. How much should or shouldn't he say? "After the uh...incident at Aridel, I had an opportunity to spend some time with Mr. Chamberlain. They were doing some serious damage control after the accident and wanted the whole thing to go away. So they compensated the families of the employees who had died and paid me to keep my mouth shut. I kept it shut, the company disappeared and that was it. Chamberlain came to my house to finalize the paperwork and I never saw him again."

"They paid you to stay quiet?" Ms. Benoit asked surprised.

"They never said that's what it was specifically. It was more of an 'early retirement.'"

Puzzled, Ms. Benoit looked at the Professor, then back at Ethan. "I can see trying to satisfy the families to keep *them* quiet, but it isn't their usual policy to pay off a single person and keep them alive. Why were *you* so special?"

There was a long pause. "I don't know."

Ms. Benoit looked at Ethan questioningly. "The Order with compassion? That just doesn't sound like something they would do. It's too personal."

"That's all I can tell you."

"If there's nothing else then," the Professor said, standing and motioning for Alex to hand him the photos.

"Wait a minute," Ms. Benoit insisted, "we need all the information we can get. If you know something else about any of this, please, tell us." Ethan looked over at Alex with a slightly distressed expression, seeking her support.

"It's up to you," she replied.

Ethan looked at Ms. Benoit as he thought, then let out a heavy sigh. "Alex and I were following a lead on an energy source that we believe may have been responsible for the destruction of the Aridel lab. It's possible it was caused by an element we were working on as part of one of the projects. There's likely more of this element out there and if Chamberlain really is a member of the Black Sun, and his death was faked for some reason, then it doesn't take a physicist to figure out that he's probably involved."

"What kind of energy was it?" Ms. Benoit asked. The Professor sat back down to listen.

"It was a substance that possessed traits of a self-sustaining power signature we couldn't identify or isolate. It may have destabilized during a test."

"You aren't sure?"

"I don't know what else could have caused it. The blast had certain *unique* qualities."

"This is the same explosion Professor Greenhagen mentioned earlier?"

"Yes, it is."

"Obviously you survived it."

"I was the only one in the lab who did."

"How did you manage that?"

"I wasn't at the lab at the time. I got sick the day before and was home when it happened."

"Did Chamberlain know you weren't at the lab before the explosion?"

"I'm not sure. Why does that matter?"

Ms. Benoit folded her arms and leaned back in her chair. It wasn't that she didn't believe Ethan, it was just that after eleven years of investigating the Order and trying to understand their motives and reasoning, there were just too many inconsistencies. Something wasn't adding up.

"Is it possible this explosion wasn't really an accident?" she then suggested. Ethan instinctively started to say 'no' for the simple fact that he had never considered the explosion as being anything else. Thoughts became confused. The question revealed possibilities he had never visited before—considerations too heinous to have warranted serious merit, until now.

"I...I don't know," he stammered, now unsure. His thoughts were in turmoil, spinning wildly with new possibilities and consequences once foreign to him. He looked at Ms. Benoit, then the Professor who were both watching him intently. It was too much.

Ethan pushed the chair back, stood up and walked to the far corner window where he stood partially hidden behind a curtain to look outside while trying to understand what this new revelation could really mean. It would appear that at least for the moment, this meeting was in recess.

"Rianna, thank you very much for taking the time to meet with us. As always, it's been a pleasure," Professor Greenhagen said cordially, standing to see Ms. Benoit out. She was a little confused by Ethan's abrupt reaction and kept glancing toward the window where he stood. It seemed counterproductive to leave now just as this new information was being uncovered. But the

Professor understood a little more about the situation than she did.

"You're welcome," she said as she collected the documents and put them back in the attaché bag.

"It was nice to meet you, Ms. Fullerman," Ms. Benoit said as she held out her hand to Alex.

Alex's attention on Ethan was momentarily interrupted. She stood and shook Ms. Benoit's hand. "It was nice to meet you too."

Professor Greenhagen then walked Rianna to a side door on the opposite side of the room from where Ethan was standing. He opened the door and they stepped outside to where her car was parked.

"What was that?" she asked after the door closed.

"I think Mr. Grey just got his first good look into Pandora's Box. Don't worry, I'll keep you informed."

After the Professor and Ms. Benoit left the room, Alex walked over to Ethan. He was so far into his own thoughts that her touch startled him and he flinched. "Sorry, I didn't mean to scare you." Ethan moved away from behind the curtain and forced a smile. She thought she might understand a little of what he was feeling, and rested her head against his shoulder to offer non-threatening support. It was appreciated, but he still felt embarrassed and confused.

"Is it really possible that someone could have planned all that and killed everyone on purpose? Was I working for the very same people I keep professing I want nothing to do with?" Alex knew he was really asking himself these questions and just listened. "I had accepted the fact that some of the people we were contracting with may not have always used our research in the way I would have preferred. But I had never even considered that the accident could have been anything else. What if it wasn't? What if the people I was working for somehow manipulated my work and I was partly responsible?"

"It wasn't coincidence what happened to you and why you were gone that day. That's what I keep trying to tell you. There's a reason for all this. We just don't understand it yet." Ethan continued to look out into the serene courtyard now illuminated by twilight. Alex gently tugged on his arm. "Come on, let's go sit down."

The Professor had pulled two chairs from the table and placed them in front of his desk where he was now sitting. There was a banker's lamp on the desk with a green shade that bathed the desk's surface in a warm and friendly light.

Ethan tried not to make eye contact as he sat down, but after a moment of silence, he glanced up briefly to see the Professor smiling at him. It was the first *real* smile he'd received from the man.

"Sorry about that," Ethan offered reluctantly.

"It's quite all right," the Professor reassured. "You just showed me a little honest truth and there's nothing wrong with that. Now, let's talk turkey. Your brains were spinning so hard you were almost vibrating." Enthusiastically he clasped his hands together and dropped them on the desk. "So, what are we really dealing with here? I'm all ears," he said before proceeding to glance back and forth at them, anxiously waiting.

"Well, I believe—"

"*We*...believe," Alex corrected.

"Sorry. *We* believe this energy I mentioned isn't based on your garden-variety atomic particles. It's something I've never seen before and *we* think whoever originally supplied the lab with the sample probably has more of it."

"You mentioned that before. How much do you think we're talking about?"

"The sample we were originally working with was several grains that resembled the visual makeup of salt or sugar. I believe *that* sample alone was responsible for destroying our entire forty thousand square foot underground lab, and there's no way of knowing how much more of the stuff could be out there."

The Professor sat back in his chair. "I see. And you're trying to track down where this sample came from?"

"That's right."

"And you think it was this sample that caused the explosion."

"I don't think it was an explosion at all—more of an implosion. I think it was some kind of released energy that consumed

208

everything, and left empty space. We think whoever has this stuff might be planning to experiment with it again and may be planning to use that old radar site as their new lab."

"That's pretty specific information. Do you have any facts, any proof of this?"

"Nothing I can show you."

"A source, a contact?" That uncomfortable feeling was coming back and there was silence. "Alright then, what did you find at the radar facility?"

"We didn't really find anything there," Alex quickly redirected.

"Nothing?"

"Some crates with old equipment."

"How about the parchment with the name and address? Where did it come from?"

"A stranger handed it to me while we were in Balkhash," Ethan replied.

"Someone just handed it to you?"

"Yes, sir."

The Professor was having a hard time with these inconclusive, and somewhat evasive answers. Frustration was becoming more evident in his expression. "What about this Hazzar? Who was he?"

"Now *that* was an interesting experience," Alex commented enthusiastically.

"Well, this old man told us that a long time ago when he worked at a dig in Syria, some scrolls were uncovered that talked about something called the Judgment Fire and the Power of Souls. That's why we asked for information about the digs. The scrolls were supposedly taken by someone he described only as a European man. Then he drew a picture of a black sun on the ground."

The Professor seemed distracted as he mumbled something behind his hand now resting over his mouth. Then he leaned forward and slammed his hand down on the desk, startling both his guests who jumped in their seats.

"I *knew* I had heard that someplace before!" the Professor exclaimed, swinging his hand around to push the chair back in order to stand. "Now, where is it...where would it be?" he said as he walked to the tall bookcases at the back of the room, stood and scanned them. "Let's see..." he pondered quietly, surveying the mass of material stacked from the floor up to beyond his reach. "Maybe here..." He pulled out a tall wooden step stool, placed it in front of one of the bookcases, climbed to the third step and began sifting through booklets and pamphlets while briefly examining each one. "Nope...nope...nope," he would say, setting them down on a nearby partially empty shelf.

He stepped down and slid the stool over a few feet to climb up and repeat the process. "The world has a plan, you know," his voice reverberated through the room as he continued digging through books and papers. "Most people are too busy and move too quickly to notice. They run here and run there with their busy this and busy that, fathoming no awareness of the mechanics that run it all. *Ah hah!*" he exclaimed, pulling out a blue letter-sized pamphlet.

Climbing down and walking back to his desk, he continued. "Many people think it's all chaos—totally random. Foolish people," he said while sitting down to start flipping through the pages of the pamphlet. "There is order in chaos and if people would just take the time to observe, they can recognize those patterns and find the order." His voice became quiet and he spoke more slowly, still methodically turning the pages, scanning each one. "Everything we need exists somewhere. All you have to do is look for it. You just have to look. Just...look..."

He then put his finger on a page and read a little while mumbling to himself. "Here we go," he said and started to read aloud. "In nineteen seventy-three in Ocala, Florida, the local Sheriff's department responded to a call regarding a reclusive elderly man whose neighbors reported not seeing for over a week. When a sheriff's deputy arrived at the home, he found the elderly man, Cecil Holmes, in his late nineties, deceased, having passed away in his sleep.

"The real story begins when the now former deputy relates that Mr. Holmes' secluded back yard contained 'rock sculptures of incredible construction that seemed to defy gravity'—an admission he would not make until fourteen years later. The deputy, who has since left the department, described many 'large rocks' that were 'about six feet long and three feet round on average,' stacked and arranged in formations including arches and gates, some similar to the 'balanced rocks seen in pictures of Stonehenge.' The former deputy described the stones as being so precariously balanced it was 'as if an unseen force was holding them in place.'

"The former deputy continued that one large boulder was balanced on top of another so precisely that he could push on one end and 'it would spin around almost perpetually.' Then he claimed to have seen 'something odd' as he looked through one of the large formations that was 'constructed in the shape of an archway.' In his own words, 'What I saw through the arch didn't look like the yard behind it. I put my hand out and received what I can only describe as a very sharp shock, like touching a strong electric fence. The next thing I knew, another deputy was calling my name and shaking my shoulder. I had apparently been unconscious for some time. When I came to my senses and looked around, all the boulders were lying on the ground in heaps, as was the arch.'

"He goes on to explain that because of the odd nature of what he had seen and experienced, he chose not to say anything about it, fearing that his professional reputation and judgment would be questioned. He states that after this experience he began to wonder how an elderly man could have placed rocks that 'must have weighed at least a thousand pounds each' into such complicated and delicate formations, some being ten feet high.

"The former deputy also states that he later returned to the elderly man's house, on his own time, to ask neighbors more thorough questions about if they had ever seen anything odd or out of place at his residence. The response from the neighbors was that the property was always quiet. For as long as most of them had lived there, there had never been any heavy machinery or other equipment at the residence that would account for the possible placement of the boulders, or even where they might have come from. What the deputy actually saw and experienced there has never been explained."

The Professor looked up briefly, then started turning and scanning additional pages. "This was written by a student of mine who had an inclination toward unexplained phenomena. And if I can just locate this next part, I think you'll find it quite interesting. This student researched the deceased man and later found someone who had worked with him while in Greece doing salvage diving around the nineteen fifties, as I recall. Ah, this must be it. These are the man's own words," the Professor said before starting to read from a page with notes scribbled in its margins.

"I was eating with Mr. Holmes and some of the other men one night at a restaurant in the harbor we liked to go to. It was about three days after we had gotten back from a strange salvage job off the coast of Egypt. An object was recovered from the sea floor that the people who had hired us immediately hid in a crate. No one would talk about it and they were real secretive about everything. After the other men left the restaurant, Mr. Holmes told me that he had seen what was in that crate.

"Everyone was told to stay away from it. But when the ship was on its way back to port, and while the guy in charge was busy, Mr. Holmes said he went below to find out what was so damn secret. He said he opened up the small crate and inside it was a rough, cylinder shaped container about half a foot wide and a foot or more long that looked to be made of stone. On the top was a plug of sorts, so it was sealed tight.

Then he said he held the container up and some kind of light started coming from inside it. It scared him, so he put it back and closed the crate. He said he thought he saw what looked like God's fire and judgment. That's all he said and I never saw Mr. Holmes again—never saw the crate again either. It was probably shipped off to who knows where."

The Professor paused, still looking at the page, then pulled off his glasses, closed the booklet, smiled and looked up. "Patterns in the chaos, Mr. Grey."

Ethan glanced over at Alex who was grinning at the Professor's pleased demeanor. It would seem she had seen this strange kind of jubilation before. Ethan wasn't feeling the same magical, cosmic convergence the Professor seemed to have found. Yes, there were interesting coincidences in these elaborate stories. But none of it seemed to lead to any rational conclusions.

"I don't see how this really helps us," Ethan commented.

"We just connected a piece of your puzzle," the Professor stated proudly.

"How could there possibly be a connection between these stories and what happened at my lab?"

"Simply because a connection isn't obvious to you yet doesn't preclude its existence. I have no doubt they're connected somewhere. You'll just have to figure out how." Ethan looked at the Professor with a blank gaze. The Professor looked back at him, sighed, then looked over at Alex. "Is he always this dense?" Tact never had been one of the Professor's strong points.

Disappointed at Ethan's inability to grasp the art of conjecture, the Professor picked up the booklet, turned his chair, stood and began walking back toward the bookcase. "I find it interesting how some people make choices based on what they *don't* know, and what they believe they *can't* do, instead of what they *do* know and what they believe they *can* do," he said loudly. "Most people are afraid—afraid of finding something they won't understand, or something beyond their control—afraid of failure, afraid of change. They think that ignorance will somehow hide them from the consequences of the world."

The Professor set the pamphlet on a shelf and started back to his chair. "But the fact is, truth exists whether you choose to see it or not. You can deny it, but no one escapes it. Fear and ignorance are simply the byproducts of provincial wisdom that spin the compass of influence."

Professor Greenhagen sat back down in his chair, clasped his hands together on the desk again, leaned forward and look directly at Ethan. "Fear is a lie, Mr. Grey. When a person begins to understand what makes him afraid, only then can he begin to find clarity. With clarity comes knowledge, and knowledge can be a *very* powerful companion."

Ethan was again embarrassed at his apparent lack of confidence and failure to grasp what he believed was just reckless enthusiasm. The Professor continued to wait for a response that was not forthcoming. Alex inconspicuously shrugged her shoulders when the Professor looked at her. She knew she couldn't speak for Ethan this time.

"Well, it's been enlightening. I think we have some interesting possibilities here. If you two find or figure out anything else, I'd like to hear about it."

"Thank you, Professor," Alex said before standing, followed by the Professor, then Ethan. The Professor held out his hand to Ethan, but said nothing. What should have been a gesture of co-operation and goodwill ended up as nothing more than a simple social formality.

"Drive safely," the Professor said as he sat back down in his chair and put on his reading glasses.

Ethan started walking toward the main doors where they had come in. Alex gently took his arm and pulled him toward the side door. It seemed appropriate to take the quick way out.

Ethan was subdued and Alex refrained from offering advice or stating the obvious as they walked around the side of the house to the front driveway where her car was parked.

After about five minutes on the road, he finally decided it was safe to say something. "I don't like that guy. I'm sorry, but I just don't." She still didn't say anything. "Isn't this where you offer advice or encouragement or something?"

"Not this time," Alex replied solemnly. "I think you've had enough of people telling you what to do."

That wasn't quite the motivational speech he was expecting and it left him a little empty. "I don't mind," he said dryly, trying to get her to talk to him.

She sighed with frustration. "I know you have things bothering you, and the Professor could have been less blunt. But I think he's right, you're being plagued by some underlying fear." That was all she said.

Now back at her townhouse, Alex stepped out of the car and headed to the door while Ethan followed.

"You're welcome to stay here if you'd like."

"Thanks, but I better be on my way home. It's a long drive. Besides, I'm not sure if Mutters ever read my instructions on how to open the cans of food I left out for her. She might be getting hungry. She's not real big on the mouse diet you know." Alex's resulting smile was as hollow as his attempt at distracting humor. What the Professor had seen so clearly was now becoming more obvious to her as well.

Ethan had no more tricks to smooth things over, or places to hide in his insecurity. He went to her spare bedroom, collected his things, picked up his suitcase and carry-on bag and returned to the front room. Alex was putting away dishes she had washed earlier and set out to dry. He set his bags down by the front door and she came out to see him off.

"Thanks for everything," he said somewhat apologetically.

"You're welcome." Her response was sincere, although lacking its usual spark, and it hinted of finality. "I'll call you if I hear anything."

"Okay," he said, turning toward the door. As he reached for the handle, Alex put her arms around him to give him a friendly hug. He looked down to see her melancholy face. She was sad, but it wasn't for her, it was for him. He hesitantly put his arms around her and held her awkwardly, trying to impart some degree of comfort.

"Have a safe trip home," she said, backing away and clearing her throat.

"Thank you," he replied. There was a subtle feeling that he was missing something important—something felt incomplete.

She watched him put the luggage in the back seat, climb in the front and drive away. As the car disappeared around the corner, she wondered if her friend would ever find the strength she believed he possessed, but was so afraid to embrace. It must be incredibly frustrating to have a map and a compass, and still find one's self completely lost.

CHAPTER TWELVE

Echo of Lilies

E THAN SET THE CRUISE control at eight miles per hour over the legal speed limit. Hopefully it would cut the travel time down a little—just not enough to get caught doing it.

With a wealth of concepts, thoughts and challenges to dwell on, he chose to spend his time thinking about Alex and the somewhat odd professor, and why they seemed to be so concerned about his unwillingness to join in their reckless abandon. It was foolish to assume that anyone could go poking around in the affairs of an organization that sounded as dangerous as the Black Sun without the real possibility of dire consequences.

The Professor's story *was* interesting, but what were the chances there really could be a connection? There just weren't enough facts for anything to be taken seriously. None of it would answer his real questions anyway, and he didn't seem to be any closer to figuring out where the journal actually came from or why he was having such vivid hallucinations.

The possibility of Chamberlain still being alive was certainly a shocker though. Could it have been the element that was so important he would fake his own death? What exactly *was* the element anyway? He shook his head in frustration at the overwhelming incongruity and decided to work the radio to find something loud that would drown out the annoying thoughts and questions.

Time passed painfully slowly. The last hour seemed more like three. The radio stations had nothing worth listening to. Then while poking buttons, he inadvertently selected the memory module. Piano music started to play. Rachel had left one of the modules in the radio so she could critique her work while running errands. He immediately recognized the arrangement as one she called *Dance of the Dragonflies*. It was a time when she was becoming very serious about her composing—a time of contentment when Allison was five or six years old. He listened for a while. You could hear her searching her talent—trying different rhythms—exploring new ideas. He could see her feelings in the melody and it brought back memories of a better time. Then it came creeping in, that old familiar adversary, loneliness.

It seemed no matter where he went or what he did, he couldn't enjoy anything anymore without that cold, ugly shadow finding him. He turned off the radio and drove a few more miles in silence, listening only to the numbing drone of the engine and roar of the wind.

He thought about being home. Even those thoughts felt isolated now—being alone in that large house with no one to talk to except the cat, and even she wasn't much for conversation unless it was dinnertime. Maybe he *should* have stayed with Alex. That hadn't really seemed appropriate either though.

Thoughts of going home should have been comforting. They weren't. The longer he drove, the less he wanted to go back to what wasn't there. His thoughts began to betray him and he was now alone. He didn't belong in Alex's world and was lost in his. Secret societies...visions... Only delusional heretics have visions.

There really *was* something wrong with him. This doesn't happen to *normal* people. He never asked to be a part of any of this. Those ugly feelings were reemerging—inadequacy, failure, fear... It was time to take a break.

The sun was about to greet the horizon when Ethan pulled off the interstate at a small town he'd never been in before. There were a couple of travel motels by the freeway, but venturing into the small town revealed an interesting and isolated little place that seemed to more aptly fit his current state of mind.

After paying the lady at the desk, he took his bags to the second story room and settled in. The room was clean and didn't smell too bad. It would do. He turned on the television and lay down on the bed to watch whatever was on when his stomach reminded him of its culinary needs. This would have been a great time for room service. No such luck. A Mexican entrée smothered with packaged sour cream, hot sauce and salsa from the only open drive-in in town would become his in-room dinner while he watched visual gibberish.

He hadn't seen the first movie before and watched two more until it was really late, or really early. The movies reeked of low budgets, bad acting and poor directing. His attention strayed and his thoughts would bounce from the show to the journal to images of the lab to the radar site to Chamberlain's office to Rachel and round and round and round.

The television was now becoming nothing more than background noise to mix and shape strange thoughts and images. It was in this half-conscious state of awareness that he heard a loud, clear voice; *"You're being plagued by some underlying fear."* It was so distinctive that it sounded like Alex was there in the room with him. Startled, he opened his eyes, sat up and looked around. Nothing...no one. Not even all alone in a motel room in the middle of nowhere was he able to escape the antagonistic and involuntary introspection. He could hide from others, but could never hide from himself. No one can.

He put his hands over his eyes and looked into the darkness of his mind. As he slowly began to slip backward again toward sleep, the memories and images became chaotic—a slurry of events, shapes and forms with no real definition. They fluttered about randomly until one image settled in his mind. It was Rachel kneeling by their bed. She did this every night and it sometimes annoyed him that she was so lost in believing that sort of thing. She looked funny doing it too, but it was *her* thing so he never said much. Whatever it was she was saying, she said it quietly as if speaking to someone only in her thoughts, or in silent words.

Then he heard voices again—soft whisperings that couldn't quite be understood. A strange place this was on the far side of consciousness where thoughts escape the boundaries of reality to mix with imagination and become alive. The voices were getting louder. He strained to understand what they where saying. A little clearer now—one becoming prevalent over the rest. As the others faded, he began to recognize the soft and distinctive intonations of his wife's voice; *"Father, please help Ethan that he might have his eyes opened. Help him find what is most important..."*

"Ugh," Ethan grunted out loud as he sat up awkwardly in the strange bed. It was her voice, just as clearly as if she was sitting next to him. Of course, there was no one there. It was just a dream. But strange...not like a dream. He shook his head and rolled off the bed to go to the bathroom. With the television now off, the clear and soothing sound of his wife's voice and the image of her kneeling next to their bed would continue to echo in his mind over everything else.

The room was quiet, and peaceful. He sat in the chair next to the table and looked at the bland motel bed—the image of his wife kneeling still vaguely superimposed in his mind. Her voice was now silent as if to let him know it was now his turn to use his own. A humble feeling came over him and for the first time in a long time, he didn't fight it. It was easy to feel, but difficult to accept—awkward and strange.

Before that moment, he would have never consciously admitted that he was scared. To ask for help was a sign of weakness, or so he had always thought. *This* seemed different somehow. Even the cognizant realization that brought him to this point was a positive step. His wife was intelligent and embraced life. She never seemed to be afraid, even if she was. Maybe she really did know something. Maybe that's what's been missing.

It was difficult to do, but Ethan knelt down to the side of the bed. It felt strange. He had never done anything like this before. Rachel used to close her eyes. He kept his open, afraid of distraction by those things that always seemed to find their way out from an inner darkness.

Several minutes passed while he wondered what he should say, and what he should do. Anxiety that had always been a constant companion tried to work its way in to convince him that he was being foolish and acting absurdly. *No, not this time,* he thought to himself and he fought off the ill feelings. Then with some trepidation, he clasped his hands in front of him and started, "Ummm..."

He was embarrassed at hearing his own voice. Maybe he'd just think it like his wife did. But it was hard to focus with all the other thoughts. "Okay, I've never done this type of thing before so...well...I don't know what to say."

Briefly he glanced up at the ceiling as if to look at who he thought he might be talking to. After a deep breath, he started again. "I don't understand a lot of things that are going on right now. I guess I'd just like to know why all this is happening to me. There has to be a reason. I'm guessing, if you're really up there, somewhere, you know what's going on so if it would be okay, maybe let me in on some of it? I'd like to know what I'm supposed to do. If that's okay...I guess." It felt silly to talk to the bed, not knowing if what was being said would really make any difference.

There was another question he wanted an answer to as well. It had been burning within him for so long that it would be difficult to say out loud without bringing a flurry of tormented feelings. And the possible enormity of an answer to such a question was more than he thought he was prepared to hear. Maybe someday he would ask it. "Thank you. I guess that's all."

He climbed into bed and shut off the light near the nightstand. At that moment, it occurred to him that no one else on Earth knew where he was. Well, except for the lady at the desk, but that didn't really count. He was alone—truly and completely alone.

Ethan smiled happily, sitting in his lounge chair in the tall grass of the large open field while he listened to Rachel play. Allison was jumping and dancing around the piano and laughing as her mother enthusiastically pounded out the spirited number. Her music filled the entire valley with sound and everyone everywhere could hear it. He was so proud.

Allison ran to him and grabbed his hand to have him join her in their frolic. They danced in the serene meadow and slowly circled the piano as the warm sun looked on with a peculiar yellow light.

In the skies around them were people, lots and lots of people sitting in seats like an audience. They started to clap. They clapped slowly at first then louder and louder. He looked up at them, delighted that they shared his appreciation for his wife's talent and their improvisational dance performance.

The clapping intensified and was becoming somewhat excessive and unreasonable. They weren't *that* good. He studied the crowd. They were looking at something in the distance while their cheering and encouragement continued. He turned to see what they were looking at. There was nothing that could be seen. But he heard it—an engine screaming in the distance. It was coming closer and getting louder as it approached through the meadow. The people began to stand and clap even harder and cheer even louder. Their shouts of approval blended with the shriek of the engine…and it started to rain.

The melody of the music was all but drowned out and Allison was now by her mother dancing in a carefree pirouette. "No, not this time," he said clinching his fist in determination. He strained against the unseen force that was already upon him. The meadow had changed to a water soaked street. He shouted and screamed in an empty voice. The people, now lining the sidewalks, were jumping, shouting, clapping and cheering wildly. He screamed at them to stop. They wouldn't.

His voice was still empty. They continued to cheer and his family continued to play and dance around the piano. The sound of the enraged machine was almost upon them. The rain poured with a thunderous roar. The people cheered wildly…and he was helpless. There was nothing he could say, nothing he could do. He was completely worthless to them.

Thrashing in bed, he awoke, panicked in the darkness of a strange place. His heart was pounding. He could barely breathe. He kicked off the covers, grabbed his chest and slid to the side of the bed. His breaths slowed slightly as he fumbled for the light switch. Then emotion began to rise in an uncontrollable fury. He was tired of this, this incessant torment that never, ever went away. When was it going to end? How many times would he have to watch them die? How many times? *How many times!*

In an explosion of rage filled with years of frustration and re-sentment, he grabbed the pillow and blankets and began beating them against the bed as hard as he could while his face strained with unleashed torment. *"Why! Why! Why!"* he shouted angrily through gritted teeth with every blow.

As the last of his rage rapidly flowed from him, he flung every-thing across the room, grabbed the bed and threw it over onto the floor. Then in one last burst of anger, he swung his arm around at the lamp to extinguish the light that so indifferently illuminated his rampage. The lampshade crumpled as his fist went through it, striking the bulb that shattered and sprayed glass across the room. His rapid breathing was now the only sound he could hear, while he stood silent and alone in the dark room.

With his anger now expulsed, there was nothing to hide the overwhelming isolation and self-pity. He crumpled to the floor and began to sob. He was ashamed of his digression and of what he had just done. He felt around for the chair that was some-where behind him, and sat down. *This has to stop*, he thought. He turned toward the small table and rested his head on his arms. This wasn't like him. He wasn't this kind of person. He didn't want to be this kind of person. These were horrible feelings he thought were gone. Emotionally drained, he sat limp at the table for several minutes before groping around the room for the other light switch.

Squinting in the new light, he looked at the mess strewn around the room and dropped his head in disapproval of his de-plorable behavior. The bed was put back on the frame along with the sheets and blankets. Larger pieces of the shattered bulb were picked up and thrown into the trash. The bottom half of the lamp was still upright, being bolted to the nightstand. The top was broken off and hanging to the side by only two bare wires through its center. He located the cord for the lamp and pulled it from the wall.

The small clock radio on the nightstand read 3:13 A.M. The television looked uninviting and he didn't really want to go back to sleep. He filled a plastic cup with a small amount of water from the sink, took a few sips and walked to the window by the door where he parted the curtains slightly to look outside.

A fog was floating through the parking lot where a streetlight glowing in the crystalline air appeared as a giant, fuzzy white ball. The street under the light was barely perceptible. Still, on the far side of the road appeared to be something yellow and white. It was too hazy to make out details. Everything else was dark and still.

He closed the curtain and set the cup on the table. Walking over to the dresser, he picked up some literature left for the guests and set it down on the table to read. He looked at the television momentarily, then at the window again. The yellow and white light across the road was strange—out of place. He parted the curtain again, looked out, then back at the room. There's nothing like being wide-awake in the middle of the night.

After getting dressed and putting on his jacket, he quietly slipped out of the room and walked along the balcony to the main stairs and down to ground level. The air was eerily calm and the fog had a slight chill to it as it passed around him. His muffled footsteps in the parking lot were the only sounds he could hear. Even the freeway only a mile or so away seemed to be silent.

As he stood under the glowing light and looked across the road, there appeared to be a path that led away from the sidewalk and disappeared into the darkness out of the light's illumination. Maybe it was a small park, although he didn't recall seeing one the night before when he had arrived. He jogged across the street and onto the adjacent sidewalk, then turned back briefly to look around. The only other visible lights were from the motel and other streetlights some distance away. Nervously, he turned back to look down the dark path to focus on the white and yellow lights. Funny, they didn't really look like lights now. They actually kind of looked like...*flowers*.

Slowly he began to walk toward them—his focus so intense that there seemed to be nothing else around. Then the fog thinned and his vision cleared. He stopped and stared. They *were* flowers, and they looked like the same kind he saw in the field next to the house where his car introduced itself to the mailbox.

As he came closer, he could see they seemed to be reflecting daylight and were swaying gently. His mind became confused. He knew this had to be some sort of impossibility. Then the fragrance hit him—that unmistakable and incredible smell he had become so accustomed to every fall. They *were* Rachel's lilies. His mind rapidly brought images and memories—a fresh bouquet on the dining room table, the fragrant aroma that would fill their home.

Everything was very peculiar and he looked around again, still uneasy. There was a barely visible empty park bench on the left and the bed of flowers was ahead to the right. He walked a few feet closer and just stared in amazement. They were perfect—hundreds of beautiful, perfect white and yellow lilies. They glowed with incredible elegance, drenched in the light of an invisible sun. He knelt down and put his face close to them to take in their aroma as they swayed gently—their petals fluttering, dancing in a warm breeze.

There was actually no breeze of any kind, let alone a warm one. But Ethan was so taken by what he was witnessing, the simple rules of his temporal world had escaped his common sense for just a moment. He felt as though the essence of his wife and all she embodied were right there in front of him, beckoning him to come join her in their warm ensemble.

Thoughtfully, he reached out to hold one of the flowers when a distant, omnipresent voice was heard.

"*Ethan.*"

Startled, he quickly stood and looked around. There was no one there, anywhere. He looked around again, confused, then back at the swaying lilies.

"Ethan."

This time the voice was clear and distinct. It came from behind him. He turned toward the voice and was completely dumbfounded by what he now saw. Despite all the common sense he believed he possessed, and all the empirical knowledge that formed the foundations of a logical existence, what he was now seeing before him, however improbable, was *not* a place of his world.

Standing about ten feet away near the park bench was a man with short, well-groomed white hair. He was tall with a tanned complexion accentuated by white robe-like clothing that reminded him of middle-eastern dress. His head was uncovered and he had a certain pleasantness and authority about him. He looked at Ethan as though they were old friends. Ethan then realized it was no longer dark or cold and the fog was gone. An overhead sun was bright and warm, the sky clear with a light breeze.

Behind the man were hundreds of large trees and a low grassy surface that looked like green velvet that extended as far as he could see. The trees were nestled in groves, forming islands in the massive expanse. There were flowers and shrubs and plants of every kind scattered in large groups of beddings that lined walkways and surrounded ponds and small streams. He was captivated by the incredible beauty of this place and momentarily lost his attention on the man. He slowly turned around to see a small bluff with a waterfall cascading into a large pond that fed other nearby streams. There were no people, no buildings, no cars. *It was an astounding sight.*

A tingle came over him while his mind tried to comprehend this place and the incredible landscapes of almost unimaginable beauty. A place like this could only exist in a dream. *"Unbelievable,"* he said quietly, smiling with the giddiness of a child at Christmas. Nothing rational could explain this. He had turned full circle having completed his inspection, and was now facing the man in robes.

"So, you must be The Wizard," Ethan jested.

The man smiled at his remark. "My name is Joshua. Please, come sit." The man motioned to the bench next to him.

Ethan glanced around again, still amazed by the enormity and beauty of it all. He walked a few feet toward the man, then stopped. "Who did you say you were again?"

"My name is Joshua," the man replied. "I am here to advise you. Please..." Again the man motioned for Ethan to come sit on the bench. Hey, why not. It hadn't turned into a nightmare yet.

Ethan walked to the bench, took off his jacket, casually tossed it over the back and sat down toward its end. The man also sat and turned slightly to face Ethan.

"Nice place you have here. This is *really* something. It amazes me how a mind can come up with such wild things, you know? One minute you're beating a pillow to death and the next... Man, my wife would love a yard like this. *I'd* like to live in a place like this for that matter. Yeah, it won't last long. They always start out like this you know...all pretty and happy." Ethan paused to admire the large leafy trees.

"Rachel is a wonderful person, but your family will not be joining us here." Joshua let Ethan look around for a few moments. "Ethan, would you understand if I told you this was not a dream?"

Ethan looked at the man then back at the amazing landscape. "Well then, I'd have to say that a dream telling me this wasn't a dream would have to be a first." He smiled and laughed silently, but started to become a little uncomfortable.

The beauty around him was vivid and sharp, full of color and detail. He could still smell the fragrant flowers, and the grass. It had consistency, stability and ordered motion. Not the chaotic capriciousness of other dreams.

He waited for the inevitable nightmare to break the calm. It never came. A small knot began to form in his stomach. He then realized he could feel the wind on his neck, real warmth from the sun, the weathered wood of the bench—details you can't usually define in a dream.

He turned to look at Joshua and noticed the detailed lines on his face, and the strands of hair that flitted in the breeze. As he looked into Joshua's eyes, the knots began to grow and twist. Fear swept over him when he saw and recognized the soul of a living being. "This is...a dream...isn't it?" he stammered.

"It is not," the man replied.

Sudden panic shot through Ethan like cold blood as he jumped to his feet and walked quickly away to stand by the lilies. He looked down the path that had once led to a street and to his motel, then back at the man who was again standing next to the bench.

He looked back at the lilies. His hands and legs were quivering and shaking. *How could this be possible?* Before, it was just strange images, bad dreams. How could *this* be possible?

"Where...are we?" Ethan managed to choke out through a tight throat.

"We are in a place where I can talk with you."

"Can I leave?"

226

"Yes. You may leave at any time, but I have much to tell you—to help you find answers to your questions."

"I don't understand. What questions?" Ethan replied in a shaky voice, his body still quivering.

"You travel a unique path and have been given special talents that are confusing to you. You asked for understanding. I have been sent here to give you that for which you have asked."

"Are you...are you God?"

"No," the man replied smiling. "I am Joshua, a messenger. Please, sit. I will explain."

Ethan could scarcely believe what he was seeing and hearing. He stood and looked around again hoping to understand—weighing the options—trying to comprehend. His first instinct was to run. It was almost overpowering. Yet, another part of him wanted to know—honestly wanted to find truth, if truth really existed. Was this where truth comes from?

Slowly, he made his way back and cautiously sat down at the very end of the bench. Joshua sat down where he had been previously. Ethan was afraid to look at him again, so he looked down at the pathway in front of them instead. "Rachel never said anything about this kind of stuff happening...when you ask questions."

"Only a very select few receive guidance in this manner," Joshua said motioning to the area around them. "You were born with talents of great value. Some you do not understand. For that reason, and because you have now asked for that understanding, I am here."

Ethan sheepishly looked up at Joshua. "You mean...the images, the visions...?"

"Yes. Do you still wish to understand?"

"Yes, yes I do."

"It is important for you to know that with a higher knowledge also comes great responsibility. People are expected to use their gifts as they are intended. To have a talent and gain knowledge from it, then allow it to wither in ignorance and fear, is far worse than having never received a talent at all. For with the knowledge and understanding you seek, also comes responsibility. To receive *one*, you *must* accept the other. They must be received together, or not at all."

"You mean...there's something I'm expected to do?"

"Yes. The responsibility and the knowledge are one."

"So if I don't accept this...responsibility, then I'll never understand what's been going on with me? Is that what you're saying?"

"You have great fear. You fear to believe. Your life is one of the greatest gifts you will ever receive, yet you fear life itself. When you begin to understand death, *then* you will begin to understand life. Life's journey is one you must make in order to gain the knowledge you seek. Without knowledge, your path will be left to blind interpretation. Your beliefs and actions are your path. You have agency to choose, and those choices will elect the path you walk. In the end, you will be judged by your path. Do you understand this, Ethan?"

"I'm not sure," he replied slowly.

"Then what do you believe?"

"I'm...I don't know, really."

"Then what do you desire?"

"I'd like to know what's going on with me and...be happy again, I guess."

"You seek to be happy, yet you do not know what you believe. In order to achieve true happiness you must first understand your existence and purpose in life, for knowledge of purpose will define your path whereas one is the other, and the other is the one.

"To travel the path you seek, you must gain knowledge and understanding, for if you do not understand your path, then you will wander, whither and die. Your desires are sincere, and if you honestly seek the knowledge that will cause you to understand, *and* if you accept its principles and challenges, *then* you will find the happiness you seek."

Ethan understood what Joshua was saying, but was still completely overwhelmed. Joshua continued. "Be comforted in knowing that no trial you encounter will be above your ability to endure. You have the strength and the capacity to comprehend and understand more than you believe is possible. Understanding is within *all* men, *if* they search for it. But be warned, if you should gain the knowledge, *then* turn away from its truth, your path will be lost, and *you* will become lost."

"It doesn't sound like you're giving me much of a choice, really."

"All men have the freedom of agency, but no choice is ever free of consequence. Many choices define our very existence. They are the ones that carry the greatest responsibility and lead us to the greatest rewards. It is understandable then, with the weight of responsibility, that all men do not make the same choices."

Ethan looked out over the grass and pondered these things. It was practically impossible to believe this could really be happening. "Why me?"

"All people are given talents; some easily known, some not. You are able to study and understand the intricacies that bind your world, the organization from which all has been created, can you not? Is this not a talent?"

"Well, yeah, I guess. But I don't understand how that has anything to do with...*this*," Ethan said as he looked around.

"There was a point in your life not long ago when you were able to break the bonds of time and see outside that which confines you."

Ethan looked at Joshua as he thought. "You're talking about what happened at the lab, and the other...visions."

"Yes."

Ethan just looked at him. "Break the bonds of time? See outside what confines me? Okay, I'm done. Take me to my little padded room or whatever because now I *know* someone's just messing with me. I'm not playing this game anymore." He started to laugh and shook his head. *Wake up, wake up...*

"If you wish to leave this place, you need only return down the path from whence you came. You will be advised no further. But before you make that decision, I invite you to see something more. Walk with me, if you will."

Joshua then stood and started down the path that continued past the lilies and farther into the park. Ethan stayed on the bench and watched him walk away. The man's hair moved with the breeze and his robes flowed and shifted as he walked. It still looked so... *real*.

Stubbornness and skepticism were part of what made Ethan a good scientist. It was also what was preventing him from standing and following Joshua. Should he go further into an unknown, one that was probably just an elaborate figment of imagination anyway? Or do nothing, and possibly risk abandoning everything?

It didn't seem fair that the decisions he now faced would have to be made based on what he felt, instead of what he understood to be true. Feelings were poor determinants in establishing logical outcomes. Which decision would he regret the most...or maybe the least? To what end would the wrong choice lead?

Hesitantly, Ethan stood and looked around again, then started walking after Joshua who was already a fair distance ahead. He caught up to him and fell in stride a few feet behind. "Where are we going?" he asked.

"You will see," Joshua responded without turning or breaking his stride.

The path passed by all types of vegetation, all different kinds of flowers and even trees with flowers he had never seen before. Some things he recognized, most he did not. There were now numerous trails leading off the main path and as he passed each one, he could see where they wound in and around large bushes and shrubs that hid their destinations. They walked past streams and ponds and small waterfalls. *I wonder if Alex would believe this one?* he thought as he looked around at everything in wavering acceptance.

Joshua turned down one of the narrow paths and Ethan followed. The path led around several bushy flowering trees to a dense area of vegetation that obscured its end.

"Where does *this* one go," Ethan asked impatiently.

"You will see," Joshua responded patiently.

They arrived at a large wall covered with vines. Joshua pulled an area of the vines aside to reveal an opening and motioned Ethan to pass. "Here."

Ethan stopped at the opening and looked through it, trying to see what was on the other side. There was something there, but it was blurry, like looking through wax paper. He looked over at Joshua who motioned again with his hand for Ethan to pass. After searching for a fleeting courage, Ethan took a deep breath, and stepped through.

His body tingled for just an instant, and he found himself in another, and totally different place. This time he was standing in someone's yard. It was a fairly large yard in front of an average size house. The house was of a unique architecture and seemed familiar. Someone was sitting on the front porch in a wide swing, gently rocking back and forth, their face hidden behind a book.

The other homes in this typically suburban neighborhood were different in size and style, but all had the same distinctive appearance. Joshua was standing a few feet behind Ethan. Behind Joshua was a short fence and sidewalk next to a street. On the other side of the street was a field of tilled dirt. In the distance across the field were buildings that appeared commercial—some sort of industrial complex with a smokestack spewing a large cloud of whitish vapor.

The sky was overcast with a threat of rain. Thunder rumbled softly. The sun was low in the sky over the complex and cast a red-purple hue as light passed through openings in the clouds. A rounded, low and shiny car hummed by on the street catching Ethan's attention. He had never seen a car like that before.

After it passed, he turned to Joshua. "Where are we?"

"You will see," Joshua repeated. Ethan sighed with a bit of irritation, turning his attention back to the person on the porch.

"Okay, who is that?" he asked, motioning with his head.

"See for yourself."

"Aren't we going to look a little strange?"

"We are only spectators here," Joshua replied.

Ethan cautiously walked toward the porch. He could now see it was a woman with long blond hair that was braided and resting in front of her right shoulder. Her head was down as she read the book. Gently she swung her foot, pushing off the floor to rock the swing.

A huge flash of choppy bluish-white light lit up the house. Ethan turned to see where it had come from. A few seconds later, rolling thunder shook the air. As he turned back toward the porch, the woman had lowered her book to look out over the railing. He could see her face clearly now, highlighted in the reddish light. He gasped. *It was Sara!*

Another car passed by. Sara watched it travel quietly down the street. Ethan watched her intently—studying her face as she followed the car with her eyes. This was the girl whom he had learned to love like his own daughter—who took him through seven years of some of the most important times of her childhood. And there she was, *right there*. He wanted to run up to her, hug her and tell her how great she was. She looked even more beautiful in person.

Joshua stepped to Ethan's side. "Sara is a very special young woman. There are many different truths to be revealed as one travels through life. Some are meant for you to know along with a full understanding of your talents. Sara has the unique ability to see and understand certain laws that border this world and the others. She is aware of the unique force that embodies nature and man, and not unlike you, she has seen that which masters time. Because of these abilities, a new understanding has been found. She has seen what should not have been, and for you, what should not be."

"But...traveling in time isn't really possible, is it?"

"Your lives are subject to a time that is linear. That from which time is created is *not* linear. To understand its full truth is not possible for the mortal mind. Sara has glimpsed only a fraction of what exists, otherwise she would have become as the knowledge.

"You are capable of recognizing the attributes of time by what you observe, but are restrained by its laws, and know little of its true diversity. Because of your gift, you have experienced moments of clarity where the time that governs *your* world has been briefly parted, like a curtain moved from over a window allowing you to see through it. You know this is true, but don't understand why."

It was an interesting answer that only stirred more questions. For now, his attention turned back to Sara. He wished he could talk to her somehow. To tell her he had received her journal, how much he appreciated her company, how incredibly brave she had been. The fact was, she wasn't just someone he watched and listened to on an electronic device, she had helped him through one of the worst times of his life.

"When she'd talk about her friends and I'd get to watch the birthday parties and fun things she did with her family, she made me feel like I was a part of it—like she made those journal entries just for me. When she was sad or distraught I wanted to help her so badly, to cheer her up, to make her feel happy again. She's just a kid. How can a child understand the things you say she knows?"

"A child is as close to the Creator as any mortal can be. In the innocence of a child, you can see the Creator's purity and power in knowledge. Sara has retained some of that knowledge."

Seeing her was a great feeling—even to simply be in her presence as she gently swayed back and forth on the large wooden swing. It was difficult for Ethan to understand how he could be there and not be a part of what was around him. Then his fears were realized...it started to rain.

"Oh no...no," he said as he heard the drops begin to hit the roof over the porch and saw them start to splatter on the walkway and steps. This time though, it was different. He couldn't feel them. Puzzled, he held out his hands as the large drops of water, falling with an ever-increasing intensity, passed through them to the ground. It was a confusing sensation. Somehow, the rain had no power over him here. He looked up to the sky, eyes open, and watched the rain fall to Earth. He could see it streak from the heavens to flow through him. No dream had ever been like this. It was an amazing and exhilarating experience.

He turned back to Sara. She had set her book down, pulled a sweater around her and was watching the storm. Ethan watched her briefly, and then turned to Joshua. "She looks sad. Is she okay?"

"Because of what she understands, a great deal of responsibility rests with her. Do not worry for her. She is strong and knows her place. Her life will be full and her rewards will be many."

Ethan stepped to the middle of the porch stairs to be closer to her. Seeing her in this manner was bittersweet. He was there with her...but not really. He watched her as she gazed into the shimmering air, intrigued by the thousands of tiny raindrops leaving trails of prismatic color as they hurtled to the ground. She seemed content now, watching the rain and flashes of static that danced in the sky.

"It is time to go," Joshua announced.

"Already?"

"Yes, but know that there will be a time when you will have the opportunity to see her and converse with her as a friend, should you choose to do so."

"I'd like that."

He watched her for another moment, studying her face and her expression, then turned back to Joshua. "I'm ready," he said preparing himself to leave. But after having barely spoken those words, he found himself back in the grove of trees, standing near the bench.

The beauty of this place was still staggering. Even so, Ethan gave a heavy sigh as he sat down. It was difficult to leave another person he had become so attached to. He now wanted to understand how all this could be possible and what it all meant. It was time to look up and around and accept the fact that he was apparently part of something much larger than he had ever allowed himself to see. The answers were here and he had been given a unique opportunity to know them, if it could all somehow be believed. Cynical idealism was firmly ingrained from years of arrogance. Change wasn't going to be easy.

"What do I need to do?" Ethan asked submissively.

"I know you have many questions. I will answer them if it is within my authority to do so. For you to understand what lies ahead, you must first know what came before, as it is why mankind exists. You have already heard some of what I will tell you, but at that time you chose to ignore its truth out of conceit and self-righteousness—a condition that plagues many. These truths have been given to all mankind in record and in these records you will find the history of many people and the purpose for all that is."

"Rachel..."

"Yes, she understands, as do many others."

Ethan lowered his head. "I really was a fool. All those wasted years," he said quietly as unpleasant thoughts arose of the times he had dismissed Rachel's efforts to explain what she understood, or when he had been rude and inconsiderate to her friends, ridiculing them for what *they* understood. And the times he would tell her he wasn't interested in going to church because it was a 'waste of time.'

Every Sunday morning she would politely ask with the hope that someday he'd open his eyes and see what was most important. He could have been sharing a wondrous knowledge with his family, but chose not to. How disappointed she must have been.

"What has transpired before *can* be forgiven if the heart is true." Joshua's words did not comfort him much at that moment. His family was what he loved most of all. When he had the chance to listen and share in something that was an important and substantial part of their lives, he let them down. Guilt and sadness welled up inside. "Ethan, look at me."

Ethan looked up, wiping tears from his eyes as Joshua held out his hand in a fist. He then turned it over and opened it, palm up. A single droplet of water formed in the air and floated a few inches above his hand. Joshua looked at the small sphere of water, then at Ethan. "If this drop of water was to represent the total knowledge of man, then the total drops of water contained in all the oceans of all the world would represent the knowledge of our Creator."

Ethan stared at the drop of water and tried to visualize Joshua's words. It was impossible to comprehend. "Immortal concepts cannot be fully understood by the mortal mind. You are not expected to understand those things that are beyond your capability to do so. What *is* expected of you is for you to study and to learn all that you are capable—to have faith, charity, love and hope so that you may understand and believe that which is necessary for you to navigate your life. With these principles, and the capabilities we know you possess, you will find your true path and the happiness you seek."

Joshua raised his hand slightly and the water droplet vaporized. "Are you willing to accept the truths you will be given?"

It was an incredibly frightening decision. But even as incredulous as he was, there was no worldly way to empirically explain what was happening here. His willingness to hold on to skeptical deniability was fading. He knew this was going to be the most important decision he might ever make—a choice of immeasurable consequence. "Yes," Ethan finally replied with some apprehension, but also with a great deal of hope.

"Our Creator is an exalted being, having once passed through portals of trial from which His authority and glory have been forged. In another place of dwelling, not unlike this place, we lived as families. We are not yet as our Father, but His desire is for us to have the opportunity to one day share in His knowledge and glory, just as you would wish *your* children to share in yours.

"Before this earth was formed, a plan was established to allow us all to individually choose our fate. Another offered a different plan by which all would be glorified without the agency to choose. This plan was rebuked by many, but favored by some, causing a war between them. The Creator then made His decision and the plan was enacted by which we would make our own choices, to choose our own fates, and this earth and others like it were then formed along with all the other celestials in the heavens.

"A time of seasons was then created by which this world and everything formed on it would experience continual change to gauge its progression. Our minds were veiled of this previous knowledge, allowing all men to learn and choose without prejudice. The fallen one and those who believe in his ways and who rebuked the chosen plan, became spiteful and evil. They did not come to the earth to live as man and woman with the opportunity to become like our father. Instead, their choice caused them to remain as spirits, becoming dark and vowing to sway man to evil, to cause them to fall into the depths of hell.

"When all those who have chosen to come to Earth have passed through the veil of mist that creates all men equal, a sifting of those who live on the earth will commence and a judgment of all who have ever lived will follow thereafter. This is the plan.

"As mankind has progressed from the beginning and asked for further knowledge to guide them, this knowledge has been provided in various forms; some in records and some by revelation through ordained prophets. The Creator endowed His prophets with the power of knowledge to aid and guide in the development of man. But man became wicked and evil and the teachings and knowledge were removed from man's presence for a time.

"Most of these teachings, along with their knowledge and power of authority, have since been restored. However, not *all* things were to be revealed during that time. When the knowledge was removed, many truths were hidden away. One of these truths was reserved to be brought forth again only in the Last Days to cleanse the earth of the wicked and prepare for Final Judgment. A destiny failed by one who was chosen, allowed this truth to become lost.

"Evil will do everything in its power to confound and deceive man and cause him to lose his way. At the End, those of evil and those who have turned away from the truth to embrace the desires of evil, will be sifted as tares are sifted from the wheat to be burned and the earth will be cleansed of them. This judgment will be pure with an unquenchable fire that knows the desires of one's soul.

"A man with a devout allegiance to evil has found what was lost. His quest and that of his followers is for control over mankind. To attain great power is their goal and is what they seek and is what they believe they have found. *They* are deceived, for this truth they now possess can only be revealed with an authority they do not have.

"The one of evil knows the true purpose of this power, or truth, and has vowed that all his followers will *not* be sifted, but instead walk the earth among the righteous at the End. *You* must find that which has been taken and complete its journey to the place where sacred truths are kept. *This* is your task."

Ethan sat in bewilderment of these new revelations. Even the Professor would have had a hard time wrapping his head around this one. *This* time though, he fought the ingrained compulsion to automatically dismiss it all as fantasy, and honestly tried to comprehend what he was being told. "And I'm supposed to somehow do this?"

"It is your destiny. You are aware of it and have glimpsed its power."

"The visions..."

"Yes. As a comprehensible explanation, this truth exists in a transcendent state. You are able to occasionally sense its presence and catch a glimpse of it as through a window. What you see are fragments of its existence in moments of your time. You and Sara are not unalike in your gifts. That is how she knows you."

"The journal..."

"Yes."

The bond he felt with Sara was one of the few anchors that helped him maintain at least some level of sanity in all this. Knowing that they somehow shared a similar gift was strangely comforting. He still wondered how she was able to send the journal to him. Then again, all the other overwhelming proclamations made the question of *how* seem somewhat trivial to the considerations of *why*.

"Why do you need *me* to do this? It would seem to make more sense that you...*people*...could just take it back."

"The agency mankind has been promised prevents us from directly interfering in mans' affairs. All men must decide for themselves what choices they will make and all men must then bear the consequences of those choices. Once the decision had been made to leave this truth on Earth, its stewardship became the responsibility of those entrusted to its safekeeping. If we were to take possession of it, we would then also be taking away the agency of those involved.

"The freedom of agency must be protected in all men and in all things, for if the Creator was to remove from one man his right to choose, whether for good *or* for evil, then he would have to remove the same from all. The right to choose is an underlying and fundamental law of the plan and what defines our existence."

"So what you're saying is someone lost this...uh...."

The pieces all started to fall into place; Element Zero... The scrolls... The salvage story... The Fire of Judgment... The Black Sun... "It's the Power of Souls, isn't it? The stories were true. It really is all connected." Ethan looked toward the ground and shook his head subtly as his mind raced. Joshua waited patiently. "But...how do I find it and how can I really do all this? I've never done *anything* like this before."

"Now that you have finally asked for guidance, you will receive it. With this guidance you must find your strength and with that strength you will rise to the occasion."

Ethan had never thought of himself as more than just an average man with typical expectations and problems. *This* was something that would take the wherewithal of a man he wasn't sure he could be. "What if I fail?"

"You will only fail if you believe it is your destiny to do so."

"That *has* crossed my mind once or twice, you know," Ethan remarked, a little facetiously.

"What is easy is seldom what is best. The trials you endure will define your character and allow you to become the person you really are."

"You sound so sure, like you already know what's going to happen."

"We know of what great things you are capable."

It was all still almost incomprehensible. As he looked around at the grove, he noticed the lilies again, and thoughts of his family returned. It was time to ask those questions. "You said my family wouldn't be here. Do you mind if I ask where they are?"

"They are in a place of magnificence with others who have also gone before."

There was still the one question he wanted to ask. He had rehearsed it in his mind over and over and if there was ever a time, it was now. "Can you tell me why they were taken from me? Why would a Creator who is supposed to be fair and merciful take my wife and daughter from me like that?"

"The Creator does not *take* life from us. There is a perception we sometimes believe that the loss or pain we endure is so great that it must be a punishment put upon us by the hand of Greatness. This is not true. The lives of those on this earth and of all nature are governed by the laws set forth from the beginning, and those same laws will continue until the End. The natural order of your time ensures your agency. It cannot be circumvented to prevent a tragedy or untimely passing. The laws that protect man's affairs *do not* preclude those events.

"All consequences must be the result of the choices and actions of men and of nature, for the power of self-government has been given to both. Only on occasions where a man's faith, knowledge and benevolence have caused him to evolve to the highest degree of mortal purity and perfection, has man been allowed to pass beyond the boundaries of mortal existence without experiencing death. To become perfect is to become like unto The Creator."

That answer may have explained the concept, but didn't lessen the feelings of loss from their absence, and Joshua knew this. "I was a farmer in my mortal life and I saw many wonderful things."

"Ah, that explains the wheat and tares sifting thing," Ethan quipped.

Joshua continued. "I also saw much death from sickness and by the hands of those who took joy in the pain of others. My mother was lost to a sickness when I was a boy and we knew little of the Father or the plan for our existence. My lack of knowledge and anger of injustice troubled me as a man and I carried that pain with me to my own death. It was only when I saw my mother again that I learned of the glory of which we are all a part. Had I known these things before, my mortal life would have likely been much different. That life I can never change. What I *can* do is make reparation."

Ethan had lost his focus and was staring at nothing. Joshua watched him knowing his thoughts were confused. "Walk with me again," Joshua said as he stood. Ethan stood and they walked off the path across the grass into a nearby grove of trees. They stopped and stood near one of them in a place that afforded a view into the entire grove where Ethan could see hundreds of tall, beautiful green leafy trees.

Joshua reached up and put his hand behind a leaf on one of the lower branches so Ethan could see it clearly. "I want you to look at this leaf and imagine it represents a person in your world. You will know their emotions and state of mind." Ethan began to feel a strange sensation about him and then he sensed concern. A man was concerned about his work. "And now this leaf," Joshua said as he moved his hand to another. Ethan felt the emotion of another person. It was a woman. She was happy at something she was watching. "And now this leaf," Joshua continued.

Ethan now could feel the emotions of three distinct people. "And now this branch." Suddenly the emotions of dozens of peo-

240

ple were within him. Somehow he was able to sense each one and feel their distinct emotions. "And now the limb...and now the tree," Joshua continued.

Ethan was being filled with the essence of individual lives. He looked at the leaves on the tree as they fluttered and moved in the breeze, each one separate, still all together. "And now that tree," Joshua said pointing to another nearby. Ethan gasped as the essence of those thousands of people then joined the others in a flood of emotion that was immense and caused him such awe that he fell to his knees. "And that tree...and that tree..." Joshua continued until he had pointed to several of the trees in the large grove.

The state of mind and emotions of millions of people of every kind were now present within him. Some were very disturbing while others were exhilarating and pleasurable. His spirit of self had grown as big as the grove itself to retain all that he was now experiencing.

Then the essence of one person became predominant over the others. It was a young man and the emotion within him was so intense as to be almost crippling. Worthlessness, disparity, sorrow, anger, resentment, sullenness and hopelessness dominated his whole being and caused Ethan to grimace as the ugliness settled within him. He had experienced these feelings himself and they were so intense that it was difficult to bear. He knew that such darkness would eventually consume this man and lead to his self-destruction if allowed to progress. But who was he? What could be so terrible in his life to cause him to live in such anguish? Then the focus shifted to another with intense anger and hatred, then to another and another. The experience was causing Ethan to lose his own senses as he sluggishly fought to look up at Joshua.

"Enough, please, enough," he begged.

"The perception of aloneness is a lie perpetuated by the adversary to create despair, hopelessness, indifference, anger, hatred, resentment... To understand the true nature of your own feelings and desires, you must overcome the lies impressed upon you by those who wish nothing more than to darken and destroy your spirit and the spirits of all they encounter. Only when these lies are recognized and purged from your own being, only then will you begin to see and understand the true path before you.

As you recognize the lies within yourself, you can then begin to help others recognize the lies within *themselves*, because no greater joy will you find than bringing light to those in darkness."

With a subtle wave of Joshua's hand, the intense emotions of those millions of people were lifted from Ethan. The dizziness left him, and he felt oddly alone and small—drained of enormity. He rested on his knees while regaining his senses, then slowly stood. He said nothing, his mind numb from the experience.

"On this course you will now take, you will encounter difficulty and deception and *you will* be tested. Gain strength in knowledge from those you trust. Make your choices honestly and know that true understanding comes from the heart. Continue to ask for guidance and you will receive it there."

"But...there are so many more things I would like to know."

"In due time," Joshua responded. "The answers you seek will be given to you if you have the desire to search for them, the patience to wait for them, and the courage to understand them. Ponder these things and go forward with conviction. Journey well, Ethan."

Joshua smiled and Ethan could see and feel the warmth, sincerity and power of this man's incredible countenance. This strange and magnificent experience was coming to an end. He didn't really want to leave this fantastic place. Then, with the inevitable blink of an eye, he found himself in the cold darkness of night.

He could barely see. The bed of lilies was gone and a dark patch of weeds was in its place. There was no path and he found himself standing on rough and uneven hard dirt. A chill went through him. His jacket was lying across the top of an up-ended, discarded pallet and there was nothing else around—nothing remained of where he had just been. Everything was empty, quiet and still—just as before.

After unlocking the motel room door, he walked in and turned on the light. The clock read 3:37 A.M. That meant only twenty-four minutes had passed since he had left, which seemed impossible. It felt like hours had passed. He tossed the room key on the small table and sat down in the chair. *Everything* was different now.

A small strip of sunlight crept across the floor near the bed, sneaking underneath the cheap curtains. It was well after ten and he was still wearing his shoes, having covered up only with the bedspread sometime earlier that morning. Momentarily confused about where he was, he looked around...then everything came flooding back.

He sat up to the side of the bed, steadied himself and then walked to the window to look outside. The blinding light caused him to wince and cover his eyes. He opened the door and using his hand as a shield, waited for his eyes to adjust, blinking and squinting, trying to make out the details of what was on the other side of the street. It was as he had thought; a vacant lot covered with scattered patches of weeds, a pile of dirt in one corner and bits of trash scattered here and there.

His mind was swirling with ideas, images, perceptions... It was all being analyzed and reevaluated. Things that didn't make sense before were starting to become clearer. The walls of impossibility were thinning. New ideas and thoughts were emerging faster than he could keep track.

Anxious to get back to a life and to a home that now seemed more inviting, he skipped the shower, grabbed the bags and headed out. A quick stop at the front desk and a modest reimbursement for a lamp would have him on his way.

The vacant lot was now directly in front of him as he prepared to enter the street. His mind was full and busy—as clear as it had ever been. It was hard to concentrate on things like 'remove cap, insert nozzle, lift handle.'

He was trying to be careful not to over-analyze or make irrational judgments about this irrational experience. After the car was topped off with fuel, he grabbed something that could only marginally be called breakfast, and was on his way home.

The rest of the drive went by quickly with all his time spent in thoughts of that 'other place.' Even the thought of stopping by the cemetery was lost in the mental fray that continued until he found the familiar roads of his bedroom community. Actually, his reasons for visiting the cemetery would now take on a different meaning, if what he had been told could be believed. It would seem what constituted the lives of his family weren't *really* there anyway.

There was some apprehension as he approached the driveway to the house. Then a good feeling came over him when he pulled in to see that everything looked great. There were no weeds of any consequence and the lawn actually looked nice. Various flowers were in bloom in the now clean and neat mulch-covered beds and the trees were healthy and green. He'd never look at a tree the same way again.

After pulling into the garage and taking his luggage in the house, Mutters ran to meet him in the hallway. "Hello, kitty," he said. She meowed and stopped at his feet to look up at him, darting her head back and forth anxiously. He reached down to pet her and she purred enthusiastically with affection.

He paused while passing the pictures of Rachel and Allison in the upstairs hallway and smiled in his new knowledge. But in that knowledge he now also felt a distant feeling of anguish. It wasn't his and wasn't theirs, but somehow it still had something to do with them. *Odd*, he thought. As he made his way to the bedroom, the feeling left him.

That night as he sat on the bed and looked at Rachel's picture on the nightstand, the same strange detached feeling came back. The next morning it happened again and once again while looking at their picture above the fireplace. Then he realized that feeling of anguish and despair was the same as he had felt while in the grove of trees. It was real...and he wondered...

That evening Ethan decided it was time to make a phone call...

"This is Jeff."

"Hi Jeff, Ethan Grey."

"Hey, Ethan. How are you doing? I was just thinking about calling you the other day."

"I beat you to it. How's business?"

"It's good. Busy."

"Glad to hear it. I was wondering if you could help me with something."

"Well, I'll certainly try. What do you need?"

"I need some information on a particular person and I remembered you hired some people to do that for you one time. Do you think they might still be available?"

"I believe they are. Do you want me to handle it or do you want their number so you can contact them directly?"

"I'd like you to do it if you don't mind. I think I'm going to be pretty busy here in the near future."

"Oh, you starting up something fun?"

"Well, that remains to be seen. I'll let you know."

"Who's the person and what info do you want."

"The person's name is Stephen Lee. He used to work at a hardware store on the north side of town. That was a year or so ago. He should be about twenty years old now. I just need a general rundown on what he's doing and what's going on in his personal life. I'd like this done discreetly."

"Stephen Lee... Why does that name sound familiar?"

There was a long pause, then Ethan responded. "He's the one who was driving the car." The conversation suddenly turned awkward.

"You mean, the boy who uh..."

"Yeah, that one." There was more silence.

"You don't mind me asking what you're planning to do, do you?"

"Oh I'm not going to *do* anything. I think he might be having some trouble and I just wanted to find out what was going on with him."

"You know Ethan, the last time we talked about this, your feelings about this kid were less than gracious and you let everyone know it. If something were to happen to him after you got this information..."

"Oh no. That's not what I'm thinking at all. To be honest, I've been seeing things a little different recently and, well, I just want to find out how he's doing. That's all."

"Guess I'll just have to trust you on this one. How soon do you need it?"

"Whenever you get it will be fine."

"Alright. Anything else?"

"I may be heading out of town pretty soon and will probably need to convert some money. I'll give you a call later."

"Okay. I'll wait to hear from you then."

Jeff was a good man. He had taken care of the 'retirement' account since it was opened. It isn't always easy to find someone you can really trust with your money...or your secrets.

CHAPTER THIRTEEN

Hands of Fate

IT HAD BEEN FOUR days since Ethan left and she hadn't talked with him at all during that time. She knew it was up to him to decide what he wanted to do. Still, she thought he would have called to at least say "hi," if not to discuss the larger matters at hand. It wasn't easy to concentrate on seemingly insignificant things like her *career* when something so vastly more important was looming. It was still his choice though, and she wasn't going to push him.

There was a knock on the open office door and Professor Greenhagen stuck his head in.

"Professor, come in," Alex said cheerfully.

He entered, sat down and got right to the point. "Heard from your friend?"

"No. I was hoping he would have called by now too, but nothing yet."

The Professor sighed and looked down at the desk. "I don't trust him."

"You sound like you know something."

"I dug up some information on that lab he used to work at. The details of the explosion are different than what he describes. Either he's telling the truth and someone's covering something up, or he's lying. Either way, it just makes me all the more suspicious. Did he share anything more with you after our meeting?"

"Not really. He has personal issues to work through and unless he comes around on his own, I just don't see us going anywhere with this."

"He's a flake and I think he's hiding something. You'd tell me, wouldn't you?"

Alex started twiddling her pen. "Of course. I think some things are just bothering him. He may not have the stomach for this kind of stuff."

"He *has* brought up some very interesting ideas, I'll give him that. But unless he can come up with something tangible, this is all nothing more than a fascinating fishing expedition. Somehow I sure would love to get into the heart of the Order and rip out a major artery," the Professor said, then sighed and slowly shook his head in frustration.

They sat and said nothing until Alex finally spoke. "I understand."

"Maybe you should give him a call. See what his problem is." She just smiled politely. "At least keep me informed. Let me know if he ever pulls his head out," the Professor concluded before leaving.

"I will," Alex responded, still twiddling the pen. She took out her global to make sure it was still on. It was.

It was late that evening at home and Ethan still hadn't called. She was disappointed that after all the incredible experiences they had been through, he could just let it all go. Four days... Was he really that messed up, or was it something else? She sat on the sofa and tried to read while glancing at the clock. After an hour, that was it.

The music was muted and she picked up the global. She held it in front of her looking at it, thinking what she would say. Suddenly, it rang. Startled, she jerked her hand back and the global dropped, bouncing off the edge of the sofa and onto the floor where it cartwheeled a few times before coming to rest face down in the fuzzy carpet.

Quickly she picked it up and hastily answered. "Hello?"

"Alex?" the voice on the other end said hesitantly.

She pulled the phone away and looked at the number on the display. *"Ethan,"* she replied.

"You okay?"

"Yeah, fine. You know, it's a funny thing though. Last week I got back from this trip to Europe that I took with a friend. We had some pretty wild experiences and you know what? Apparently it didn't mean much to him. He didn't even keep in touch after we got back—didn't even call me, *for four days.*"

"Sorry about that. I was kind of preoccupied."

"So how *are* you doing?"

"That always seems to be the question of the day, doesn't it? Warranted no doubt."

"No doubt. But seriously..."

"I think I'm okay, believe it or not. Overwhelmed a little, but okay."

"Really?"

"Yeah, really."

"No one turned you in to the Humane Society?"

"No, kitty's fine.

"Good."

"I want to find that vessel Hazzar's father talked about—the Power of Souls."

Alex was stunned and almost fell off the sofa. "Uh...Ethan? I think something just happened to my phone. Could you repeat that?"

"You heard me."

"Noooo I don't think so because it sounded like you said you *wanted* to go look for the Power of Souls."

"That's right." There was a moment of perfect silence.

"You're really serious."

"Yes, I am.

"Well, what happened with trying to find the element?"

"It's a long story. Bottom line is, I think the Professor could be right. I think it's all connected."

"Okay, but why the sudden change of attitude?" she asked, hinting of possible insincerity.

Ethan knew his flip-flop behavior had made her skeptical about almost everything he did or said. "I don't really have a choice. I need to find it."

"Of course you have a choice. We all have choices."

"Well sure, but some choices end up being a little more obvious than others. You know what I mean? I've just decided that I have to do this," he said with conviction. It sounded like he really *was* serious. "So do you think the Professor is still interested in being involved?"

Ethan's positive sentiment was refreshing and unexpected, which is why she knew something wasn't right. "Are you sure you're the same Ethan Grey I engaged in the throws of primordial passion with in Russia?"

There was a brief pause while he thought. "Well, technically it was Kazakhstan."

"Whatever. I thought you didn't like the Professor?"

"He still bugs me. The thing is, I'll bet he can arrange the kind of support I'm going to need. Whether I like him personally or not has little bearing on getting the job done."

"What are you going to do if you find it?"

"Steal it." Dead silence followed.

"Okay, really, what color of toads have you been licking?"

"Believe it or not, I haven't felt this good in a long time."

"My point exactly."

"I've made up my mind, Alex. I know what I have to do."

"You know, Ethan, I'm just not sure he's going to go for it. There just isn't any *real* proof of a definable threat and that's what he needs."

"Regardless, I *am* going through with this, and I'm going to need help even if I have to figure it out on my own. That's all there is to it. I just thought he might want to be involved since he's so gung-ho about the Black Sun and all."

"I promised to help you, but this is just..." There was another long pause.

"All I'd like you to do is talk to him and see if he's interested. That's it. If he isn't, I don't expect you to do anything else."

"Oh, but I will," Alex stated emphatically.

"Hey, this isn't a field trip anymore. I have no idea how it could all turn out."

"I understand, but I made a promise."

"This goes way beyond our deal, Alex."

"My mind's made up."

"Alex…"

"You really want to argue with me?"

"No…no. That would be pointless."

"You're learning. I'll see what the Professor says and give you a call."

"Alright, thank you."

After taking a few minutes to figure out what she was going to say exactly, she dialed the number.

"Hello, Professor."

"I'm guessing you talked to your friend."

"Yes, sir."

"And what did he have to say?"

"Well…you're going to find this hard to believe, but he's decided to go find this Power of Souls…and I'm going with him."

"Alex…" the Professor responded, disappointed in her obvious lapse of judgment.

"I'm sorry sir. I've already made my decision."

"Alex, you haven't really thought this through. Screwing around with the Order isn't something you two should be doing on your own. People could die."

"I know sir, but I think he's serious this time. He's even asking for your help. That alone should tell you something. He'd like to meet with you."

"It tells me he's schizoid and I don't think you should trust him. *I* certainly don't. Like the story of a total stranger in the middle of Russia giving him that parchment? Honestly now."

"Technically, it was Kazakhstan…sir."

"I know that, Alex. It's just that you haven't made the best choices in men in the past and this one doesn't sit right with me either."

"He'll pay for everything."

"That's not the point. I don't want to see a price put on your life, or his either for that matter. You're painting me into a corner here."

"I'm sorry sir, but we're going to try to do this and I'm sure we'd have a much better chance of success with your help."

"I'm not sure you completely understand just how involved and dangerous this could get. I'm not even sure if I can protect you over there." There was a long silence, then a heavy sigh. "I'll let you know."

"Thank you, sir."

✵ ✵ ✵

Even though the trip to Balkhash and Turkey ended up being a little more eventful than expected, it *had* still been just a simple research trip. This new expedition to find the Power of Souls would undoubtedly take him into realms of uncertainty that he might not be able to control. If something were to happen and he couldn't return, the journal might be discovered. The chance of someone disseminating it for its technology and maybe figuring out a way to view and corrupt its mysteries was a possibility he wanted to eliminate if possible. Given his experiences and what the journal meant to him personally, keeping it intact and hidden away from the outside world seemed the proper thing to do. The journal of a young girl who had become such an important part of his life would not be defiled.

He set the large flower arrangement down to the side of Rachel's headstone along with the small plastic box and paused to study the names. As he read them, the thoughts of despair and loneliness he used to feel were mostly subdued. What he now felt was not a peace as of yet, but still of less futility—almost an absence of emotion.

Trying to be inconspicuous, he took the small box to the back of the headstone, set it down and removed the lid. Inside was another small rectangular container made of heavy plastic, sealed shut and waterproof. Also inside the box was a large kitchen knife and small gardening spade.

Taking the container out and setting it on the grass as a guide next to the headstone, he took the knife and cut out a deep rectangular section of sod about six inches larger than the dimensions of the container. With the spade, he removed the piece of sod and dug the hole down about a foot and a half, placing the excavated dirt in the box. He set the small container in the hole carefully and replaced enough of the dirt to allow the sod to bulge slightly, then lie flat when pressed down under foot. The spade and knife went back into the box with the excess dirt. *You can't even tell*, he thought proudly, standing back to admire his work.

Linear timelines, as they are commonly and simply understood by many, would suggest that the journal would no longer exist if theorized future events could be altered, thus negating the necessity for its existence in the first place. So did its existence in the present mean he was going to fail? If that was the case, then everything else he now knew was a lie.

No. Regardless of its paradoxical reasoning, certain events and experiences could not be denied. It would seem then that time was just incomprehensively more complex than what we can extrapolate by simply watching it pass. Not a *scientific* conclusion, but one he would just have to live with.

☀ ☀ ☀

The Professor had finally come around, although not happily. Now Ethan was smack in the middle of freeway rush-hour traffic on his way to meet with Alex, the Professor and Ms. Benoit. Discussions to formalize whatever plans might be necessary would precede their flight out the following evening. Money had been transferred and converted and Jeff had been given Ethan's open-ended itinerary. Mrs. Kensington agreed to watch the house and Mutters. Everything seemed in order.

Unknown to Alex, the Professor had agreed to meet with Ethan alone beforehand at Ethan's request. Even though there was some friction between them, the Professor was obviously an intelligent man with formidable resources. Since he had agreed to support this ill-advised venture, it seemed important to try and establish some kind of common ground between them before putting his life in the Professor's hands.

He would have arrived sooner, but wasn't paying much attention on the first trip to the Professor's home and didn't want to call anyone to admit he was lost. The driver requested an address from his dispatch, but one wasn't listed for the name given. Surprise. They kept cruising through the neighborhoods until Ethan finally recognized the right street. The driver didn't seem to mind too much, the meter had never stopped running.

"Let's go in here," the Professor said as he motioned to the guest room off the foyer. He sat in a chair near the end of a wood coffee table. Ethan sat on the sofa behind it at the other end. The room was decorated nicely with paintings and other rare and valuable antiquities. There was a large marble chess set on a tall skinny table and behind it, a bookcase full of books.

"So, Mr. Grey, what has become so important that suddenly you've decided you need to go find this artifact?"

"Well, sir, I think I saw some of those connections you were talking about. I also want to apologize for my previous behavior. This whole thing is turning out to be a little more involved than I was expecting."

"I can appreciate that. But it's only been a week, and suddenly you're okay with everything?"

"I wouldn't say I'm okay with *everything*. You're obviously just more accustomed to these kinds of situations than I am and I don't always see things the way others do."

"Ethan, people seeing things differently is a fact of life. To completely change your attitude in a week though, that could raise some suspicions about one's motivation."

"Yeah, I suppose it could. By the way, I think it was real nice what you did for Alex—taking her in and helping her with her marital situation and all."

"She's a fine young woman and deserved better. Sometimes you just have to let certain people know what's appropriate and what isn't, especially the ones she's taken a liking to. It would be... *most* unfortunate to see her heart broken again."

"Yes, being betrayed *is* one of worst things that can happen to a person. Many times it brings up feelings of distrust, anger...even retribution. But some situations aren't always as they appear."

"A circumstance many could avoid by simply being honest. It goes to one's character."

"True, but character isn't only defined in what one says, many times it's also defined in what one *does not* say. I think an intelligent man knows when discretion is the better part of valor. Wouldn't you agree, Professor?"

"Intelligence is not determined in words alone, Ethan." the Professor leaned forward and rested his forearms on his knees to look at him squarely. "You know, honesty can be an interesting commodity. There are times when exploring its discourse in application is not always a prudent endeavor."

"But isn't that honesty something we should find in ourselves before trying to impress its virtues upon others?"

They were now staring at each other across the room. After a few tense moments, The Professor leaned back in his chair and slowly formed an almost invisible grin. "Humph. Simple perception *can* be an impoverished witness. Maybe there's more to you than meets the eye."

"An insightful observation, Professor."

"Well then, it's nice to know you've found your mettle, Mr. Grey. I was beginning to wonder."

"You're not the only one."

"So, why is Alex so eager to put her life in danger to do this with you? I trust her judgment, most of the time. But this seems uncharacteristic even for her."

"She's a complex and strong woman. Maybe this is just who she really is."

"Maybe so. You know Ethan, I really do believe there's a force that connects and binds all things on this earth. I also believe it contains all the knowledge that ever existed and ever will exist. It's something that's always around us and if a person just takes the time to study its effects, to see the interactions of nature and of man, you can tap into that knowledge and find what you need. You can do anything you want to do, discover anything you want to know, even use it to become wealthy and powerful.

"For some, those connections are practically imperceptible, for others, clearly discernible. It is a *marvelous* world we live in, and it sounds like you, my friend, might be starting to see some of those connections."

"I appreciate your words. I'm not sure I'm *that* intuitive though," Ethan offered.

"The order of things is driven by simple common sense—strong and weak, right and wrong, intelligent and ignorant. All you have to do is filter out the noise. You'll find what you want."

"I'm afraid we may need a little more than just common sense if we're going to make this work."

"That's where *I* come in. Don't worry, we'll discuss everything later. Where are you staying?"

"I have a reservation at a hotel a few miles from Alex's place."

"She should still be at her office. Does she know you're here?"

"No, but I'm going to meet her later for dinner before we come back."

"Very good then. I'm glad you stopped by and I'll see you later tonight." The Professor stood and shook Ethan's hand.

❦ ❦ ❦

"Just so you know, I met with the Professor a little while ago to kind of clear the air."

"You've already talked with him?" Alex asked.

"I just wanted to make sure we understood each other before getting into all this."

"Huh. So how did *that* go?"

"Pretty good actually. He's interesting, that's for sure. Takes this 'force all around us, patterns in the chaos' thing pretty seriously doesn't he?"

"Ah, you got to hear his theory of Unified Knowledge."

"Is that what it is? He talked about the 'knowledge that exists everywhere and we can tap into if we listen.'"

"That's the one. What did you think?"

"He has some interesting ideas. I can't say they all made *complete* sense, but I didn't want to get into a philosophical discussion about it or anything."

"That was smart considering Philosophy and Theology is a major part of his education and teaching. He probably would have cleared his schedule to argue his points with you."

"You seem to have a good relationship with him. What do *you* think?"

"I think the Professor is an incredibly kind and thoughtful person who has dedicated his whole life to learning and teaching."

Ethan was puzzled at her evasive answer. "You skirted the question."

"It's difficult because I think his focus is more on the conceptual abstracts of life rather than the logical processes of life. Professor Greenhagen tends to look for 'ghosts in the machine' if you will—enigmatic explanations for what happens in our lives. We can both look at the same life events and where I see a simple order of intelligence, he'll see a grand intertwined mystical event that's being influenced by some magical force channeled by tapping into the *great cosmic library*. I love him dearly, but he definitely has his own ideas on things. He also has a tendency to imply that since we're all part of nature, it's okay to follow nature's rules when it suits us. That's always bothered me because I think nature can be cold and cruel sometimes."

Ethan thought for a minute. "He actually seems pretty nice once you get past the crust. So if he really believes that, then why did he take *you* in? Wounded kitten syndrome?"

"I don't know...maybe."

"His ideas can't be *all* bad for him to still be teaching after so many years."

"Oh they're not *all* bad ideas by any means. Some of what he says about being strong and positive, listening and filtering out the noise makes a lot of sense. The thing is, *his* common sense comes from a different place than mine does. I've known him for a long time and I believe he's a good person. I just don't think he sees the big picture. A lot of his ideas are mainstream and what people pay to hear. I think those same people are looking to believe in something easier to live by...something that's more mystical and vague and less consequential. Someday I suspect those people are going to get a *seriously* rude awakening. Maybe we all are."

"Already had one of those," Ethan said quietly under his breath.

"And if you tell the Professor I told you *any* of this, I'll break your arm."

"Noted," Ethan replied.

"See, now you've got me going again. You *like* doing this, don't you? Getting me all worked up."

"I figure we might have a less eventful dinner this time if you get it out of your system *before* we get to the restaurant."

Alex's expression was serious, then she smiled. "Touché."

Dinner was delicious and thankfully, uneventful. Another vehicle was already parked to the side of the Professor's office when they arrived. Alex knocked on the side door, then opened it and walked in as Ethan followed.

"Ah, good," the Professor said as he stood to greet them. Ms. Benoit was there and stood as well. The opulent office brought back a few old unpleasant feelings, although recent events had given him new confidence as well. They all shook hands and sat down.

On the wall behind the table was a large monitor cleverly hidden behind a set of paintings on sliding rails. The Professor motioned to Rianna and she clicked a button on her small PDA. An image appeared on the monitor and she began speaking. "In light of our last meeting, we were able to get some better photos of this man we know as Richard Grayson. As you know, he operates a company called Ireon in Hamburg." She clicked on the device and brought up the next picture. "This is a security ID photo of Thomas Chamberlain we pulled from agency archives—the same man who was the director of Aridel Systec," she said directing her statement to Ethan.

The next picture was a split screen of both previous pictures. She clicked again and the two pictures merged and a point match comparison diagram formed over the face of the superimposed photos. '71% MATCH PROBABLILITY' was then displayed below the diagram. "Facial point comparison says there's a seventy-one percent chance that these are the same man. So it is *very* possible that your Mr. Chamberlain is still alive and well. That was a good catch, Mr. Grey. Pancros was seen leaving Ireon just two days ago which leaves little doubt as to their affiliation."

"Here's what we're up against," the Professor started. "This artifact could be at Grayson's facility in Hamburg, at the estate outside Bremen or possibly someplace else entirely. I've retained a small incursion team that will lead the operation and should be able to retrieve the artifact once its location can be verified. Since this is a private operation, we won't be receiving any official support and it will be up to us to figure out where the artifact is being kept. You two *will not* be directly involved," he said to Alex and Ethan. "My team will handle the operation, the surveillance and retrieval, and you two will stay out of harm's way. *Is that understood?*"

"Yes, sir," they both said dutifully.

"If we take the team into the wrong location, it's unlikely we'll get a second chance at the other one. *If* we can determine where the artifact is, then we'll formulate a plan and execute it. If we're wrong the first time and don't acquire the item, then the operation will be over. We'll have tipped our hand and I won't risk another incursion. Also, in light of Mr. Chamberlain's miraculous resurrection, *you'll* be going with a new ID and passport," he said to Ethan. "I'll give those to you tomorrow. Alright then, the team leader will contact you after you arrive. He'll identify himself as Mr. Smith."

"Oh, *that's* original," Ethan quipped as Alex smiled half-heartedly.

The Professor continued. "Ms. Benoit and I will monitor the operation from here and stay in contact with Mr. Smith. We'll determine and advise the best course of action depending on what you find. Assuming we're successful, the artifact will be delivered to a safe location out of the country known only to myself, Mr. Smith and his next in command. He'll let you know where you're going once you're in the air. The artifact will remain hidden at this new location until we're sure it's safe to extract it and bring it back here. That will give us some time to determine what we're dealing with."

Ethan knew that the Professor's plan for hiding the artifact, or Power of Souls, would not suffice for what he was supposed to do. Unfortunately, the details of how he would handle that situation were over a bridge he wouldn't be able to cross until he got to it.

The Professor then walked to his desk and opened it. "Alex, you already have one of these. Ethan, I'd like you to take this one." The Professor handed him a global. "You'll have secure communication and we'll be able to track your location. Rianna and I will try to keep tabs on you both and if *anything* unexpected happens, we'll abort and get you out."

The Professor sat back down and became even more serious. "Are you sure I can't talk you two out of this?" he said while looking at them almost forlornly.

"I wish you could," Ethan replied.

"I don't need to remind you two that this organization is not to be trifled with. Under no circumstances are you to do *anything* on your own. All you're expected to do is stay low and out of sight and follow Smith's lead. They'll handle it. Understood?"

Ethan nodded then turned to Alex. "Well, excited to get out of the office again, Money Penny?"

Alex looked over at him. "Sometimes I wish *I* had a license to kill, Mr. Grey," she said with an evil smirk.

The Professor just shook his head. "I'll have a car pick you up at your place and I'll give you your tickets and hotel information then. Make sure you have your passport and ID with you when we pick you up, and please call me if you think of anything else in the meantime."

"We will," Alex responded."

"Last chance..." They both said nothing. "Then I'll see you tomorrow."

"Good luck," Ms. Benoit said as she stood.

"Thank you, we're going to need it," Alex replied.

✵ ✵ ✵

It had been a restful night at the hotel—no weird dreams, no visitations by strange men in robes. But as he lay there looking at the ceiling, he did wonder, at least a little, what was going to happen on this trip. The experience with Joshua may have given him an infusion of new thoughts and possibilities, maybe even some much needed confidence. Still, this new stalwart persona wasn't cast as thick as he would have liked Alex and the Professor to believe.

Knowing about his family and learning about life and everything that went with it was incredible, fascinating and enlightening. Yes, it was nice to know a brain tumor wasn't causing the visions. And yes, it was nice to know that there might *really be* something more to life than just what he previously understood. That didn't keep him from being scared.

The realities of this trip, and what could happen had not been displaced. They were, in fact, about all he could think about. The anxiety had never gone away. It was hope in new possibilities that throttled the fear and kept anxiety under control. Hope was his new companion. Faith would not be so easily acquired. *That* would still take time.

Ethan rang the doorbell and Alex promptly answered. "Hi. Come on in. I'm running a little late so have a seat."

"Can I help?" Ethan asked.

"No, but thanks. I'll just be a few minutes. I've gotta get this done before we leave," she said a little panicked.

"No rush, we still have about an hour."

Alex was trying to finish up a guideline that was to be submitted to the University. She was obviously stressed. A half hour later it was finished and fifteen minutes after that she had her bags out in the front room, ready to go.

The limo showed up shortly afterward. The driver came to the door while the Professor stood outside the car and waited. Within a few minutes, the luggage was loaded and they were heading to the airport.

"Well, you two ready for this?" the Professor asked.

"I think so," Alex replied, somewhat uptight.

"More ready than I was last time," Ethan said almost jokingly.

"Here are your tickets. The return is open-ended. Ethan, give me your wallet and passport." Ethan pulled them out and handed them over. The Professor set the wallet and passport on the seat and pulled another wallet from a jacket pocket, then took the money from Ethan's wallet and transferred it to the new one. He then removed a new passport from his pocket and handed them both to Ethan. "Your name is now Ethan Hamilton. You're a tourist. You have a new driver's license, credit cards and passport. Do you have any other identification on you? Travelers checks, embroidered luggage?"

"No."

"You're sure?"

"Yes, I believe so."

"From now on, use this name everywhere. Study and memorize all the new information and keep your fingers off buttons. Let Alex do everything." Ethan looked through the wallet and started studying the passport.

"Welcome to the club," Alex commented. With a new last name, it seemed they now had something else in common.

❖ ❖ ❖

The setting sun cast a shimmering orange glow over the wings of the large airliner. It teased cirrus clouds on its ascent to find the ethereal winds that would carry it eastward over the Atlantic. Alex had said very little so far. While usually embracing the role of ardent protagonist, *this* trip had caused her to step back—to think about her life and what she still wanted to accomplish. Her silence was unusual.

"*What* am I doing?" she suddenly blurted out uncharacteristically. Surprised, Ethan looked at her, watching and waiting. "I mean...has your insanity rubbed off on me? What was I thinking?"

"Now be nice. Once we land you can just stay at the hotel or we'll find you a flight home if you want."

"It isn't just *this*," she said holding up her hands and looking around. There was a long pause while her thoughts churned. "What do you expect the rest of your life to be like?" The question caught him off guard. He hadn't been thinking that far ahead. "I mean, what do you plan to do when this is over? Let's say everything goes perfectly and you find this Power of Souls.

Then what? Will I just go back to teaching and you'll just go back to...whatever you do?"

"Well, I can't say that sounds all that appealing," he responded. The fact was though, he really hadn't given it that much thought. It was an honest and sobering question. "Huh, I don't know." She looked at him for a second, then returned to staring at the back of the seat in front of her.

"I want to have children."

"Didn't we already do that? You just need to wait a hundred million years."

Alex sighed and continued staring. "Derric didn't want any children. Actually, I didn't either. I suppose at the time it was probably a good thing. No telling what would have happened to them. I feel like I'm missing something, you know?" He *did* know. "Do you suppose Rachel would have done anything differently if she had known she was leaving?"

"I really couldn't tell you."

"Would *you* have done anything differently?" It was an uncomfortable subject and made him squirm a little. "You know what? I'm sorry, that's none of my business. I should just keep my big mouth shut."

"No, it's okay. It's just..." Ethan paused while he thought. "I suppose I would have tried to understand better, tried to listen more."

"That's good...that's good," Alex said as she nodded.

Ethan was watching her out of the corner of his eye. He'd never seen her like this before. "Alex, don't worry about all this stuff. It'll work out somehow."

"I wish I had your newfound optimism. My life's a mess, Ethan. And here I am flying halfway around the world, *again*, involved in something I have absolutely no business being any part of. Coming along this time was a stupid idea."

Ethan smiled. "No it wasn't," he said as he reached over to squeeze her hand. "Don't ask me how I know this, but I think I'm right where I'm supposed to be, and so are you."

"I sure hope you're right," she said before turning to watch the last light of day slip away.

Hamburg was slightly overcast as the plane continued descending in preparation for its final approach. Ethan was sitting by the window on this last leg of the flight. He was impressed by the green landscape. Except for the wide use of stone architecture and a few other differences in the style of buildings, the scenery wasn't unlike familiar areas of the eastern United States.

They headed to their hotel and checked in after picking up the rental car and a good map. After unpacking her things, Alex came back to Ethan's room and sat down on the sofa to relax.

"So, now I guess we wait," she said.

They wouldn't wait long. Ethan's global rang a few minutes later.

"Hello?"

"This is Mr. Smith," a man stated.

"This is Mr. uh...Hamilton."

"Be in front of your hotel at three o'clock. We'll pick you up."

"Okay." The phone hung up from the other end.

"Boy, these spy types aren't very chatty."

"What did he say?"

"Out front, three o'clock."

"That's still two hours. What do you want to do until then?"

"Besides eat?"

"Well, there's always that."

"I'd like to go check out the factory where Chamberlain... Grayson works."

"Oh now you *know* that's not a smart idea. We're not supposed to do *anything* unless we work with Mr. Smith. Or did you miss that part?"

"We'll just drive by, check things out," Ethan suggested.

"We wait," Alex said insistently. "*They'll* show us around. Let's just go get some food and relax." He reluctantly agreed.

It was a little before three when they walked out the front doors of the hotel to wait for their contact. "Hmm, deja vu," Ethan commented.

They had been sitting for about five minutes when an old, ugly white van pulled up in front of them. A man with dark, short hair sporting a red stripe down the middle got out and started walking toward them. Ethan and Alex both stood and watched as the man walked past and into the hotel.

"Whew, that was close," Ethan remarked.

Then a large, black, late model SUV pulled up behind the van and a man got out. He stopped about five feet in front of them. "I'm Smith," he said impassively.

"I'm Grey, I mean Hamilton. *Dang.* This is Alex."

Smith rolled his eyes. "Get in," he said before walking back to the vehicle.

Ethan climbed in and sat in the front passenger seat. Alex got in back behind him. There was a man sitting behind the driver's seat who appeared to share Smith's equally chipper demeanor. Alex didn't say anything at first, then held out her hand. "I'm Alex."

The man looked at her momentarily from behind his sunglasses, then shook her hand. "Nice to meet you," he replied without a name or hint of a smile. *This is going to fun,* she thought as they drove away.

"We received the intel yesterday morning and already have people working locally to see what we can come up with," Smith stated.

"Isn't that risky working with the locals?" Ethan asked.

"No, these are *my* people. I trust them. So, we're trying to locate an old stone container—cylindrical in shape, six inches by twelve to sixteen inches long. Is that correct?

"Yes, that's correct."

"Any other information that might be useful?"

"Not really."

"Ireon is outside of town in the industrial district and the compound is about ten kilometers north of Bremen. We're familiar with both locations. Other than being babysat, what exactly are you two supposed to be doing on this assignment?"

"We're your clients and the ones writing the checks."

"All the more reason to keep you out of this."

"I need you to get me as close to the buildings as possible. I might be able to tell where the artifact is."

Smith looked over at Ethan briefly, then back to the road. "I don't think so."

"How about a bonus directly from your client," Ethan said as he looked over at Smith.

"I was told specifically to keep you two out of harms way."

"I know what you were told, but it's my money paying for this little foray and I need to see those two sites."

Smith let out a sigh. "What kind of *bonus* do you have in mind?"

"Enough to make it worth your while."

"I don't know," Smith said warily.

"Look, all I need you to do is get me close to the buildings, that's all. If I can locate the artifact remotely, it would save us all a lot of legwork. If not, we'll stay out of your way and let you do your job."

"There was nothing mentioned in the briefing about a way to remotely detect the artifact."

"No one else knows about it—couldn't risk letting the information out." Alex was getting more nervous by the second. This information was all new to her as well and she had no idea what Ethan was up to.

"And how, exactly, are you going to tell where this artifact is just by getting close to the buildings?"

Ethan looked over at Smith through his sunglasses, then back ahead as he remarked, "Well, I *could* tell you, but then Alex would have to kill you, both."

He kept looking forward and never changed his expression as an uncomfortable silence permeated the once stimulating conversation. Alex was shocked. The man in the back seat slowly turned to look at her from behind his very dark lenses. She knew Ethan was cocky sometimes, but to say something like *that* to people like *this* was just plain lunacy.

Her own dark glasses hid her screaming thoughts and golf ball size eyes while she slowly turned to the man next to her, and stared back at him. After a moment, Smith and the man in the back seat started to laugh. Ethan never did change his expression. Alex then breathed out a huge and silent sigh of relief.

"Okay, I might be able to get you near the factory, but the compound is heavily guarded and I wouldn't be able to get you any closer than about a kilometer, regardless. I'm still responsible for you two so you do this my way. We'll drive by Ireon first and go from there."

"That's fair," Ethan replied.

"So, what's your role in all this," Smith said motioning back to Alex.

"I'll let you know when it's all over."

The factory was impressively large with a warehouse in the back and an office complex in front, all secured by a tall chain-link fence that encompassed the property. There was a main gate at the southeast corner of the parking lot that appeared to be for employees and guests. It had a security crossbar across the entrance with a guard shack and a wide row of tire spikes on the 'exit' side.

Smith drove the SUV up to the guard shack and stopped in front of the crossbar. A guard stepped out to greet them. "Guten tag! Wie kann ich Ihnen helfen?" the guard asked.

"I'm Jameson Britcher from Paradyne," Smith said as he handed the guard a business card. "We have an appointment with Luana Hidelemann in product development."

"Picture ID please," the Guard replied in fairly good English. Smith reached into his front pocket, pulled out an ID and handed it to the guard. The guard walked to the rear of the SUV, wrote down the plate number, walked back to the shack and handed Smith his ID and a sign that read BESUCHER 8. "Put this on your dash. Visitor parking is in front of the smaller building with the windows over there to the left."

"Thank you," Smith said as he took the sign and put it on the dash. The guard pushed a button and the crossbar rose out of the way.

"I'm guessing we don't *really* have an appointment?" Ethan asked, just verifying the obvious.

"Nope," Smith replied. "This is how we get you close to the building."

Smith pulled the vehicle into a visitor parking stall and shut off the engine. "Now what," he asked.

"Give me a minute," Ethan said as he tried to figure out what he was supposed to do. If he really could sense the Power of Souls, would he see visions again? How long would it take? Nothing was happening so he started to get out.

"Hey, where you going?"

"I'm just going to step inside. I'll come right back." Smith immediately got out to go with him. "You're not dressed for a meeting," Ethan remarked.

"If you go in, I go in."

"No. If someone asks what I need, I'll just say I forgot my briefcase and come back out, okay? It's not like they're going to shoot me or anything."

"Probably not, but if something goes wrong, I'll shoot you myself."

Ethan walked to the double glass doors, trying to stay calm and ready in case a strange vision came. There was still nothing. He opened the outer vestibule doors and nerves started to dance. *Calm down...calm down.*

Now through the inner doors, the lobby was two stories high and quite nice with a security desk not far inside with a single guard. The guard was talking to another man at the desk and only glanced at Ethan as he walked in. Ethan looked around and then the guard stood. "Kann ich Ihnen helfen?" he asked.

Ethan still couldn't sense anything and this was as far as he was going. "Whoops, looks like I forgot my briefcase." Then as casually as he could, he walked back to the vehicle and climbed in. "Okay, let's go," he said anxiously.

"Was there a problem?"

"No, just nerves." Smith backed up and headed around to the side of the office to take a quick look at the warehouse from an angle he couldn't get from the street. There was an automated gate there with card access. He then turned and headed back to the exit.

The guard looked at them oddly as they pulled up, having only entered a few minutes earlier. Smith took the sign from the dash and handed it to the guard. "Had the wrong time. We'll come back later." The guard took the sign and waved them out. "Thank you," Smith chimed as they pulled out on to the street. "So I guess this means you didn't find anything?"

"No."

"So it isn't here?"

"I'm not sure. I'll let you know when we get to the estate."

Alex remained quiet, but was incredibly curious what Ethan was doing. He hadn't said anything before about being able to tell where the artifact was. Why hadn't he told her about any of this? This behavior was *very* strange, even for him.

It took about fifty minutes to drive to the estate's location. The countryside was beautiful with rolling hills and lots of trees and green grass. The estate was on a hill about a kilometer off the main road.

"This is as close as we get," Smith said. "You can see the main building from here through those trees. It's hidden from view everywhere else. No roads on the other side and there are cameras and sensors all over the property. If what you're looking for is that valuable, then I would suspect it's probably in there." Ethan stared through the trees as the SUV drove past the main entrance and behind an embankment. "What do you want to do?" Smith asked.

"Let's follow this road for a while then come back."

Smith did exactly that as they drove about a kilometer past the estate, turned around and came back. Ethan peered through the trees when the estate briefly came into view again. He studied what he could as they drove past. Nothing. He couldn't sense it at all. Granted, it was a long shot since he wasn't sure exactly what he was doing anyway. Still, it was disappointing. He faced forward and let out a heavy sigh.

"So, I guess this means we proceed as originally planned?" Smith asked.

"I'm afraid that's what it means."

Alex was champing at the bit during dinner. "Well Ethan, you going to clue me in on what's going on or what?"

"What do you mean?" he replied, knowing exactly what she meant.

"Driving to Ireon and the estate? Talking about being able to tell if the artifact was there or not without doing anything that I could see? What was that all about?"

Ethan set his napkin to the side of his plate. "Something I didn't want to tell you about until it was absolutely necessary."

"We were supposed to be honest with each other. Remember? Consider it absolutely necessary."

"We'll talk about it in the room. Okay?"

Alex sat with her arms folded and looked away. "Maybe coming here *really wasn't* a good idea. I'm beginning to think we should have just stayed home and let the Professor handle this whole thing."

"I couldn't do that."

She looked at him again, suspiciously. "Why not?"

"I'll tell you upstairs."

Her mannerisms hinted of anxiousness as they walked to his hotel room. "Alright, spill it," she said once they were inside.

Ethan took the five leaflet-size brochures he had picked up on their way through the lobby, and put them on the table. He then opened each one about an inch and set them on their long sides to face each other about ten inches apart across the table like a row of dominos.

"What are you doing?" she asked.

"You'll see. Do you have a lipstick or something?" She pulled a tube of lip balm from her pocket and handed it to him. "Good. Have a seat."

Alex sat down in the chair by the table so she was facing the ends of the brochures. Ethan took the tube of lip balm and set it upright on the table at the end behind the last brochure to his left. He then pulled the other chair around and sat to the left of Alex.

"Imagine your life as a line of dominos, with each successive domino representing your next moment in time. When we're born, the first one is knocked over—that is our very first moment in this world. Then we go to the next moment, and to the next, and the next. For each new moment, a new domino is added, and they tumble continuously our entire lives until the last one falls.

"The thing is, regardless of how long we've been traveling in our respective lines, our moments all tumble in unison—a synchronicity controlled by time. We can see what everyone is doing in that moment, and we have memories of the past, but no one can physically move ahead or back to see what's going on in any other moment. You see what I mean?"

"This isn't going to be another science lecture, is it?"

"Not really. Just bear with me for a minute. Let's say Mr. Lip Balm here is a person, and this row of brochures represents a line of moments in his life. So, let's move Mr. Lip Balm to his next moment." Ethan picked up the tube of lip balm and bumped it into the brochure, knocking it over. Then he set the lip balm down in front of the next brochure. "Now, in his present moment of time, he can see where he is, and he can remember where he's been, but he can't go back to relive that previous moment or physically see into his future. That view is blocked."

Ethan picked up Mr. Lip Balm again, bumped over the next brochure and set him down. "Now, here again, he can see his present, and remember *more* of his past, but he still can't see the future. Time prevents it.

"By studying past events, we can formulate ideas and strategies that allow us to *estimate* how certain future events might unfold. But the fact remains that we cannot physically know what will happen in a future event until that event becomes the present, or the past. Likewise, we cannot physically go back to relive expired moments. *This* is how our lives work. You following me?"

"Astonishingly enough, yes."

"Okay then, theoretically, what would Mr. Lip Balm see if we were to slide him out here to the side, outside his normal timeline?"

Alex looked at the table, thought, and pointed. "Well...he would see his past...his present...*and* his future, all at the same time."

Ethan leaned back in the chair and smiled at her. "That's right."

She looked at him curiously, then back at the table. "You think *this* is what could be happening to you? Your visions?" she asked thoughtfully.

"Somehow…yeah, I think it is. I found out that when I'm near the element or someplace it's been, it will sometimes interact with me, and *this* is what I think happens," he said pointing to Mr. Lip Balm. "Usually what I see is fairly random, but then sometimes the images will focus and I'll see specific times, like what happened at the radar facility. Today I was hoping that being near one of the buildings would allow me to sense where it is. Unfortunately, nothing happened, so now I have no idea where it could be."

"This is all just *astounding*. How did you figure it out?"

"Well, actually, someone told me." Alex was eager to hear the rest of *this* story. "It was…an experience I promise to tell you about someday when this is all over. I just don't want to get into it now because frankly, I'm still not entirely sure what to believe."

Alex shook her head slowly. "It's just absolutely incredible."

"Then you really believe all this."

She looked at him questioningly. "What? You mean you made it all up?" Then she started to grin.

Ethan smiled. "It's just that it sounds even *more* unbelievable when I hear myself say it out loud."

"I understand. But you can still trust me you know."

"Yeah, I know…I know."

"I'll see you tomorrow. You're an amazing person, you know that?" she said as she gave him a friendly hug. It made him blush, just a little.

Ethan sat on the sofa in his room and stared at the television. He wasn't really watching it or even listening to it. His mind was buzzing with possible ways to locate the artifact of which none seemed realistic. Even so, he had been told it was within his ability to accomplish this task. So, if that was true, then there must be a way—he just couldn't see it yet. As he thought, it then occurred to him that just as before, to receive answers, you must ask questions, and the answers he now needed would likely have to come from a place beyond his own knowledge.

Still not completely comfortable with the idea, he turned off the television and awkwardly knelt down next to the hotel bed. This time, he closed his eyes and waited to see if anything *unusual* would happen. Nothing did. His mind remained refreshingly clear and calm. He could sense the room and his place in it and could hear nothing but the sound of his own breathing. Then he began...

"I know Joshua told me I was to find the Power of Souls. I just don't see how that's going to happen now unless I let these other guys find it and hope they'll give it to me later. Is that what I'm supposed to do? But what if they won't give it to me? What if they can't even find it? Am I supposed to do something else? I could really use some help figuring this out, please. Thank you. Um...Amen?"

Ethan opened his eyes and looked across the bed, and waited. He didn't feel anything yet. *How do you know if anyone is even listening?* What is an answer really supposed to sound like? Until something changed, there wasn't much else he could do. He got up off his knees and climbed into bed.

In the depths of sleep, his dreams were awakened and he found himself as a young boy with friends playing on the school grounds near his childhood home. It was a Saturday. They were kicking a ball back and forth on the grass field when a hard kick by one of his friends sent the ball over his head and behind him. It bounced and rolled near two older and bigger boys that were walking by.

The scroungier one picked up the ball and turned to Ethan and his friends. "Thanks," he said before continuing on his way.

The other boys with young Ethan were afraid and did nothing. But young Ethan wasn't going to let these boys take their ball. That just wasn't right. "Hey! Can we have our ball back, please?" young Ethan shouted to them.

The two bullies turned and looked at him again. "What did you say, you scabby little pus-bag?" the scroungy bully with the ball replied.

"That's *our* ball. Can we have it back, please?" Young Ethan was trying to be brave.

The two bullies then walked up to him. "I don't see your name on it anywhere. Looks to me like it's finders-keepers. We found it and we're keeping it," the bully said as he bounced the ball off young Ethan's head, causing his teeth to clack together.

Dazed for a second, he just stood, and his friends just stood and waited. "Give it back," young Ethan then said defiantly.

"Make us," the other bully responded.

Ethan grabbed for the ball but the other bully grabbed *him* and threw him to the ground. He tried to get back up. The scroungy bully then kicked him in his side, knocking the wind out of him and hurting his ribs.

"Leave him alone," a new voice said from behind them. The scroungy bully, still holding the ball, turned around to see another kid about their age standing there.

"I don't know who you think you are, but you better get out of here," the scroungy bully warned.

Swiftly, the new kid reached out and grabbed the scroungy bully's long hair with his left hand and pulled him forward. Then he grabbed the bully's right wrist and spun him around over backwards, still holding on to his hair. The bully's arm was now twisted into his upper back. The ball fell loose, bounced and rolled away. The other bully turned chicken at the sight of his buddy now helpless at the mercy of this new kid.

"You shouldn't take what doesn't belong to you," the new kid said resolutely. The scroungy bully grimaced at the pain. "You two are going to go away now, right?" The bully was gritting his teeth and said nothing. His arm was then firmly twisted and raised a little farther. *"Right?"*

"OW! OW! OKAY! OKAY!" He was held there another moment, then dropped onto his back. The other bully suddenly found his nerve and stepped toward the new kid.

"You really wanna do that?" the new kid said as he glared at the other bully. The other bully stopped and backed off as the scroungy one on the ground slowly rolled over and got up. Then they both walked away.

Young Ethan was still lying on the ground, curled up on his side, holding his ribs. The new kid picked up the ball, walked over to him and offered his hand to help him up. As Ethan looked up at the boy from the ground, a shadow was cast over the boy's face by the sun from behind him. He couldn't see who it was.

Then, the dream ended and Ethan awoke. Confused, he sat up in bed. The dream was strange—more like a fabricated memory from his childhood. As he thought about what it could mean, it started to make sense. Could this be his answer?

He was up and ready to go by the time Alex called. There wasn't really anything he could do until Ireon's office opened at 8 A.M., so he went down to the hotel restaurant with her for breakfast.

"Talked with the Professor recently?" Ethan asked.

"Yeah. He spoke to Smith last night and he is *furious* about your little excursion. He was too upset to call you himself and told me to tell you to behave, or we're done. Smith will contact us again sometime this morning. That was it."

"Who's *we're* exactly?"

"All of us, I suppose."

Ethan looked at her, concerned. "You too?"

"No."

"Good."

"Not really. I still have no idea what I'm doing here. You don't seem too overly concerned about the Professor threatening to pull the plug."

"I'm just doing what I think I have to do. Whether he's upset or not really doesn't change the situation. Now that Smith's here, I'll pay him directly if that becomes necessary. You know, you can still go home. You don't have to stay here."

"I'm not going anywhere."

"It was just a suggestion."

"Come up with any new ideas?" Ethan didn't respond to her question and kept eating. A full mouth was a good reason to keep it shut. But he wasn't going to lie to her, and he had to swallow sometime.

"Well, I do have an idea, actually."

"Great. What is it?"

"I'm not going to tell you," he replied.

Alex looked surprised and dejected. "Why not?"

"Because you won't approve."

"When has that mattered? We're a team, remember?"

"Not so loud," he said quietly.

Alex looked around, then leaned toward him. "Everything we do, we do together. That was the deal."

"Alex, in all honesty, what I'm planning to do, I have to do alone. You're just going to have to sit tight on this one."

"Then I *am* useless here," she blurted out, frustrated.

What was it about her and restaurants? Ethan asked for the check and they left before she could say much more.

As they approached their rooms, Alex started prodding for information. "Now what are you planning to do? And don't tell me you can't tell me."

"Alex, there is nothing you can do but stay here and wait for me to either come back or contact you. I'm not going to tell you anything more than that. You're just going to have to trust me on this one."

He walked over to his bag and pulled out his passport and a small envelope with some money in it while Alex watched. He slipped the passport into the envelope, took out his wallet, removed most of that money and put it in with the passport. Then he handed the envelope to Alex.

She took it, looked at it, and looked up at him. "You're going to go do something stupid, aren't you?" she said with anxious concern.

"I don't think it's stupid. A bit risky maybe..."

"*I knew it*. Why can't you just let Smith handle it? I don't understand why you keep doing these things?"

"It's just what I believe I have to do. Listen, I should be fine. Giving you the passport and money is just worst case. I'll be back. Don't worry."

"This is *not* a good idea," she proclaimed adamantly. "In fact, it's a *lousy* idea. Just let Smith find it."

"I'm sorry. I *have* to do this."

"You know something don't you? You've seen something."

Ethan gently, but firmly held her by her shoulders and looked into her eyes. "It's going to be fine, and you're going to promise not to call anyone or do anything until I contact you. Okay? Promise me." Alex huffed out a sigh and looked around. "Promise?"

"Fine," she said reluctantly. "This is still a terrible idea. How do you know you won't end up in the river chained to a barrel of cement or something?"

"I didn't see that."

"I'm not kidding Ethan. Something awful could happen."

"I just don't think it will." Alex shook her head in disbelief. Ethan then walked her to the door. "Promise you won't call anyone."

"Yes, okay, but if I don't hear from you by noon, I'm calling *everybody*, and *that is* a promise."

He looked at his watch. "Okay, noon."

Alex started to leave, but stopped and gave him a brief hug before heading into the hallway. "Noon," she reiterated, pointing her finger at him as she walked away sideways.

Ethan closed the door, went to the desk next to the sofa and pulled out a directory. Setting it on the desk, he started thumbing through the pages, looking for the company name. He dialed the main number and a receptionist answered. "Ireon, vielen dank für den Anruf. Wo'mit kann ich Ihnen dienen?"

"Uh...can you transfer me to Richard Grayson's secretary please?" Ethan asked, not sure if they would understand.

But the woman responded in well-spoken English. "One moment please." Music came over the receiver. Funny how German elevator music sounded a lot like American elevator music.

Another female voice came on the phone. She had more of an accent. "Richard Grayson's office."

He suddenly became nervous at hearing the name, and had to work at speaking coherently and calmly. "Hi. I'm...an old acquaintance of Richard's and was hoping to surprise him. Is there a chance he might be around this morning?"

"I'm sorry, Mr. Grayson only sees people by appointment. I can check his schedule to see if he has an opening."

"Yes, thank you." There was a momentary pause.

"It looks like he recently had a cancellation. Let's see...yes, he has a half hour this morning at nine. Would you like to me to schedule you in?"

"Yes, please."

"And your name?"

"Well like I said, I'm an old friend and just wanted to surprise him."

"I at least need your last name to make the appointment."

"Hamilton."

"Hamilton. Okay, Mr. Hamilton, I have you scheduled at nine this morning."

"Thank you.

"You're welcome," the woman said before hanging up.

So, that was it. If Grayson really was Chamberlain, then he'd soon find out if the dream was what he thought it was.

The guard stepped out of the shack as Ethan pulled up in a rental car. "Guten morgen."

"Morning," Ethan replied. "I'm here to see Richard Grayson."

"Picture ID please." As Ethan pulled out his wallet, the guard wrote down the plate number as before. "Here you go," the guard said and handed Ethan one of the visitor signs. "Put this on your dash in plain view. Visitor parking is in front of the main building there."

"Thank you."

"Have a good day," the guard replied.

Ethan sat in the car for a few minutes after pulling into a parking stall, wondering how he was going to handle this. With a deep sigh, he tried to expel the insecurity and anxiety, then got out of the car, and slowly walked to the door.

Reaching for the handle, he saw his hand shaking and quickly pulled it back, rubbing it with the other. He couldn't back out now...not now.

Hands still a little twitchy with lungs working hard to maintain a semblance of normal breathing, he opened the doors and walked to the guard desk.

"Kann ich Ihnen helfen?" the guard asked.

"I'm here to see Richard Grayson."

"Do you have an appointment?"

"Yes."

"ID please." While trying to concentrate on staying calm, Ethan pulled out his wallet and handed his ID to the guard. The guard took it and placed it over a scanner. Ethan then noticed a reflection off a pair of glasses lying on the desk that revealed several camera monitors in the counter facing the guard, each one with multiple split-screen views. The guard was intently studying a data screen next to the scanner for what seemed like an unusually long time. This did nothing to steady his already prickly nerves.

"Slow system, eh?" Ethan jested awkwardly.

The guard ignored him and handed the ID back along with a visitor badge, then slid him a clipboard. "Sign here." Ethan signed his name. "Up the stairs, turn left, go down the hall. You'll see the offices on your left."

"Thank you," Ethan said before clipping the badge to his shirt pocket and walking to the stairs.

There were only a few other people in the hall as he headed down the corridor. *Calm down, calm down*, he kept telling himself. He then came to a wide, doorless entry into a reception area. *Deep slow breaths.* An attractive young woman sitting behind a large built-in desk looked up from her paperwork, glanced at his badge then smiled. "Hi. How can I help you?"

Ethan was surprised. "How did you know I spoke English?" he asked.

"The EN in the corner of your badge is for English. How can I help you?"

"I'm here to see Mr. Grayson."

"Name?"

"Mr. Hamilton."

The young woman looked at her screen, then tapped on a small device near her hand. "Yes, Mr. Hamilton. Have a seat and I'll let him know you're here."

"Thank you," Ethan replied as he sat down on a cushioned chair next to a large leafy plant.

"Mr. Grayson, I have a Mr. Hamilton here to see you," she announced through a small microphone attached to her earpiece.

There was a brief pause. "Yes, sir." She clicked off her headset and looked up at Ethan. "Mr. Hamilton, you may go in now," she said smiling and pointing to a large set of double office doors.

"Thank you," he replied with a crackle in his voice. He looked at the huge doors and carefully pushed himself out of the chair, trying to be gentle on his already shaky legs. It was going to be a long twenty feet.

He stopped at the door that separated him from his destiny. This was an incredible risk. But it would seem that just simple survival wasn't enough anymore. The life he had once lived in ignorance wasn't really living at all. This was the only way. His knees shook and his heart raced. He momentarily steadied himself against the door and closed his eyes.

He saw himself under a bright warm sun at the edge of a vast, high mountain vista. There, the endless and majestic beauty of the world would hide him for just an instant. The view was spectacular, and soothing. Then he slowly opened his eyes, took in a deep cleansing breath, gripped the knob hard, twisted the handle, and offered himself into the hands of fate.

CHAPTER FOURTEEN

Providence

GRAYSON'S OFFICE WAS ALMOST as large as Professor Greenhagen's, only not quite as spacious and high. Everything was modern with a wide, curved black metal-framed desk with glass top and a matching credenza behind it next to large windows. Two flat video screens and a computerized phone were the only items on the desk. Several small halogen light fixtures hung from the ceiling by thin wires and cast an embellished light over the desk like a stage.

Grayson was sitting behind it in a tall black leather chair. He was busy writing. After walking through the door, Ethan stopped and watched him from across the room.

"Close the door," Grayson said, not looking up. "Have a seat," he then added after the door shut. Ethan stepped slowly down a couple of steps that led to the main part of the office. He looked around carefully, making his way to one of the two black steel-framed, leather chairs in front of the desk. As he got closer, he studied Grayson. It *was* Chamberlain.

Ethan cautiously sat down, not sure what to expect. Grayson finished scribbling notes on a document and set the pen down. He leaned back in his chair, looked up at Ethan, and let out a heavy sigh. "Ethan Grey, *why the hell* did you have to show up here?"

In a distant corner of Ethan's mind, a tiny ray of light had been shining—hope that this meeting might somehow go well—that somehow his desire to do the right thing would will everything to work. Grayson's malicious intonation instantly shattered that hope.

"I wish I could say it was good to see you again. You should have just done what you were supposed to do and let it go," Grayson added.

"Too many questions," Ethan replied, trying to control his visibly shaking knees.

"Asking questions is not a healthy ambition in this game."

"I'm a scientist. That's what I do."

"Some answers aren't worth your life. Whatever questions led you here, you should have just left them alone. I can't help you."

"I think you can. The dense energy projects? Element Zero? You know where it is."

Grayson furrowed his brow and looked back at Ethan. "There's more involved here than you could possibly imagine which is why I gave you an out the first time."

"You'd be surprised what I can imagine, Mr. ...Grayson."

"This isn't just about me Ethan, there are others."

"I know, and I also know what you're planning to do."

Just then, another door in the room opened. Two men in dark suits entered and approached. Ethan watched them for a second, then quickly turned back to Grayson and leaned forward. "I know about the radar site in Kazakhstan and the wave accelerator," he whispered before the men reached him. "I know what you're going to do."

The men grabbed Ethan under each arm and started pulling him out of the chair. "Come on, this isn't necessary," he said as a struggle ensued. Now on his feet, they began pulling him toward the side door. Panic struck and Ethan swung his elbow back, hitting one guard in the chest and causing him to loosen his grip. Ethan spun around trying to get free of the other guard when an incredibly sharp pain hit him in the back and surged through his body. Convulsing violently, he quickly lost consciousness, and fell limp to the floor.

Ouch. That stick's sharp. Why do they keep poking me?

"Mr. Grey…" a voice sang melodically.

Jerks. Leave me alone…let me sleep.

"Wake up Mr. Grey. Time to wake up."

"*Ow!*" Ethan grunted as he lifted his head at a sharp, but brief pain in his chest by his right shoulder.

"That's better," the male voice said pleasantly.

Ethan couldn't move. He had been stripped to his underwear, arms tied down firmly to a wood chair with something tight around his wrists. It felt like wire. His ankles were tied to the legs of the chair in the same manner. He couldn't see. His eyes were covered with something—tape maybe. He had never experienced anything like this before. It was terrifying. He tried to move, but the restraints cut into his wrists.

"Nice of you to join us this morning. I hope you don't mind. We moved you to someplace a little more…*intimate.*" The voice was coming from a short distance in front of him. "So, Mr. Grey, tell me how someone who is supposed to be so smart could be, well, such an imbecile?" There was a snicker from someone to the side of the voice.

"Who are you?" Ethan asked. A sharp, piercing pain surged briefly through his left shoulder causing the muscles to contract and his arm to pull hard against the restraints. His jaw clenched tightly and his neck strained. The pain finally stopped. He gasped to catch his breath. It felt like he was being electrocuted.

"Here's how this works. I ask you questions, you give me answers. If you give me the wrong answer…" A surge went through his leg causing it to contract and the restraints to cut into his ankles. "You see, Mr. Grey, common sense would dictate that an intelligent man, such as yourself, would understand the consequences for dropping in uninvited on a private party. That's why your arrival here is so *very* puzzling. What could *possibly* be so important that you would come all this way to our little corner of the world and start asking questions about things that are none of your business? What would cause a person like yourself to do such a thing, Mr. Grey?"

Ethan sat defiant. The stick was jammed into his stomach and the current surged throughout his body. He pulled against the restraints uncontrollably and strained against what felt like millions of needles being rapidly and repeatedly thrust deep into his flesh. After a moment, it stopped.

The pain was incredible and his wrists and ankles were beginning to bleed. His jaw was still clenched from cramping muscles. He tried desperately to open his mouth to breathe more air. His muscles finally released, his head dropped and he started heaving up small amounts of partially digested food.

"Isn't it fascinating what effects a device like this can have on the human body? I designed it myself you know. Just to enlighten you on what you can expect, there have been some who managed to break off several teeth before it was over. Some have bitten off pieces of their tongue or chewed it up so badly that it swelled and they suffocated. At the least I get a few dislocated jaws. Unfortunately, some just expire and take all the fun out of it. Still, it's all wonderfully entertaining.

"Now, you're a handsome man, and I'd sure not wish you to end up disfigured. It's *your* choice though." A very brief but intense pain hit him in the throat, causing the muscles in his jaw and neck to tighten severely. "So, Mr. Grey, while you can still speak, I suggest you enlighten me as to why you want to know about Element Zero."

Blood was trickling from Ethan's mouth and it spit as he tried to talk in slurred speech. "I just wanted...to know...what happened at the lab," he said through short breaths.

"How did you know where to find Grayson?" Ethan thought about what he could possibly say that might persuade this man to keep him alive, but his mind was too confused and numb to think straight.

Another brief shock hit him in the right arm. "I don't know!" he blurted out, then started gagging and coughing again.

"Of course you know, Mr. Grey. What will be interesting is to discover the point at which your body finally convinces your mind to tell us what we want to know. It's all up to you."

Ethan let his head hang. It hurt incredibly. His muscles felt like they were on fire. His mind was spinning. He didn't understand—the dream seemed so obvious. What was wrong? Why was this happening to him? What had he done wrong? How could he possibly fulfill a supposed destiny like this? It was unlikely these people would ever let him go. Another brief shock in his chest snapped his head up.

"Mr. Grey," the voice chimed, "Element Zero. Why are you looking for it?"

As his body tried to shutdown and his mind floated near unconsciousness, his thoughts were suddenly pulled away and he found himself in another place. He was a boy again, this time standing at the base of Niagara Falls. It was a vacation their family had taken when he was about eleven. "Cool, huh?" his dad shouted from several feet away. Young Ethan stood and looked up at the breathtaking sight; millions of gallons of water roaring endlessly off the cliffs, crashing into the waiting, churning pools below.

The sound was ferocious and the force of the impacting water made the ground and railing vibrate from its tremendous kinetic energy. An aromatic, sparkling crystalline vapor floated through the air, creating a brilliant rainbow in the bright sun. He gazed in awe and gripped the railing tightly to feel the incredible energy that coursed and flowed through his body. It was wondrous and invigorating and the feeling of immense and endless power made him giddy.

Then in an instant, it was silent and dark again. Ethan began to laugh subtly in defiance of the pain in his tortured body.

"Something to share, Mr. Grey?" the voice asked.

Ethan stopped laughing and raised his head. "You have no idea what you're dealing with," he said boldly.

There was a momentary pause in silence, a few 'clicks,' then the voice responded in an irritated tone. "Neither do you."

The prod was jammed hard into Ethan's chest. His body wrenched and twisted wildly. It stopped several seconds later when someone walked up to the voice and whispered. There was a sigh of disappointment. "Unfortunately, it seems we will have to resume our conversation later, Mr. Grey. Don't go anywhere." The voice stood and started walking away. "Make sure he stays quiet," it said before leaving the room.

Someone then unrolled a large section of tape and wrapped it around his head over his mouth. A crushing blow struck him on the left side of his face, knocking him unconscious and almost toppling the skinny chair. There, he would hang limp for a time.

The room was completely silent. When he awoke, he still couldn't move his arms or legs. Muscles were stinging. The restraints had dug well into his wrists and ankles. His mouth was full of blood. He kept his head lowered to keep from swallowing. There was no way to know how much time had passed. An hour? Five hours? The darkness and immobility were unbearable. His legs and arms were tingling and stinging from lack of circulation. At least he could still feel them.

The door to the room opened...and closed. Footsteps came toward him to stop some distance away. Ethan was trying to listen, but didn't hear the man swear under his breath when he saw Ethan naked and bloody, restrained by several large plastic zipties, his face covered with duct tape. The footsteps came closer. Ethan's head was still lowered. He had given himself to providence—given in to whatever ill will still awaited him.

The footsteps stopped and he waited. A gentle hand was placed on the left side of his face while the other grabbed an edge of the tape over his eyes. It was slowly removed. Parts of his eyebrows and eyelashes stuck to the tape when it was pulled off. He grimaced and kept his eyes closed until the tape was gone. Trying to open them was difficult. They were pasty and stuck together.

The tape over his mouth was carefully pulled off from around his head. Hair was slowly ripped out and blood began to trickle from his mouth onto his legs and the chair as the tape passed his lips. "*Aw, man,*" the voice said in quiet pity. It was distressing for any human being of *any* conscience to see another human being like this.

Ethan tried to open his eyes to see who had removed the tape. "I'm really sorry Ethan." It sounded like Grayson. Ethan could barely make him out as he kept blinking, trying to clear the blurriness. "You shouldn't have come here. They knew it was you the moment your picture was scanned. It's still in the system."

"My mistake," Ethan slurred in a raspy voice, still trying to clear his mouth. Grayson shook his head and let out a sigh of frustration.

"You don't mess with these people. They aren't afraid of anything or anyone."

"I guess torture is just for kicks between meetings?"

"I don't condone this, Ethan. I would never do anything like this. But the decisions aren't mine to make. I have my place." Ethan coughed and spit. "I shouldn't even be down here, but I need to know how you know about the facility in Kazakhstan. Only a few people are even aware the project exists. There is *no way* you could have known about it."

Ethan's eyes were beginning to focus and he could now more clearly see the circle of bright light around him and the darkness outside it. Grayson was sitting at the edge of the light in front of him.

"Mr. Grayson, nice to see you again," Ethan said with some contempt.

"Come on Ethan, what's going on? How did you know I was here and how do you know about the facility?"

"You first. Where's the element?"

Grayson leaned back on the stool and thought. They would probably end up killing him anyway... "I didn't even know it existed until it was brought to the lab. After the explosion, I was approached and given a chance to keep working on the project over here. If we can still find a method to harness its energy, there seems to be almost no limit to what we could do with it. It could be the purest, untapped power resource we've ever encountered. Do you know what that means? *We could do anything.*"

Ethan looked into Grayson's eyes. He could see that the man honestly believed what he was saying—that the element was simply an enigmatic source of energy they could still conquer and control. "You really think that's what it is?" Ethan posed.

"You should know. You saw what incredible power it was capable of producing."

Ethan looked down for a moment, then up a Grayson resolutely. "It's a lie."

Grayson looked back at him puzzled. "What do you mean it's a lie?"

Ethan started to smile at the irony of their situation. "It would seem you've been played for a fool. The people pulling your strings know what the element really is. But apparently they didn't want to share that information with you."

"What information?" Grayson asked smugly.

"Do you know where the element came from?"

"Of course. It was discovered in a mine we own in West Africa."

"Well, I suppose that *is* more believable than the truth." Grayson waited, listening intently. "It actually came from an ancient stone container found at the bottom of the Mediterranean Sea. It has power, yes, but nothing you or the people in your organization can control. Its power is for something of a more...divine nature...I suppose you could say."

Grayson started to laugh. "I should have known. *I should have known,*" his voice reverberated loudly in the room as he stood and walked into the darkness. "And by what means did you come by this *divine* information?"

"A credible source."

"I see. And how about the radar site? Did this *source* tell you about that as well?"

"No, actually we figured that out from the journal of a young girl."

Grayson was sincerely impressed by Ethan's audacity. He would have laughed again if the absurdity of the conversation hadn't digressed to a point unworthy of even that response. "I see, I see. Well, I'm sorry Ethan," he said as he reappeared in the light, "I'm not sure *anyone* can help you." He then reached for the strips of tape to put back over Ethan's face. Ethan knew this was his last chance.

"Right now you're making arrangements to set up another lab at the decommissioned Balkhash long-range radar facility. You're going to use a new multi-path, parasitic energy wave accelerator to bombard another sample of the element. I don't know what arrogance makes you think you can try the same experiment again and have a different result, but that's exactly what you're going to do.

"You'll be standing in a control room that overlooks the test area in the underground facility. There's a raised work platform in the middle of the lower room where the spherical target chamber is situated. It'll be fed by a three-beam converger from the accelerator and you'll use three Kryon staged capacitive generators to power the beams.

"In the control room will be two technicians, German I believe, one sitting on each side of the control console and you'll be standing behind them with two other men. You're wearing a dark suit with burgundy dress shoes and on your left lapel is a small half spherical black, glossy pin—the symbol of your malevolent organization.

"As the firing sequence initiates, you'll say, 'Gentleman, today we make history,' and you *will*, but not in the way you think. *This* time the ensuing energy wave won't just decimate the facility, it will travel a little over a thousand miles in every direction from the site, obliterating everything in its path. In less than two seconds, every city, every person, every plant, every animal, every insect, every living thing for almost four million square miles will be completely destroyed.

"The world will be baffled and sickened at the devastation. That sentiment will slowly turn to anger when the United States will be blamed for what you're going to do. The entire country will be isolated and thrown into bitter skirmishes that escalate into global nihilism. It'll be pretty ugly, and you'll be there, proud to watch the beginning of it all."

Ethan fidgeted and grimaced as he tried to find a less irritable position. "My guess is the container will be taken to the site for some reason. The detonation causes a cascade reaction and then...it'll all be gone. The ironic thing is, whoever is actually in charge of your organization knows this. They know Element Zero can't be stabilized and in fact, know it will eventually become the reaper that will destroy them and all those like them, *unless* they destroy it first. And you'll help them do it in spectacular fashion. Almost two hundred and ninety million people will die, including you."

Grayson said nothing. He slowly sat back down and looked at Ethan momentarily, then faced sideways, looking into the darkness.

Ethan continued. "Once the sample at the lab was destroyed, they knew there was a way, and we helped them figure it out."

"How could you possibly know all this?" Grayson asked without changing his focus.

"Because I've seen what's going to happen."

Grayson slowly turned and looked at Ethan. "That's impossible," he said derisively.

"Yeah I kept telling myself that too, but after you experience the impossible a few times, it gets hard to ignore. Look, regardless how ridiculous this all sounds, it's the truth. I'm not sure I have the capacity of imagination to make up stuff like this."

Grayson shook his head, stood again and began pacing in the dark. "How is telling you the location of the element going to change anything? You can't stop them."

"I'm supposed to take the vessel and hide it, which will hopefully keep those events from ever happening."

"That's insane. Who hired you to do this?"

"I wasn't hired, exactly. That explanation might be a little more difficult for you to believe," Ethan said hesitantly.

"You know, I wanted to give you a chance, but this is just too preposterous." Ethan sighed and tried to shift to another position. Somehow Grayson had to be convinced.

"Did you ever wonder why I was the only one spared in the explosion? *I* sure did. You probably never knew this but the day before the so-called accident, I had some sort of interaction with the element and I saw things—visions of things I didn't understand. The experience made me so sick that I had to go home. The next day, immediately after the accident had occurred, I felt fine again. I told myself it was just some delusional episode and coincidence. Now I've come to understand there was a reason I survived—just like there must be a reason why I found you again and why we're here, now. Sure I'd rather be discussing this on a nice sunny golf course somewhere. Be that as it may…"

He tried to shift his weight again. "I can't show you proof of anything, but what I'm telling you *is* the truth. This element doesn't belong to your organization, or to me, or to any one person for that matter." Ethan dropped his head briefly to let it rest, then raised it again. "Look at me, Mr. Grayson. Can you honestly say that you want to be involved with people who do these kinds of things to other people?"

Grayson looked at Ethan for a moment, then turned away as he thought. He walked around in the darkness, then stopped. "Chamberlain. My name is Tom Chamberlain."

That was all he said before walking away. Ethan listened to the diminishing footsteps as they echoed in the dark, empty room. The door opened—there was a brief sliver of light. Chamberlain walked through, and closed it behind him.

☀ ☀ ☀

The passing hours were agonizing. Alex tried everything she could think of to occupy her thoughts with something other than what Ethan must be doing. Every imaginable scenario had been run through her mind a dozen times while pacing the floor. It was 11:47 A.M. She desperately wanted to call someone—to do something to find out what was going on. But she promised she'd wait, so she did.

Ten minutes later, the phone on the nightstand rang. Startled, she looked at it knowing no one should be calling her there. Slowly she walked over and picked up the receiver.

"Hello?" she said warily.

"Is this Alex?" a male voice asked.

"Who is this?"

"I believe we have a mutual interest, Ethan Grey."

This was the kind of call she had been dreading. "Who are you? Is Ethan okay?"

"We need to meet."

"Why? Where's Ethan?" she demanded.

"Ethan is being detained. I think we can resolve this if we meet. Otherwise I may not be able to help him. We need to be prompt about this. There's a bar called Das Sporthaus directly behind your hotel on the next street. Can you meet me there in fifteen minutes?"

"I don't even know who you are. How can I trust you?"

"You don't have a choice. Come by yourself and *do not* call anyone, especially your friends from yesterday. Fifteen minutes."

"But how will…" The phone hung up from the other end.

This was *not* good. She needed help. They may have already killed him and were just setting her up for the same fate. No, if someone had done something to Ethan and wanted to get rid of her too, why would they want to meet in a public place? *The global*, she realized. It has a built in tracker and she could probably find out where he was that way. But tracking another global was something she had never done before and had no idea how to do it. The Professor would know. Smith might know. But the man on the phone warned not to call anyone. How would he know if she did? Still, it wasn't worth the risk. Whoever it was on the phone was right, there appeared to be no other choice.

Das Sporthaus was directly in front of her on the other side of the street. Avoiding the busy traffic, she ran across and walked in the front door. It had two levels toward the back with lots of tables and several large, wall-mounted viewing screens displaying various sporting events. There were only twenty or so people in the whole place although more were coming in, probably for lunch.

Carefully she scanned the tables and people, but didn't see anyone who seemed out of place or sitting alone, except for one guy who looked like he had already been there awhile. He was more interested in a game on one of the screens than anything else.

She sat down at a table near the door and watched anxiously.

"Kann ich sie etwas servieren?" a waitress asked.

Alex didn't know exactly what she had said, but assumed the waitress was asking if she wanted something. "No thank you. I'm just meeting someone," Alex responded. The waitress acknowledged her by smiling and left.

Another anxious five minutes passed as a few small groups of people entered. Then a tall man in a long dark coat walked in. He stopped and looked around casually, and thoroughly. It only took a few seconds for Alex to match the man's face with the pictures from her memory of the meeting at Professor Greenhagen's home. A chill came over her when she realized who this man really was.

He walked over to her table and stood nearby. "Are you Alex?"

"Yes," she responded timidly.

"Follow me," he said as he walked past her toward the more secluded rear area of the bar. Alex hesitated, looking around again, then nervously stood and followed him.

They were now at a small table in the back corner of the lower level. Alex sat down as the man removed his coat and rested it over a chair, then sat down next to her. She stood up and moved to sit across from him. Just being in the same building was too close.

"Do you know who I am?" he asked.

"Yes I do," she responded uneasily.

"Then forget what you think you know and just listen. I know why you and Ethan are here and you don't have a prayer."

The feelings of desperateness were almost overwhelming. She tried to breathe slowly, tried to stay calm.

The waitress came to the table. "Kann ich sie etwas servieren?" she asked.

"Nein, vielen dank," Grayson replied, handing her some money.

"Vielen dank," she replied and left.

Grayson waited until the waitress was several feet away, then looked back at Alex. "How involved in this are you?" he asked.

"I'm his friend."

"What do you know about what he's trying to do?"

"Why should I tell you anything? I know who you are."

"Answer my questions or he'll probably die."

"You'd really kill him?"

"No, I wouldn't, but I work with people who likely will unless you tell me what I want to know. What is he really doing here and who is he working for?"

"He isn't working for anyone. We're doing this on our own. We're just here trying to find something," Alex said frustrated, trying to maintain a professional state of mind.

"Then how did you find me?"

"He recognized a picture of you. Even without your beard."

"Really. Well, he claims to be on a mission to stop some sort of disaster. Is this true?"

"It is. Look, Mr. Grayson, Ethan is an extraordinary man. I don't think he even knows how unique he is. And to hear him talk about some of that stuff sounds crazy, I know. But he's for real. I've never known him to lie. Whatever he told you is the truth."

"Or what he believes is the truth."

"I don't know what else to tell you. I don't want him to die."

Grayson started fiddling with a napkin, then looked back up at Alex. "How does he know our plans? Where does he get his information from?"

"I told you, he just knows. He says he has visions sometimes. That's all I can tell you about it."

Grayson was quiet while he spun the napkin around in circles. "I do have to concede it's pretty remarkable how he seems to know so many specific details about certain things." There was another pause. "I don't want to see him die either," he then said as he energetically spun the napkin. "The men you were with yesterday. Who are they?"

"We hired them to help us find this thing we're looking for."

Grayson smiled at her attempt to protect Ethan. "You don't have to hide it. I know exactly what you're looking for. So they're here to help you retrieve it?"

"Umm, yes."

Grayson looked down again. It was obvious he was troubled in his thoughts and torn in his loyalties. He leaned over to his coat and took out a pen from an inside pocket to write on the napkin. "Here's what we're going to do. Tonight at eight-thirty, there will be a small white delivery van parked in the lot behind this address. Barring unforeseen problems, Ethan should be in the back." Grayson slid the napkin across the table to Alex. "Now listen to me carefully. Give this to your friends at eight-twenty...no sooner. *Do not* talk to anyone else about this. Take everything from your hotel with you and *do not* go back to the hotel afterwards. Do you understand?"

"I understand. Is he okay?"

"He's been better. You sure you can follow through with this?"

"We'll be there."

Grayson stood, pulled his long coat off the back of the chair and put it on. Alex watched him then remarked, "You're doing the right thing."

"We'll see," he said before walking away.

Alex just sat for a minute. The fate of her friend was now relegated to a scribbled address on a stained napkin from a bar. She carefully folded the napkin to protect the writing, put it in her pocket and headed back to the hotel.

☀ ☀ ☀

The pain in Ethan's wrists and legs would subside briefly if he didn't try to move. To sit motionless tied to a chair for hours upon hours was excruciating. He was so, so thirsty, but the smell of urine, blood and vomit was so repulsive and nauseating that even the thought of water was distasteful.

It was becoming more difficult to hold on to the fragile new beliefs that had lead him there. Now even time seemed to be an enemy that mocked him in prolonged and merciless indifference. He hung his head, closed his eyes and gave in to the emotions induced by pain and indignity.

Suddenly, his thoughts were transported away again. He was sitting in his mom's car as they drove along a state road to a cousin's house. He was only five years old and could barely see the tops of the trees and power poles from where he sat low in the passenger seat. It was a long ride and he had been in the car for a very long time.

He looked up at his mother. "How much longer?"

She looked over at him and smiled. "I know it's been a long time sweetie. We'll be there pretty soon. Just hang in there a little longer for me, okay?" She reached over and put her hand on his head and ran her fingers through his short hair. He looked up and smiled back at her. He could see the love in her eyes, and feel the reassuring warmth of her hand as he tried to hold on to the vivid memory that gave him hope, and momentarily pushed the ugliness aside.

In a fragmented state of sleep and pain induced exhaustion, he heard a door open, the click of a light switch, the door close. Footsteps were coming toward him. He couldn't wake himself to see who it was. His mind was conscious, but his body had shut down to force regeneration. The footsteps stopped in front of him as they had before.

"Ethan," a voice said. It was Chamberlain again. Ethan tried to reply. But his voice only spoke in his mind. Slowly the pain and tingling started coming back. He raised his head, took a deep breath and opened his bloodshot eyes. He could see the foul smell reflected in Chamberlain's expression.

"You came back," he choked through a dry throat.

"Yeah," Chamberlain responded solemnly. Using a small pocketknife, he carefully cut the ties from around Ethan's wrists and ankles. Ethan groaned and slowly moved his arms, stretching the painfully bruised muscles and tendons. "Can you stand?"

Ethan put his hands on the sides of the small chair and leaned forward, trying to push his way up, but his muscles were too bruised. "Give me a minute," he said, resting back in the chair. "What's happening?"

"I spoke with your friend."

"She's here?" he asked panicked.

"No, I met with her earlier and arranged to have you picked up in town. Your clothes are on the shelf over there and there's a sink on the wall. Try to clean up the best you can and I'll be back in about an hour and a half. The door will remain locked. You'll need to stay here and stay quiet until I come back. Will you be okay until then?"

"I'll manage," he responded. He kind of wanted to know what Chamberlain's real reason was for letting him go. For the moment though, he was just thankful to be free of the chair, and have hope of escape.

The appointed time was at hand. He was now dressed and mostly cleaned up, sitting on the concrete floor against a wall near the counter. The feelings of indignity were hard to dispel, as was the constant pain. But it was nothing compared to what had been experienced earlier.

The door opened. Ethan looked up at it warily. Chamberlain walked in. "You look better."

"I feel better," Ethan responded. "Have you seen my global?"

"No. I'm sure it's long gone. Are you ready?"

"I guess," he said grimacing as he rolled over on his hands and slowly started to stand. Everything hurt. "There's something I'd like to know. What changed your mind?"

Chamberlain was silent until Ethan reached the door. "I was so fascinated and intrigued with the possibilities of the element that I would have done just about anything to stay with the project. The reality of my association with these people took a backseat. Everything we did seemed justifiable. It was all in the name of science and progress for the greater good. I knew about some of the things that went on, but tried to ignore them—just did my job. It was never really personal...until today."

Chamberlain opened the door, looked around and held it for Ethan. They walked out into a corridor with pipes and conduit near the ceiling that ran its length.

"What happens when these people find out what you've done? What will you do?" Ethan asked.

"I'll be long gone by then."

"Won't they look for you?"

"Without a doubt. No one *leaves* the Order." They started up some stairs at the end of the corridor. "This element was the most important thing in my life. I guess I was so blinded by it that I couldn't see anything else. And it came to this. At least I can try to do something now."

"Then you believe me," Ethan said, hopeful.

"I'm not going to say that. On the other hand, you seem to know things that no one else could possibly know. I'm not going to take the chance."

They walked through aisles between huge steel shelves and pallets and arrived at a door near the loading dock. Before opening the door, Chamberlain pulled out his mobile phone and dialed a number...

"This is Richard Grayson. I was just leaving and thought I saw a car parked by the fence west of the warehouse. Would you check the west warehouse roof camera to see if there is someone there?" He paused a few seconds, then opened the door and motioned Ethan to follow. They walked to one of the delivery vans sitting across from the dock. "Good, thank you," he said and put the phone away. "There's a camera on each door. The monitor for the camera on the west side of the building is at the other end of the desk from this one. I didn't want the guard to see us leave."

Chamberlain opened one of the back doors of the van and instructed Ethan to climb in. He then drove the van out an automated exit gate that served the dock area. Ethan sat out of sight on the floor close to the cargo cage near the passenger seat.

"I can't just give you the element. It's at the estate and it's always guarded. What I can do is call in an urgent authorization to have it moved due to a possible security threat. The guards will go with it, but at least it will be out in the open. I'll do that at around eleven forty-five tonight. They'll take it to another secure location in Bremen, probably using two armored cars and about six men. That's as far as I go. How you handle it from there is up to you."

"Wouldn't they use their helicopter?"

"Only Pancros uses the helicopter. He's going to be out of town with it for awhile."

Ethan couldn't have asked for more. This was exactly what they had hoped for. "How come you just don't take it yourself?"

"I've already made enough mistakes and if you're right, it doesn't sound like I can do anything useful with it anyway. It's time to cut my losses, regroup and move on."

"How can I repay you?"

Chamberlain was quiet before responding. "Don't get killed."

Within a few minutes, the van pulled into the parking lot and Chamberlain shut off the motor. A nearby streetlight lit up the front interior of the van.

"Your friends should be here in about twenty minutes. Just sit tight and wait."

"Thank you, for everything."

"Don't thank me yet."

"I'll probably be all right. It could have been worse, I could have never come to see you."

Chamberlain thought about the comment, and grinned in Ethan's auspicious perception. "You're right. Good luck Ethan." Chamberlain climbed out, closed the door and disappeared into the night.

It was lonely and quiet. Time crawled. Then Ethan heard a vehicle pull up outside somewhere. The back of the van had no windows so he waited, apprehensive, hopeful of who it should be—afraid of who it could be.

He covered his eyes when a man directed a bright light through the windshield. "One in back," he heard the man say quietly into his radio. Then the back doors flew open and two flashlights blinded Ethan when he turned toward them.

"It's me, it's me!" he said loudly as a man jumped in the back, grabbed his arm and pulled him out.

A black SUV was parked sideways directly behind the van. The men hurriedly pushed Ethan through the back passenger door and closed it. They wore dark clothing and carried small automatic weapons. One of them ran to the other side of the vehicle and jumped in. The driver then quickly drove away.

It was hard to see who his rescuers were, although he assumed it was Smith. He didn't recognize any of them right off. After they were back on the street, the man in the front passenger seat turned around briefly. "You are one *seriously* stupid son of a bitch, you know that?"

He knew that irritated voice. It was Smith. "Well, it's nice to see you too."

"No you don't get it. I don't tolerate this kind of idiocy and you don't get second chances with me. We're done. You're on your own."

Ethan certainly understood his anger and waited a few minutes to let him cool down before saying anything else. "I have information," he offered.

Smith turned around again to glare at him in the passing lights, then turned forward again without replying. It was clear he wasn't interested in discussing anything at that point, regardless of what it was.

About twenty-five minutes later, the vehicle pulled off the street and into what looked like a barn next to a small house in a remote neighborhood just outside town. The barn door slid closed behind them and the men began to climb out of the vehicle. Smith opened the door for Ethan who was told to follow the other men.

They opened a door in a wall that revealed steps leading down to a narrow passage. Ethan followed the unusually quiet men into a long tunnel that led past two other doors on the sides and to a door at its end. The lead man opened the door and they walked into the basement of the house where their weapons and other gear were placed in cabinets next to shelves of food and other boxes. Afterward, they walked up a set of stairs to a door that led into the home next to the barn.

As the first man walked into the room, Ethan heard Alex ask if they had found him. The first man motioned behind him as Ethan walked in the room and saw her. "Honey, I'm home," he said melodically in an effort to lift the heavy tension.

"Are you okay?" she asked as he approached, his face turned slightly to hide the swelling.

"I'm fine," he replied, hoping to go into the restroom first, not wanting to explain the ugly details of what really happened.

"Then don't *ever* do that again!" she shouted as she hit him hard on the left arm.

"*Ow!*" he grunted loudly, grabbing his arm and bending over away from her. The other men standing nearby snickered quietly at Alex's outburst. Ethan's exaggerated reaction surprised her, and then she saw the open wounds cut into his wrists as he held his arm.

"*Oh no,*" she said ruefully, putting her hands over her mouth. "You're not okay."

"Well I was doing pretty good *until you did that!*" he said, walking awkwardly toward a large cushioned chair. Alex quickly ran to him and helped him sit down.

"I'm sorry, I'm sorry," she said kneeling, trying to get him to let her look at the wounds.

Smith came over and sat down in a chair next to them. "You said you had some information." Smith then saw the scars and got a better look at the swollen cheek and eye as Alex gingerly inspected them. "What happened?" he asked.

"Some weasel with an accent and high powered cattle-prod tried to turn me into Eddy Kilowatt. That's what happened. I have a matching set around my ankles too."

"We should get these cleaned up," Alex insisted.

"No time. The element is going to be moved from the estate, probably a little after eleven forty-five tonight. That's our chance."

"That's only a few hours from now," Smith commented. "Why didn't you tell me this sooner?"

"I tried, but you were a little miffed, remember?"

"Where's it going?"

"Chamberlain just said somewhere in Bremen. The rest is up to us."

"How do you know we can trust the information? Maybe he's setting you up."

"I don't think so. I know this guy. He's the one who let me go." Smith slowly scratched his cheek as he thought, then stood and walked into the other room and started talking to the other men.

"I really am sorry," Alex said again, trying to reconcile.

"It's all right. Just don't hit me anymore, okay?"

Smith came back in the room and sat down. "Since we don't know exactly where they're going to take it, we'll setup on the road between the compound and Bremen."

"A second chance?" Ethan replied submissively.

"Don't get used to it."

"Chamberlain told me the vehicles were armored."

"Not a problem," Smith replied smugly. "We'll leave in forty-five minutes."

"Good, that means I have time to change clothes and try to recover from being *beat up*," Ethan commented sarcastically to Alex with a reserved grin.

Alex dropped her head. "That isn't funny."

Four more men arrived. Smith and the other men discussed the plan at the kitchen table, then Smith came out and sat down with Ethan and Alex. "You two will ride with me. The others will set up and we'll wait off the road above what we've designated as the recovery point. Once the vehicles and men are neutralized, the artifact will be retrieved. We'll head directly to rendezvous with the plane after that. Get your bags and let's go."

They put everything in one bag each. Alex gave the money and passport back to Ethan and put her own in her back pocket. His wallet was gone, probably with the global, but at least he still had his passport.

CHAPTER FIFTEEN

Incursion

ETHAN, ALEX AND ONE other man rode with Smith in his SUV. The others followed in three other vehicles and one on a motorcycle. The first and fourth vehicles had barricades in them and the vehicle directly behind Smith's SUV was loaded with several odd devices that Ethan didn't recognize.

Smith was watching his navigation unit then pushed the MIC button on a small radio hanging near his left shoulder. "Charlie Three, Alpha, mark," he said into the radio.

"Charlie Three," came an immediate response. Smith watched his mirror as the last vehicle with barricades pulled off to the side of the road. They drove for another kilometer and Smith keyed his radio again, "Charlie Two Bravo, Alpha, mark."

"Charlie Two Bravo," another voice responded. Smith and the vehicle behind them turned left onto an upward sloping side road and stopped at a gate.

The man in the front passenger seat with Smith jumped out with a pair of bolt cutters, ran to the gate, cut the chain and swung the gate open, then put the cutters back in the vehicle. He waited to join the second vehicle as Smith drove through the gate, up the road then turned around and parked. The second vehicle followed and also turned around, parking to the side of the gate behind the fence.

With the lights off, the men opened the back of the vehicle and removed several items, carrying them down to the main road. The lead vehicle and motorcycle continued on.

Alex asked what the men were doing. "They're setting up RF Mines next to the road," Smith replied. "We face them toward the roadway and after they're activated, they trigger when a vehicle passes, firing a burst of focused high power, high frequency radio waves that disables the electronics in the car. Armored vehicles are typically designed to withstand small weapons fire and explosive charges, but they still use electronics to control the engine. We knock that out, the engine dies. Charlie One and Three will set up barricades to keep other traffic off the road when the time comes."

"Then what?" she asked.

"If there are two vehicles, we'll hit the first vehicle and hope the second vehicle pulls in behind it. Then we hit the second one with a mine. If we hit them both at the same time, they'll know something's up. This way they think the first vehicle just has mechanical problems."

"And if the second vehicle doesn't stop?" Ethan asked as a car drove by.

"We're dispersing a couple of mines farther down the road just in case. If they do somehow manage to get past the mines, Charlie Three will stop them."

"With what?" Alex asked.

"You don't really want to know."

"So you're hoping the second car will stop and the people will get out to see what's wrong?" Ethan surmised.

"No, they'll probably stay in the vehicles, which is actually what we're expecting them to do.

You see, most people who use armored vehicles are trained to remain in the vehicle during an assault—that's where the protection is. As soon as you open a door or lower a window, even to return fire, you lose that protection. If we can get the second vehicle to stop behind the first, we'll use a RIDS, which is a Roof Incursion Dispersement System. It's dropped onto the roof of the vehicle and a plasma-charged chemical stream burns a small hole through the steel, and anyone unfortunate enough to be sitting under it. Then a knockout gas under high pressure is dispersed into the cabin. The whole procedure takes about five seconds.

The gas is extremely effective. Only a couple of breaths are enough to knock a person out for around twenty minutes. Once the gas is dispersed, the occupants usually panic, try to escape and open the doors. They usually don't get far. The gas takes them down within a few seconds and it becomes inert after being exposed to air for more than fifteen seconds.

If they stay inside, we use a small shape-charge to blow the latch out of the door. Hopefully it'll go as planned and this should be short and sweet. If they get out of the vehicles before the gas gets them, we may have to take them out. Just don't be too shocked if it comes to that."

"What happens if the mines don't disable the vehicles at all?" Alex asked.

"Unless they're driving something more than fifty years old with no electronics, it'll work. Almost no one has EMP or RF proof vehicles. The mine also wipes out other devices including phones, radios, just about anything electronic. So after being hit with the mine, all their communications will be dead as well."

"Seems you've thought of about everything," Ethan commented.

"You can never plan for everything. We had men too close to a mine one time when it was triggered and it blew-out their own radios. Stupid stuff like that is what screws up an operation and gets people killed."

"What if the second car calls for help before you can disable it?" Alex asked.

"This location where we are is the farthest point from both the compound and town. We figure we'll have about four minutes before someone could get here if they were notified."

"*Alpha, Charlie One mark,*" a voice came over the radio.

"Copy Charlie One," Smith replied. "Once Zulu is in place, we should be ready."

"Where's Zulu supposed to be?" Alex inquired.

"He'll be opposite the compound on a hill watching for the vehicles."

More calls came in. *"Charlie Two, Bravo Two deployed."* *"Bravo One deployed."* *"Copy Bravo. Alpha, Charlie Two Bravo is ready."*

"Copy Charlie Two Bravo," Smith responded.

"Alpha, Zulu is in the stands," a quiet but animated and energetic voice said over the radio.

Smith shook his head. "Always the comedian," he commented before keying the radio. "Copy Zulu. Charlie One, Charlie Three, Alpha, status."

"Charlie One ready." *"Charlie Three ready,"* came rapid responses.

"Copy Charlie. Gentlemen, the field is hot," Smith responded over the radio. "That's it. Now we wait."

Various vehicles passed on the road in both directions as it approached midnight. Smith was quiet while Ethan and Alex intermittently talked about things to try and break up the tension. Alex mentioned to Ethan that they should have brought the ice pack with them because his face was still pretty swollen.

Then the call came: *"Alpha, Zulu, players approaching the field. Two long sedans, standby."* The SUV was dead silent while they waited for another message. *"Alpha, Zulu ident, two players in the game."*

"Copy Zulu. Charlie Three status," Smith said quickly, but calmly.

"Charlie Three, field is clear."

"Charlie Three, execute."

"Charlie Three."

"Charlie One, ready ident."

"Charlie One ready." Smith waited patiently for the call from his team member ready to identify the sedans and set up the second barricade. It was about four and a half kilometers from the compound so it took a few minutes for the cars to reach position one. Then that call came in.

"Alpha, Charlie Three, ident two players."

"Charlie Three, wait for clear then execute," Smith replied.

"Charlie Three."

"Charlie Two Bravo, Alpha, the play is yours."

"Charlie Two Bravo. Bravo status." "Bravo One ready." "Bravo Two ready." "Charlie Two Bravo,"

"Here we go," Smith said as he pulled a semi-auto pistol from a holster under his jacket, checked the clip, put it back and started drumming his fingers on the steering wheel.

Bravo One remotely set the first mine and cleared to a safe distance. The vehicles approached rapidly and when the first one passed, the mine fired making a loud *'SNAP,'* like a massive static discharge. The passenger side headlight went out and the other headlight dimmed as the engine died. *"Bravo One, player one is disabled,"* a quite voice announced over the radio.

As the first car slowed to pull off the road, the second car applied its brakes and began to slow down behind it. The cars rolled past Charlie Two's position as he picked up the second mine and scurried farther down the side of the road in the grass to reposition it. Bravo One readied the RIDS unit for the second car. Charlie Two set the mine, scurried away and fired it remotely. *'SNAP'* The engine in the second car died. *"Charlie Two, player two is disabled. Bravo One go."*

Bravo One sprinted to the back right corner of the second vehicle and slung the RIDS unit onto its roof. It stuck with a *'thud'* as its magnetic ring grabbed and held tightly to the steel. The unit began emitting a high-pitched *'whoosh'* and immediately filled the car with a dense yellow gas as Charlie Two ran to the back corner of the first car and slung a RIDS unit onto *its* roof seconds later.

As the second unit activated, Charlie Two shot out the headlights of the second car as Bravo Two shot out the one working headlight of the first car and ran back to flank the right side of the first vehicle. Bravo One took his position in the road to flank both vehicles. Charlie Two then ran back to flank the right side of the second vehicle.

Both the front driver and passenger side doors of the second vehicle opened as gas poured out and a man stumbled from each door, coughing violently before falling to the ground. Seconds later, the front passenger door of the first vehicle opened. Coughing could be heard and stopped before the man fell unconscious out of his seat and onto the road, legs still inside.

Weapons were trained on the unconscious men until the gas dissipated. Bravo team moved in to secure the vehicles and pull the men to the side of the road as Smith started his SUV. *"Alpha, Charlie Two Bravo, players secured."*

"Alpha, copy," Smith responded as he turned on the lights, put the SUV in gear and gunned it through the gate and onto the road where he stopped abruptly next to the two disabled sedans.

"Here sir!" Bravo One shouted to Smith as he jumped out of his SUV. He ran to the first car and looked in the back to see an unconscious man with a silver suitcase attached to his wrist with a securing ring and metal cable.

"This one's clear!" Charlie Two shouted from the second car and closed the trunk.

Smith ran to his SUV, grabbed the bolt cutters and returned to cut the cable and free the suitcase from its escort. Then he opened the back passenger door of his SUV and handed the suitcase to Alex who was sitting on that side of the vehicle. Ethan turned the front of the case toward him and pushed and pulled on the latches.

"Good game. Clear the field," Smith said into his radio. Bravo team and Charlie Two had already removed the RIDS from the roofs of the disabled cars and Bravo team was heading back to their vehicle. Zulu had 'left the stands' and was heading toward them to recover the first mine. Charlie Two jumped into Smith's vehicle and they drove off.

"I can't open it!" Ethan said frantically. "It has combo locks. It'll have to be cut open or something."

"Yeah I know. We'll have to open it before we get on the plane to make sure the artifact is in there."

Ethan looked at the case and wondered. If only a few grains of the element allowed him to sense its presence before, then a much larger amount should be overwhelming. But he sensed nothing. How to control the odd but timely dreams and visions was still something not understood in the slightest. He closed his eyes and tried to concentrate. All he saw in his mind was a silver suitcase.

The plane was located at an airfield south of Bremen—about a thirty-five minute drive from their current location. Ethan kept the case secure on his lap as they made their way from the rural area to an expressway onramp. It wasn't long before Alex noticed Smith nervously watching his mirrors.

"Something wrong?" she asked.

"Not sure. Someone may be following us."

"Isn't one of your team back there?"

"Bravo One and Two are going to meet us at the airport, but that isn't them." Alex and Ethan looked at each other in the intermittent passing lights. Alex grabbed Ethan's hand and squeezed it hard.

They continued on the expressway for a few kilometers before Smith decided to exit and test his theory. He watched his mirrors closely as he came to a stop at an intersection, then keyed his radio. "Bravo One, Alpha." There was silence. "Bravo One, Bravo Two, Alpha." Smith then made a quick turn to the right and sped up to legal speed. There was still no response from the radio.

He pulled out his phone and dialed a number. There was no answer. He dialed another, then spoke. "This is Smith. We're on Achimer just south of the A1 east of Bremen. We're being followed and there's no response from Bravo. How soon can you guys get here?" There was a brief pause, Smith shook his head, then swore under his breath. "Alright, contact me by radio when you're in the area and *don't* waste time getting here."

He put the phone back in its holster, swore in a mumbling roll then made another right and a left onto side streets to try to lose the pursuing vehicle. *"Ah... It's got a locater!"* he suddenly exclaimed irritated. "Ethan, hand the case up to Conner. Alex, get the tool bag from the back." Ethan handed the case to Conner who turned on the passenger map light and quickly, but thoroughly started examining the perimeter of the case as Alex scrambled to grab the tool bag from the floor behind her seat.

"Nothing, sir," Conner reported.

"Then get it open!" Smith demanded as he turned another hard corner and floored it.

"Hand me the bag!" Conner shouted as he held out his hand between the seats. Alex awkwardly shoved the bag to him which he took and set on top of the case.

"There's a rotary cutoff saw in there," Smith said as Conner started to dig through the bag.

"Got it," he said, pulling it out with his right hand and tossing the bag back to Ethan with the other.

Conner slid the case down between his knees and the dash, started the battery-powered saw and began to cut a horizontal groove into the case just above the left lock. A small stream of sparks spewed off the blade when it hit the steel latch. After about twenty seconds, the wheel slipped through and he started on the other lock. When the blade had defeated the second latch, Conner shut off the saw and hurriedly pushed it back between the seats for someone to grab. He then pulled the case apart to reveal its contents.

There, on a dark side street in an unfamiliar city as they gambled with their very lives, Ethan saw for the first time the object containing the matter for which his entire life had now been committed to protecting. The container was a little different than how he imagined it would look.

The chaotic world around him seemed to go silent for just a moment as he gazed, mesmerized by the handmade simplicity of the stone vessel resting deep in its foam cradle. It was uniquely simple in construction, finished not by a skilled craftsman as an object of adulation, but by someone more average for an unpretentious purpose. It was a moment of solemnity.

Conner raised one end of the vessel, lifted it out and inspected it for a tracking device.

"Is that it?" Smith said loudly, turning his head toward Ethan.

"Yes...yes, I believe it is," he replied a little overwhelmed.

"Take it and get rid of the case," Smith shouted to both Ethan and Conner. Conner carefully handed the vessel back to Ethan while Smith turned another corner. Conner then lowered the window and threw the case out onto the side of the road into some weeds. Smith knew they were still far from safe. The airport was at least ten minutes away.

Ethan held the container in his hands only briefly until Alex grabbed his carry-on bag from the back and pulled it up to where they were sitting. "We'll put it in here," she said, unzipping the bag. She pulled out his clothes and started wrapping the vessel in undershirts, underwear and socks, then laid it on a pair of pants at the bottom of the bag. The other clothes were stuffed around it and the bag zipped shut. Ethan took the long strap, put it around his shoulder and rested the bag on his lap.

Smith had slowed his pace, trying not to attract attention as they skirted the city limits of Bremen. He knew that if they had been followed this long, it was likely someone had also figured out they were on their way to one of the two airports.

"We're going have to rethink this. We need to take these people out before heading to the plane or we may never make it," Smith said as he drove down a secluded street. He abruptly pulled over to the curb and turned off his lights.

It was an unlit area with several other parked vehicles. "We'll wait here until the other guys get close then we'll set up an ambush. Just stay low and stay alert."

"Did you see what kind of vehicle it was?" Conner asked.

"No. It was too far back. The lights were tall though so it was probably another SUV."

They intently watched several vehicles travel in various directions through an intersection ahead of them. A few vehicles drove past and down the street where they were parked. Conner had his automatic weapon ready on his lap and Smith had taken his out from a modified center console, checked it, and had it lying to his side.

Several agonizing minutes went by while they sat and watched the sparse traffic. It would probably still be another ten before Smith's men were in the area. All they could do was wait.

The radio finally came to life. Smith responded and activated his encoded GPS transmitter. They were now only about three minutes away. Only three minutes...

A dark SUV turned at the intersection and slowly made its way down the street toward them. "Heads up everybody," Smith said. He started the vehicle, put his hand on the gearshift, and waited. The approaching SUV didn't look any different than any other one. But Smith had been doing this long enough to know when to listen to that inner voice, especially when it was nervous.

He continued to watch the vehicle intently. Ethan was still sitting low in the back seat, looking out at the approaching headlights through the bottom of his window. In an instant, the dark SUV turned toward them and accelerated. It was a surreal moment for Ethan as he watched the headlights careening toward him—his mind temporarily blurring the comprehension of an impending and brutal collision. It was something from a nightmare he had seen so many times before.

In one quick and simultaneous motion, Smith pushed on the brake to release the shifter, yanked it into Drive and floored the accelerator. It was too late. Just as the SUV dropped into gear and spun the rear tires to take off, the other SUV slammed into the driver side door and front wheel, pinning it against the curb with enough force to push the left side off the ground. Its engine roared and tires spun in a vain attempt to finish its attack and overturn its enemy.

The impact had deployed the side-curtain airbags and killed the engine. Smith's head bounced off the driver-side airbag. Ethan had started to turn away, but his head hit the window low with enough impact to severely daze him.

People were yelling in quiet, muffled voices. He was bent sideways over his bag. Someone was pulling on his arm and his shirt, trying to drag him out of the passenger side of the vehicle. Suddenly it was raining sparkles that seemed to strobe.

Alex was crouched down yelling something. *Why is she yelling?* He couldn't understand her. Sluggishly he lay on the ground, looking at grass that glittered with shards of glass and flashes of strange light that pulsed and flickered.

The slow motion confusion gradually faded into flashing muzzles and loud gunfire and shouting as his senses returned. Conner was at the front of Smith's vehicle returning fire and hit one of the approaching men in the upper chest and head, sending him to the ground. Smith had already radioed that they were under fire, but help was still two minutes away—an eternity when a split second is all it takes to end your life.

Directly behind them was a housing complex with a driveway between buildings. *"Stay down and run through there!"* Smith shouted over the gunfire. Ethan and Alex took off toward the passage as Smith moved to the back of his SUV just in time to catch one of the gunmen trying to outflank them. Smith opened fire at point blank range sending the man sprawling to the ground, but not before taking three rounds in the upper chest and shoulder. The impact knocked him back, but he stayed on his feet and continued firing at the other vehicle as he ran to gain a better position behind a car parked behind his smashed and bullet-riddled SUV.

Ethan and Alex ran along the dark passage, momentarily moving through lighted areas. People would come out to see what was going on, then run back at the sound of gunfire and the occasional *'zing'* of a stray bullet.

The narrow road curved around and through the housing units to a connecting street where a fueling station was located on the corner. "We still need to get to that plane," Alex said, breathing hard as they approached the station.

"I don't think we were meeting a plane. I think Smith or Connor was the pilot," Ethan replied, grimacing. Alex looked at him, now totally despondent.

"Well then, what should we do?" she said, almost in tears.

"I don't know. Just get out of here somehow, I guess."

"Do you think Smith and Conner got away? I think Smith was hit," Alex said soberly.

"They're tough. I'm sure they'll be fine," Ethan responded, trying not to sound pessimistic.

Sirens were now approaching. Two people standing near the pumps ducked and ran inside as another round of heavy gunfire erupted in the distance—and then there was silence. A man with a handful of snacks ran from the station to an old ten ton delivery truck parked about fifty feet from them. Ethan was struggling to focus. It looked like the latch on the loading doors of the truck was unlocked.

"There, come on," he said, grabbing Alex by the sleeve and pulling her. They ran toward the back of the truck.

The driver's door slammed shut just as they reached the latch. Ethan pulled out the securing pin, pushed the latch up and pulled on the door. The truck engine started. He took the bag off his shoulder and slid it in the back of the four-foot high bed, then started to move to the side to let Alex in when she pushed him.

"Get in!" she shouted, shoving him in the back. He grabbed the adjacent door and painfully pulled himself up and into the truck.

The brakes released and the truck started to move. With her right hand on the inside edge of the secured door, Alex stumbled forward as the truck took off, pulling her with it. Ethan held his hand out as far as he could and Alex grabbed it. But just as she jumped on the rear bumper, the truck bounced out of the station lot and onto the road, causing her to lose her footing and fall against the deck.

Now only halfway in with her legs dangling out the back, the heavy open door swung around, hitting her hard on the thigh. Ethan let go of her right hand and quickly grabbed the back of her pants, pulling her up and into the truck.

"Are you okay?" he said as she rolled onto her back.

"That's going to leave a bruise," she responded through gritted teeth while holding the back of her thigh tightly.

The only available light was from the occasional passing street-lights shining through white fiberglass panels that lined the top of the cargo area. As a light would pass, they could briefly see boxes of various sizes stacked about halfway to the ceiling. Ethan held the door closed as the truck traveled for about a minute, then slowed and made a very long right-hand turn. It straightened out and started to accelerate. He opened the door narrowly to see a wide road with several lanes.

"We're on a highway, heading south, I think. You don't have your global anymore, do you?" Ethan asked.

"It was in my bag. I don't have anything," she said, starting to sit up. "All I have is my passport, some gum, about five hundred bucks and Mr. Lip Balm."

"Mr. Lip Balm, huh? Well, at least you have something to wear."

CHAPTER SIXTEEN

Land of Mist & Light

THE RUMBLING AND BOUNCING kept reminding Ethan of his tenuous physical condition, and the overwhelming pain kept him from the sleep he so desperately needed. Maybe an hour had passed since they exited the expressway and began traveling on a smaller two-lane road. The truck had slowed once to make another turn, but neither of them was prepared or had realized what was happening until it was too late and the truck was already accelerating back up to speed.

Now they were resting again as Ethan bobbed back and forth. Alex, still mostly awake, was gently holding his arm. Ethan's headache was becoming more severe due to the trauma of the day, and neither of them had a plan at that point, other than to try and stay away from the vicious and very resourceful Order.

Sometime later as Ethan's mind tried to find peace, he saw his dad driving the family car. He was a boy again, riding in the back seat this time as the car came to a stop.

"Is this it?"

"This is it," his father replied.

"Alright!" young Ethan shouted as he threw open the door and jumped out.

Ethan was suddenly completely lucid. Alex had her eyes closed and was trying to doze off.

"Alex," he said, grabbing and shaking her leg.

"What, what?" she replied, startled and disoriented.

"This is it. We're getting out."

"Where are we?"

"I have no idea. Come on."

Ethan stood awkwardly in the diffused moonlight and helped Alex to her feet before opening the door to look behind the truck. All he saw was a dimly lit country road with no other vehicles. "You'll go first and I'll toss the bag to you."

"But we haven't...even..." The truck started to decelerate. It didn't stop completely, but was going very slowly and started to make a turn.

Alex quickly climbed to the ground and ran with the truck for a second before letting go. Ethan immediately tossed the bag to her as the truck completed its turn. He started climbing down as quickly as he could, but the truck started to accelerate. He tried to run, then stumbled and fell to the asphalt, sliding and rolling a few times before ending up on his back in the middle of the road. Alex ran to him.

"The fun just never ends," he groaned sarcastically.

"Are you okay?" she asked, for lack of something more insightful.

"No, I'm *not* okay. I'm *sick* of this crap. Why does everything always have to be so...*damn difficult?"* he spouted while Alex helped him up. "Is it really necessary to go through all this? You know what it is? Somebody screwed up—*that's* what this is. Somewhere out there is some poor twit sitting with his happy family thinking, '*Man* my life is pathetic. I would just *love* to lose everything, start having nightmares and freaky hallucinations, then actually *decide* to go seriously piss-off a bunch of crazed evil *wackos* bent on world domination so they'll chase me all over hell trying to kill me for something I'm not even sure I believe is possible!' Oh yeah, that's *perfect.* No, I'm *not* the one with the masochistic death wish because *I NEVER ASKED FOR THIS!"* he shouted skyward. *"Oooooooh,"* he then grimaced quietly, lower-

ing his throbbing head and pushing on it with both hands. Alex didn't offer anything else.

Patchy clouds played hide-and-seek with the moon as they stood near a 'T' intersection somewhere in an isolated part of the country. The road they had come down continued straight ahead along the base of a tall ridge, and the adjoining road the truck had turned onto ran perpendicular to it. There were open fields with fences along ghostly roads, and trees scattered about.

Ethan looked around and thought he saw something toward the ridge. "Is that a building over there, or am I just seeing things?" he asked sarcastically.

Alex turned and squinted, trying to focus through the darkness. "No, I think you're right. It looks like a building."

"Well then, let's go over there," he grumbled as he started to walk.

Headlights came toward them over the hill about a mile down the road. Immediately, they both moved out of sight off to the side where they found old broken pavement that led to a metal vehicle gate. Next to the gate were bushes that they hid behind until the car had passed.

Ethan climbed through the gate first, then Alex handed him the bag before climbing through herself. The broken road was home to large clumps of grass growing up through long jagged cracks in the old asphalt.

"How did you know the truck was going to slow down?" Alex asked.

Ethan took a second, then responded. "Along with all the other weird stuff, I've been having these flashbacks to my childhood where I see events that seem to correspond with something going on in the present. This time I was riding in the back of my dad's car. We stopped and I opened the door and jumped out, so I knew that's what we needed to do."

"Huh," she said smiling and shaking her head. "You really are amazing, you know that?"

"Yeah well if I was *that* amazing I would have dreamed myself walking in the dark and brought a flashlight."

Alex didn't respond, but started feeling her pockets. "You're not going to believe this," she said almost apologetically.

"You're kidding. You have a flashlight?"

"No, but I have a lighter," she said reaching into her pocket. "It was lying on the floor at the hotel. I picked it up when we were leaving. I had completely forgotten about it."

"Well there you go then. I'm not the only amazing one here," Ethan concluded. Alex wasn't sure if he was being sincere or not.

They approached the building that was tall, white, and spooky. It appeared mostly square with small windows in various places that they could see—most of them broken. At the front of the building were steps that led to a door. It was locked. They walked around to the side to faintly see two large silos toward the back that were probably once used to store harvested products of some kind. A set of railroad tracks ran next to them—a spur likely leading to other tracks nearby.

The moon cast a heavy black shadow on the side of the building so Alex gave the lighter a flick. It immediately lit and although not very bright, still provided enough light to locate another door.

"Never thought I'd be glad that someone smokes," Ethan commented as Alex held the lighter near the door. It had a large deadbolt that had been pried off long ago, and the door pushed open easily. Alex held the lighter in front of her and cautiously stepped into the doorway as she looked around.

"Do you want to go first?" she asked nervously.

"You're doing fine," Ethan responded, pushing the palm of his hand against his still aching head. "Just watch out for the usual man-eating arachnids and snakes and stuff."

"Yeah, thanks," she replied as they walked into a large open room where another set of stairs led to an upper level.

"Let's head upstairs where we saw the high windows from outside," Ethan suggested while pushing the door closed.

Something in the corner of the room scratched on the floor, trying to scurry out through a small opening in the wall. Startled at the noise, Alex blindly grabbed Ethan by his shirt. She let go after a moment, took a deep breath and continued toward the stairs.

The second level was large and open as soft moonlight flowed through a dozen or so partially broken windows set high on the wall, revealing antiquated equipment covered in spider webs and dust. The old machinery seemed to rest peacefully in the fragmented bluish-white light. Alex moved along an inside wall that appeared to run all the way to the edge of the building.

About halfway across, she stopped and searched the floor. Finding a piece of broken wood, she then handed the lighter to Ethan and proceeded to scrape the dirt away in a large rectangle. Ethan set the bag down on the semi-clean floor then started to sit down next to it with his back to the wall. Alex took the lighter and helped him.

"Thank you," he said.

"You're welcome," she replied softly, sitting down beside him.

He leaned his head against the wall and gently pressed his palms to his temples. "Does my head look overly large to you?" he asked. "Because I feel like it's going to explode."

Alex held the lighter up so she could see his face. The light of the small yellow flame made his condition painfully visible. His eye and cheek were even more swollen than before, probably because of the crash.

Her emotions started to surface and she closed the lid to extinguish the light that would expose the feelings now unintentionally expressed on her face. Her lips quivered and tears began to form. She tried to withhold the sounds that would give away her new feelings, but the involuntary bursts could not be restrained.

"I look that bad?" Ethan tried to joke. Alex leaned her head on his shoulder, and took his right hand in hers to hold it—inadvertently feeling the bandages she had wrapped around the deep cuts in his wrists. It only made her feel worse.

"I'm so sorry," she said with a broken voice.

"Well, it could have been worse. The guy who hit me could have been ambidextrous," Ethan said as he grunted out a single laugh.

Alex dropped her head by his shoulder and began to sob. He put his arm around her and patted her shoulder, holding her reservedly. "We'll figure this out. Don't worry," he said as he rested his head back against the wall.

"But it's my fault we're here. None of this would have happened if I hadn't pushed you into this."

"Now you know that isn't true. You're not responsible for the choices I've made, or for what those people have done. I could have said no. Actually, if it wasn't for you, I'd probably be dead by now."

Alex was trying to wipe the tears from her face when Ethan grunted more laughs.

"What?" she choked out.

"I'll bet you don't look so good now either," he said, grunting a few more laughs. Alex then blurted out a couple of her own.

His head was really starting to throb as a sharp pain shot through it. *"Oh,"* he groaned, putting his hands back to his temples and closing his eyes.

"Do you think we'll be okay here for a while?" Alex asked in a rough voice.

"Probably," he replied, barely moving his lips.

"You need to rest. I'll see if I can find something to cover you up, okay?"

"Alright."

Alex picked up the still warm lighter, flicked it again and ventured into the dark, abandoned plant. On the floor against a wall on the opposite side of the building were several pallets of large feedbags once used to transport feed for livestock. She carefully removed the bags from the top of one pallet that were covered in a layer of dirt to retrieve several from underneath that were reasonably clean.

She took an armful back with her to find Ethan slumped over half asleep. She used the broken board to move more dirt away from around him, then placed one of the bags on the floor next to him, with his carry-on at the top, so he could rest his head.

"Ethan...Ethan," she said quietly. He looked up at her, barely opening his eyes. "Lie down." He looked over at the dimly lit feedbag on the floor and at his carry-on, then scooted over to lie down as she helped him.

She took the bags and spread them over him like a blanket. Hopefully this would keep him warm. She should have taken a shirt out of his bag for herself, but didn't think of it before and didn't want to bother him again. So she sat on her own feedbag and wrapped another one around her. It was pitiful, but what else could she do?

Fatigue was setting in again. But it was hard to think about sleep in a place like this. The huge dark expanse of the room made her feel small and vulnerable. It was abnormally quiet. Minute sounds of scurrying mice and insects seemed amplified in the dead, dark air. She hadn't felt this helpless in a long time and hoped it was something she would never have to feel again.

And Ethan… He was probably just trying to be nice in what he had said. It was *her* prodding that had led them to all this. She could think of very little to bring her comfort in this moment. Maybe morning would bring new hope.

☀ ☀ ☀

What is this place? Am I standing…sitting? I can't feel anything. There's nothing here. But I have to be somewhere…everyone is somewhere. Hello! Hellooooo! Am I hearing myself? Or just thinking I'm hearing myself? Air… Am I breathing? I have no breath. I have no breath! Is this death? Is this what death is? No, no I don't believe that. But if this isn't death, then what is it? I'm thinking, so I have to be something, somewhere. Joshua? Are you doing this? I don't understand. Why am I here? Where is this place? Joshua!

The darkness slowly turned into a thick, gray fog. Ethan held his hands close to his face. He could see them now. He looked down at his legs and was relieved. That jubilation was short lived when he realized that even though he could see himself, he could see nothing else—just a fog all around him. Above…below… He was still nowhere with no reference…no direction. He was alone in this strange place.

321

What's the point of this? he wondered. Slowly he turned all the way around, straining to see something—anything. There was nothing to see. He sat down and put his arms on his knees, lowered his head, closed his eyes and laughed to himself. *This is lunacy. Just wake up. Wake up!* He raised his head and opened his eyes, but *nothing* was still there. He laughed in defiance, or maybe it was ignorance.

A faint shadow then appeared in the mist. It was small and some distance away. It seemed to be coming nearer. He was frightened of what it could be and moved to his knees, ready to run. But where would he run? The figure moved closer and closer and as it approached, its shadowy essence began to change, becoming brighter and clearer.

It came ever nearer to him, then stopped and stood a few feet away. His heart felt like it was going to burst and he froze in total disbelief.

"Hi Daddy," she said smiling. What he was seeing was impossible. It was his daughter. It was Allison! It was really her...right there in front of him. Not like the other dreams...but real, like when he met Joshua.

"Allison? Is that really you sweetheart?" he said in a hopeful, but shaky and reserved voice. He cautiously held out his hands. Allison walked toward him and put hers in his. The touch caused an incredible warmth to flow through him that was as real as anything could possibly be.

"It's really me, Daddy," she said as she put her hands around his neck and gave him a big hug. He was hesitant at first, not sure to believe what was happening. But how could he deny what he felt? To again feel the warmth and love of his daughter was magnificent. That feeling had been lost to him for so long that he had almost forgotten what an incredibly wonderful feeling it truly was. "I've missed you," she said smiling.

"Oh I've missed you too, sweetheart," he said as tears streamed down his cheeks.

As he held her back to look at her, he put his hand gently on the side of her face. Her eyes were sparkling, and her long, flowing golden hair was just like he remembered—just like her mother's. "You're even more beautiful than I remember," he said thoughtfully. Allison giggled her shy little giggle, just like she used to. "Allison, what is this place?"

"It's where *you* are, silly." Ethan looked at her puzzled. She giggled again and grabbed his hand. "Come on Daddy, let's go."

"Where are we going?"

"I'll show you. Just follow me."

Ethan stood slowly as Allison began to lead him. He could still see nothing but a foggy, dense haze and wondered how she knew where she was going as she walked with such unwavering confidence.

After a time, the thick veil of fog began to thin. Ethan was happy to see sunlight again. And as they emerged from obscurity, he was astonished at what he saw.

It was a huge city bright with light that seemed to float in the air some distance away. It stretched for as far as he could see in both directions. Above it was clear sky with a bright sun, below it was an endless abyss, dark and foreboding. The fog was a wall that also seemed to extend forever in all directions. Then as he followed the wall with his eyes, he looked below him, *and saw nothing.*

Panicked, he cried out and jerked his hand away to stumble back into the fog, falling on his stomach in the familiar safety of obscurity. He turned and looked back to see Allison dimly through the mist. Slowly he turned around on his hands and knees and crawled to the edge as far as he dared. Allison walked back toward him, but stopped before entering the mist. She was standing in mid-air. He could clearly see there was nothing below her—nothing supporting her. *This is not possible*, he thought frightened.

"What's wrong, Dad?"

"Allison, you're...not standing on anything." Puzzled, she looked down at her feet.

"Well of course I am."

"Allison, I can't see anything below you."

"This is how we get over there," she said as she pointed to the city.

"But, there's no road...or bridge or walkway. I can't do that."

"Yes you can."

"No, I can't."

Allison walked back to her father and stood in front of him. "You could until you looked down. Don't look down. Just hold my hand and follow me," she said holding her hand out to him.

He stood up slowly and took her hand again—still reluctant to move. As Allison once again stepped outside the wall of mist, Ethan was physically unable to follow her. His mind wouldn't allow his feet to move. There was nothing there to walk on. It was impossible to do what she was doing.

She turned to face her father and took his other hand in hers. "Dad?"

"Yes, sweetheart," he said nervously.

"This is the only way for me to take you to see Mom."

Ethan became numb. "You're taking me…to see…your mother?"

"She asked me to come get you. That's why I'm here, to take you to her."

"Your mom's over there?" he asked with anticipation.

"Yes, and this is the only way to get there."

Ethan looked out over the endless expanse as apprehension tried to overwhelm all other emotion. He then knelt down on shaking knees and looked at his daughter. "Allison, I would really, really like to see your mom, but I…I can't go across there. Is there some other way?"

"No, this is the only way."

"Then why is there no path? If there was a path then I could do it."

She turned briefly to look at the expanse, then back at her father. "But there *is* a path, Dad. All we have to do is follow it across."

"But Allison, *I can't see it.*"

"*I can.*"

Ethan looked into her eyes and saw the total trust and faith of a child—something *he* had abandoned long ago. If he was to go where she wanted him to, it was *her* faith he would have to follow. "You can really take me to see your mother?"

"Sure can. She's been waiting for you. Let's go," Allison said, enthusiastically pulling on his arms.

"Wait, wait. Just go really slow, okay?"

"Okay."

He stood and took a deep breath. She turned, took a step then looked back at her father as he stumbled, wavered, then regained his balance. "Dad, look at me." He held on tight to her hand, and took another step. Allison took a few more steps, as did Ethan.

It was hard not to look down at the endless abyss, eager to gobble-up those who stumble off the path. He tried to stay focused on Allison and the city as she guided him across. She would occasionally change direction, as if following a winding course.

He became less concerned about what was below him as they walked together, and instead focused on the brilliance of the city. The wall that surrounded it seemed hundreds of feet tall and was made of a white stone that shimmered like billions of tiny crystals. At the edge of the city was a large space of well kept green grass with an old stone walkway that led to a huge solid arch in the wall.

As Allison led her father onto the stone path that wound through the grass, he stopped and turned to look at the abyss. Allison stopped as well, still holding his hand.

"Allison, you said you could see a path. What do you see?" She pointed to the stone walkway where they were standing.

"It looks like this and goes over there where I found you."

Ethan carefully studied it. He could still see nothing, but obviously something *was* there. *That* he could not deny. "Allison, why can't I see the path?"

Without hesitation, Allison responded. "Mom knows."

"Is she in there?" he asked, pointing toward the wall.

"Yep, and lots of other people too. Come on." Again she pulled on his hand to lead him.

With anticipation and anxiety, he now walked side by side with his daughter toward the enormous arch. As they approached, he could see the wall was seamless, as was the gate inside the massive archway. It was as if they had been carved from a mountain by giants and placed there by hands unknown to man.

Allison stopped a few feet from the gate. Ethan let go of her hand then slid his along the stone to feel its smooth texture. He looked up and around in awe, then turned to Allison and gave her a big smile. "I'll bet there's a reeeally big door knob on the inside, isn't there?"

She giggled, grabbed his hand with both of hers and with a quick, firm pull, stepped backward into the gate. A blinding white light appeared around her. Ethan gasped as he was pulled off balance. Quickly he closed his eyes, grimacing and turning away, waiting to impact the stone.

"Dad...dad." He could hear her, but was afraid to open his eyes. "Dad!" she said insistently, shaking his hand. Slowly, he opened one eye to a squint and looked toward her voice. She was looking up at him. "We're here." He slowly opened the other eye and looked around cautiously.

It was majestic, like the place he first met Joshua. There were long rolling hills of lush grass and wildflowers and groves of trees scattered across the countryside. A gentle, warm breeze caressed his face as he looked around with child's eyes. "Wow. This is a *great* place."

"Pretty, huh?" Allison responded.

"Oh, this is incredible," Ethan said while he slowly turned, looking at the overwhelming majesty.

Allison let go of his hand and pointed to a large circle of rocks in the distance. "Mom's over there. Race ya!" She took off at a dead run. Ethan stood pondering the unbelievable possibility of this place, and seeing Rachel again. He watched Allison run through the knee-deep grass. Then when he realized he was standing there alone, he took off after her.

He caught her before they reached the structure. "Allison, wait." She stopped and turned back to look at him, moving the hair away from her face. He put his hands on his knees and leaned over toward her. "Is your mom really here?" he asked thoughtfully.

With innocent inflection, she replied, "Dad, are you still afraid?"

"Well...yes. I guess maybe I am...a little," he said, surprised by her perception.

She took him by the hand again and smiled. "There's nothing to be afraid of. I was a little scared too when I first came here." And once again, she led her father by the hand.

They came to a place where odd-shaped purple flowers grew out from under large tropical-like bushes with large leaves. As they walked past, Ethan was overwhelmed; gardens everywhere full of every kind of flower a person could possibly imagine— bordered by small winding walls of stone and vegetation. He was completely mesmerized by the incredible colors that seemed to dance in a symphony of sight.

"There she is!" Allison shouted as she let go and bolted away. Ethan turned to watch her and there, at the edge of a flower garden full of white and yellow lilies, stood a woman in a beautiful white dress, wearing a large white garden hat with a yellow bow. His heart began to race. "Hi Mom! I'm back!" Allison said happily when she neared the woman. The woman turned around and when they met, they hugged and conversed. Then Allison looked and pointed toward Ethan.

He thought he recognized the long flowing golden hair that he had tried so hard to keep in his memories. But how could this really be? There was also a small child that had been standing behind the woman. The woman took Allison and the small child by the hand and they started walking toward him.

The large hat shadowed the woman's face and he strained to confirm that what was happening could somehow be real, and not some horrible, cruel joke. As they came nearer, he saw those features from his memories...the shape of her chin, her cheekbones, her mouth and lips, that quirky smile. She took off her hat and handed it to Allison as the sun lit up her face for the first time again. *It was his wife.*

The flowers in the background seemed to pale behind her as she approached, and then he saw those vivid, striking green eyes that could always see deep into his soul. His fear, confusion, pain, frustration, indecision and longing would be hidden no longer. Everything within him was now known to her. It was as if they had never been apart.

In her eyes he could see the warmth and love in which he had grown so close, and had shared for so many years. She reached out to touch his face and as her fingers met his skin, a feeling of deep warmth surged through him. His face quivered as tears welled and flowed. She put her hand squarely on the side of his face and the other on his chest to look into his eyes with the devotion only sincere and honest love can manifest.

"Hello, Ethan," she said softly. When he heard the melodic tone of her voice, his insecurity left him and his emotions erupted. Rachel put both arms around him and rested her head on his chest. Ethan instinctively put his left arm around her back and cradled her head with his right hand.

All the old feelings were coming back. He rested his cheek against her head and caressed her hair. He wanted to close his eyes, but was afraid if he did, she might disappear. Everything was so familiar, and wonderful.

Having now composed himself to a point, Ethan looked at his loving wife, studying her face in disbelief that somehow she was really there—that he was somehow with both of them again. "Am I dead?" he asked.

"No, Ethan," Rachel giggled, "you're *very* much alive. I'd like you to meet someone." She turned and held out her hand. The young boy took it and looked up at Ethan. Ethan questioningly looked down at the young boy, then at Rachel who smiled and said nothing. He kneeled down to look at the boy who seemed familiar.

"What's your name?" Ethan asked.

"Patrick," the small boy said shyly. Ethan's smile slowly turned to disbelief as he looked up at Rachel. Patrick was the name they had chosen if their first child had been a boy.

"Rachel?"

"Patrick is our son."

"Our son? But...how?"

"The day before the accident I found out that Allison was going to have a brother. I was waiting until that weekend when we would have time to celebrate. It was going to be a surprise, but I never got the chance to tell you."

Ethan was speechless as he looked at the son he had never known. It was a staggering revelation. A son. *He had a son!*

"Allison, would you take Patrick over by the pond, please?"

"Sure, Mom. Come on Patrick," Allison said as she held out her hand. Patrick put his small hand in hers and Allison skipped away slowly so her brother could keep up.

There were so many questions, so many things he wanted to know. He watched his daughter and son, then looked around and back at Rachel. The thoughts were brewing, but before he could start asking his discourse of questions, she put her finger on his lips and looked into his eyes. "I can only show you what is possible." She then rested her hand over his heart. "The answers you're searching for, must come from here."

He knew what she meant, and he was ashamed. So many times before she had tried to share and explain what she understood and felt, but he wouldn't listen—always arguing with her about evidence and proof and facts. *Some answers must be felt and not just heard.* That's what she used to tell him. What a fool he had been. So much more could have been accomplished in their short time together had he only listened.

Rachel stepped back and held out her hand. Ethan took it. She led him into the garden where they walked along its paths and marveled at its beauty. He was feeling submissive and somewhat guilty at his inability to grasp what she seemed to understand so completely. "You were right...weren't you?"

"It isn't just about being right Ethan, it's about truth. What I know to be true, I know because I also feel it in my heart. That is what I tried to share with you. Even now you struggle. What you cannot see with your eyes are the very things that blind you." He sighed and lowered his head as they began to walk.

She leaned her shoulder against him and held his arm while they reverently strolled hand in hand. Later they stopped and sat on a low stone wall.

"We're all on a journey that many cannot yet comprehend. But even the longest journey in the mortal world is in fact only a few short steps on a road to an endless horizon. What you think, and the choices you make, is who you become."

"When you and Allison left, everything I had that was good was taken from me. I'm trying, but I'm not sure I really have a life without you."

"Your life is still full of beauty and opportunity for you to experience. It is filled with hope and promise if you choose to see it. You are of the chosen and can accomplish great things if you seek for them.

"You're a traveler, like any and all of us, on a journey started long ago—endless in its experience. This place is where we work and wait until all have completed the earthly journey."

"But...how is that possible? There are billions and billions of people and millions of years. How—?"

Rachel cradled his hand. "You *must* be patient. The physical laws of mortal life, such as the progression of time, are different here. To know them you must learn and understand the concepts Joshua has explained, and first complete your own journey. The choices you make and the paths you choose will determine your place here as they also do in life.

"What you encounter may not always be within your control, but the decisions you make about your life in any situation are *always* within your control. *That* is where you begin to learn discipline, and discipline is how you will learn the truths that will lead you here. They are simple truths, but it is not a simple journey, as you already know.

"Your path is unique among most and will serve you well if you should stay true to it. You are strong and intelligent. I have no doubts in you." Ethan was hopeful, but still troubled.

He looked down, sad, as another thought came. "I should have listened before when you tried to help me understand. I feel like I've let you down."

"You have not let us down. You're a good man, *and* a good father. You just need to find your course. You have been shown many things to guide you, but you must choose to see with no disguise. When you open your heart, *then* you'll open your eyes."

Ethan was startled at her words. "It was *you* in Sara's dream." Rachel just smiled and rested her head back on his shoulder.

A subtle rumble rolled through the air. It sounded like thunder. Ethan looked up, but there were only a few white puffy clouds that he could see.

"Mom, it's going to rain!" Allison shouted from across the gardens. She started skipping toward them, winding her way along the paths as Patrick ran behind.

"Okay!" Rachel replied as she stood. "I'm afraid our time is coming to its end."

"No, I don't want to leave you again," Ethan said anxiously. Allison ran up to her father and held out her arms, waiting for him to pick her up. He knew that leaving them and this place was inevitable, and lifted his daughter up to hold her a last time.

"Thank you for bringing me here."

"You're welcome Daddy. I love you," she said squeezing his neck. He swayed her back and forth gently and gave her a kiss on the cheek.

"I love you too, sweetheart," he replied, his voice choking.

He put her down and kneeled to look at his son. Patrick didn't know this man yet and just watched Ethan from his mother's side. Ethan held out his hand. "It was nice to meet you, Patrick." The little boy looked at his father's hand, then up at his mother.

"It's okay," she said reassuringly.

Patrick slowly reached out and put his small hand in his father's. Ethan gripped it gently. "Bye," the young boy said, and pulled his hand away. Allison held out her hand to her brother and they stepped a few feet back.

Ethan stood and turned to the woman he loved more than life itself. He took her hands and kissed them, and held them against his face.

"Ethan, all that you've seen can be yours if you stay true to your course. You *will* find us again, and can be with us forever." She held his face and softly kissed his lips, then put her arms around him. He held her tightly, kissing her neck as he felt her long, sun-warmed hair run through his fingers.

"I love you Rachel."

"I love you too, Ethan." As he held her, she whispered in his ear. "Find happiness in the happiness of others. Share my love and I will always be with you."

He held on as long as he could, but his eyes became heavy, and in the warmth of his wife's embrace, and the aroma of berries, it slowly started slipping away.

CHAPTER SEVENTEEN

Das Heim von Oma

THE SMELL OF CHILLED, damp air and the soft drumming of falling rain greeted him in the early dawn when he opened his eyes. The room was a stark and cold contrast to where he had just been.

A tiny puddle had formed on the dirty floor in front of his face where water was dripping from a crack in the high ceiling. He turned his head slowly upward to see a single droplet fall through a bright stream of white light every few seconds. He extended his hand into its path, and let the water hit his open palm. Thoughts of Joshua and his words began to resonate in his mind as he watched each droplet hit, and splash into the air.

A twinge of pain ran through his back from lying on the concrete floor—although he was surprisingly warm. Alex must have covered him up. He couldn't remember. She was lying with her back to him—kind of slumped over his legs. She looked very uncomfortable. He turned his head back to watch the dripping water hit the floor, and thought about the dream... Or was it...?

"Alex. Alex." He gently put his hand on her shoulder to wake her. Startled, she breathed in quickly and lifted her head to look at Ethan's hand, then sat up.

"Crap, we're still here," she grumbled, rubbing her face.

The short cloudburst was tapering off. Ethan pulled the sacks off him and sat up against the wall next to Alex. His face still hurt, but not as bad as last night. The headache was mostly gone.

"How are you feeling?" she said, leaning over to look at him.

"Hungry."

"Let me see. Well, you're a couple different colors, but the swelling seems to have gone down a little." Then she noticed the streaks on his face. "Ethan, what's wrong?"

"What do you mean?"

"You've been crying."

He put the back of his hand on his cheek. It was wet. "Nah, it must be the dripping water," he offered.

She turned and sat facing him. "We'll get through this. We'll figure it out." Her compassion was sincere, even if his tears had been misinterpreted.

As he looked at her, he realized that her decision to be with him was a testament of her commitment, not only to Rachel's credibility and beliefs, but in him as well. She had taken a huge chance in staying with him, and was being incredibly supportive and helpful. She was a talented and incredible woman in her own right—something he was finally beginning to see.

Alex was looking down, not sure what Ethan was thinking and was surprised when he took her hand, kissed the back of it and continued to hold it. He was smiling at her in the soft morning light. "I saw Rachel and Allison and...uh... I saw them in a dream. I could touch them, hold them...even smell their hair. I looked into Rachel's eyes and I saw her. I felt her presence. They're in a beautiful place. They're happy. It was amazing."

"You know Ethan, if it was anyone else telling me this, I'd say they were nuttier than a fruitcake." Ethan looked straight ahead in a daze, lost in the images passing through his mind. "Did you talk to them?"

"Yes, I did. It was an incredible. It's hard to describe." Ethan's lips started to quiver slightly. Alex felt a little uncomfortable holding his hand while he talked about seeing his dead wife and daughter. But she tried to keep the situation in perspective. Part of it was just that if any feelings beyond simple friendship ever *did* develop between them, she wanted to make sure that they were genuine, and not just a proxy for the personification of his wife.

After a moment, Ethan realized she was staring at him. "What."

"Sometimes I wish *I* could see some of the things you see."

"Yeah, and go through life wondering if you're not all hooked up right? You should be careful what you wish for."

"No, you know what I mean. I think we all sometimes wish we were more than what we are. When you showed me the journal, I can't say I wasn't a little excited for an adventure. It was so mysterious and all. Now I kind of feel like the lowly sidekick being dragged along as you have all these fantastic experiences. I just don't feel like I'm worth much to you anymore."

"You know Alex, it wasn't just the journal that got me going. You can take as much credit for saving my life as anyone. You're the one who opened the door to a cage I didn't necessarily want to leave. The incredible things we've experienced may never have happened if it wasn't for you. I wish you could see some of these things too. Someday I think you will. I owe you a lot." Alex smiled, lowered and shook her head. "*I'm serious.* Without you, I have no idea what would have happened to me. You stuck with me just like you said you would. No one can ask for anything more than that."

"That's nice of you to say, but I don't feel like I've done that much."

"Are you kidding? Alex, I don't know of anyone, honestly, who would have come this far, including Rachel. Yes, she was a wonderful and amazing woman, but you two are completely different and you're pretty incredible yourself so don't *ever* think of yourself as anything less, because I certainly don't."

"Wow. Maybe you should have dreams like that more often."

"Yeah, well, I've gotta be reaching my quota."

"It's just that you seem different."

"Let's just say...I never could really see the big picture. Rachel tried to explain things to me before she left. I guess I was just too arrogant to listen. Now I think I'm starting to understand a little more of it all the time."

He rolled to his knees and slowly stood. Alex quickly got up to help him. He groaned at the pain in his muscles, arms, legs and face.

"Still glad I got you into all this?" she asked facetiously.

"Absolutely," he said grimacing. "By the way, thank you for covering me up last night.

"I did what I could."

"It was enough," he said putting his arms around her and giving her a sincere hug. She was still a little uncomfortable. Maybe it was just confusion in her own feelings. Time would tell.

Ethan took in a big breath and gingerly felt the side of his face. "Maybe we should—"

Alex quickly raised her hand and turned her head slightly. After a few seconds, she turned back to Ethan. "Voices. Someone's in here," she said in a panicked whisper. "I think they're down there." She pointed to an opening in the floor about thirty feet away where an old conveyer passed through. Then she pointed to the far side of the floor. "I think there's a door over there that leads outside."

"Okay," he whispered back.

He picked up his bag, Alex took him by the arm and they started walking slowly. It would take them close to the opening. The floor was concrete and made no sound as they walked, but it was still prudent to be as quiet as possible. If they were careful, they might be able to get outside without being noticed.

As they came close to the opening, Alex increased her grip on Ethan's arm. Now *he* could hear something, just not well enough to make it out. The trauma to his head had caused a constant ringing that had dulled his hearing.

Alex stopped. She was looking toward the opening and Ethan was looking at her. She stood motionless, then leaned over and whispered in his ear. "They're speaking German."

"That's probably because we're in Germany," he whispered back.

Then there was loud laughter. Alex listened intently for a few more moments and then whispered back to Ethan. "It sounds like some kids."

She moved into the opening just enough to see two boys standing in the middle of the room below them.

They appeared to be about twelve years old and were smoking cigarettes—laughing and being quite jovial. Ethan cautiously peeked over Alex's shoulder, then moved back away from the opening to avoid being seen.

"What do you think?" she whispered.

"I think they're alone and there's no one else around or they wouldn't be making so much noise."

"So what should we do?"

Ethan moved back to the opening and watched the boys for another moment. "I think we should see if we can talk to them."

"You sure? We don't want anyone to know we're here."

"We don't want the people who did *this* to know we're here," Ethan said pointing to his face. "Look, we have no idea where we are and have no idea which way to go from here, do we? They're just kids. Maybe they could at least tell us where we are." Alex let out a sigh and looked back toward the opening. "Besides, what are the chances someone could have followed us here, huh? It must be a *sign*," he said dramatically raising and shaking his hands.

Alex rolled her eyes. "Don't bet on it. Besides, I'm not up on my German. How about you?"

"Yeah, that could be a problem."

"So...what?"

"Let's give it a try anyway."

"Alright."

Alex started walking slowly toward the stairs that led to the lower level. Ethan followed closely behind her. The stairway landing to the lower level was about fifteen feet from where the boys were standing.

"I'll bet they run," Alex whispered.

"I'll bet they do too," Ethan responded.

A little unsure of his steadiness, Ethan put one hand on Alex's shoulder as they started down the narrow metal stairs. The stairs exited away from where the boys were facing, so Alex was looking over her shoulder all the way down. The boys were still talking loudly and hadn't noticed either of them. But as Alex reached the floor, one of the boys caught a glimpse of something and turned to see what it was.

Upon seeing the two adults, one boy screamed like a schoolgirl at recess and bolted for the door. The other boy, shocked, but more disoriented by his friend's ear-shattering retreat, jumped, dropped the cigarette and stared at both of them like a deer in headlights.

Just as Alex started to raise her hand to try to convince the boy that they meant no harm to him, he shouted out in a frightened voice, *"Wer sind Sie?"*

"We didn't mean to frighten you," Alex responded quickly. My friend and I are lost. Do you speak English? Can you tell us where we are?" she continued in the friendliest tone she could find. The boy stared at both of them with big eyes, unsure whether to stay and listen or follow his friend. "Is there a town near here? A phone? Do you know where there might be a phone we could use?" Alex put her hand to her ear like she was using a phone. The nervous boy continued to stare at them, and said nothing.

"Well, so much for that idea," Ethan said disappointed.

The boy focused on Ethan, pointed at him and in good English asked, "What happened?"

Alex looked at the boy, then back at Ethan and realized he was referring to the bruises on Ethan's face. "Some very mean people did that," she replied. "You speak English."

"So do you. Who are you?"

"My name is Alex, this is Ethan." Ethan raised his hand about waist high and waved. The boy instinctively raised his and waved back. "What's your name?"

"Garrett," the boy said hesitantly.

"Well Garrett, it's nice to meet you. We didn't mean to scare you. We just need to find out where we are and use a phone. Can you help us find a phone?"

His expression still showed bewilderment in finding people, adults no less, in his friend's and his secret place. Of course, it was probably what *any* eleven-year-old boy would think if he was approached by vagrant strangers having spent the night in an abandoned barley plant way out in the country. It was no doubt what his running, screaming friend thought.

Garrett responded very cautiously. "Maybe."

"That would be very helpful. Thank you." Ethan stayed back while Alex continued to converse with the boy. He could see the boy was wary of him, no doubt because of the way he looked.

"Why are you here?" Garrett asked.

Alex knelt down and started to explain. "There are some very bad people who are planning to do something that will hurt a lot of other people. We found out what they're planning to do and we're trying to stop them. They hurt my friend before we got away and we came here last night to hide. The problem is, we don't know where 'here' is, and we need to call another friend to get some help."

Garrett looked at them both then asked, "Will I get in trouble?"

Alex smiled and replied, "No. All we need to do is use a phone and then we'll leave. Tell you what," she said standing and reaching into her back pocket to pull out a small fold of money. "Just so you know we're honest, how about I give you twenty American dollars." Alex unfolded a twenty-dollar bill and started to hand it to him. A mischievous grin came to boy's face as he reached for the bill. Alex lifted it up slightly out of his reach before he could grab it. "*But*, you have to promise me you won't smoke any more cigarettes. They're bad for you. Okay?"

"Okay," he replied solemnly. Alex lowered the bill and he gently took it from her hand.

"Where did you learn to speak English so well?"

"My mom and dad speak English and I learn it in school. They travel a lot."

"That's great. Do you live near here?"

"No. My sister and I are staying with my grandma. She lives up the hill. My mom and dad are on a business trip."

"I see. Do you think your grandma would let us use her phone?"

"Maybe. We can go ask her. She's kind of grumpy sometimes."

"That's okay. All we can do is ask."

A muffled shout came from outside. "Garrett!"

"Es ist in Ordnung!" Garrett shouted toward the doorway. "That's Hans. He lives down the road from my grandma. Follow me."

Garrett walked to the doorway and peeked outside while Alex and Ethan followed. Hans was hiding behind the corner of the building with his head poking out just far enough to watch as his friend and the strangers emerged. Alex and Ethan both warily looked around as well, becoming familiar with their now illuminated surroundings.

Gray overhead clouds were moving off to reveal a blue morning sky. It was still a bit chilly. The new rain had dampened the air. To their left was a hillside full of trees and to their right was a large open valley full of fields with a smattering of roads, trees and what looked like farms.

Garrett talked to his friend and they seemed to be in agreement. "This way," Garrett said motioning. His friend walked to his side and looked over his shoulder frequently as they started up the hill into the trees. Alex and Ethan followed a short distance behind, looking over their shoulders as well.

The grass was wet and quickly soaked through pant legs and shoes. The trail wound along the hillside through dense trees until cresting about a mile from where they had started. As the ground began to level out, the trees thinned and opened into a clearing of small farms with cattle and sheep in fenced fields and lots.

Garrett and his friend climbed through a log fence and started across a field toward a dirt road. Ethan and Alex followed closely behind while a herd of grazing sheep and goats eyed them curiously—not overly concerned with their trespass.

As the boys started to climb through the fence on the other side of the field near the road, Alex asked, "How much farther to your grandmother's house?"

"Not much farther. Just down this road and that way," Garrett replied, pointing down the road and to the left.

"You two walked quite a ways this morning."

"We like to explore the woods and go to the old building."

"I see." Alex thought the boys where cute and smiled at Ethan to show her approval of them.

The farmhouses were quaint in appearance. The land was bordered by trees to the east and south and was open to the west and northwest. They could now see the top of a house with smoke coming from the chimney as they turned down a dirt lane. The driveway sloped and turned over a mild crest and down to an animal gate. Garrett opened the gate and waited for his new friends to walk through.

On the left side of the lane was a green barn with several white geese in front of it. About a hundred feet past it was a small rock house. There were trees lining a hillside to the left and behind the house were pastures that sloped down to level off into another valley a couple miles away.

Garrett stopped and turned to Ethan and Alex before they reached the house. "Wait here," he said, "I'll find grandma." Hans stood a few feet away from Alex and waited as well— occasionally squinting to look up at them. Garrett walked up the few steps to the house and shouted, "Oma!" He opened the screen and inside door and again shouted, "Oma!"

"Hallo," came a voice from behind them. They turned to see an older, stout woman with gray hair in a blue scarf. A young teenage girl was standing beside her. They both held small baskets filled with eggs. "Was wollen sie?" the woman asked with authority.

Caught off guard, Alex stammered. "Uh…we're here with Garrett." The woman reared her head back slightly and garnered an expression of surprise. Just then, the screen door to the house slammed as Garrett came running back out.

"Oma! Können diese Leute Dein Telefon benutzen?"

"Sie sind Amerikaner," Hans added resolutely. The woman handed her basket to the girl and motioned her to go to the house, then looked Alex and Ethan over carefully.

With a look of concern, she then turned her attention to Garrett. "Wie sind Sie hier hergekommen?" She wanted to know where they came from. Garrett started to speak and pointed in the direction from where they had come when the woman suddenly held out her hand and stopped him. "Halt mal eben!" she said, grabbing his coat sleeve at the shoulder and pulling him toward her. Leaning over, she sniffed a couple times at his head and shoulder to then push him back. "Habt ihr wieder Zigaretten geraucht?" she asked in a very irritated tone.

Garrett lowered his head and replied, "Ja."

The woman then glared at Hans as he lowered his head and looked around abashedly. She held out her hand. "Gebe mir die Zigaretten!" Hans very slowly reached into his pocket to pull out a partially crumpled pack of cigarettes. "Schnell!" the woman shouted. Startled, Hans winced and quickly handed them to her, still keeping his head down. The old woman quickly snatched the pack from his hand and whacked him on the head with it. He winced again, but didn't say anything. Then the fun began.

Having crushed the pack in her hand, the woman leaned forward and scolded Hans while shaking her finger at him. Then she turned and did the same to Garrett. He also ducked his head, trying to avoid the scolding. Then she looked back at Hans. "Du gehst nach House!" she said sternly, pointing toward the road. Hans turned and with his head hung low, began walking up the lane. They all watched him quietly. "Du kleiner Lümmel," the grandma muttered.

Ethan, with his arms folded tightly, trying to stay warm, leaned over to Alex. "You didn't need a translator for that one." The women looked at Ethan who quickly stood up straight. She put the crushed cigarettes in her pocket and turned back to her grandson. "Erzähle jetzt den rest," she said, motioning him to continue.

Garrett started to tell the story again of how he met the two strangers. He waved and pointed, gestured to his face and pointed at Ethan while the woman listened intently. Then he pulled the twenty-dollar bill from his pocket and showed it to her. The woman took the twenty and studied it.

"Uh oh," Ethan said quietly.

The woman looked over at them both, handed the bill back to Garrett, pursed her lips and sighed in contemplation. "Kommen sie herein, kommen sie herein," she finally said, and motioned them to follow her.

The door to the house opened into a small mudroom adjoining a neatly-kept kitchen. They had all taken off muddy shoes and Ethan and Alex stood silently in the corner of the kitchen, not sure what to do. The girl had set the baskets on the counter and was moving eggs into cartons.

The woman examined Ethan's face carefully, then took his arm and led him into her small family room where a fire was burning in a wood stove. She motioned for them to sit on a couch near the stove, then walked back into the kitchen to talk to Garrett. He took their shoes, knocked the mud from them, brought them back in and set them by the fire to dry.

The grandmother came in a few moments later with half a glass of water and two pills. Ethan looked at the pills and realized they must be pain medication. He pointed at the pills then to his face. The woman nodded and responded, "Ja, medizin." Ethan nodded in acknowledgement and swallowed the two pills.

"Gut," the woman said, taking the glass and heading back to the kitchen.

"You're brave," Alex commented

"Nah. She's seems like a good woman."

"Fine. But if you start seeing flying cows…"

Ethan grinned. "You'll be the second one to know."

Garrett came back into the room carrying a cordless phone and handed it to Alex. "Grandma said you can use her phone, but you have to reverse the charges if you call very far."

"Tell her that will be fine and thank you very much."

Garrett started to walk away, then stopped and turned back to Alex. "What does reverse the charges mean?"

"It means the person we're calling will pay for the cost of the phone call so your grandma doesn't have to."

"Ohhh," Garrett replied and walked back to the kitchen.

Alex stood, took a folded piece of paper from her front pants pocket, sat back down and unfolded it. "It's the Professor's private number. He told me to use it only in an emergency." Alex looked at the phone and realized she didn't know how to make an out-of-country phone call from there. "Do you know how to do this?" she asked Ethan.

"No idea. You need a calling card."

"I had one yesterday."

"I can help," the young woman offered from the doorway. "I call my parents at their hotel sometimes when they're away."

"That would be great. Thank you." The girl walked into the family room and Alex handed her the phone. "By the way, I'm Alex, this is Ethan."

"I'm Lydia."

"Hi, Lydia."

"So your Garrett's sister?" Ethan asked.

"Yes. We stay here with grandma sometimes when we're out of school. Where are you calling?"

"The United States."

Lydia held the phone, thought for a moment, then dialed a short string of numbers and handed the phone back to Alex. "That should be the International Operator."

Alex took the phone and listened. "Yes. I would like to make a collect call to the United States please." She paused, then looked up at Lydia. "Thank you," she said quietly. Lydia smiled proudly and went back to the kitchen to help her grandma.

The operator came back on the line and asked for the number and name. Alex responded, "Adeline."

Ethan was slumped down on the sofa and looked over at her with an odd expression. "Adeline?" he inquired curiously.

"It's a code word we have so he knows it's really me."

"So…if you said is was *Alexandria,* he'd think you were somebody else?" She gave him a subtle but sharp rap on the side of his knee with her knuckles. Ethan jerked. "Ow! I was just kidding. You know, the drugs haven't kicked in yet." She ignored him as he rubbed his leg.

"It's ringing…"

"Hello?"

"This is TransTel International with a collect call from Adeline. Will you accept the charges?"

"Yes I will."

"Thank you. Go ahead please."

"Professor?"

"Alex. Are you okay?"

"Oh, am I glad to hear your voice. Yeah, we're okay for the most part."

"Where are you?"

"We're at a small farmhouse somewhere south or west of Bremen, I think. I forgot to ask. Hang on."

"No, wait. I'm running a trace. I'll tell you in a minute where you are and you can confirm it."

"Okay"

"How's Ethan?"

"He's a little worse for wear, but I think he'll be all right if nothing else happens." She looked over at him and he had his eyes closed.

"Do you have the artifact with you?"

"Yes."

"Good."

"Professor," Alex said quietly, "I didn't think anything like this was going to happen." Ethan opened his eyes.

"Sometimes things just don't go the way we plan. But I'm glad you're okay. Right now we need to work on getting you two home." Alex started rubbing her forehead with her fingers. Her silence told the Professor much. "Listen, don't worry. We'll get you out of there. What happened to your phone?"

"It was in my bag in the back of Smith's SUV. Is Smith okay?"

"He took a few rounds, but should make it."

"What about the other guys." There was no reply to her inquiry.

"I've got you about forty-five kilometers northwest of a town called Espelkamp—that's south of Bremen. There's a small airport just west of the town. If I can get a plane to you, do you think you can get to the airport there?"

"I don't know…probably. I'll have to see."

"Ask someone if they know where this town is."

Alex turned, looking for Garrett or Lydia. Garrett was standing in the doorway. "Would you ask your grandma where Espelkamp is?"

"It's south about an hour away. We go there with grandma for groceries," he replied.

"Thank you." Alex turned back to the phone. "The people here know where it is."

"Good. It will take a few hours to get this arranged. Will you be okay until then?"

"We should be fine."

"Can you trust the people you're with now?"

"Yeah, I think so."

"Then I'll call you back as soon as I have some more information. Don't talk to anyone you don't have to, and don't go anywhere yet. And keep an eye on your friend and that artifact."

"I will."

"Just hang in there. It'll be all right."

"Okay."

Alex looked at the phone and pushed the button to hang up the call.

"So what did he say?" Ethan asked.

"There's an airport near a town south of here called Espelkamp. He's trying to get a plane there."

"That's impressive. I guess sometimes influential friends are nice to have."

"Sometimes. He'll call back when he has it arranged."

"That's good news."

"Garrett, would you tell your grandma 'thank you' for letting us use her telephone, and let her know that we'll be expecting a call in a few hours? Would you also ask her if it would be okay if we stayed here until then?"

"Ja," Garrett replied.

They could hear him and his grandmother talking before he came back into the room. "She says that would be okay and wants to know if you would like something to eat. She says you sound hungry."

It would seem that the 'grumpiness' Garrett perceived in his grandmother was only the inexperienced perception of a child. The rough exterior was just a thin shield of emotion to isolate the realities of coping with life after the passing of a beloved spouse. Years of hard work maintaining a small farm alone and trying to carry on a familiar lifestyle once shared, can take its toll on anyone. All that and the need to also be strong for sons, daughters and grandchildren. The warmth and kindness within a person is many times disguised only by another's failure to see. Garrett just wasn't yet old enough to understand.

Ethan looked like an old man trying to eat his pancakes. It was painful to open his mouth that wide. Slowly and methodically, he ate all four of them, three eggs and a glass of milk. The milk was a little thicker than what he was used to, but tasty nevertheless.

Alex ate her smaller breakfast as well, but had water to drink instead. She suspected the milk may have come straight from the barn, and that was a bit more than she could stomach.

She sat and watched Ethan finish the last of his breakfast. He drank the last of his milk, set the glass down and wiped his mouth carefully. He seemed to be taking everything in stride, as if the monsters pursuing them had been forgotten for a time. *She* couldn't shut them out so easily.

"That was really good. Thank you very much," Ethan said to the woman.

"Yes. Thank you," Alex added.

The woman smiled and nodded back. "Sie sind willkommen."

They were now both sitting in the family room letting their pant legs finish drying. Ethan had dozed off on the sofa, and Alex was looking over a very old map that Lydia had given her.

The phone rang. It had been a little over an hour from when Alex had spoken to the Professor. Lydia was sitting at the table reading a magazine and answered the phone. "Hallo." She paused briefly. "Yes, a moment."

She handed the phone to Alex who was now standing in the doorway. "Professor?"

"You still doing alright?"

"We're fine. The people here have been very nice."

"Good. Here's what I have for you; a private jet should arrive at the airport outside Espelkamp at about twelve forty-five your time—that's an hour and a half from now. Can you two get there by then?"

"Just a minute." Alex lowered the phone. "Lydia, would you ask your grandma if there is any way she could take us to the airport at Espelkamp? Tell her we have a way home to the United States but we need to be at that airport in an hour and a half. Here..." Alex pulled out the small fold of money from her pocket, removed five twenty dollar bills and handed them to Lydia. "Ask her if this is enough."

Lydia talked with her grandma and returned to the room a minute later. "She says she could use a few more groceries, but says you gave her too much. She wants you to keep the rest." Lydia handed two of the twenties back.

"Great. Please tell her thank you very, *very* much."

"Okay," Lydia replied.

"Professor, it looks like we have a way there."

"Very good then. You'll need to go to a place called Neuhof Aviation. That's where one of the pilots will meet you. He'll introduce himself as Gregory. You'll make one stop for fuel near the coast then fly directly back to the U.S. You got all that?

"Yeah, I got it."

"Good luck, Alex."

"Thank you, Professor," she said before hanging up the phone.

CHAPTER EIGHTEEN

Shattered Glass

GARRETT AND LYDIA BOTH waved from the edge of the lane as their grandma and the two visitors headed down the road. The old pickup was in exceptionally good condition. That's because it was apparently never driven fast enough to wear anything out. No wonder it took an hour to get to town. The slow pace was excruciating, though they were very grateful for the ride and tried to be patient. People would blare their horns as they went around them—no doubt in appreciation of the vintage automobile.

The town was in a low valley with a mountain range on the south side. Ethan spotted a private jet parked on a taxiway near a row of buildings when the pickup finally arrived at the small airport. "That must be it," he said to Alex as he pointed. Their thoughts were now of going home and the hope that this long ordeal would finally be nearing its end.

Alex then pointed out a building with a sign out front that read Neuhof Aviation. The old woman stopped the pickup in front of the building. Alex climbed out first, holding the bag with the artifact. Ethan followed. Alex put her head back in the cab and thanked the woman, then moved back a few steps as Ethan stepped to the open door to do the same. The woman offered her hand and Ethan held it in gratitude.

She looked at him and said, "Junger mann, vertraut deinem Instinkt."

Ethan didn't understand the words, but he knew what she meant. "Thank you. Thank you very much for everything."

"Auf wiedersehen!" the woman said cheerfully, letting go and waving to both of them.

"Auf wiedersehen! Thank you!" Alex replied enthusiastically.

Ethan closed the passenger door and waved, watching as the old pickup backed up and drove away. He couldn't help but think about the woman and her grandchildren, once strangers....

"Ethan, come on," Alex said, anxious to get going.

The airport seemed fairly small, though obviously large enough to handle a private jet. Neuhof Aviation was one of the companies there that rented aircraft and contracted jobs for various clients. It was unclear exactly if someone the Professor worked with was providing the jet, or if it was chartered from Neuhof. It didn't matter really, as long as it got them home.

The building was quiet. There were two desks just inside the entrance, but no one was around. "Hello?" Alex called out. There was no reply.

"Maybe they're in the back somewhere having lunch," Ethan suggested.

They walked down a short hallway, looking into the rooms to find no one. They continued around a corner and down another hall toward a door at the end when it suddenly opened. A handsome man wearing a pilot's jacket walked through the spring-loaded door, which closed behind him. "Kann ich Ihnen helfen?" the man said.

Alex was surprised and started to respond. "Um, hi. We're looking..."

"You're American," the man interrupted. "You must be the ones we're taking back to the United States."

"Yes," Alex replied gratefully.

"Good. We've been expecting you. My name's Gregory," the man said, extending his hand to greet them.

"I'm Alex, and this is Ethan."

"Excellent," the man said smiling as he shook Alex's hand, and then Ethan's.

But when Ethan grasped the man's hand, he winced. A chill shot through him, and a dark, ugly feeling fell over him. He shuddered and pulled his hand away. Time began to slow. The man was now talking to Alex again. Ethan glanced down at the man's lapel, and there he saw the maleficent symbol of all consuming darkness—a Black Sun. They were not going home. *They had been betrayed.*

The man opened and held the door that led to a large hanger. Alex eagerly walked through, diligently carrying the bag that contained the very power these men were after. The man smiled and motioned for Ethan to follow. As Ethan walked past, he looked into the man's face. Behind the smiling mask, there was addiction to merciless power, malevolent ambition and loyalty, all well disguised within a pleasant shell of decency.

Alex was a few steps ahead, the man a few steps behind. In the far corner of the hanger stood two other men. As one of them turned to walk away, Ethan saw the distinctive profile of an automatic weapon held loosely under a jacket. He knew if he didn't do something now, they would die, and everything that had been sacrificed, everything they had survived would be for naught. The Power of Souls would again be lost.

With all the courage and strength he could summon, Ethan spun around and launched his fist as hard as he could at the man's head. The man was watching his colleagues at the corner of the hanger while releasing the safety on his weapon. Ethan's fist struck the surprised man hard and a loud 'CRUNCH' echoed in the hanger. The man was instantly knocked backward off his feet to land hard and unconscious on the concrete floor.

As he hit, the pistol that was about to end their lives fell out of his hand and slid a short distance away. Alex turned at the sound, but first only saw Ethan struggling to regain his balance. Then she saw the man on the floor, blood gushing from his face, the pistol on the ground near his hand.

She gasped and covered her mouth with both hands. Ethan grabbed her arm and pulled as the man at the corner of the hanger started running toward them—raising his weapon and yelling to the others just out of sight.

"Come on, come on!" Ethan shouted. Alex stumbled, still in shock.

He pulled her through the door and pushed her down the hall before slamming the door, twisting the lock and taking off after her. Bullets sprayed through the wall behind them. They instinctively ducked as they ran.

"What happened?" Alex cried out as they turned the corner toward the door at the front of the lobby.

"He was one of them!"

Ethan shoved the door open. Outside were two parked cars. He ran to the first one—it was locked. He tried the second one—it was open, but there were no keys. He grabbed Alex who was almost paralyzed with disbelief and they ran toward another group of cars in front of the next building about two hundred feet away.

As they ran, Ethan lifted the heavy bag from her shoulder and put the strap around his neck, the bag under his arm.

"Check those on the far end!" he shouted, pointing to the group of cars—hoping it would give her some protection, and both of them an escape.

They sprinted from car to car frantically grabbing at door handles. Alex was closest to the door of the building where the cars were parked when a woman walked out pulling her keys from a purse. Alex ran toward the woman who was still looking down, and snatched the keys out of her hand.

"Was machen sie?" the woman said surprised.

"I'm sorry," Alex said frantically pushing on the key fob, trying to find the woman's vehicle. A car's headlights flashed and horn beeped. The side windows suddenly exploded in the first two vehicles on the end from a hail of bullets, setting off a blaring alarm in one of them.

Alex hid behind the passenger side of the woman's car and Ethan ducked behind one of the others. The woman screamed and ran back into the building.

"The green one!" Alex shouted before opening the passenger door and climbing in. She fumbled the keys trying to get the right one in the ignition. Ethan briefly saw a man running toward them before he reached the driver side door. Alex had slid into the seat and was trying to start the car. Ethan opened the door, pushed the bag over to her and jumped in. Scrunching down in the seat, he put the BMW in reverse and floored the accelerator.

The engine roared and tires dug down, spinning wildly, throwing gravel everywhere as the car sped backwards. Ethan turned the wheel while hitting the brakes and slammed the shifter into Drive. The engine revved then labored when the transmission engaged and tires spun again, chirping intermittently as they found hard dirt. The rear driver side window and front passenger windows shattered. The back window exploded and several holes appeared in the passenger side windshield.

Now a distance away, Ethan sat up to look in the mirror. He was heading full-out for some other hangers farther down the road. "They've stopped shooting!" he shouted over the wind and engine noise. Alex had her head down between the seats and didn't move. "We're never going to get out of here on the ground!" She still didn't respond. He looked down at her. She was covered in shattered glass—her dark hair sparkling with reflected light.

He reached down and shook her shoulder. "Alex! *Alex!* Are you okay?"

Slowly, she sat up and looked at the holes in the windshield. *"This was supposed to be over!"* she shouted back emotionally.

Ethan hit the brakes hard and turned down the side of the first hanger, threading the sedan between two rows of equipment and partially disassembled aircraft. There were about twenty small airplanes covered and tied down on the tarmac near the taxiway. They needed one that was ready to fly.

He slid the car around the hanger and headed down the tarmac between the planes and buildings. The first hanger was closed. In the second hanger were two aircraft obviously under repair. A third airplane was facing outward with a man cleaning the left wing. Ethan slammed on the brakes and turned hard into the hanger, sliding the shot-up BMW to a squealing stop under the plane's right wingtip.

Alex quickly wiped her eyes and got out of the car. Ethan was already halfway to the right side of the airplane's cabin to try the door. It was open, and a key was in the ignition.

He turned around, motioned to Alex and shouted, "Come on!" She ran to the door and handed him the bag. He put it on the floor behind the seat. He told her to get in then pulled the wheel chock and scurried underneath the plane to pull the other.

The man cleaning the wing was still wiping it with a large white rag, but had slowed his pace considerably while he watched the unfolding events in sheer bewilderment.

"Thanks. It looks great!" Ethan shouted as he opened the door to the plane and climbed into the seat. "You should probably move!" he added before closing the door. The man kept slowly polishing the wing, then stepped off his stool, picked it up and calmly walked away to stand near the outside hanger wall.

Ethan turned the key and several lights came on. *"Ahhhh..."*

"What?"

"Everything's in German," he said frustrated, searching for the starter. He found and pushed a red button. The engine cranked and fired—sputtering and idling very slowly. "Throttle, throttle," he said searching. He pushed in a rod at the center of the instrument panel that caused the engine to kick and sputter sharply.

Then suddenly, it roared to life in a blast of deafening noise. The plane shook and rocked, sliding on its tires. "Brakes...brakes, brakes, brakes, brakes," he said to himself, looking around frantically at the pedals and lower panel. He grabbed and squeezed a lever near the bottom of the instruments that clicked and released the rudder pedals.

The brakes disengaged and the plane moved forward, gaining speed rapidly. As it cleared the hanger doors and sped across the tarmac, Ethan quickly pulled back on the throttle and pushed the right rudder pedal to avoid hitting the planes tied down in front of them. The left wing dipped and the right wheel lifted off the ground from the hard turn. The plane was tipped and momentarily balanced on the nose wheel and left strut wheel.

"Ethan!" Alex shouted, grabbing the edge of her seat with one hand and holding on to the assist-bar with the other. The wheel dropped back to the ground.

"Seatbelts!" he shouted before pushing the throttle in again to speed across the grass, blazing a shortcut to the runway.

He pulled back on the throttle again and pushed hard on the rudder pedals to apply the wheel brakes. He looked down the runway and up into the air both directions for other aircraft. Pushing hard on the left rudder, the plane began to turn onto the runway. He shoved the throttle in as far as it would go.

The engine roared and the plane vibrated and began to pull hard with a steady force that pushed them back in their seats. Ethan alternately pushed on the pedals, trying to keep the plane in the middle of the runway as it accelerated. The small jet that was supposed to be their ride home sat motionless on the taxiway near the first set of hangers. Nearby, a helicopter was spooling-up its engines.

Ethan had entered the runway about a third of the way up and could clearly see the end as he started to pull back on the yoke. *"Flaps! I forgot the flaps!"*

"What are flaps?" Alex shouted back over the incredible noise. But as Ethan pulled back farther on the yoke, the airplane slowly lifted into the air, barely clearing the tall chain-link fence near the end of the runway.

"Never mind," he replied.

The plane continued to climb out slowly and gracefully. Alex had white knuckles and fingers in a vise-grip around the assist-bar. Her other hand was firmly gripping the side of her seat. She watched the ground intently as it dropped farther and farther away beneath them. She finally let go to cover her ears. Ethan looked over at her and saw a headset hooked on the cabin wall behind her. He found his and put it on, then tapped her leg and pointed to the other headset. She took it and put it on.

"Can you hear me?" he asked.

"Yes," she replied.

They said nothing as the plane continued to climb smoothly for several minutes. Ethan located the flaps while Alex stared out the window. She could still see the image of the man lying on the hanger floor, bloodied and motionless, the gun near his hand.

"That guy was going to kill us, wasn't he?" she said stoically.

"You did fine. Really," Ethan said encouragingly. She ignored him. She wasn't really that angry at him, it was just... *everything*.

Until today, a certain trust had never been questioned—there had never been a reason to doubt it. But what was obvious couldn't be ignored. The Professor *was* a dear friend, but someone *had* betrayed them.

Ethan knew they couldn't stay in the air forever. The only thing he could think to do was to land the plane somewhere, try to hide the artifact and figure out a way to come back and get it later—if he wasn't already dead or serving fifty-to-life in the German penal system.

"I didn't know you knew how to fly," Alex commented.

"Well, actually I'm kind of surprised we got off the ground. My uncle used to fly and I'd go with him once in a while. He'd showed me how to take off and land and what all the gauges meant. I was never really that serious about it though. College ended up taking all of my time. I should probably warn you, taking off is the easy part, landing might be a whole different story."

He looked at the map again, trying to figure out what to do. Then a vibration suddenly resonated throughout the cabin. It felt like someone was pounding rapidly on the wing with a hammer. Ethan looked up and over at Alex. She had felt the same thing and was looking at him. Then her eyes got real big as she looked past him and outside his window. Ethan turned to see fuel streaming from several holes in the underside of the wing. Suddenly, the pounding started again. They both turned to see several jagged holes appear in the other wing. Fuel began streaming from them as well.

Ethan twisted the yoke hard to the right. Alex screamed and grabbed onto whatever she could find. The airplane creaked and the wings warped as it violently twisted over onto its side and partially onto its back to reveal the silhouette of a large black helicopter directly above and slightly behind them.

Now in a steep dive, the engine shrieked as they plummeted toward the forest. Ethan pulled the airplane out of its dive at what looked to be about fifteen hundred feet above the rolling ground. He turned back to look for the helicopter, but the wings blocked his view.

"Now what?" Alex asked terrified.

"We land or we crash," Ethan said in frustration. "Look for a road or a clearing or something." Alex was frantic. She was scared to death and started to hyperventilate. "Keep it together Alex. I still need you."

"We're going to be dead in a minute anyway!" she shouted angrily.

"If they wanted us dead, we'd be dead. They want the artifact in one piece which is why they only shot up our fuel tanks."

"And that's better?" she shouted back at him.

"Look faster," Ethan said, noticing that the stream of fuel from the holes was beginning to thin.

He pulled back on the throttle and lowered the nose a little to get a better view. "Look, up there," he said as he pointed to several patches of light green standing out among dark trees. They appeared to be about twelve miles away at the base of a mountain. "That's probably a clearing." He banked the plane slightly to head directly for them, trying to glide as smoothly as possible.

As they approached, they could now see there were several clearings of different sizes and shapes with masses of tall trees that formed natural borders at their edge. There was also what appeared to be a road that ran along the base of one of the mountains some distance away. One of the clearings farther ahead looked large enough to land the plane, but it was at a higher elevation and they were too low to reach it.

Ethan pushed in the throttle to try to maintain altitude and the engine responded, then sputtered several times, and died. A light began flashing and a buzzer sounded to warn of the stalled engine, as if that wasn't already apparent.

"Okay, listen. See this lever right here?" Ethan grabbed Alex's hand and put it on a lever between the seats. "It has three positions. When I say 'one', you pull it up and toward you to the first position. When I say 'two', you pull it to the second and when I say 'three', pull it all the way back. Do you understand?"

"Yes," Alex responded anxiously.

Ethan chose a clearing to set the airplane down. He banked it slightly to the left in preparation for a sweeping right-hand turn, lining up with the longest stretch of a narrow, treeless patch of green.

"One!" Alex grabbed the handle with both hands, pulled the lever sideways out of its locked position and back where it clicked into place. The flaps lowered to their first position. Ethan completed the smooth, sweeping turn.

"Two!" Alex pulled the lever back to the second position as the plane pushed upward slightly, and started slowing more noticeably. They were coming in dangerously close to the tops of the trees, and Ethan knew it.

"Three!" Alex pulled the lever all the way back, extending the flaps fully. The airplane pushed upward again, but became sluggish and hard to control.

If he pulled up to clear the last stand of trees, he might lose too much airspeed and the aircraft would stall and drop like a rock. Crashing into the trees at speed didn't seem like much of an option either.

"Hang on!" he shouted as the wheels starting clipping the tops of the tallest trees. They still had about two hundred fifty feet to go before reaching the clearing.

He kept pulling back on the yoke. The branches slapped against the propeller and wheel struts. The nose started dropping and the left wing dipped slightly just as they cleared the trees. He pulled back as hard as he could and turned the yoke to the right to try and level out the plane, but their airspeed was too low.

With both pedals hard to the floor, Ethan pushed back as far as he could, bracing himself for the impact. Alex began screaming and instinctively tried to put her feet against the instrument panel, trying to push herself away from the ground rushing up to meet them.

The clearing was covered in tall dense meadow grass that gave the ground a plush, soft appearance. They could now easily see petite little purple and white wildflowers on skinny stalks accenting the lush grass that flowed in waves of green velvet.

The tail dropped slightly before the left wheel slammed into the ground, followed by the nose. The left wheel strut bent upward and back severely as the nose-wheel folded up against the belly. They both lurched forward, the force of the impact ripping off their headsets and hurling them into the windshield and instrument panel.

An eerie intermittent screeching reverberated in the cabin as the metal body bounced, scraped and slid against hidden rocks and dirt. Grass and flowers were whipping by Ethan's window at what seemed like a hundred miles per hour. The left wheel strut gave way completely. The left wingtip dropped and dug into the ground, causing the airplane to arc as it slid toward the tree line.

They bounced back in their seats when the aircraft finally came to an abrupt stop. The moment was surreal and everything was now still and silent. Ethan quickly came to his senses and unlatched his door that hit the ground as it fell open. Alex had hit her head on the yoke at impact and was severely dazed.

"Alex!" Ethan shouted while releasing his seatbelt. He leaned over to unlatch hers. She slid down toward him, almost unconscious. Her body was limp as he pulled her over the seat and out of the plane. Carefully, he rested her against the fuselage under the wing.

The distinctive sound of the large helicopter could now be heard in the distance and was getting closer. Alex had her eyes partially open, but she was fading in and out. Ethan kneeled down and held her face while he looked her over. She had a cut on her forehead and a split lip that was bleeding.

"Alex, we need to go. I think you're okay. You just bumped your head. Come on baby. Look at me."

She blinked sluggishly, tried to focus on his face then mumbled, "Did you just...call me baby?" Yeah, she'd be fine.

He retrieved the bag from behind the seat and put the strap around his neck and shoulder. His feet and legs really hurt, but the helicopter was getting closer. "We need to make a run for the trees, *now*," he said as he bent down and put his arm around her to help her up.

"I'm dizzy," she said slowly while trying to stand and crouch awkwardly under the wing.

"We need to get to those trees. You've gotta run."

"I don't think I can."

Ethan looked out at the tree line. The helicopter was almost on them. *"Then hang on."*

He pulled her out from under the wing, put her over his shoulder, and ran. The trees were only a hundred twenty-five feet or so from where the airplane finally came to rest. Ethan ran hard through the grass while struggling to carry his friend and the heavy bag. When they reached the trees, he glanced back to see the helicopter swoop down sideways like an angry black bird of prey. Their survival had surprised the hunters and the trees provided refuge. The helicopter prepared to land near the crashed plane.

The forest floor was full of brush and dead limbs and was difficult to navigate. Ethan's taller stature made it easier for him to traverse the entangled growth and debris. Alex had fallen several times before regaining most of her senses. They ran as fast as they could along a trail made by animals. The helicopter had returned to the air and was hovering not far overhead. Ethan had no doubt someone was on the ground tracking them. They had to keep moving.

He was exhausted and knew Alex wouldn't last much longer. The helicopter continued to stalk them. There seemed to be no way to escape these people. He stopped and looked around for a place to hide. Maybe if they were lucky, the aircraft would move off and the men would go past them. They could hide the artifact and get help from whoever would eventually show up to investigate the crash.

About three hundred feet along a ridge of rocks at the base of a steep embankment, Ethan found a small alcove covered with bushes. They climbed in behind and sat on the ground side by side with their legs tucked up close to stay hidden. Alex was trying hard to be as strong as she could, but her despondency was easy to see. She had all but given up. It was in her eyes when she looked at him—a look he had seen before a time or two in the mirror. He gently put his arm around her and held her to him as they sat and hoped...and prayed.

Ethan leaned his head back and rested it against the rock wall to close his eyes for just a moment. Then he realized the sound of the helicopter was gone. He opened his eyes and found himself standing in a large open field full of sagebrush. It was a cold winter day with a light covering of snow. He was carrying a rifle, the one he had when he was a boy.

"Hey Ethanial," an intense, whispering voice said from behind and to the side of him. He turned to see one of his older cousins who appeared to be about sixteen. One of his cousin's friends was standing behind him. They also had rifles. "Quit standing there like a dork and go around the outside," his cousin said, waving his gun in the direction he wanted young Ethan to go.

Young Ethan started to walk. He watched his cousin and his cousin's friend spread out and quietly move forward. They were searching for something. A few steps later, young Ethan's cousin whispered loudly, "I see one!" His cousin's friend took off after a small cottontail rabbit. Young Ethan watched as the rabbit tried to escape, darting around sagebrush and rocks before stopping to hide under one of the large clumps of sagebrush.

His cousin's friend held up his hand, indicating he knew where the rabbit was. Young Ethan watched as the boy snuck up behind the mound of sagebrush, slowly raised his rifle, leaned over the top, aimed, and fired.

Ethan jerked and opened his eyes. He turned to Alex who was sitting with her head down, resting it against her knees. He grabbed her arm. Startled, she looked at him.

"We can't stay here," he said standing.

"No…no," Alex pleaded as he gently pulled her up.

"I'm sorry."

They ran along the edge of the embankment then through a stream being fed by a small waterfall. On the other side of the stream, Ethan could see they were heading for another clearing. They had run out of places to hide. The embankment was too steep to climb and he could feel that someone was closing in behind them.

They stopped about fifteen feet from the edge of the clearing. Alex fell to her knees. She was completely exhausted. Ethan pulled the bag off his shoulder, let it fall to the ground and rested his hands on his legs.

The helicopter was still overhead. It was hopeless, utterly hopeless. He had done everything he could possibly think of doing. Even if he did try to hide the artifact there somewhere, these people would eventually find it. Nothing would stop them.

He didn't understand why Joshua would give him a task that seemed impossible to accomplish. It was going to be a pointless and futile death. Nothing had been gained and nothing would change. But he wasn't going to just give it up. *It would have to be taken.*

Ethan picked up the bag and slid the strap back over his shoulder, then turned to Alex and held out his hand. From her knees, she looked up at his outstretched hand, then up at him. She knew the situation was hopeless as well and felt no compelling reason to go on. But the resolve in Ethan's face was undeniable. There was commitment and strength in his eyes—no despair, no shame, no weakness. They were the eyes of a man who had made a decision to never give up—a man who now possessed a fortitude that nothing could ravage—whose spirit would not be extinguished.

The power she now saw in those eyes and in his countenance almost lifted her from the ground. She took his hand and stood. He held her face gently and kissed her on the forehead as she closed her eyes. He slid the hair away from her face and pressed his cheek to hers. She held his hands and felt an inner warmth that was incredibly empowering and rejuvenating.

Together, they walked to the edge of the clearing, and with absolute conviction, held each other's hand tight, took a deep breath...and ran.

CHAPTER NINETEEN

Power of Souls

THE HELICOPTER WAS STILL hovering casually behind them over the trees. It could have easily blocked their path, but for some reason, it just hovered—watching and waiting patiently. Ethan kept his focus to the trees on the other side of the clearing, trying to think of nothing else. Making it there was the only thing that mattered now.

A man emerged from the trees behind them. He stopped and acquired his target, aimed, and fired.

The first bullet passed between them, just grazing Alex's leg. The second found its mark, hitting Ethan in the back of his right thigh. It was like being struck with a baseball bat.

He grunted at the impact and tried to keep running, but on his next step the leg gave way. Still holding the bag in front of him, his other hand pulled away from Alex's and he hit the ground on his right side and slid several feet in the tall grass. Alex thought he had tripped so she stopped and waiting for him to jump back up. Then she saw the man running toward them with his weapon raised while a second man exited from the trees a little farther down. Ethan still wasn't getting up.

She screamed his name and ran back to help him. Then she saw his bloody right leg—the stain spreading rapidly. "Oh no. *Ethan, come on!*" she shouted, grabbing his arm and pulling hard.

"Please!" she pleaded, glancing up at the approaching men. Ethan pushed himself off the ground as he cried out in pain. He staggered when he tried to stand, the bag still over his shoulder with his right arm now around Alex's neck and shoulders.

She was holding his arm and trying to lift him up. His jaw was clenched and he groaned loudly in defiance, trying to refocus on the trees now less than two hundred feet away. Leaning forward, he tried to walk on the injured leg. The pain was so intense he almost passed out. Then there was another *'POP.'* He cried out again, and fell to his knees.

A single second shot had hit the other leg with cold-blooded precision. Alex didn't let go and tried to keep him on his feet, but she just wasn't strong enough. He tried to let go of her. She held on as he crumpled slowly to the ground. She fell to his side. There was nothing more they could do. It was over.

The first gunman reached them and stopped about twenty feet away. He had his weapon trained and ready, and stood motionless. The helicopter made a wide, lazy turn around them as the second gunman approached and stopped—his weapon also trained and ready.

Unable to hold himself up, Ethan fell on his side as Alex slid under his neck and shoulders to let him rest. He continued to look toward the trees—indifferent to the gunmen standing behind him as if to somehow will the forest to find and protect them.

Alex looked into Ethan's face. The hopeless courage he still embraced turned her emotions from pity and despair to anger and disdain for these men who stood cold, dedicated and emotionless. She didn't understand how *any* human being could have the mind to do such ruthless and merciless things—faces covered to conceal their individuality—to hide their conscious acceptance of commissioned malevolence. They were nothing more than heartless puppets to an evil master.

Callous and cold, they stood purposeful with no remorse. Alex was infuriated at their silent insolence. *"What are you waiting for?"* she demanded through tears. The men remained motionless and silent. The helicopter landed a short distance away. *"What are you waiting for! Just get it over with!"* she shouted over the shriek of turbine engines and spinning blades. She looked back down at Ethan, both legs useless and now completely soaked in blood. He was going into shock and was starting to shake.

Alex pushed the bag aside so she could hold him close to her. She hated these men and their merciless ambitions. They deserved to die for what they had done. But she was helpless and at their mercy. It enraged her. "*Damn You! Damn You!*" she screamed at them.

Ethan closed his eyes as her words pounded in his ears. She held her face down against his, trying to comfort him the best she could as tears spilled onto his cheeks. There in the soft grass and petite flowers of this beautiful meadow, they waited for death that was assuredly at hand.

A man climbed out of the helicopter and approached as the engines spooled down to idle. He wore a dark suit and strolled casually, walking between the two gunmen and motioning them to lower their weapons. He stopped and starting clapping his hands together slowly. Alex lifted her head and looked at him. The man didn't recognize her presence and kept clapping. Ethan slowly turned his face to see who their pursuer was.

"Bravo, Mr. Grey, bravo. That was quite the performance you two put on. You know, I was quite disappointed to find you missing on my return to Bremen. It would seem Mr. Grayson experienced a serious lapse of judgment on your behalf—something that will definitely have to be rectified when we find him...and *we will* find him. His failure to comprehend our marvelous future is most distressing.

"But let's talk about *you*, Mr. Grey. You've been very busy during your little holiday and that has caused our organization a good deal of concern. Of course, as all holidays go, this one too, I'm afraid, must come to an end. I have to concede though, it's been quite stimulating. Tracking you down, watching you run through the woods like frightened deer. You didn't *really* think you could escape, did you? Truthfully, I don't want you to feel that your efforts were in vain or anything. It's just that our bird back here is loaded with all kinds of nifty gadgets, including a thermal imager. We just watched as you ran here and there... It was a good experience for the boys—a little excitement in an otherwise dull day, and good exercise as well.

"You know, if you really think about it, you two were dead the moment you decided to steal from us. This was all just fun and games. Speaking of fun, kudos on that spectacular landing. We weren't sure you were going to make it over the trees but you pulled it off *splendidly*. *Very* impressive.

"I'd like to stay and chat but I have other matters to attend to and I'm sure the locals will be here shortly. So, we'll just relieve you of what's ours and be on our way."

"It doesn't...belong to you," Ethan said, straining to speak.

"*Semantics,* Mr. Grey. Who owns it is immaterial to who possesses it." The man then pulled a semi-auto pistol from inside his jacket, worked the action and rested it in front of him.

"It doesn't belong to you," Ethan reiterated strongly through a labored breath.

The man looked away and laughed subtly. "You people... You think that somehow you can make a difference," he said sardonically while moving closer. "What makes you think *you're* any different? You're *all* pathetic and weak. You claim to be intelligent, but your courage is full of ignorant aggression. You profess to have purpose and dreams, yet you'll sell them for a single desire. You work for worthless trinkets and pleasures and sell your souls then wonder what's wrong with your lives. You're all the same; lost in yourselves, self-righteous in your moral indignations."

"I know the truth."

"*You know nothing,*" Pancros scolded. "Your thoughts mean nothing. Your prayers mean nothing. Your life means nothing. *Nothing.* You're less than the dirt under my feet. I know what you want. I know what you need. I know what you are and I know what you're worth. I know your weaknesses, and I know your fears. *I know you. I am your judge, your jury, your executioner. I am the god of this world.* And to show you my mercy, I won't make your girlfriend watch you die.

In one swift motion, Pancros raised the gun and pointed it at Alex's head. Ethan's emotions exploded. *"NO!"* he shouted.

Using all the strength he had left, he twisted his body up in front of hers, and threw his hand out as if to somehow block the path of the impending bullet. The muzzle flashed.

Instantly, a brilliant, blinding white light permeated everything, everywhere. It was perfectly quiet. Time had been completely suspended. Ethan flinched and closed his eyes. He turned, squinting severely, trying to look at Alex. The light was so intense he couldn't see anything at all. Then its intensity gradually lessened. He turned back toward the men and opened his eyes to an utterly fantastic and incredibly strange sight.

The air itself seemed to be alive with a pure energy that flowed all around him and sparkled like water vapor aflame. A portion of it had formed into a brilliant, glistening, flowing stream that moved as if alive. It twisted and rolled, flowing toward the three men whom he could now see clearly. They were naked. No guns, no masks, nothing to disguise what they really were. They were exposed and presented in their purest form of existence—suspended like helpless locusts against a white luminescent sky.

The men could do nothing against this power that held them. The energy swirled and moved toward Pancros and he gasped as the stream of light entered his body and flowed through him like water through a sieve. It spun and twisted and passed through the others—their faces contorted with anguish and fear. As the energy exited the last man, it dissipated into the light that surrounded them.

Then at the feet of each man, a bright ring of turbulent energy formed. It started to swirl and roll violently, rising slowly. The men's faces reflected the horrors they had created and harbored deep in their souls. The swirling energy moved upward in a column that became increasingly more intense. It passed over their heads and began to consume them. The men screamed. Their faces and bodies distorted as the energy dissolved them, returning them to the elements from which they were once formed.

Ethan cringed as he listened to the men scream, their voices and faces slowly fading into the noise. The columns of energy continued to swirl and became darkened with the transformed matter. Then there was a different kind of scream. The darkness within slowly dissipated and the very spirits of the now formless beings were freed of their mortal vessels to be caged and taken away.

It was a beautiful and horrible thing to witness—a judgment not seen on Earth for over four thousand years. Gradually the sound died away and the now white columns of energy dispersed. Then the sparkling vapor around Ethan became brighter, and brighter. Suddenly he could see with a different kind of sight.

He felt warm and his mind was instantly opened to a vastness and glory that defied all comprehension. His spirit merged with the energy and he began to witness some of the events that had occurred in a meridian of time transcending his own—the forming of galaxies, nebulae, stars, planets and other celestial events. He saw their relationships to each other and how they were set into motion in a magnificent ballet of perfect balance and harmony. He watched the formation of man and witnessed his existence on many different worlds. Everything was everywhere, and still all within his sight. It existed in its own time, yet, he could see past and future as one. This power did not simply transcend time, it *was* time.

He began to see the flow of existence that extended backward to an endless beginning, and forward into eternity—a glimpse of immortality normally reserved only for those who have passed the gates of this temporal world—set free of the mortal mind—a place of endless wonderment where he could not stay. Before the comprehension caused him to become more than man, he made a conscious decision, and opened his eyes.

He could see the tall grass and little purple and white flowers on long skinny stems gently swaying in a warm breeze. The brilliant, glistening energy was gone, replaced by a strange, but familiar light. The thoughts of what he had experienced were astonishing, although he couldn't quite comprehend them now.

Then a familiar voice spoke. "Hello, Ethan."

He looked up. It was Joshua, standing in front of him, his feet hidden in the grass. Ethan looked at him, trying to regain his sense of awareness. "Hello, Joshua," Ethan replied.

"Stand," Joshua said motioning.

Ethan started to stand, but remembered both his legs had been shot. "I...can't," he replied.

"I would not ask it of you if it were not possible," Joshua responded. Ethan looked at him, contemplating, then looked down at his legs. There was no blood, and there was no pain. Slowly he moved to his knees, and carefully stood, looking down at his legs as he did.

"Thank you," he said gratefully.

"*I* have not done this. This was by your own hand."

Ethan was troubled at the weight of Joshua's statement. "I...I did this?" he said, leaning over to calm jittery knees.

"For an instant, you possessed perfect clarity and purity of thought—a moment when your only desire was for the well-being of another. The giving of one's self completely for that of another is the single most powerful and most pure act possible by mortal man—a thought so pure it brought forth the power from which all existence is formed and from where all just things emanate. Because you were willing to give of your life completely and freely, your lives were spared, you were healed, and the men who sought to do you harm have been judged.

"As your will was emulated, so too was your mind expanded and your eyes opened to glimpse that of the Divine. It was for this reason you were given warning. For now that this truth is known to you, you can never deny it, or you will become lost forever.

"You and Alex have risen to the occasion in extraordinary measure. Be assured that one day untold numbers will celebrate in the knowledge of your accomplishments. But now, know that you must complete this journey and deliver into the Heart of Fear that which has been entrusted to you. There the Power of Souls will rest until called forth at the End.

"Be ever mindful of those who might wish to exploit your knowledge and be mindful of what you say and with whom you share your experiences. Be also strong and do not fear, for you have seen the glory in all things and glimpsed that which governs all.

"You must continue to seek guidance and trust in your feelings. There may still be occasion to doubt, but with patience will also come understanding. One day, all may be revealed to you."

"I understand," Ethan replied. Words alone could not describe what he had been through—and he was grateful. "Thank you," he replied sincerely.

"Journey well, Ethan," Joshua said as he smiled, turned and walked away.

Ethan knew he would not see him again in this lifetime. Then his thoughts returned to Alex. He let out a deep sigh, and turned to her.

The sound of the idling helicopter was suddenly behind him again. He knew the men were gone and Joshua was gone. Alex appeared as if asleep. He knelt down beside her and ran the back of his hand along her beautiful face. She took a deep breath, opened her eyes and looked up at him. Alarmed, she quickly sat up and looked toward the helicopter and around.

"They're gone," Ethan said calmly.

"What happened?" she asked puzzled.

"Do you remember when Hazzar's father talked about the scrolls and the people described a Judgment Fire?"

Alex stared at him blankly until she made the connection. *"Oh no way. You're kidding."*

"No."

"You saw it?"

"I think so."

She looked around, then back at him. "Ethan...your face...your bruises. *They're gone.*" Ethan put his hand on the side of his face near his eye. It wasn't swollen anymore. Then as he looked closely at Alex's face, he began to understand some of what had really happened. His eyes began to fill with tears as he ran his fingers gently across her forehead and down to her cheek. Then he gently rested his hand on the side of her face and lightly ran his thumb across her lips.

"You're perfect," he said quietly through the tears.

"Ethan?" Alex said with some concern.

"Your bruises...the cut in your lip..."

Alex quickly put her fingers to her lips and felt them. "I don't understand." Then she realized Ethan was kneeling. "Your legs... How did... *What happened?*" she stammered.

"I'm having a hard time grasping it myself."

"Well, where was I during all this? Last thing I remember, that guy was pointing a gun at us."

"I'm not sure. It looked like you were asleep."

She thought, looked down again and sighed. "That figures."

"Don't worry. I'll explain the best I can, but we need to get going and try to find that road we saw from the air."

They headed north in the direction of the road. As they walked, Ethan told her about the incredible events that had oc-curred while she was rendered 'unconscious.' She agreed that no one else should ever know what had happened there that day, especially the Professor.

After several miles of traversing through the forest and clear-ings, they came to a paved road and started walking east toward Hannover. Even though Ethan's story was just unbelievably fan-tastic, her thoughts were still heavy and troubled. The Order's incursion at Espelkamp was planned. It worried Alex greatly that her long-time friend and mentor could possibly be involved with such a despicable organization.

That thought was overshadowed only by the possibility that she may have been betrayed by a man who was like a father to her. "He helped us out so many times. I just can't believe he could be working with them," she said thinking out loud.

"You know Alex, at this point we don't know for sure *how* they found out. If anything, I've learned that appearances can be deceiving. Until we know what really happened, I don't think you should condemn him just yet. However, I still think we need to handle this on our own from here on."

Several cars approached from the east and passed them. Then another approached from the west. They turned and held out their hands indicating they wanted the car to stop. It didn't and moved to the centerline to pass. They turned and continued walk-ing as several more vehicles passed in both directions until an old Mercedes heading east slowed and stopped.

They ran to the side of the car and looked in. It was a younger driver and he smiled at Alex as she stuck her head in the side window. He smiled a little less at Ethan.

"Hi. We're trying to get to Hannover. That's the next town isn't it?" Alex asked politely.

"Hannover...yes. I can take you," the young man stated.

"Wonderful. Thank you very much," she responded.

"I think he likes you. Maybe you should sit up front," Ethan remarked quietly.

"That's because I'm prettier than you are," Alex replied smartly as she grinned and opened the front door.

"My name is Warren," the young man said to Alex. Warren was a likeable young man traveling to Hannover to visit friends.

"I'm Alex and this is Ethan." Ethan smiled and waved. "Thanks for stopping. We really appreciate it."

"You are welcome. You kind of remind me of my mother," Warren said, pulling back onto the road. Alex's smile curled a little and she turned slowly to look at Ethan. He just smiled back and shrugged his shoulders. Alex turned and faced forward, now a little older in the young man's perception. "Are you tourists?" Warren asked.

"Yes. We're from the United States," Alex replied.

"We were heading to Hannover and ran out of fuel a ways back off the road," Ethan added.

"Do you need assistance? I can call someone," Warren offered.

"No, it was...borrowed. I'm sure the company that owns it will come pick it up pretty soon."

"I see," the young man replied. Alex turned around again and gave Ethan the evil-eye. Hey, it was the truth, more or less.

A few miles down the road, several emergency vehicles passed them heading west. Ethan and Alex both turned and watched them go by.

"Wow, they are in a hurry," Warren commented. Alex and Ethan looked at each other briefly, but said nothing.

"Thanks for the ride," Alex said as they climbed out of the car.

"You are welcome. Enjoy your visit," Warren replied. Alex waved as the young man drove off.

"Well, now what?" she said watching the car head down the street.

"We should probably find a place to stay and get you some new clothes. I'll call my accountant and see if I can get him to wire some money here. Then we can find you a flight home."

Alex looked up at him surprised. "Now wait a minute. What do you mean find *me* a flight home? I promised to stay with you and I intend to keep my promise."

"You've kept your promise, Alex. You've been *incredible*. But this last part, I need to do alone."

"I don't understand. Why can't I go with you?"

"It's just something I need to do by myself. Besides, we just stole and crashed an airplane. I doubt *that* little incident will go unnoticed. It won't be long before the authorities start putting pieces together—the eyewitnesses, fingerprints... Right now, we're fugitives."

"That's a cheery thought."

"Sorry, but it's the truth. It'll be easier for them to recognize us together so the sooner you go home the better."

"No, you're right," she said, as she looked around disappointed. "I'm not sure that guy who was cleaning the plane could tie his own shoes though, let alone identify us."

"Maybe not, but I'll bet the lady whose car we stole probably can."

"Good point. Let's go shopping."

The hotel they found wasn't stellar. At least it had vacancy, accepted cash, and the people didn't ask too many questions. As they picked up the key-cards, Ethan inadvertently collected up a brochure off the counter with the other papers. While walking to the hallway to find their rooms, he noticed the extra brochure, glanced at it, then prepared to drop it onto a small table in the lobby as he walked by.

Suddenly he was looking up at his mother. "Now Ethan, you know better than to lay your things around the house like that. I'm your mother, not a maid. Now pick up your things and put them where they belong."

Then he was back, looking at the brochure in his hand. He chuckled at his mom and as he started down the hall again, he looked over the brochure more closely. It was an advertisement for a travel agency written in German on one side and English on the other. It read, 'Make Greece Your Next Vacation Destination.'

Jeff was happy to hear from Ethan and arranged to have funds transferred to a local cash store where he could pick them up. Alex was scheduled for the only flight to the United States they could find that evening, and Ethan was still trying to find a flight that would take him to Athens. It required a personal visit to several different travel agencies before finding one that was willing to make the arrangements in cash, although the inconvenience to the owner did end up costing him a 'special handling fee.'

He had considered asking Jeff to make the arrangements, but decided the correspondence might still be too risky and it was probably best to leave him out of it anyway. Maybe this level of anonymity wasn't really necessary with Pancros gone. Then again, making assumptions could be a deadly mistake. No chances would be taken, except for one.

The simple fact that there were no documents showing that the artifact had been properly acquired would likely cause problems at customs if he tried to take it on the plane. Artifact smuggling was still a problem for many countries, and monitored closely along with everything else. As odd as it would seem, his chances of getting the vessel to Greece were best if he could have it shipped to the hotel.

The little shipping center was a hole-in-the-wall. Ethan had gone in alone and now had the container packaged and ready to go. He gave the address information to the clerk and had her put 'Attn: Mutters' at the top. The box could still be identified when it arrived and no one would be the wiser...unless they asked for picture ID.

There were a few simple questions from the clerk that brought up some very interesting considerations. One was if the item was 'breakable and replaceable.' The really strange one was being asked to state its value. *Its value?* The irrational implication made him grin and shake his head. He said no, yes and declared the standard minimum amount.

It was strange irony to lie about something that he knew could read the intent of his inner being. Can lying for good be considered an honorable intent, or is any lie simply dishonesty?

The whole point was to get the container to Athens in the safest, most reliable and most inconspicuous manner possible. Even being *asked* to apply a simple, materialistic value to something so supernal seemed almost blasphemous. Hopefully, he would be forgiven if the end justified the means.

Ethan carried Alex's new bag to the check-in terminal. Such short notice meant booked flights so they settled on the first one out that would get her home. It was pretty ugly with three transfers; one with over a four hour wait plus she would have to fly into JFK before transferring to Dulles. No doubt, more advanced notice or a simple call to the Professor could have facilitated a much tidier arrangement. Unfortunately, that jury was still out.

A once devout trust was now riddled with uncertainty, and trying to separate personal feelings from facts was going to be difficult for Alex. "What am I going to do?" she asked solemnly. Ethan just shook his head. He couldn't answer for her. Once trust has been lost, it can be very difficult to maintain a balance of fairness when searching for the reasons why.

"Just do what you think is best. You might have some tough decisions ahead."

She looked down in thought before putting her arms around him and hugging him tightly. Then she leaned up on her tiptoes to give him a friendly kiss on his stubbly cheek as he lowered his head. "Be careful," she said.

"I'll try. Have a good flight." And with that, she entered passport control.

He watched carefully as they visually verified and processed her passport and sent her on to the security checkpoint. A sigh of relief was expressed after she passed through all the usual procedures and headed to the concourse. Before entering, she turned to see Ethan still watching from the far side of the terminal entrance, and waved to him one last time. Ethan waved back, and she disappeared around the corner.

It didn't take long for her absence to be felt. The cab ride back to the hotel wasn't just solitary, but seemed empty. It was the difference between being alone and lonely. The crowded mental inventory of recent experiences was pushed aside while his thoughts centered only on her. She really *was* a good friend and could easily be more, but the possibility of another relationship always reminded him of his devout loyalty promised to Rachel. He would not tarnish that promise.

It was difficult to sleep. He just lay there and stared at the dark and barely perceptible ceiling from the hotel bed. The possibilities with Alex were becoming more than momentary thoughts to be dismissed. *That* particular mental door, having always been slammed shut so quickly before, was still open this time. Cautiously, he tip-toed through and began to investigate his feelings on the other side.

There were certain aspects of his life that had always seemed definitive. Marriage was one of them. When he married Rachel, he committed himself to her completely. There were no reservations of any kind. He knew people who had gone through divorce, some of them even in his own extended family, and it was unfortunate that for whatever reasons, the vows were broken. Even so, those reasons and courses of action with their consequences were known quantities—they knew what was coming.

When a couple lives a full life and one spouse passes away in old age, it seems natural and is generally accepted, even though it may still be difficult for a surviving spouse. When someone is terminally ill, time lessens the shock of death when it comes.

But to have those you love taken away from you, ripped away from this life with no warning, with no chance to say goodbye, was the very worst of all. It was only by the true knowledge of an existence without end, when the grand principles of life's extended plan were explained and received without prejudice, only then does one have the chance to completely escape from the shadows of ignorance.

In the moment when he chose to sacrifice himself to save Alex, he hadn't forgotten his love for Rachel, but had in fact added upon it. He was now beginning to better understand what he had shared with her—what she had taught him and shown him. Her love could not be diminished simply because she was no longer with him, but would instead be deepened when it was shared with others.

It was an epiphany that almost seemed too simple to be real. Rachel didn't want him to be alone and miserable, she wanted him to be happy, to take what she had given him and use it for himself and to help others. *That* was how he would find his real joy in life and how he would continue to show his love for her. He was beginning to understand—*to open his heart and open his eyes*.

He had been led across the abyss so he could see what was possible to attain. Allison could see the path because she was pure in heart. Likewise, those who understand and accept the truth will also have their paths known—a map to navigate the abyss—to find that new world on the other side. So what would happen to the others? A formless existence without end or to gaze across a hopeless void at paradise denied was a horrifying prospect. If only others could see what he had seen.

The lingering poison of anger and hatred would still take time to be completely purged from Ethan's being. Understanding only *promotes* opportunity. True acceptance is achieved in actions driven by honest and unfettered desire. Unfortunately, those qualities don't always coexist. Many with good intentions still fail when their actions are overcome by pride or fear—masks that burden the soul. *There's nothing simple about this,* Ethan thought as his mind finally began to wander, and he fell into sleep.

Passport control was busy the following morning, which was a good thing. A bunch of detailed questions might be avoided if the staff wanted to keep the restless waiting to a minimum. Many passports now had standard optical coding to verify personal information. Not all countries and airports had standardized on the system however, and thankfully this airport was one of them. He noticed that when Alex had gone through.

Keeping even his fictitious name out of the EVE database hopefully would allow him to travel anonymously. The passport officer verified his information and sent him through security where his bag was x-rayed and cleared. There was little doubt that had the artifact been in the bag, it would have been inspected and a whole host of other problems would have reared their ugly heads.

Now on the plane, Ethan let out a sigh of relief as he waited for the other passengers to finish boarding. He looked around at them and wondered what secrets *they* might keep. How many of *them* have had miraculous experiences or experienced terrible tragedy. The average person can't know the life experiences of another, or what that person's state of mind may be simply by observation. That is, of course, unless you happen to sit by someone who *wants* you to know everything and *tells* you everything, whether you really want to hear it or not.

Now that he was personally aware of the power that could see into one's soul, that knowledge was giving him added perspective about perception. Matters of the soul are seldom visible for others to see. Simple perception truly is an impoverished witness. So many times he had looked at someone and decided who he or she was only because of what he could see. Undoubtedly, people had looked at him and done the same. How incredibly naïve that judgment really was.

The plane rocked gently as it was pushed backward out of the terminal in preparation to taxi. If all went well, he'd be in Athens in a few hours, and hopefully the power that helped create and organize all that exists was also safe in its little brown box somewhere. He grinned and shook his head.

CHAPTER TWENTY

Traitors & Nobles

THE DRIVEWAY WAS LITTERED with stately vehicles. Professor Greenhagen exited his own and walked to the door of the mansion where he was told the others were waiting in the library. This was the first time he had actually been asked to attend one of their meetings. He wasn't a member of the Committee, but had an arrangement with The Noble.

This meeting, and the fact that access to the secure database had been restricted earlier that day, could only mean that something of great matter was at hand, and it likely had to do with the operation in Germany.

His concerns for Alex were still foremost in his mind, having not heard from her and not knowing where she could be. Reports of what happened at Espelkamp were still sketchy and unconfirmed. He would never forgive himself if something had happened to her.

As he entered the opulent and richly decorated room, he briefly scanned the people. All of them were men, except for one woman. There were only a few he had seen before. Personally, he knew none of them. Their expressions were stoic and serious which seemed to fit with the Committee's persona.

"Welcome, Professor Greenhagen," The Noble stated as he motioned for the Professor to sit in a specific empty chair. Then he began. "Some of you are already aware that I've been working on a project to recover an artifact that was believed to be in the possession of an organization known as the Order of the Black Sun. There was speculation as to whether or not this artifact actually existed, until yesterday.

"Approximately twenty hours ago, a small stone container, referenced as the Power of Souls, was successfully acquired from members of the Black Sun near Bremen, Germany. The assault team leader reported that two assets, one male and one female under their protection, escaped with the artifact during a subsequent Order ambush. The assets reportedly made their way to a farmhouse south of Bremen near a town called Espelkamp where we sent two agency pilots to pick them up. A few hours ago, our pilots and several locals were found dead in a hanger near the parked aircraft.

"Witnesses at the airport reported a man and woman running from two other men who were, quote, 'shooting at them with machine guns.' A shot-up BMW was found in the same hanger where a Cessna was stolen and later found crashed and abandoned in a forest clearing one hundred three kilometers east of Espelkamp. A helicopter known to be used by the Black Sun was also found abandoned and still running about five kilometers away in another clearing. No one was found in the Cessna wreckage or anywhere in the vicinity of either aircraft.

"The local authorities in Hannover, Espelkamp and Bremen have issued descriptions of the two assets, but as of now, no one has officially reported seeing them. Professor Greenhagen has reason to believe they could still be alive. If they are, it would be desirable to have one of our agencies find them first. For that reason, the male asset's records have been cleaned from the international database. The female's records had been cleaned previously.

"We believe that our plans to extract the two assets from Espelkamp were leaked to the Black Sun organization. Only four people were involved in the actual process of arranging the plane and pilots including myself, Professor Greenhagen, Mr. Woolsey and the controller who actually dispatched the aircraft and two pilots. The pilots were given instructions for the pickup only and no details of the package."

A few of the members then started to inquire of each other in a buzz of questions and speculation. It was unthinkable that one of their own could be responsible for such an act of treason.

"So our group's operation has been compromised?" one of them asked.

"Yes, but that problem may have already been rectified, as I'll explain in a moment."

"So it's likely then that this Black Sun organization has the artifact *and* the two assets," another member postulated.

"It's possible, although unlikely," the Noble responded. "About an hour ago, it was confirmed that sixteen people known to be high level Black Sun members have disappeared in various countries around the world, and these are only the ones we've been able to verify so far. One witness in England stated that some kind of white smoke surrounded a man and he disappeared. The man was a known member. Two other witnesses in Los Angeles and Sri Lanka reported similar events that occurred at the same time.

"We were able to retrieve a security video feed from an office in Hong Kong." A video screen lit up on the wall and everyone looked toward it. "The man sitting in the chair in the upper left hand corner is Gongsun, a Black Sun member under active surveillance for suspected racketeering. Watch him closely."

The image was clear, then it distorted with interference. The area where the man was sitting was briefly washed out in a flash of light, then the image reappeared and the man was gone.

"This video has been analyzed and no one has tampered with it. What you just saw is exactly as it happened."

"And what exactly *did* we just see happen?" one of the men asked.

"It appears that he simply vanished. Of course, that's impossible. We're still analyzing the feed and gathering all the information we can.

"Whatever this phenomenon is, it appears to be a coordinated effort on a global scale. Someone is targeting members of the Black Sun and they're disappearing without a trace. The crash of the Cessna is estimated to have occurred around the same time as these disappearances. They may or may not be related. We need to find the two assets and the artifact. This artifact was very important to the Black Sun and knowing why might be the key to what's happening.

"Now, regarding Mr. Woolsey. The pilots and the dispatcher were not briefed on the specifics of the package they were retrieving. Mr. Woolsey was the only other person aware of the operation. After I was informed of the incident at Espelkamp, I started an investigation into his activities and those of the air-fleet controller.

"Mr. Woolsey hadn't been seen since he left his house this morning. Earlier today, I was informed that his car was found just before noon, abandoned near an onramp to I-81. The police reported that a motorist behind Mr. Woolsey's vehicle watched it drive off the on-ramp and down into some bushes where it stopped. The motorist stopped to investigate and when he approached the vehicle, it was still in gear, the engine was running, the doors were locked and no one was inside.

"Mr. Woolsey's agency recovery team went through the car and found a forged passport, forged identification and other documents suggesting he was leaving the country. I think he had his own agenda and giving up the assets was his last cowardly act before running. The timing of this incident also corresponds exactly with the other disappearances. It appears the controller was unaware of Mr. Woolsey's dual loyalties. We'll keep that investigation active for the time being.

"The fact that Mr. Woolsey was able to deceive us to this degree is unsettling to say the least. Procedural changes are already underway. Once I became aware of his actions, access to our secured network was shut down and new protocols are being initialized. The network should be available shortly.

"Now please, don't overreact. This is not the time to begin questioning the loyalties of other members. As I understand the nature of the Black Sun, it's likely that Mr. Woolsey was probably working alone.

"Clearly, however, there are forces at work here using a technology we are unfamiliar with and at a level of coordination and secrecy that rivals anything we've ever encountered before. Use your resources. Let's focus on finding these assets and this artifact and get to the bottom of what's going on as quickly as possible. I don't want the foreign agencies getting the jump on us. Is there anything else?"

The members were dismayed that their elite organization had been defiled. They should have been above such deceit. It would seem *no one* is impervious to the treachery of others. There were questions, lots of them, but none that could be answered at the moment. "Then good luck," the Noble said before the group began to disperse.

The Professor remained seated as the last members exited the library. Now it was just the Noble and him sitting in the large room.

"I'm sorry about Alex. This must be difficult for you."

"What bothers me most is how this must appear to her. If she's dead, she'll never know the truth."

"Let's just stick with missing for now. So what do you make of all this, Samuel?"

"The implications are staggering."

"You really believe this artifact has something to do with the disappearances?

"I do."

"And you honestly think it has some sort of power?"

"*Some* kind of power, yes. You saw what I saw. This goes *way* beyond a well orchestrated conspiracy and new technology."

"What then?"

"Something we've never seen before."

The Noble looked down briefly, then back up at Samuel. "Well then, Professor, we need to find that artifact."

"Agreed."

Chapter Twenty-One

Heart of Fear

ISLANDS COULD BE SEEN everywhere as the turbo-prop made its final approach into Athens. The landscape was fascinating, contrasting sharply between water and land with steep rocky terrain and rolling green valleys. Greece was a beautiful country. He felt a little guilty that Alex wasn't there to share it with him, but getting her home and safe was more important.

Hopefully, customs officials here wouldn't give him too much grief either. There were several Passport Control stations so Ethan stood in the line and waited for his turn. After negotiating the little maze and being called to the next station, the officer dropped a bar across the entrance behind Ethan as he walked through. Closing the station with so many people in line seemed peculiar. *Why would he do that?* Ethan wondered. Was someone onto him? Just simple coincidence maybe?

The officer held out his hand and Ethan handed over his passport. The officer seemed to take a long time, looking back and forth between Ethan and the picture. Ethan was already nervous. This wasn't helping.

"Ethan Hamilton," the officer said succinctly, reading the name.

"Yes."

"Tourist?"

"Yes."

"Anything to declare?"

"No."

The officer paused for several seconds. "You Americans like to fish, no?"

"Uh...I'm sorry?"

"Americans—you like to fish."

"Well, I suppose."

"You should look up my friend. He owns a boat. He takes people to catch big fish. Sitia Bay in Crete is where you can usually find him. Boat is called the...the P something. Odd name. You would know it when you saw it. He could take you about anywhere you would want to go. Maybe even halfway to Egypt."

Ethan really wasn't interested in small talk with the man. It was all he could do to try and stay calm—not forgetting that at least a half dozen law enforcement organizations were probably looking for him. He looked nervous, and *was* nervous.

"I'll keep that in mind. Thank you," he replied, anxiously taking the passport and trying to avoid making eye contact with the over-talkative officer. What Ethan didn't know was that the man already knew who he was, *and* why he was there.

As Ethan fumbled with the passport and quickly started to leave, the officer said one last thing, "Journey well, Ethan."

Those words seized his conscience and he froze. Slowly, he turned back to look at the man. It was a different face, but the same eyes—those powerful eyes of a stranger he met once not long ago on a street in Balkhash. The man smiled at him reassuringly, and walked away.

Ethan's heart was pounding. He now realized the man hadn't just been spewing chitchat, it was instructions. He started reciting the man's words to himself while walking out to find a taxi. Honestly, he hadn't been paying that much attention and hoped he could correctly remember what he had been told.

Right or wrong, what he remembered was well engrained by the time he arrived at the hotel, but there must have been some mistake. This didn't look like a hotel. He pulled out the piece of paper where the address had been written by the 'travel agent' and showed it to the driver again.

"Are you sure this is the right place?" Ethan asked.

"Yes. Here, here," the driver replied as he pointed at the paper, then at the building. Ethan looked out the window and up at the old two-story structure that was butted against many others along a narrow sloping street. These looked like old houses or apartments. If the address *was* correct, then something was definitely wrong.

"Thank you," Ethan said, and paid the driver.

The number on the door *was* the same as the one written on the paper, so he knocked and waited. After a moment, a woman, probably in her late fifties or early sixties, opened the door.

"Hi. I'm looking for the hotel?"

The woman looked at Ethan's bag, and then back at him. "Room?" she questioned. It then occurred to Ethan that the person he got the tickets from must have arranged for a room in a house. He had just assumed it was a hotel. The guy he made the arrangements with *had* been a little hard to understand.

"Yes, a room," Ethan replied. The woman then motioned for him to follow her.

They walked into a small hallway and up a set of stairs to the second floor where she showed him a very nice room that was reasonably large, considering the small size of the house. There was an adjoining bathroom that was old, but clean. The accommodations would do just fine.

"Okay?" the woman asked.

"Yes, okay," he replied, taking some money out to pay her. "Ethan," he said pointing to himself.

"Iliona," the woman replied

"Nice to meet you, Iliona." He handed her the money. She took it shyly, smiled and put it in a blouse pocket.

A place like this wouldn't likely be on anyone's watch list. His only real concern now was the delivery of the artifact. "I'm expecting a package to be delivered here. Have you seen a package? Package...box about this big? Would have been delivered by a truck or courier or somebody." Ethan showed her the size of the box with his hands. She watched intently. "You have absolutely no idea what I'm talking about do you?"

She smiled politely and shrugged her shoulders.

"Okay," Ethan said, thinking how he was going to explain this. They needed someone to translate, but how would she even understand that?

He dug in his bag and pulled out a map of Germany. It was picked up in Hannover after the other one had been lost in Bremen. Unfolding it, he set it on the bed and motioned to it. "Map," he said. Iliona walked forward and looked at it. "Map," he repeated, pointing.

"Map," she replied, appearing to understand.

"This is a map of Germany. I need a map of Greece. Where can I find a map...of Greece?" he asked pointing, then holding up his hands in a questioning manner.

"Map...Greece," the woman replied and nodded. She motioned him to follow her.

Now outside, she led him up the street to a small grocery store a few minutes away. It was a corner market that sold groceries and sundry items. Iliona walked inside to a small display hanging on the wall as Ethan followed.

"Map," she said pointing to it. Ethan pulled out one of the maps and opened it up. It was a map of Greece written in Greek and English—for tourists, no doubt.

"Yes, this is it. Thank you," he said happily. He set the map on the counter and paid the clerk. "By any chance, do you speak English?" he then asked the man behind the counter.

"Yes, I speak English" he replied with a slight accent.

"Would you mind asking this woman a few questions for me?"

The man looked at Iliona, whom he didn't know personally, but had seen in the store many times before. "Yes, I can."

"Would you ask her if she has received a package, a box addressed to her residence? Would have been about...this big."

The man spoke to Iliona. She replied shaking her head 'no.'

"Alright, would you tell her I'm expecting this box to be delivered to her house? It will say...uh..." Ethan realized that if Iliona couldn't speak English, she probably couldn't read it either. Just telling her the name wouldn't help. He asked the clerk for a pen, wrote 'Mutters' on a small piece of paper, and handed it to Iliona. "Will you tell her that this name will be written at the top of the address?"

Ethan was lost as the clerk spoke. When he was done, Iliona nodded and said, "Okay." Good. The box had been shipped 'next-day' delivery. Hopefully it would still show up that day.

Iliona was very nice, but awfully shy. Ethan asked the man to tell her 'thank you' and gave her some money to pick out some groceries. At first she refused, but Ethan insisted so she collected some bread and a few other items and they walked back to her residence.

He started up the stairs, but before the woman entered the separate door to the bottom floor, she turned and said something to show her appreciation—at least that's what it sounded like.

"You're welcome," he replied.

He looked over the map of Crete while methodically searching for the place the 'passport officer' at the airport had mentioned. Then he saw it; Sitia, and next to it, Sitia Bay. That was it, that's what the man had said. Since Crete was a little over three hundred kilometers south over water, he'd now have to find a service to take him there, preferably by air.

Returning to the corner market, the clerk was helpful in explaining where to find a taxi, and it wasn't long before Ethan was back at the airport. There were a few companies that flew regular passenger services to and from the island, and no doubt there would also be private planes as well, if you could find the right people. Hopefully, not *all* the standard services would be booked by tourists and regulars who flew to the island for pleasure and work. Just one seat was all he needed.

He was assuming the container would still arrive that day so he tried to find a flight to Crete for the following morning. The first two companies were booked, and not only for the morning flight, but for the entire day. The third company had just told him the same thing when a lady from behind the counter of the second service company shouted out, "Sir, sir!" and motioned him to come back. She had just received the cancellation of a couple for the second flight in the morning. There was a list of alternates, but for reasons Ethan would never know, she gave him the first chance at one of the open slots. He gladly accepted it and paid.

Later that evening, he went back to the corner market, picked up some food to eat in the room and tried to relax while he waited. As the hours crept away, concern began to grow over the package. He tried to keep things in perspective and told himself that even if something had happened and it didn't show up before the end of the day, he'd just have to locate a shipping center, find out where the artifact was and change plans as needed. Maybe it just got delayed and would still arrive tomorrow.

While still thinking about what he might have to do, there was a knock at the door. "Yes?" he responded.

"Box," came Iliona's muffled voice through the door. Ethan jumped up, ran to the door and opened it.

"Box?" he asked, making sure he heard her right.

"Yes. Box," she said, pointing down the stairs. Sitting on the floor just inside the front door was the box. His package had arrived.

Quickly he walked down the stairs with Iliona following. He was relieved to verify the name on the address. It really was here. "Thank you," he said to her. She smiled and went back inside.

After carrying the box up to the room, he carefully opened it and removed the packing. There it was, just as he had wrapped it. Carefully, he removed the rest of the packaging and cradled the stone vessel in his hands.

This was the first real moment of calm he had felt in some time. He knew what he had experienced the day before was only a tiny fraction of what this power was capable of manifesting in the hands of someone with real authority and clarity of mind. To know that he had been entrusted with something that transcended the boundaries of our existence, and the very laws of time, was overwhelming. He tried to push back the ever present feelings of inadequacy to understand the fact that he alone had been chosen for this task—something that couldn't have been even *remotely* comprehended just a month before. What mortal obligation could ever compare to being the trustee of an immortal power?

It was incredibly sobering to know that the eventual fate of billions would be determined in part by something he was now holding in his hands. Why, among what must have been countless others, was this destiny of almost inconceivable consequence *his*? He couldn't fathom how one's worth in being chosen to perform such a task could be measured.

Even having experienced the expansive wonders of worlds outside his own, he knew that some of those questions would not be answered or fully understood until much later—maybe even into the realm where Rachel and his family now lived.

He had slept well and was now mostly dressed after showering when a knock came at the door. He opened it to find Iliona with a tray of breakfast. He wasn't expecting that. Maybe it was because of his kindness at the store the day before, or maybe she did this for all her guests. It was a very nice gesture at any rate.

Before leaving to find a taxi that would take him to the airport, he thanked her for her generosity. She didn't understand exactly what he had said, but could sense his honest sincerity and knew he was appreciative of her hospitality.

The flight south was relatively short. The islands scattered about in the open sea between Athens and Crete were intriguing. From his vantage point high above the surface, they seemed so tiny and isolated in the great vastness of water. Then he imagined an ant that might live on one of those islands. From *its* vantage point, the island would appear as a great and sprawling continent.

Was the island really an inconspicuous speck of dirt, isolated and alone, lost on a massive globe of water? Or an enormous landmass of wonder and beauty that would seem to go on forever? It was the same island, different only in the perspective from where it was viewed. Such is life.

Ethan now stood looking over one of the Sitia Bay marinas with its numerous docks and boats tied to their moorings. His view of the expansive Mediterranean Sea stretched and disappeared into the horizon. The smell of salt water was light on the air. It reminded him of a vacation his family once took to the

Virgin Islands. He could almost see them playing on the long, warm sandy beach. There was no long, warm sandy beach here though, only a rough coastline with long wooden docks that protruded from a rocky shore. Even so, it was still a grand and pleasant view.

He didn't know specifically where he was going, only that most of the boats for hire were supposed to be on the south and east side of the docks. That's where he'd start looking.

Many of the boats were used to shuttle tourists on diving expeditions and fishing trips with the larger commercial ships located at another marina a little farther up the coast. As he walked down a flight of concrete stairs to the docks, he noticed a small group of men standing outside a dive shop.

He approached them. "Excuse me, could you direct me to where I could rent a boat?"

"We have boats," one man responded in English and a heavy accent. "What do you want to do?"

"Well, actually I'm looking to hire a boat that has a name that starts with 'P'." The men looked confused.

"You want a boat with pee?"

"No, no, I'm looking for a boat that has a name that starts with the *letter* 'P'." Ethan drew a letter P in the air.

"Oh," the man said melodically before he turned to the other men and said something Ethan couldn't understand. They laughed, conversed for a moment more then shook their heads. "Check that way," the man said as he pointed down the dock.

"Thank you," Ethan replied.

In true tourist form, he wandered aimlessly, displaying a façadical grin while perusing the docks, looking at boats and talking to people. Most of them didn't speak English. It was a needle in a haystack. There were a lot of boats and it wasn't a small bay. A name and address on a piece of parchment would have been handy. There might be a boat registry of some kind somewhere and if he didn't find something pretty soon, a more official search would have to be undertaken.

Hours had gone by as he searched and asked questions and looked at boat after boat after boat and traveled from marina to marina and dock to dock. In one of the smaller marinas outside the city, the name on one boat finally caught his attention—*The Prestige*. It was a beautiful, bright white boat about fifty feet long. It was probably considered more of a yacht. It didn't jump out at him as *the one*, but it *was* the only name he had found so far that seemed close.

The side of the boat was a few feet higher than he was so he couldn't see anyone. There were voices coming from somewhere inside with occasional laughter. "Hello. Excuse me. Hello." No one seemed to be on deck so he climbed up a small ladder on the side. After a few steps, he stopped dead in his tracks when his eyes widened and filled with the stunning image of a tanned, gorgeous woman lying in a lounge chair, eyes closed, headphones in her ears.

She had long, silky black hair and must have been somewhat impoverished as to only afford a very minimalist swimsuit. It revealed incredible curves on a soft, toned, glistening, sun-warmed body that was more than a match for the tiny strips of cloth that strained to barely cover and contain her rich and very well proportioned womanly endowments.

"Whoa," Ethan said to himself as he looked down for a second, just a tad embarrassed. This didn't seem like it could be the right boat... But maybe he should go check, just to be sure.

Warily, he approached the woman who was alone on the deck. He stood a few feet away, mesmerized, his mind numb in her stunning beauty and incredible features. Physically she had everything that would entice, twist and confuse the common sense of any average male—sensuous defining curves, long legs, supple lips, and everything else.

She exuded an intoxicating essence and he was drawn to her as primal male desire began to cause his heart and mind to race, his body to tingle and his breathing to become irregular. This was the kind of woman who could bring a man out of a six-month coma, *or* put him into one. *Walk away. Just walk away*, came a distant voice from a rational thought process that had somehow escaped complete debilitation.

He looked away, took a couple of deep stabilizing breaths, reached out and waved his hand in the Mediterranean sunlight to produce a shadow on the woman's face. He saw her blink behind her sunglasses. She turned her music off and looked up at him. His stupid grin didn't seem to surprise her.

She was fully aware of her effect on men and the expression on Ethan's face was only confirmation of the putty conversion process going on between his ears.

Her mind was far less pliable. She knew *exactly* how to dance to this tune and smiled at him.

"Uh...hi," Ethan replied cleverly.

"What can I do for you?" she said with an exotic accent and alluring voice.

"Well," *breathe...focus*, "I uh... Are you the owner of the boat?"

"That would be Julian. Would you like me to get him for you?"

"Yes, please, thank you." Time slowed considerably as he watched her stand and walk to the cabin door, open it and call inside. It almost stopped completely when she walked back toward him.

A handsome dark-haired man wearing swimming trunks came to the glass cabin door and stood in the opening. He seemed to be in good spirits as two other impoverished women, one practically destitute, followed him to the open door, clinging to him and peeking around his broad shoulders.

"What do you want," he asked while casually flipping his hair.

"Hi. I was..." *Look at him. Focus...* "just wondering if your boat was for hire."

"What do you have in mind?" *Yeah, Ethan, what's on your mind?*

"I...just want to go out to sea for a little while. You know, just cruise around...relax."

"Ah, *relaxation* is what you're looking for," Julian replied, looking back at one of the women. "For the right price, I'm sure we can find you *plenty* of relaxation." The two women giggled. There went the heart again.

"Oh...uh yeah, I...well, there's..." He glanced back at the Grecian goddess who was now on her lounger again—head tilted back and sideways a little so she could watch him. Her smile and the view was so inviting, he forgot what he was going to say. Actually, he had forgotten why he was there. This woman...*she was so unbelievably incredible*. She could make you forget your name and you wouldn't even care.

"*Ethanial Tobias Grey!*" his mother suddenly shouted. Startled, young Ethan looked up at her from in front of the television. "That is *not* appropriate material for you to be watching, young man."

In the blink of an eye, he was back. The sudden flash of his mother was a bit of a shock. He hated being scolded. Always did. But this woman, *this magnificent woman*... She stirred something in him he hadn't felt in a very long time. It was worth a scolding. *Ten* scoldings. But...no.

He looked at Julian and let out an almost convulsively deep sigh. "There are a few other places I need to check first. I'll have to get back to you."

"Hey, whatever. You know where to find us," Julian said before disappearing back into the ship, no doubt to continue working on his international diplomacy.

Ethan turned and walked back by the goddess. He was about to thank her when she reached out and grabbed his hand. "You're welcome to stop by anytime," she said seductively, letting her fingers slide down his palm and off his fingertips.

A shiver went through him. "I'll...keep that in mind," he replied awkwardly. Still grinning, he walked several steps backward, turned and headed toward the ladder.

A few rungs down, he stopped and took another look at this beautiful woman. She waved with her fingers, he waved back. Her image and those feelings would be seared into his memory for a *very* long time. As a matter of fact, it took the weight of the bag pulling on his shoulder to finally break the spell and remind him what was most important.

His footsteps reverberated lightly on the weathered wood as he walked—thoughts confused. Then as clearly as if someone was standing next to him, he heard, "*You profess to have purpose and dreams, yet you'll sell them for a single desire.*"

Stopping dead in his tracks, Ethan slowly turned back to gaze at the gleaming white yacht. It then dawned on him just how close he had come to losing his way—all for the seductive disguise of something he once shared with his wife. A temptation not complete in its lie, but without truth in its purpose—the most powerful and dangerous form of seduction.

Ethan breathed in a deep, slow breath and let it out. Of all the challenges he had faced, the one presented in its simplest and most basic nature was the one in which everything could have most easily been lost. He lowered his head, turned and continued on his way.

People give boats some pretty strange names. He couldn't understand or even read many of the ones he had seen so far, and some only had numbers with no names at all. After being directed by a couple of friendly strangers, and with his mind still wrestling carnal thoughts, he stopped, stared and laughed out loud at the half worn name on the old boat in front of him—*Perihelion*. This had to be the one.

Most people probably had absolutely no idea what the word meant. But it obviously meant something to the owner of this well-weathered, retired commercial fishing boat—at least that's what it appeared to be. Probably not a place he would find impoverished women.

He walked next to it, peering over onto the deck and into the windows of what looked like the cabin. There was a short set of steps leading up to a low access door in the side where he stopped. "Hello? Hello, is anybody home?"

"Yeah, yeah, hang on," came a gravelly voice from somewhere behind the cabin wall.

Ethan waited as a man worked his way up from below deck. The man stepped out of the cabin doorway and looked down at Ethan. He had a thick, course, gray beard and longish dark hair generously salted with gray that was pulled into a ponytail. He was dressed in khaki-style pants, an open button-up shirt, and was at least sixty years old. His face was seasoned by years of hard work and his appearance portrayed a tough independence.

"Who are *you*?" he demanded.

"Ethan Grey. I understand you and your boat might be for hire."

"Who'd you understand that from?"

"Some people up on the docks over there," Ethan said as he pointed. The man looked that direction with a scowl.

"Humph," he snorted, looking back at Ethan. "You American?"

"I am."

"Well why didn't you say so? Come on up," the man replied happily, extending his hand in greeting. "Always glad to meet a fellow American. Name's Frank Jacks. What was yours again?"

"Ethan Grey." Ethan shook Frank's hand, but had to work not to visibly show his disgust at Frank's apparent lack of commitment to proper hygiene.

"So what finds you on my little boat?"

"I'm looking for someone to take me out into the Mediterranean."

"Okay. You want to fish? Go diving?"

"Well...I want to just go out and explore. You know, just go out for a while. Maybe head toward Egypt."

"*Egypt,*" Frank responded confused. "Why on earth would you want to take a little boat like this all the way to Egypt? Just take a plane and save yourself the trouble and time."

"I realize this sounds odd. I'm not even sure I'll need to go all the way to Egypt. I just want to go that direction—just to see what's out there. It's kind of a...personal thing."

Frank leaned back and looked at him with distrust so poignant that it made Ethan feel ashamed for disguising the truth. Maybe he should tell him the whole story. Maybe he might actually believe it. Alex did. Of course, that was different.

"I can tell you what's out there, water—lots and lots of water in every direction for as far as you can see." Then Frank squinted and looked at him cockeyed. "You're not involved in something illegal are you? Going out to meet someone, maybe? I don't do that sort of thing, you know."

"Oh no sir, nothing like that at all."

Frank continued to study Ethan carefully, trying to size him up to determine if he was being truthful or not. "Three thousand euro a day plus fuel plus you bring your own food. First day in advance."

That seemed a little steep, but he could tell Frank wasn't impressed with his explanation and almost *any* price at that point was better than being told to take a hike. Frank was just trying to offset the risks. He could understand that.

"Deal," Ethan said, holding out his hand.

Frank shook it and explained the details. "We'll leave tomorrow at first light. Figure on about four days to go all the way to the coast of Egypt. Bring enough food for a couple days longer than you think you'll want to stay out. At six days we'll probably need fuel and more supplies if we don't pick them up in Egypt. I have water and coffee onboard. If you want something else to drink, bring your own."

"Sounds good," Ethan replied. He reached into his pocket, pulled out a fold of currency, counted out three thousand euros and handed it to Frank.

Even though it was a fairly lucrative deal, Frank was a little surprised that he now had exactly what he had asked for. Usually people tried to work him in a situation like this. It was suspicious...almost *too* easy. Maybe Ethan was one of those guys with more money than sense, or maybe there was more to this trip than what it appeared. He'd find out soon enough.

"Thank you, Mr. Jacks. I'll see you in the morning."

"Bright and early, Mr. Grey."

Frank was already preparing the boat to leave when Ethan came down the dock in the dim morning light. He was carrying two small duffle bags and a full bag of groceries. "Good morning," he said to Frank as Frank offered to take the bags.

"Good morning, Mr. Grey."

"Just call me Ethan."

"Okay, Ethan. Let me show you where your things will go and we'll get underway."

Ethan followed him down narrow stairs to a narrow hallway where Frank set the bags on a freshly made bed in a small room to the left. It had a foldout desk built into the wall with two drawers under it.

"This will be yours. The bathroom is that door there and in the back is a refrigerator and burners if you want to cook something. You just have to wash your own dishes."

"This will be fine."

"Then I'll get us underway," Frank said, heading back up top.

Ethan was pleasantly surprised at the modest accommodations and cleanliness of the room, and the boat in general. It also occurred to him that the rank odor emanating from Mr. Jacks' person the day before was now gone. That in itself was a blessing.

He secured everything under the bed and put a few grocery items in the small refrigerator before going up on deck. He had never gone out to sea on a boat like this before.

Frank was preparing to remove the mooring lines from the dock. "Ethan, get that line for me," he ordered, motioning to the aft securing rope. Ethan untied the rope from the metal spool, tossed it on deck and quickly climbed back onboard. Frank increased the motor speed slightly and maneuvered away from the dock. Slowly they began making their way out of the harbor.

As the boat moved into open water, Frank pointed to the farthest landmass east on the island that you could see. "The Sideros Peninsula is about thirty kilometers out. We'll go around it then start heading south."

Ethan was impressed by the beauty of Crete and intrigued with being so close to the water's endless expanse. He'd been on a cruise ship before, but that was like a floating city, high above the water with hundreds and hundreds of other people. *This* was *completely* different.

The boat made its way around the peninsula and turned south. Frank had locked the navigational control and came out to talk briefly with Ethan who was sitting on a vinyl-clad bench in front of the cabin. "That island way out there you can just see on the horizon is Rhodes, and the one just to the right is Karpathos," Frank informed, pointing off to the left. Ethan nodded to indicate he saw them. They talked a while longer, then Frank went back to the cabin as Ethan sat and watched the wonderful scenery along the east side of the island until they had passed well into the Mediterranean.

High, wispy clouds stretched intermittently across an otherwise blue sky. A few large commercial ships could be seen in the distance on their way to various destinations. With the island now behind them, the unreferenced and completely open water around the boat became less intriguing, and was even a little disorienting. Ethan decided he was more comfortable below in his small quarters, or in the kitchen where he looked at maps or read one of the magazines he had brought with him. Whatever he was supposed to do would most likely make itself known at some point. It always had before.

It was around noon when Frank went down to see if there was anything else he was supposed to do besides head toward Egypt. "You had anything for lunch yet?"

"No. Just been snacking on a jar of olives."

"I'm going to grab me something and go back up top. You're welcome to join me."

"I might do that."

Frank took a can of something out of a small cabinet and opened it with a hand can opener. Then he took a beverage out of the fridge and headed down the hallway. Ethan opened some processed meat, made a sandwich, got a bottle of water and went up to the main cabin.

Frank was sitting on a tall chair to the side of the wheel, so Ethan sat on a small bench next to the radio equipment.

"You know, I feel a little guilty just cruising along doing nothing. We could do some fishing if you want."

"No, I'm fine," Ethan replied. Frank shrugged his shoulders and ate another fork full of some kind of hashed meat. "I'm curious about the name of your boat, though. It's pretty unusual."

"Yeah, most people have no idea what it means. Do you?"

"I do, actually."

"Want to hear the story?"

"Sure."

"My father loved astronomy. When I was a kid, he made this huge telescope from a kit and was always looking at the planets and stars and showing me what he had found. He used to tell me a story about two brothers born among the stars. The universe was their playground. They'd play hide-and-seek in nebulas, swirl galaxies and throw shooting stars across the sky.

"One day, their father called the brothers to him to tell them that he was creating a solar system. He needed a sun to provide light and warmth to a tiny little planet of people, plants and animals. He asked his sons if one of them would like the honor. One said no and went back into the darkness of the universe to play. The other accepted his father's offer.

"He grew brighter and brighter until he became our sun and filled the entire solar system with his brilliant light. For that, he was forever praised and admired by his father and by all those who received his warmth and light on the tiny little planet.

"I always liked that story, so when I was older and found out that perihelion meant 'nearest to the sun,' I thought it would be a fitting tribute. This used to be my fathers boat, and when I'm out here at night and the skies are clear, I can look up and almost see him in the heavens. He loved life and was always interested in knowing more about everything. That's one of the things I'll always remember about him.

"It sounds like your father was a good man."

"Yeah, he was."

"Wouldn't it have been easier just to name the boat after him?"

"Maybe, but then I wouldn't get to tell this story every time now would I?" Frank said smiling.

"Good point. So what does your family think of you being out here by yourself?"

"The only family I still have is my son who's a hotshot executive. We talk once in a while. He has a completely different life than I do. So what's *your* story, Ethan? What drives you to wander around in the middle of the Mediterranean for no good reason?"

"Well..." Ethan started, pausing to sip some water, "there *is* a reason. I guess you could say I'm here to complete a journey that started a very long time ago. Now I'm just kind of waiting to find out what I'm supposed to do next."

"That sounds interesting...and makes *no* sense at all."

"It's kind of hard to explain," Ethan said, not wanting to get into it yet. Frank shook his head and kept eating.

Another five hours had passed and Ethan was in the middle of a nap when Frank came down and woke him up. "Ethan...Mr. Grey."

Ethan opened his eyes and sat up. "Yeah?" he replied a little dazed.

"Just thought I should let you know, there's a storm ahead of us. We can go back or try to go around. It's your nickel."

Ethan rubbed his eyes as he tried to gather his wits. "I'll come up and take a look."

He followed Frank up to the main cabin. A very intense feeling came over him when he saw the growing, rolling mass of clouds in front of them.

"The odd thing is, I didn't see it until just a few minutes ago. Usually I get a weather warning when something like this is out there. We haven't received any warnings at all."

Ethan didn't say anything and stepped outside the cabin, walked to the front of the boat and stared at the storm. It appeared to be about fifteen miles across and had a defined outer wall. There were dark, rolling clouds around its perimeter and lightning would flash across its width. The imposing thunder would echo and shake the air. Frank had slowed the engines to idle and walked out to stand with Ethan.

"Well, Mr. Jacks, I have good news and bad news. The good news is I think I found what I was looking for. The bad news is... *that's it*," Ethan said, motioning to the storm.

"You were looking for a storm? I don't get it."

This was the defining moment. Somehow he was going to have to persuade Frank to do something that defied every facet of one's common sense and instinct for self-preservation. Ethan knew without a doubt that he was on the right boat, but ultimately, Frank would still have to make the final decision himself.

He let out a huge sigh. "Frank, you know that journey that I said started a very long time ago?"

"Yeah."

"Well, I think in there is where that journey ends."

Frank didn't respond—probably too stunned by what he thought he had just heard. Then came subtle laughter. "That's pretty funny, Ethan. What are you thinking, suicide by Mother Nature?"

"That's not quite what I meant. What I mean is, I think I'm *supposed* to go in there."

The lightning intensified as intimidating thunder cracked and roared across the water. Frank watched the strange storm briefly, then looked over at Ethan. "You know, Ethan, I kind of like you. You seem to be a pretty decent guy. But when you say stuff like that, I just can't help but think you're not playing with a full deck. Going anywhere *near* that thing would be insane. I know it, and *you* know it. So why on earth would you say something so absurd?"

"I can understand what you're thinking. Really, I can. But let me ask you something. Do you believe you have good common sense?"

"Yeah, and it's telling me that stuff you've been drinkin' ain't water."

"When did you first see this storm?"

"A few minutes before I came down to talk to you."

"Did you see it before that?"

"No...I didn't."

"How long would it normally take for a storm that big to form?"

"Well...a little while."

"Longer than it did, am I correct?" Frank started to respond, but stopped when he realized it really *didn't* make any sense. "Isn't that radar and other equipment I saw in there for watching weather patterns?"

"Yeah. They detect changes in barometric pressure, sense electrical activity, cloud density, receive alerts from satellite, stuff like that."

"And they don't show anything?"

"Well...no. Something must be wrong with the equipment," Frank unconvincingly deduced.

"All of it? Wouldn't that be an astronomical coincidence?" Ethan suggested. Frank was still silent. They both just stood and

403

looked at the rolling mass of storm energy. "Honestly Frank, does that look like any kind of storm you've ever seen before?"

"No, but what you're suggesting is impossible."

"Normally I would agree with you, but I've seen enough impossible over the past year to last me several lifetimes."

Frank's expression was now one of simple confusion more than anything else. Good thing. Being tossed overboard would be most unpleasant.

"Okay Frank, now I have a story for *you*. I have something with me that is *extremely* valuable. It was supposed to have been hidden a long, long time ago but was somehow lost and later discovered by some people who never should have found it. Long story short, I have it now and it's my job to deliver it to where it was supposed to go in the first place. I believe that place is inside that storm.

"I realize the thought of going in there defies every ounce of reasoning you have, but that's what it's *supposed* to do. Frank, it isn't coincidence I found you and your boat. Behind that storm is where we have to go. It *will* allow us safe passage through because of what I have with me. We'll be okay."

"I've changed my mind. I *don't* like you anymore."

"Just look at it, Frank. Can you honestly tell me you think that thing's just a big mess of weather?"

Frank continued to stare, then looked over at Ethan. "This whole thing is insanity," he replied resolutely before walking back to the cabin.

"Frank, I believe you're about to be a witness to one of the most incredible things you'll ever experience."

"Yeah, like my untimely departure from this earth," he said before disappearing through the door.

Ethan continued to watch the storm, wondering how he was going to make this happen. Frank couldn't be forced. He had to do this willingly. Somehow he needed to see, to understand. Even showing him the vessel may not be enough. But that's all that was left.

He went down to his quarters, pulled a bag out from under the bunk and sat down. He unzipped it, removed the vessel from its protective cushioning to inspect it, then returned it to the bag.

After zipping the bag shut, he carried it up to the cabin where Frank was staring out a window.

Ethan sat down, and a thought came. *I wonder...* "Did you ever know anyone named Cecil Holmes?"

Frank turned and looked at him suspiciously. "Yeah, he was my grandfather on my mother's side. How did you know that?" Somehow his answer didn't come as a total surprise.

"Did you know your grandfather very well?"

"No, hardly at all. You still didn't answer my question."

"Did you ever hear a story about him being on a salvage or exploration ship that found something strange out here?"

Frank started to think back. "Yeah. I hadn't thought about that story for quite awhile but...yeah. Something about a stone container that glowed or some strange thing. He was an odd fellow according to my mother, so she never talked about the stories much. Dad always thought they were pretty interesting though. But what does that have to do with anything?"

Ethan unzipped the bag and gently removed the vessel, holding it up with both hands. *"This* is what I believe your grandfather saw."

"Is this another joke or something?"

"Sorry, Frank. I'm not that good. Here, take it."

Frank glanced at the vessel, then back at Ethan. "Why?"

"Because *this* is why we're here."

Frank started to reach for it, then hesitated. "It isn't going to *do* anything, is it?"

"I don't think so. Just don't drop it. It's pretty old."

Frank gently took the vessel and looked it over. "You're serious. You think this is the same thing my grandfather was talking about?"

"I think this is *the actual* vessel your grandfather held."

Frank studied it carefully. Then as he held it up into the light from the western sun, it became transparent and began to radiate some kind of energy. Ethan couldn't see what Frank was seeing, but he saw Frank's eyes grow large and his expression change. After a moment, he quickly handed the vessel back to Ethan, then looked at Ethan with confusion and astonishment.

"What did you see?" Ethan asked.

"It was incredible. I...I can't describe it," Frank replied, unsettled.

"Now do you understand?"

"I don't know. It was...I don't know."

"This vessel isn't supposed to be here. The power it contains isn't even of this earth. That storm knows we're here. It knows we have this vessel and it's waiting for us." Ethan then carefully put the vessel back in the bag. "We *will* be protected," he added.

Frank looked back out at the storm. "So, what exactly is supposed to be inside that thing?"

"Honestly, I don't know. I only know that I'm to travel into the Heart of Fear, and that storm *is* fear. Think about it. If you wanted to hide something incredibly important and valuable where no one would ever look for it, wouldn't inside a storm like that be a perfect place?"

Frank was bewildered, having never run into a situation so completely bizarre as this one. He'd been through storms before and everything he knew told him to stay well away from *any* storm, regardless. But Ethan's knowledge of his grandfather, and what he had seen in the strange stone container, and this storm were all difficult to simply dismiss. No matter how bizarre it all appeared, he couldn't deny what he had seen, and what he felt.

"You really don't think we'll be obliterated in there?" Frank questioned

"No sir. I have every intention of staying alive. There's a very special woman I'd very much like to see again."

Frank looked out at the storm and shook his head. "I really must be insane, but if this is true somehow, and I live through it, I'll at least have one hell of a story to tell."

"Well...actually Frank, you still can't tell anyone. What would happen if you told someone about this? People from everywhere would come out here and start looking for it. That's exactly what we *don't* want to happen."

He looked at Ethan then turned back to the storm. "You know Ethan, you're not giving me much incentive here. You've been trying to convince me that all this incredible stuff is possible, but not *why* this needs to be done. What's so important about this thing that it has to go in there?"

"Are you a religious man?"

"I'd like to think so."

"Do you remember a story about the End of the World where the wicked will be separated from the righteous as tares are separated from the wheat? The tares will then be gathered and burned in an unquenchable fire that will cleanse the earth?"

"*That's* what I think I saw when I held the vessel. It was like a fire of judgment or something."

"*That* is why it needs to be hidden—to be kept safe until the End of Days when it will be used to judge all mankind on Earth."

"Oh, so no pressure then," Frank replied. He sighed and pondered briefly. "You're positive this really isn't some kind of elaborate hoax?"

"No sir. What you saw was real."

Frank started shaking his head again and chuckled to himself as he watched the storm. Ethan waited patiently.

"You agree to pay for any damages plus my time to fix them if we make it out alive?"

"Frank, when this is over, I'll get you a whole new boat if you want."

"No, I like my boat. Could use paint..."

Frank kept looking ahead out the window, said something under his breath, shook his head and shoved the throttles forward.

They could now clearly see the abrupt wall at the edge of the storm less than a mile away. It was the most powerful and intimidating thing Frank had ever seen. Ethan was still relatively placid, all things considered.

"I take it you've never been on the ocean in a small boat in the middle of a thunderstorm before," Frank commented as they continued to close.

"No, why do you say that?"

"Because I suspect you wouldn't be so calm if you knew what was comin'."

Frank started mumbling to himself in the wake of increasingly larger waves and strong winds. They could feel the electrical energy in the air as incredibly powerful bolts of lightning flashed all around them in a blinding display of authority. Deafening thunder warned of impending doom. The boat slid into the storm.

Heavy rain began to fall. It had become dark and cold. A strong wind began to blow. The boat rolled and pitched high over large swells and dropped into deep troughs. Ethan held on to the edge of the console as Frank held on tightly to the wheel.

"This was not a good idea!" Frank shouted over the howl of the wind, crashing waves and thunder. *"I'm turning back!"*

He started to turn the wheel when Ethan grabbed it. *"No!"* Ethan shouted. *"I am not wrong! Please!"*

"This is insanity!" Frank shouted back.

The heavy rain and wind suddenly stopped. Frank stared in disbelief. The water near the boat calmed and settled, even though the storm was still raging on each side and over them. A clear, narrow path now appeared ahead through the darkness.

"Well I'll be a…" Frank said, peering down the tunnel through the storm. The encompassing lightning and thunder outside the calm was still a constant reminder of the merciless power and unyielding authority around them. But their own authority had been recognized and acknowledged. Ethan said nothing, patted Frank on the back, picked up the bag and walked out to the bow to marvel at the fantastic sight.

The storm outside became steadily stronger and more violent the farther they traveled inward. Its intensity was far more chaotic and deadly than anything nature could produce on her own. The sea wasn't just at the mercy of the storm, it was part of the storm. Giant plumes of water shot skyward as others crashed down in a constant flowing exchange that was simply unworldly. *Nothing* on, over or under the water could otherwise possibly survive such fury.

Then almost in an instant, they passed through and emerged into perfect peace. Still waters and a warm inviting breeze greeted them. There was a high sun and a clear blue sky with patchy clouds. The inside wall of the storm was a definitive vertical barrier that stretched upward for as far as they could see. It was circular in shape, at least ten miles across. Everything appeared bright and sharp and had that slight tinge of luminescence that Ethan knew well.

Frank idled the engines and walked out to stand with Ethan. The fantastic scene was mesmerizing. Frank was absolutely stunned. He turned around slowly to study the towering storm wall behind them, then gazed out into the wondrous calm.

"We're dead, aren't we?" Frank joked, with a hint of real concern.

Ethan slapped his hand firmly on Frank's shoulder. "No, Frank, not only are you not dead, you're not dreaming either."

Frank just shook his head. "I could have never imagined."

Then Ethan pointed. "Look, there's something there." Frank ran back to the cabin to get his binoculars.

"It's an island! Hang on!" he shouted down before engaging the throttles.

The island was in the center of the storm circle. As they approached, they could see it was small, maybe only a half-mile or so across—mostly round with low cliffs dropping straight into the water on one side with a sandy beach on the other. The rest was covered in a typical array of tropical trees and ground cover.

"Do you have a way for me to get to shore?" Ethan asked.

"Yeah, I've got an inflatable raft in back."

Frank brought the boat in as close to the sandy beach as he could and dropped anchor. They inflated the raft and lowered it over the side with a rope. Ethan secured the bag over his shoulder while Frank dropped an oar into the raft. Ethan climbed down a small ladder and stepped onto a small foldout landing at the back of the boat.

"Good luck," Frank said as Ethan stepped into the raft and sat down.

"Thank you. Hopefully, I won't be too long."

"I'll be here," Frank replied.

The water was clear and the light, warm breeze reminded him of other fantastic experiences as he slowly rowed to shore. The raft skimmed onto the beautiful white sand. Ethan stepped out to pull it up onto dry beach. The foliage was incredible. There were tall gently swaying trees and plants and vines with large flowers in bright colors. But now what? Was there someplace he was supposed to go? Maybe someone would meet him there. He had no idea, so he just stood, and waited.

Suddenly, his childhood returned. He was in the backyard at one of his friend's houses. They had lots of bushes and shrubs and trees and it was always fun to go exploring through them.

"Come on!" his friend shouted as he motioned and disappeared through a wall of bushes. Then Ethan was back on the beach.

He walked to the edge of the vegetation and noticed a stone path that emerged from the sand and led into the tropical forest. He stepped onto the path to push through thick foliage and emerged into a beautiful open garden. The path then wound its way through giant ferns and other unique growth as he traveled toward the middle of the island.

After walking for a time, he came to a large clearing. At its center was a round structure that appeared to be made of a white stone. It was about fifteen feet high and thirty feet wide with archways formed into it around its entire perimeter. The path led directly to a courtyard that surrounded the structure. As he approached, he noticed there were additional paths that led in from other parts of the clearing. There were two individual arches that stood alone, each on opposite ends of the clearing with paths that lead to the courtyard. Strangely, there were no paths leading away from them.

Before leaving the path to enter onto the courtyard, he set the bag down, unzipped it, removed the vessel and set the bag on the path to distinguish his from the others. Cautiously, he then moved toward the structure.

It appeared to be perfectly round, polished smooth and brilliant white. The archways were open, but what he saw through each one was not what should have been. Each one portrayed a different scene of beautiful places—some forest-like, others of mountains or of spacious and open valleys of colored grass and flowers. One even appeared to be a large chamber inside a mountain with openings cut into the walls where scrolls, documents and other items lay at rest, all lit in the soft glow of torches.

There was one scene that was absolutely wondrous. It appeared as morning twilight over a large rolling valley. There were trees scattered in groups throughout hills of different elevations with a low mist floating among them. The horizon was thinly lit with a cresting light of rich color that faded into a still darkened sky. There was a vastness of stars and a large moon. Above and to its side was another moon of a slightly different color that seemed to be farther away.

Curiously, he put his hand out to see what this place was. A brilliant, white energy flashed across the archway, knocking him backward, causing him to lose his balance and fall at the edge of the courtyard. Severely dazed, he looked back and up at the structure. That's when he saw something he hadn't noticed before; a single symbol carved into the stone high above each arch.

He stood and once again began to slowly circle the structure, this time looking up, carefully studying each symbol. They were completely foreign to him—nothing he had ever seen before, except for one.

Ethan stopped and held up the stone vessel. This symbol he recognized. The symbol of the sun lightly carved into the top of the vessel was the same as the symbol over this archway. This had to be it.

He grimaced, squinted his eyes almost shut, held the vessel tightly to him with his left arm and slowly extended his other hand toward the opening. Nothing happened. He moved forward slowly... Still nothing. He opened his eyes to see that he was halfway through. Cautiously, he continued and emerged into a completely different world.

It was another place of magnificence, high at the top of an incredible mountain vista similar to the one he imagined before walking into Grayson's office. He stopped and looked around as a bright, warm sun shone down from above and behind him. To his side was the mountain rock face, and ahead a narrow trail that led around a curve. He looked behind him to see a crude stone arch vaguely formed into a sloping rock wall.

He followed the path a short distance around its bend and there found a round opening formed in the rock in the side of the mountain. It was about two feet deep, and at the bottom was a round indentation about the same diameter as the stone vessel. On the ground to its side, a cover stone rested against the rock— the symbol of the sun carved into its surface.

This was it. Everything he had gone through came down to this moment. He held the vessel up and thoughtfully looked at it one last time, then carefully placed it into the opening. The heavy cover stone was carefully lifted and set over the opening, and pushed into place. The seams around its edges disappeared and blended into the mountain wall. Only the symbol of the sun now marked this place where the Power of Souls would rest until the End of Days.

A journey practically beyond comprehension, one actually started over four thousand years ago, was now at its end. This was a strange time of ambivalence. Some of the trials he had faced were terrible, but the experiences and knowledge gained in them were beyond worldly value. What mortal price could ever be too high to save one's eternal soul?

After stepping back through the arch and before leaving this magnificent and sacred place, Ethan slowly circled the structure a last time to study the symbols above each archway. It was mind-boggling to ponder what they might represent.

What else could be here? How many others, maybe ordinary men like himself, had been given the authority and privilege to perform some similar task. Who else might have already hidden or received knowledge or powers during the course of mankind's history? What other knowledge or truths may have already been removed and given to us? What else could still be ahead?

How many have the true desire to search for that knowledge, and the courage to understand and accept it? How many live with nothing to hold their course and are blown about by every spot of wind? This place, this magnificent place. Full of wonder and so many possibilities…

Ethan picked up the bag and prepared to leave. He thought he would be happy to finally be free of the vessel's heavy burden. Instead, the feeling was bittersweet. He held the empty bag and took one last look around.

Frank was sitting on the deck in front of the main cabin and waved as Ethan walked toward the raft before climbing in and rowing back to the boat.

"Well, did you find what you were looking for?" Frank inquired anxiously while they pulled the raft up the side.

"It's done. It's where it belongs."

"Okay, so now what?"

"Now...I guess we go home."

"That's it? There's nothing more?"

"Oh I'm sure there's plenty more, just probably not today."

Ethan sat down in front of the cabin and began wringing out his socks. After Frank stored the raft, he went up front and sat down next to him. "Something interesting," Frank started. "None of the navigation equipment or radios are working at all. It's like there's nothing out there. Even my pocket watch has stopped. What do you make of that?"

"Nothing really surprises me anymore, Frank. Honestly, we could be anywhere, and I don't just mean in the Mediterranean. We might not even be in our own time."

Frank just stared at him. "And I was just starting to like you again," he said, slapping Ethan on the back and laughing jovially. "Well, shall we raise anchor?"

"Yeah. Let's see if this place will let us out."

Even though both of them knew that they would probably be fine, heading into a raging storm wall of vertically rushing water was still a little unsettling. But the storm would honor their authority and courage. As they neared it, a tunnel appeared just as before to allow safe passage out of paradise.

Now well into the storm, Frank commented that he thought they were about halfway through. A few seconds later, the storm dissipated around them. It was gone. They both looked around out the side windows of the main cabin. Frank slowed the engines and followed Ethan out to the aft deck to see mostly clear skies behind them.

"I think I could pretty much die now and say I've seen it all," Frank jested.

"How long do you think we were in there?" Ethan asked.

"I don't know. I'd say maybe two, three hours."

"Look where the sun is. Isn't that about where it was before we went in?"

Frank looked toward the sun, then pulled out his pocket watch that was now working again. "Huh. But how could...? But that's..."

"Yeah, I know. Welcome to *my* world," Ethan said as he smiled and slapped *Frank* on the back.

After an hour or so, Frank shut down the engines and anchored for the night. It was peaceful and quiet as they sat out front and ate dinner.

"What did you say this was again?" Ethan asked.

"Spetzofai. It's mostly sausage, peppers, onions, tomatoes and a smattering of garlic. I don't always eat stuff out of a can. Plus, I didn't want to see you suffer through another bologna sandwich."

"It's great. Thank you. I figured you probably ate more fish and stuff since you can catch it for free."

"Oh I eat plenty of seafood. S'pose I could have cooked up an octopus or something. But I figured you'd like this better."

As Ethan chewed on a pepper, he gazed into the clear night sky. "You know, it's funny. I hardly ever take the time to just sit and look at stars like this. They're really pretty amazing."

"Hey, I told you. There's no lights, no noise... We live on a planet full of people but out here, it's just you...and them," Frank said, motioning skyward.

Ethan could almost sense his own place in the immensity of space and time. A feeling of humble grandeur, of being part of something larger—a view afforded through different eyes. It was the awareness of an endless place he knew he had experienced before, but couldn't quite comprehend—like a memory just out of reach—images just out of view.

He looked into the stars from the middle of the Mediterranean Sea as he ate Spetzofai, and wondered if this was going to be the end of seeing and experiencing such wondrous and incredible things. Normal life was going to seem a little dull after all this. But then again, it *was his* life and he could make it anything he wanted it to be.

CHAPTER TWENTY-TWO

Détente

THOUGHTS OF FACING THE Professor had been bothering Alex since Hannover. When the announcement came to board for the long flight to JFK, she just sat. The rest of the passengers had all gone and still, she sat.

It was going to take time to figure out how to handle these new emotions. Contemplating the questionable trust of an old friend, along with a deluge of new thoughts and feelings about Ethan was just too much to take in all at once. She needed time—time to think, time to put things in perspective, time to find peace with herself.

Once in another life, she had wanted to visit France. Of course Derric was too busy and too involved to be concerned with the wantings of a wife. Today though, she was here, and would find that place where her heart desired to rest.

After spending the night in chairs and walking the airport, the morning found her asking for assistance from helpful strangers. Several phone calls later would find vacancy in a manor house in the country outside Soissons, near Laon—about an hour's drive northeast of Charles de Gaulle Airport. It was a tranquil place of incredible beauty and solitude where she could spend the next few days exploring her innermost feelings and thoughts.

Being alone for the past several years had made her hungry for intimacy, and her feelings for Ethan, that started out as simple curiosity and guarded possibilities, were now moving into a place where introspection was revealing a great deal more. She knew his deep love for Rachel would never fade, and it shouldn't. But at the same time, she didn't want to simply be a replacement for something he could no longer have—a lie in which to live, and one that would never last.

What they would need to find is something new, something more and different from what either had before. That wouldn't be difficult for her, it was a different story for him. He seemed to have had everything in Rachel, and lost everything in her as well. What could she now offer that was her very own? Something he would find new and exciting—something that would not simply fill a void, but become a new foundation upon which to rebuild a life.

In the forest before making their hopeless run for freedom, she thought he may have seen that something special in her, even if it was only for a moment. Was it genuine, maybe a glimmer of what was possible? Or just a thoughtful expression brought on by strained emotions realized in moments before they believed their lives would be extinguished?

Sitting alone on an old stone wall near the top of a hill above the manor house, the possibilities seemed as vast as the distant horizon stretched out before her. The consequences of Espelkamp had been weighed and she knew as well as anyone how some people can hide behind masks that disguise their true being.

But as she thought about all the Professor had done for her, there was never a memory of any instance where he had lied or done *anything* to cause her to seriously doubt his honest friendship. To wonder *what* he was doing or *how* sometimes, sure, but never a question of trust.

Ethan could be right, things aren't always as they appear. So she put the stones away and decided it was only fair to give him the benefit of the doubt until it might be proven otherwise. In all he had done for her, he had earned and deserved at least that much.

✵ ✵ ✵

"Mr. Grey, it's been an honor. Strange as hell, but something I'll never forget."

"Thank you, Mr. Jacks. I'm just glad you didn't toss me over the side," Ethan replied as he shook Frank's hand.

"Yeah, well, knowing you, you probably would have just walked back to the boat. You can't do *that,* can you?" Frank joked, looking at Ethan cockeyed.

"No, no, I'm just a regular guy. Honest," he replied, trying to downplay Frank's jested insinuation.

"Okay, regular guy, where you off to now?"

"Home, I hope."

"Well, you're okay in my book so anytime you want to visit, just come on back, and bring that lady-friend you talked about."

"I might just do that."

"See you around, Ethan," Frank said loudly as he waved.

Ethan was anxious to see if Alex had made it back okay. Getting back himself was now a priority as well. A long time was spent sitting at the small Crete airport waiting for a seat back to Athens, and then more time waiting to find a timely flight home from there. Fortune would still find him known to no one as he boarded the plane with only a visual verification and processing of his passport. Today anyone wanting to find him would just have to keep looking.

The flight home took him to Charles de Gaulle Airport where he waited for the transfer to Washington, DC. As he sat in the terminal, thoughts of Alex began to fill his mind. It was amazing to him how a woman who he had only known through a friendship with his wife, could become so dedicated to a cause that in the beginning seemed so inane.

She saw something he never did. It took a visitation for him to understand that something really important was going on, and even then there was still *some* doubt. But Alex had been incredibly strong, and had *never really* wavered in her loyalty and devotion. It was primarily by her persuasion and coaxing that everything had been set into motion. Where might he have ended up if he hadn't missed an exit on the way to a grocery store one morning?

Even in the forest when Alex was exhausted and had all but given up, part of what kept him going was his desire to keep *her* alive. Then as clearly as if someone had put the thoughts in his head, he realized that if she had not been there with him in that meadow, *he would have died there.*

What happened was not only a condition of pure selflessness, but an affirmation that it took *both* of them to summon the power that destroyed Pancros and his men—*both* of them, *together.* Immortality is not just an endless perpetuation of self, but also a continuation of what we establish here on Earth. The perfection we seek can only be achieved through the love we have for others. Death will take us all into the realm of forever, but choice and consequence will *never* cease to apply, even in the immortal world. *Now he was beginning to truly see.*

Alex wasn't just contributory to his success, she was instrumental in it. What they accomplished together became exponentially greater than what either could have accomplished alone. Their meeting *couldn't* have been pure coincidence. Their friendship and selfless bond was the only way they could have survived. It was a balance in life meant from the beginning. She was now a possible continuation of his life, and part of a possible whole that would allow them both the opportunity to attain the highest degree of consummation possible. Family *is* the perpetual essence of eternity from where true and ultimate power is derived.

❈ ❈ ❈

Two days in the French countryside were days well spent. Time had allowed the debaters to come to an agreement on many things, or at least to an understanding. If misgivings still existed, they were identified and put in their proper place, allowing for a more constructive thought process to resume. It's hope and faith that empowers courage. Still, events *can* become so overwhelming that we sometimes question even our strongest convictions. It's a necessary evil, and part of true introspection required to keep our internal universes in order.

The airline wasn't happy about the missed flight and made their displeasure known by allowing for a 'standby' ticket only. It was better than having it cancelled altogether, requiring the purchase of a new ticket. And six hours waiting in the terminal was certainly not as pleasant as being in the beautiful French countryside. At least she was now going home.

A seat finally became available. Since she had earlier left and returned to the international terminal, it would be necessary to go through customs and passport control. Her mind was numb from waiting and from continuous contemplation. She didn't notice her passport pass over the scanner before it was handed back to her. Her anonymity had just been revoked. *She* was now back in 'the system.'

JFK was crowded and Alex was instinctively leery as she walked down the concourse. It wasn't until arriving at the gate for her connecting flight that the female who had been following her met up with a male, and they approached.

"Ms. Fullerman, my name's Jackson. This is Barrett," the man said as they both held up their agency ID's. "We're here to take you to Samuel Greenhagen. Is Mr. Grey with you?"

"No." Their question obviously meant he hadn't come back yet, or was still hiding...or worse.

"Do you know where he is?"

"No."

"If you'll come with us, please. There's a plane waiting."

"I don't know who you people really are and I'm not going anywhere but home."

"Mr. Greenhagen is waiting in the plane."

"That isn't good enough," she replied defiantly.

The man removed a small phone from his pocket, dialed a number and held the phone to his ear. "Yes, sir," he said into the phone. "*Hubert* would like to speak with you," he then said, holding the mobile out to Alex.

Hubert was the Professor's code word. She looked at the phone for a second, and slowly took it. "Hello."

"Alex, it is *so* good to hear your voice again." It was difficult to keep composure. She wanted to be equally as excited to hear *his* voice, and to know she was now in safe hands. But that just wasn't possible, not yet. Too many things had happened. The question she needed to ask was there, but the courage wasn't. "Alex?"

"I'm here," she struggled.

There was a sigh from the other end. "I know what you must be thinking and I honestly regret what happened. It seems even the people I work with are not impervious to being deceived. I failed you in that regard, and I'm so very sorry." Alex was listening and wanted to believe, but doubt was not so easily dismissed. "I just hope you'll give me a chance to explain."

"Okay," she said, working hard not to break down.

"Just go with the two people there and I'll meet you by the plane."

"Okay."

"Very good then. Do you know where Ethan is?"

"No. I haven't talked to him for several days."

"Alright, I'll see you in a few minutes."

"Okay," she ended.

The woman put her arm behind Alex and motioned for her to walk with them. They drove to an ancillary location of the airport to a waiting jet where Professor Greenhagen was standing near the stairs with another agent. The Professor was smiling, happy to see her again. Alex was more guarded. He held out his arms to greet her. She gave him a weak hug and managed a faint smile.

Once in flight, the Professor began to ask those questions he had to ask. Alex told him generally what had happened at Espelkamp and how they had escaped, but didn't elaborate on the incident at the meadow. She also maintained that she didn't honestly know where Ethan was, which was true.

Still sensing that she was holding back, the Professor tried to convince her that it would be in everyone's best interest for her to tell him *everything* she knew. She wouldn't, but did say that what Ethan was doing was more important than anything anyone could possibly imagine. A part of him didn't doubt that, given what he had seen, which was why locating the artifact was top priority. Little did he know, what he and his associates were still looking for was already safe from the deluded ambitions of man.

☀ ☀ ☀

Ethan's flight had just landed at Dulles. Alex had arrived home the day before. He was feeling pretty good, all things considered. It wouldn't last though when the Professor found out he was back and the artifact was gone. Now the question was if he would be detained immediately, or later when his fake name was registered. But once again, fate was his as a minor 'glitch' in the system would require manual passport processing. He would travel back into the United States unmolested.

His thoughts were of finding Alex. But first, a visit to the Professor seemed in order to set everything straight. *This* cab driver was mildly irritated by the five or six wrong turns Ethan suggested before they finally found the right street, even if it did get him a few extra bucks. Ethan was nervous as he rang the doorbell and waited for the door to open.

"Mrs. Greenhagen," he said cheerfully. Her expression was that of polite forgetfulness. "I'm Ethan Grey... Alex's friend?"

"Of course, how are you doing?" she chimed.

"I'm doing very well, thank you. Is Professor Greenhagen home?"

"I believe he just came back from an errand. Come in, come in. Alex was here yesterday."

"She was? How was she doing?"

"She seemed fine."

"Good, good," Ethan said smiling. They continued toward the back of the house and to a set of large doors that led to the patio.

"There he is," she said pointing to some benches at the center of the garden. "Just go ahead and go on out."

"Thank you."

"You're welcome. It was nice to see you again, Edgar."

"You too, Mrs. Greenhagen."

The Professor was sitting sideways to Ethan with his attention on a notebook. He didn't see Ethan approach.

"Hello Professor."

Startled, Professor Greenhagenlooked up and over his reading glasses. "I'm going to have to talk to my security people about who they let in here," he said standing and holding out his hand. "Nice to see you made it back," he added as Ethan shook his hand and they sat down. "Does Alex know you're here? She's worried about you."

"No, I came straight here from the airport. I'd like to go see her next. Do you know where she is?"

"Home. I just spoke with her a little while ago. This whole ordeal has taken quite a toll on her."

"Yeah, I suspect it has. You would have been proud of her though. She's quite a woman."

"That she is. A lot of people are looking for you. They want to know what you've been up to."

"You mean they want to know where the Power of Souls is."

"Well, that too.

"I'm sure Alex told you what happened."

"She told me a little. I'd like to hear your side of it."

"In time. Did you get everything straightened out with Alex?"

"What do you mean?"

"You know what I mean…Espelkamp."

The remark made the Professor uncomfortable. He looked away and sat up on the bench. "Aren't *you* curious how they found out?"

"I never really thought it was you."

"Alex didn't share the same sentiment. She's still a little nervous."

"She'll come around. She's very close to you, and that can sometimes keep a person from thinking objectively. I knew you were too intelligent to throw everything away by doing something like that."

"You didn't think I was responsible?"

"No, but Alex has to find her own answers."

The Professor nodded in agreement. "It was difficult to have her look at me with such distrust after all these years."

"Well, you can't always play with fire and not expect to get burned once in a while. What *did* happen, anyway?"

The Professor took a deep breath, looked at the ground and shook his head. "A traitor among us." There was reflective silence.

"I presume it's been handled?"

"In a manner of speaking," the Professor replied, looking at Ethan with a Cheshire grin. Ethan missed it. "So, where is the Power of Souls?"

"Safe."

"What's that supposed to mean?"

"It means it's in the hands of God."

"I'm...not sure I understand."

"It's détente, Professor; I don't have it, your people don't have it, the Order doesn't have. *No* one will find it again for a *very* long time."

"That's a pretty arrogant statement, don't you think? It's already been found once."

Ethan looked at the Professor and smiled. "They won't find it *this* time."

Another empty answer. There *was* something curious about it though. "You don't think the Black Sun Order will find it again?"

"They can try."

"Then you don't know."

"Know what?"

Even though the Professor was sure that Ethan and the artifact had something to do with the disappearances, Ethan's response and demeanor portrayed an honest unawareness.

"Ethan, *they're gone*. There *is* no Order of the Black Sun anymore that we can verify. It happened not long after your escape at Espelkamp."

Ethan's expression turned very sober. "What do you mean they're....*gone?*"

"I think you know what I mean," the Professor replied smugly. Ethan did know, but until that moment he had believed what had happened in the meadow was isolated. To now know how far-reaching and total the effect of his actions had been was quite disturbing.

"How many?" he asked, almost apologetically.

The Professor had expected to see some sort of gratification reflected in Ethan's new knowledge. What he saw instead was dolefulness from the realization of such a consequence by his hand.

"Well, that doesn't really matter. But how did you do it?"

"You haven't told Alex, have you?"

"No."

It was staggering. Ethan leaned back against the bench and stared ahead, lost in confused emotions. It was just another affirmation that only a being of extraordinary knowledge, compassion and discipline should wield such infinite power for which the responsibilities were as equally infinite.

"This is something Alex doesn't need to know about. Promise me you'll never tell her."

"That's fine. I'm trying to isolate her from as much of this as I can anyway."

"Good, thank you," Ethan said as he stood. "I have a cab waiting so I better get going. Is there a chance I can get my identity back before I leave?"

The Professor stood and they walked toward the study. "Ethan, there are people who are going to want answers, *real* answers. They're going to want to know exactly what happened at Espelkamp and where the artifact is."

"Professor, you of all people understand that it isn't always prudent to share everything you may know. This is definitely one of those times." The Professor pulled the passport and wallet from a drawer in his desk. "You should know though that it was only with your help that we were able to take the Power of Souls away from the Order."

"The fact that the Order seems to no longer be a threat is monumental. Still, there are a lot of unanswered questions."

"There are *some* answers, Professor, that can only be found in time."

CHAPTER TWENTY-THREE

State of Grace

ETHAN RANG THE DOORBELL with anticipation. The driver had been paid, but was asked to wait to make sure she was home before leaving. After a moment, the door opened and Alex looked at him briefly before a huge smile came to her face. She sprinted out the door and jumped to wrap her arms and legs around him, almost knocking him over. Ethan waved to the cab-driver who then drove off.

"*Man,* am I glad you're back," she said overjoyed.

"I'm glad to see you made it back, too," he responded while holding her. "Did you have any problems getting home?"

"Not really," she said, putting her feet on the ground and rubbing his cheeks. "You could use a shave."

"Yeah, and a shower and some fresh clothes."

"So, what happened? Tell me everything," she said excited, leading him through the door.

"I'll tell you all about it, but I want to talk to you about something else first. Here, sit down," he said while leading her to the couch. He slid a chair close so he could face her. Her expression was of concern as she wondered what could have happened to require such a formal conversation.

Now sitting across from her, he took her hands and held them in his. "Alex, I've been kind of lost for a while. You know that. I was so depressed and had so much anger that it blinded me to just about everything good. Nothing made sense. When the journal showed up, I felt like there was something I was supposed to do. But it wasn't until I met you and you started pushing me, and kept pushing that I started to open my eyes. Now when I look back at everything that's happened, I can see everything that led me here. There was no coincidence to any of it.

"Rachel is still a very important part of my life, and she always will be. But these past few months have brought me to realize something wonderful; *you* are a very real and very important part of my life now. You are the one who saw something in me when I saw nothing. You're the one who pushed me and helped me go beyond the limits of what I thought I could achieve, and to think beyond boundaries I thought were impassible. *You*, Alex, saved my life.

"And even though you weren't able to see some of the wonders I've seen, or go with me to some of the places I've been, if it hadn't been for your imagination, adventurism, courage, support and the occasional kick in the butt, I never would have made it through this journey. It's you, Alex, who helped change my life and made all this possible and for that, I owe you everything.

"There is no doubt in my mind that someday you'll receive the true recognition and honor you rightfully deserve for your part in what we've accomplished. But *I* want you to know *now* what an incredible and wonderful woman I think you are." Ethan kneeled down in front of her. "You deserve nothing less than everything good life has to offer. I would like to share my life and everything I have, and everything I am with you. I love you, Alexandria Zavalla. Will you allow me the privilege of being your husband?"

Alex had been wiping tears for some time. They were still flowing freely when she grabbed his stubbly cheeks and planted a firm kiss squarely on his lips. She held his hands again and looked at him as seriously as she could. "You may have the privilege, Mr. Grey, and I love you too." They laughed and embraced.

"We have a lot to figure out…"

"And we'll figure it out."

"Ring shopping…"

"Twist my arm."

"A wedding date, houses, jobs—"

Alex interrupted him by almost pushing him over on the floor with a long, passionate kiss. Then she looked at him devilishly.

"Children?" Ethan concluded.

"Oh yeah," Alex said eagerly.

"I suspect miscommunication isn't something we'll have to worry too much about, eh, Ms. Zavalla?"

"You're off to a good start, Mr. Grey," she remarked smiling while adjusting his collar.

"Well okay then, I better be going," he replied, standing to leave.

"What would you like to do for the wedding?" Alex then asked more seriously as Ethan helped her up.

"Anything you want, anyplace you want. I just want you to be happy," he said, stroking her hair.

"I want to do this right."

"I agree. You tell me what we need to do and I'll do it."

"Promise?"

"Yes, I promise."

☀ ☀ ☀

As Ethan pulled into the driveway, he looked at the large, beautiful house that was once home to his family, and wondered what would become of it. Would it find another happy family, or an older couple wanting to retire? Maybe even a younger couple just starting their family. Having now committed himself to a new life, this home would also become another memory, like so many others.

Mutters was sleeping in the sunshine on the front porch when he drove up. She jumped up and ran to the open garage door to greet him.

"Hello kitty," Ethan said with a smile as he got out of the car. "Looks like the neighbors are still taking good care of you." She responded with a chirpy 'meow.' Ethan rubbed her on the head.

Mrs. Kensington had been collecting the mail for him. It consisted of the usual junk, a few bills and the occasional letter addressed to Rachel. It was still strange to see her name and their address together as if someone believed she still lived there. Maybe there would always be occasional, surreal moments like this one. It was just something he'd have to get used to and learn to accept as part of life.

There was a large envelope from Jeff Hampton that he opened immediately. It contained a detailed history of Stephen Lee, the young man who had caused the accident. It was a history that seemed normal until his life spiraled into arrests for minor but notable offenses, including drug possession, and there were problems at home and at work. It was a history shared by so many others that could have been different. Hopefully, it wasn't too late to try and make things right.

❊ ❊ ❊

Ethan was quite nervous as a middle-aged woman answered the door.

"Hello," he offered with a smile.

"Come in," Mrs. Lee responded, somewhat indifferently. "I'll get my husband. Have a seat."

Ethan looked around the modest home and sat on a small chair across the room from the sofa. Above the sofa were several large family pictures. One was of Stephen and his two younger sisters. It had been a long time since he had seen the young man's face. The picture brought back some difficult memories.

Mr. Lee came into the room along with Mrs. Lee. Ethan stood to greet them. Mr. Lee walked directly to the sofa and sat down.

"Thank you for agreeing to see me," Ethan started nervously.

"I don't know what you think you're going to accomplish by coming here," Mr. Lee scorned. "How many times can we say we're sorry? I'm sorry for what happened. Stephen's sorry. Wasn't hauling the kid through court enough for you? His life is everything but ruined already. What more do you want from us?"

Ethan was expecting something like this. It was still hard to hear, and he felt ashamed and found it difficult to make eye contact with them.

"Mr. Lee, I can't tell you how much I wish things would have been different. There were a lot of things I didn't understand after the accident. One was the terrible pain and guilt your son was going through. I know he's having problems and I would change the past if I could, but I can't, and for that I am truly sorry. There are a few things I'd like to say if you'll give me a moment of your time."

The Lee's sat quietly and listened. "First, I would like to offer my forgiveness. That concept was totally foreign to me until not long ago. I want both of you and Stephen to know that I forgive him for what happened, and I'm hoping you'll forgive *me* for my deplorable behavior in the past.

"A lot of good that'll do him now," Mr. Lee said spitefully.

"Honey, let's listen to what he has to say," Mrs. Lee encouraged. Mr. Lee sat back, looked away and bit his lip.

"I realize that," Ethan said solemnly. "As I understand it, Stephen was majoring in Business Management. Is that right?"

"Yes," Mrs. Lee responded. "Unfortunately, he never completed any of the courses. He decided to work instead, but can't seem to keep a decent job. He's never been able to forgive himself for what happened and seems to struggle with everything. He makes his own decisions and we don't know how to help him now."

"He probably can't forgive himself because he doesn't think anyone else can forgive him. I believe that's mostly my fault and partly why I'm here. I need to let him know that I understand it was just an accident and that I don't hold malice toward him anymore. He needs to know that *I* forgive him and that we still believe in him.

"With that, I'd like to offer him a full scholarship to complete his degree, if you'll allow me to do that. I realize there are other issues and factors that will have to be addressed, but I'm hoping this will be enough incentive for him to start getting his life back together." Mrs. Lee put her hands to her face in astonishment.

"Is this some kind of twisted joke?" Mr. Lee asked harshly.

"No sir, it isn't, and there are no strings attached either. I'm just sorry it took me so long."

"You really want to offer this to our son?"

"Yes sir, I do."

Mrs. Lee was wiping away tears while Mr. Lee sat with his chin in his hand, trying to believe that there really are people out there who do things like this. They had been praying that somehow the burdens on their son and their family would be lifted—prayers that were apparently being answered in a way they had never expected.

Mr. Lee stood and walked over to Ethan who also stood. "Well, Mr. Grey, it's hard to understand, but I guess I owe you thanks."

"You don't owe me anything, Mr. Lee. I owe a debt to your son and to your family. This is the very least I can do to try to make up for my ignorance."

"It's still an honorable thing. Thank you," Mr. Lee said shaking Ethan's hand. Mrs. Lee was a little more emotional. She hugged Ethan several times before letting him leave.

The next morning, Ethan returned to the Lee house where he was able to talk with Stephen who was still living at home. It was very awkward at first for both of them. But as Ethan explained why he was there, and talked about what he had learned and what he now understood, Stephen's countenance began to change.

The hope he once knew was returning, and the fire in his soul was lit once again to illuminate and embrace those abandoned dreams that had been darkened by guilt, pity and worthlessness. That day, the cold hands of evil would lose their tenacious grip on another soul who would now rise above despair and hopelessness to once again find purpose and resolve. It would be the second chance that many deserve, but far too few receive.

❊ ❊ ❊

- Several Weeks Later -

The wedding was fantastic and Alex looked spectacular and radiant in her flowing white satin dress. The Professor beamed like a proud father when he walked her down the aisle. She perfectly complimented the roses in full bloom in their large gardens.

Every time Ethan looked at her, there was something new he would see that made her seem even more beautiful than before.

Alex's brother and his family were there along with half the University it seemed. Ms. Benoit even gave Ethan an affectionate hug and congratulated him on everything. He had very few actual friends in attendance, and the whole ceremony felt a little awkward with so many people there he didn't know. That was okay though. This was for Alex and as long as *she* was happy, then *he* was happy.

There *was* a familiar and friendly presence with him that was oddly comforting, however. It wasn't so much he could tell his family was there with him individually, just an inner feeling of approval—a warm reassurance of proper choices. There was no more worthwhile feeling.

It was strange to hear those words again, 'till death do you part.' This time Ethan knew it was only a declaration of mortal man—an automatic annulment for those without the greater knowledge. This ceremony was really only the beginning to later events that would give them the opportunity to bridge their earthly union into the eternities he had seen. Equally as thought provoking was the knowledge that Rachel, Allison and his son could somehow also be a part of that transcendent family. The knowledge was still new and strange and difficult to comprehend, but undeniable.

Belief defines existence. Work and trial define life and life defines the soul. As he watched Alex, and shared in her happiness, he couldn't help but take just a moment to think about Rachel's life. If she had already believed what he was only now beginning to understand, then her willingness to marry him, not knowing if he would ever accept those beliefs, was puzzling. It seemed like a risk he wasn't sure he would have taken if their places had been reversed. Maybe she knew something he didn't, or had seen something in him he hadn't seen in himself.

Regardless, his commitment to Alex was much more than simple words spoken in a ceremony. She would help him learn, and together they would add upon a very powerful grace and love that would transcend the boundaries of time.

✷ ✷ ✷

Ethan sat quietly and watched from the steps of the country villa Professor Greenhagen had procured for a week as a wedding gift. It was early morning—a time when darkness was preparing to find refuge from the sun. Only the very brightest stars could still be seen before they would bow to new light.

The eastern horizon began to brighten and glow in hues of purple, orange and blue. At that moment, as he watched the last star fade and the colors run, nothing seemed impossible. Hope, faith and understanding were formidable powers that allowed him to see beyond simple perception, and into a future of what could be.

The beautiful countryside was becoming more visible as the sun continued to rise, illuminating the marvelous world around him. While he watched in peaceful reverence, the unusually warm country air became home to tiny droplets of heavenly water that streaked to the earth in streams of rainbow colors, glistening as they reflected the sun's pure light. Then more and more until a brilliant, prismatic rain filled the sky. He watched as it teased and beckoned him to come join in its replenishing dance.

Alex was awakened by the patter of rain on the roof of the villa after a wonderful night's sleep. The morning sun was shining through one of the bedroom windows onto the comforter. She stretched and rolled like a contented feline to rest her arm across her husband, but he wasn't there. A quick look, then a look around. She slipped out of bed to see where he might have gone. It wasn't long before she saw him through a window at the front of the villa.

He was standing in grass not far from the front steps—his head skyward, hands outstretched. She quietly opened the door and walked outside to watch him. He seemed to be lost in himself, motionless in the rain.

"Ethan, what are you doing?" she asked with a hint of concern.

Ethan lowered his hands to his sides and turned to her. She looked radiant with the morning sun reflecting off her lion-like hair and long white silky nightshirt. *She was beautiful.*

"Good morning, Mrs. Grey." Alex smiled and lowered her head shyly at the new title. Ethan took a deep breath, let it out as he looked around and began to explain. "I used to hate the rain. It would drown my hopes...smother my dreams... It would never let me forget. Now...now it's wonderful. It's the same rain, but everything's different. I see things in ways I never knew were possible before. I have an understanding I never knew existed before. Every day is full of new possibilities and you helped me find them, Mrs. Grey."

Alex grinned modestly. "Mind if I give it a try?" she said, stepping off the porch to walk across the grass in bare feet. She stopped a few feet from him, clasped her hands behind her back, closed her eyes and held her head skyward to let the sun-warmed rain bathe her body in its delicate waters. The feeling was incredible. Her mind began to open to a spaciousness beyond her physical senses. Each ethereal drop of water splashing against her skin imagined a journey of each one among millions falling from the heavens to find only her. It was a feeling that energized her soul.

Ethan looked at her face and saw the pleasantness in her character expressed in a beautiful and gentle smile. As the rain soaked her clingy covering, he was reminded of a certain Greek goddess whose burning image was being washed away not only by Alexandria's physical beauty, but by a beauty that was all encompassing. And *this* was the woman he once considered only an acquaintance, then a friend.

Alex took in a deep slow breath and let it out. She lowered her head and opened her eyes to see Ethan smiling at her. "What?"

"Everything," he replied grinning.

She walked to him and put her arms around him. The rain lightened as they embraced and held each other in the rising morning sun. Then Alex pulled back, squinted her eyes and shook her finger at him.

"Uh-oh. This can't be good," Ethan joked.

"You remember what you said at the hotel in Hamburg? You promised to someday tell me what happened that made you change your mind about everything. I think today's a good some-day. Don't you?"

"Yeah, today's a good someday." Holding hands, they began to stroll through the wet grass. "It was the day we got back from Turkey. That night on the way home after I left your house, I stopped at a motel to spend the night. That's when something... a little unusual happened..."

EPILOGUE

STEPHEN LEE WENT THROUGH counseling and drug rehabilitation. Later he received his Bachelor's Degree in Business Economics at a local university. He's now married and has a good job. His wife is expecting their first child. The drug addiction still haunts him at times, but he has strong motivation and good support from a loving family.

The Kensingtons would remain on their small farm and become good friends with the large family that moved into the Grey home.

Mr. and Mrs. Hendricks would live out the rest of their lives next to the Grey's old house. A new pool would become popular with friends and they were always happy to entertain guests.

Samuel Greenhagen would retire as a professor, but continue to speak in various forums as a proponent of Universal Dynamics. He maintains a close friendship with Alex and is polite to Ethan.

Ethan reciprocates that sentiment. Mrs. Greenhagen is always pleasant and still confuses Alex's husband's name.

Frank Jacks would receive a very pleasant visit from Ethan and his new wife. He took them for a sightseeing cruise on his beautiful and recently repainted fishing boat. He would continue to roam the seas to find and experience its innumerable wonders, though none would ever compare to a trip once chartered by a very interesting and gracious fellow American.

Jeff Hampton continued to handle the Grey's major finances and even recruited some of his own financial supporters to form what would become the Lee Hampton Cross Foundation. So far, the fund has helped over forty deserving young people to find their way and fulfill ambitions for higher education.

Ethan and Alex moved to a nice home in a small rural community in Central Virginia where Alex was able to fulfill her ambitions of being a mother and raising a family. Their first child was a girl they named Andrea, and the second a boy they named Joshua. A few years later saw another boy named Zach. Mutters took to their new home well and even tolerated the new puppy, to a point.

Alex made sure they went to church regularly. It wasn't easy for Ethan to be in the environment he had once avoided like the plague. But as he became more involved, correlations to what he had learned on his own began to form, and even more pieces of the grand puzzle would find their place. It was something that would become a mostly normal part of his life.

Rachel's piano stayed in the family and Alex made sure their children took lessons.

Alex took quite a liking to the old Challenger. It ended up with a new engine and she was fond of going for spirited Saturday excursions, as long as she got to drive. There was just something about riding with a feisty, good-looking brunette in a baseball cap who knows how to throw shifts and handle a whole lot of horse-power.

Rachel's car ended up going to one of the Kensington boys named Ryan so he and his sister would have something to drive to school. It wasn't the sports car the young man had hoped for, but it was in excellent condition and they couldn't turn down the sale price of one dollar. The 'mailbox' car was repaired and Ethan still owns it. The owner of the mailbox finally received a personal apology and was duly compensated.

Ethan began working with the scientific community again. His efforts to help establish methods for determining the existence of the theoretical sub-elementary particles produced in the Henry Effect, would win him notoriety. It was around this time he received the following letter that came as a genuine surprise. It was postmarked from New Zealand, but knowing its author, could have originated from anywhere:

Dear Mr. Grey,

It's been a few years since our last encounter and I hope this correspondence finds you and your new family well. It pleases me to know that you have returned to your work. Although it was difficult to write this letter, some-thing happened to me personally those many years ago that was so incredible and unusual that I could no longer keep it to myself.

Before the accident at Aridel, I had a dream where two boys were bullying another boy. That dream came to mind as I looked at your file after the accident. Oddly enough, that same dream came to me again the night be-fore you arrived at the Ireon office in Hamburg. I left the country that night and it was the following day when the Black Sun members disappeared. Until now, no one else knows what also happened to me that day.

The room in the house where I was staying lit up with a blinding light and energy for what seemed like only a brief second. In that moment, I believe I somehow saw everything of consequence that had occurred in my life up to that point. When the light subsided, I was left with an overwhelming feeling that I had been spared for some reason. I then realized that the light had originated from the pin given to us by Pancros. A single grain of Element Zero had been placed inside each pin as a reminder of our ordained power and purpose. For a long time I tried to convince myself that the disappearances of the members was simply the result of a massive, covert operation and that the logistics of the dreams, meeting you again, and this other experience were all just happenstance.

Not a day has gone by since that I haven't thought about this experience. In that time I have come to believe that a much greater power must have been behind those occurrences and that somehow you were a part of it. You told me that Element Zero wasn't what we thought it was. It's possible that even Pancros was deceived by the Priest. We were all deceived.

I can't prove you were the reason for what happened that day, but had I not acted on the impressions of a dream so many years ago, I believe it's very possible that I never would have met you again and the course of my life would have followed that of the others. I thank you for your courage, and for a second chance.

Best wishes,

Tom Chamberlain

Epilogue

The strange visions and waking dreams Ethan once experienced would never return in such clear definition. However, there was definitely another awareness within him—a sense of clarity that made many situations and decisions easier to define and understand.

Maybe it was something that stayed with him from a supernal experience in a German forest meadow. Maybe it was a connection to a universal source of knowledge found by taking the time to clear one's mind of extraneous noise to find order in chaos. Or maybe it's the power in knowledge that comes from understanding that we are watched over by a loving intelligence of the highest order who will direct our paths and help us find our course, *if* we let Him.

The truth is, once you find that power in knowledge and allow its cleansing effects to purge the lies and doubts from within you, its purity and direction can become yours forever if you just hold it close to your heart.

No darkness of person or weight of circumstance can *ever* be allowed to extinguish the light that radiates from one's soul—for it is that light from within that truly illuminates our world.

- The End -

The atrocities of mankind that plague our world are at the hands of those who believe they will never be held accountable for their actions, or who have chosen that dark path by impudent conviction. Likewise, those who suffer at their feet, or by that of an unseen prejudice may also believe that true justice does not exist. But I submit that it does, and when its time comes it will judge us not in courts filled with lies and deception or with imperfect perception, but from within, where the genuine desires of the soul will become our savior...or executioner.

This inevitable judgment will be pure, impartial, and final—an undeniable accounting documented in the book that is our lives, read in an instant from its beginning to its end. Every word on every page formed from even the intention of thought harbored in the farthest recesses of our souls will be illuminated with the brilliance of the sun—reflected in glory, sequestered with an unquenchable fire.

Those who have chosen to walk the paths of darkness will find no shadows for retreat, no sales of mercy, no eleventh-hour repentance, no alibis of ignorance or reprieves by religion when the masks are removed and truth ignites the jury inside. For I profess to be nothing more than what I am, but what I am is everything, and it is with all that we are that we will then be known.

— *The Author*

Acknowledgements

My family, friends, and professional associates have been incredibly supportive of the work and deserve every thanks.

Lynnette, Kelly, Dave, Lindee, my wife and Mrs. Z were the first to read the manuscript and provide their honest opinions and suggestions. My new friend, Mr. Schubert, generously shared his time and patience in helping to establish proper German phrasing. Janice Sipherd, Pat Jarvis and Maryann Martinsen would later add their literary expertise.

My father, now gone for a time, portrayed a kindness and enduring integrity in everything he did and was an example to me and to everyone who knew him. He will always be remembered. And my mother, my biggest fan, whose incredible courage, faith and support of me, my family and my work, whatever it may be, never ceases.

With greatest appreciation to my wife Gayle, whose long-suffering of my independent nature and entrepreneurial tendencies no doubt also never ceases. I'm not sure if your acceptance at this point is from an honest understanding, or simply a relinquishment of trying to understand altogether. Regardless, I doubt many would have had the patience and strength to make it this far. If it had not been for your numerous and continual sacrifices and devotion to me and to our family, it is unlikely that this work would exist at all. Thank you for everything you do.

My great children, who also bravely stood behind me to weather the humbling interim consequences of another epic commitment. Hopefully, experience and wisdom will grow with them that someday they'll understand why I believe that anything worth doing is worth doing well, no matter what it is or how long it takes. They deserve the best of everything as all children do.

Many thanks to the staff at FCPrinting and especially Farrelyn, Scott, and Roger for their time and professional assistance. And to Barry, my new business partner, for sharing in the vision and believing in the work.

And finally, to you, the readers—the audience for whom the writer performs. It is by your kind words and support that the work continues.

Thank you, all.

About the Author

Ranse originates from the small farming community of Castleford, Idaho, population two hundred something. As a degreed communications professional, he started his career in the broadcast industry and moved into the private sector where he was additionally recruited as a contributing writer and editor for an international trade magazine.

The entrepreneurial spirit would later take hold to see him build and operate several grassroots communications companies as President and CEO. Shortly after consulting for the 2002 Winter Olympics, his twenty-five year business interest suddenly and mysteriously left him. This, along with other profoundly unique personal experiences, would summarily lead to a new dedication to writing.

Ranse's first novel, *Circle of Doors,* is garnering critical acclaim and has earned him an Independent Publisher Book Awards national silver medal for Visionary Fiction as well as comparisons to the works of Tolkien and Lewis.

He has four children to his very supportive and patient wife of twenty years and is active in his church. They currently live in the Northwestern United States where Ranse continues writing.

For more information visit www.RanseParker.com